BOOKS BY ABBOTT KAHLER
Writing as Karen Abbott

The Ghosts of Eden Park: The Bootleg King, the Women Who Pursued Him, and the Murder That Shocked Jazz-Age America

Liar, Temptress, Soldier, Spy: Four Women Undercover in the Civil War

American Rose: A Nation Laid Bare: The Life and Times of Gypsy Rose Lee

Sin in the Second City: Madams, Ministers, Playboys, and the Battle for America's Soul

WHERE
YOU
END

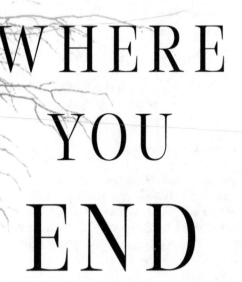

WHERE
YOU
END

A Novel

ABBOTT KAHLER

Henry Holt and Company
New York

Henry Holt and Company
Publishers since 1866
120 Broadway
New York, New York 10271
www.henryholt.com

Henry Holt® and Ⓗ® are registered trademarks of Macmillan Publishing Group, LLC.

Library of Congress Cataloging-in-Publication Data

Names: Kahler, Abbott, 1973– author.
Title: Where you end : a novel / Abbott Kahler.
Description: First edition. | New York : Henry Holt and Company, 2024.
Identifiers: LCCN 2023017074 (print) | LCCN 2023017075 (ebook) |
    ISBN 9781250873248 (hardcover) | ISBN 9781250873255 (ebook)
Subjects: LCSH: Twin sisters—Fiction. | Memory—Fiction. | LCGFT:
    Psychological fiction. | Thrillers (Fiction) | Novels.
Classification: LCC PS3611.A353426 W47 2024 (print) | LCC PS3611.
    A353426 (ebook) | DDC 813/.6—dc23/eng/20230725
LC record available at https://lccn.loc.gov/2023017074
LC ebook record available at https://lccn.loc.gov/2023017075

Our books may be purchased in bulk for promotional, educational, or business use.
Please contact your local bookseller or the Macmillan Corporate and Premium
Sales Department at (800) 221-7945, extension 5442, or by e-mail at
MacmillanSpecialMarkets@macmillan.com.

First Edition 2024

Designed by Gabriel Guma

Printed in the United States of America

1   3   5   7   9   10   8   6   4   2

For my Philly and Norristown jawns
And for twins everywhere, especially Judith and Katherine

WHERE

YOU

END

KAT: NOW

The Night of the Accident
MARCH 1983

It was just like me to go ahead and die, leaving her behind. That's what I'd hear her say, if I could hear her at all. Foolish, careless, typical. Expected, even. Another instance in which she was forced to clean up my mess, tend to my mistakes. Her guillotine voice would curse me in the sweetest tones. She would softly rake her bloody fingernails against my lifeless arm. She would say all the right things to lure me back, and keep all the wrong things to herself.

On that night we left the old neighborhood just as the rain began to fall. I ran first—I've always gone first—leading her back the way we came: through a colony of dusty relics, across a lush runway of grass, down a street where the homes are crowded with ghosts. I was not right. There was a pulsing inside my head, the tempo and weight of a thousand percussive drums, but I convinced myself otherwise, let my mind talk me into believing my own lies.

As we set off, me behind the wheel and my twin sister by my side, the rain stopped and I felt a shivery relief. The clouds cleared and the full moon shot its light through the craggy branches, illuminating the road ahead.

I saw the deer's body right before I swerved hard right, its long neck snapped unnaturally back. Then came a tree and a sheet of glass and the feeling that my head had launched away from my body, soaring into the sky, too far for me to retrieve it. I had time to form one last thought before my mind emptied itself of all things: *She will know how to fix me.*

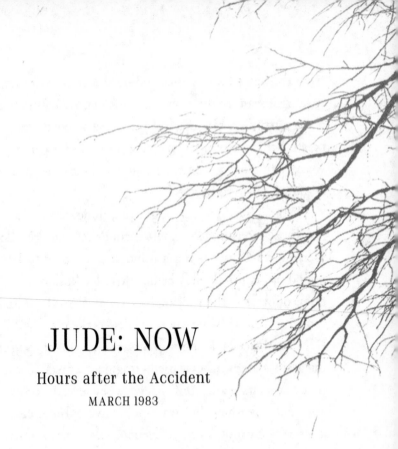

JUDE: NOW

Hours after the Accident
MARCH 1983

Jude sits in the hospital waiting room, folding and unfolding her hands, her fingernails still stained with her sister's blood. Kat has been wheeled off to some distant room but Jude can see her perfectly—a tangle of wires on her chest and a tube stabbing her throat and the nurses fluttering about like a flock of poisoned birds. A drop of sweat falls onto Kat's cheek. Machines blink and hiss. Instruments maneuver and gleam. Her long, taut body is hidden beneath a sheet. She has lost all sense of herself. The light begins to dim behind her closed eyes and Jude watches it happen, an excruciating descent, a darkening by degrees.

Kat is leaving her.

Against Jude's will, her body holds itself absolutely still; the only moving part is a ticker in her mind, tallying Kat's absence. One second, two, ten. Jude's brain pulses and her heart grows quiet, as though the two organs are trading places, confusing their functions. Thirty seconds, thirty-five. Her lips collapse into a severe blue slash, trapping her breath behind them. Eighty-nine, ninety. Her ears register a strident voice, telling her to come back and stay with him, stay with him, stay with him, that's it, steady, steady, good . . .

"Miss," the doctor says, grasping Jude's arm. "Are you okay?"

Those interminable ninety seconds rewind. Her body frees itself. Her mind resumes being a mind and her heart a heart, racing and pounding as minds and hearts do. Her lips part and allow greedy gulps of breath. The waiting room shakes itself out and returns to its proper form: four dingy beige walls, a fake plant with dusty leaves, a tidy line of stackable fabric chairs, the sounds of coughing and weeping and the nightly news predicting nuclear war. The doctor squeezes Jude's arm again and confirms what she already knows: Kat had been gone but now she is halfway back, alive but in a coma. He whispers a series of chilling words: *traumatic brain injury, intercranial pressure, damaged axons.* She will live but might never be the same. Jude should expect the worst. She should prepare.

———————

All their lives they've compensated for each other, and now, with Kat lying still and silent and swathed in bloody ribbons, Jude begins to do the work of her twin's brain. Kat must be wondering why it's so dark behind her eyes, a dark deeper than sleep, and why the voices she hears seem so slushy and far away. Her arms itch where the needle has impaled her skin and she's dying to scratch, but her other arm is weighted by something unseen. She is frustrated and scared and, above all, angry—why is she flattened and immobile instead of out in the world, raising a glass and toasting everything to come? She tries to rescue her voice, but the words stick in the grooves of her tongue.

She is counting on Jude to bring her around, to restore her so that they are again a perfect whole.

"Kat," Jude says, her mouth clamped to her sister's ear, her lips fitting perfectly in the curves and folds, her voice aimed deep into the canal. "I know you hear me. You are not allowed to die. I will kill you if you die, and then where will we be? Do you want us to spend all of eternity haunting each other's ghosts?"

Even under the bandages, Kat still looks like Jude—an opposite replica of her. Mirror image twins, they're called. A heightened, italicized version of identical, when the embryo splits later than usual. Jude is right-handed and Kat favors her left. Their hair whorls push in different directions, Kat's clockwise and Jude's counter. Their voices, too, establish balance: Kat's is frenzied and rushed, a freight train in danger of careening offtrack; Jude's is measured and parsed, doled out in careful servings, as though in danger of drying up. The same purple vein snakes along opposing temples, pulsing when they are excited or angry or shocked. A birthmark on either shoulder, a deepened dimple on either cheek, one slightly elongated incisor on either side of their mouths. Kat always joked that they even pissed from complementary holes.

Kat is three minutes older, dominating their journey from the very start, but Jude has always felt responsible. It was Kat's job to carve their path through life and Jude's to concoct explanations and tidy any mistakes. Her brain continues to translate Kat's thoughts, but they seem to be receding—not in frequency or intensity but in clarity. Jude can see it, a slow chalkboard erasing of people and places and events, leaving only outlines until they, too, are gone.

"Come back," Jude whispers. "I beseech you. I order you. You know I know what's best for us. You've always known it, even when you did what you wanted to do anyway. But this time you must do what I say, and do it now."

Two weeks to the day that Kat died for ninety seconds, she finally obeys. Jude senses it happening before it actually does: the air around her warms, throwing off a charge of energy only Jude can feel. Jude rushes to her bedside. She presses her hand against Kat's heart and feels the thump of its base; her own heart synchronizes its beats. She can see beyond Kat's eyelids, her irises stirring, pupils dilating, light finally seeping to the other side.

Kat's eyes spring open and stare directly into hers.

"Hello, Jude," she says.

"Welcome back," Jude tells her. She lowers her face to Kat's, their noses touching. A single tear drops from Jude's right eye into Kat's left. Her breath flows into her sister's mouth. "Welcome back and never leave me again."

The doctor rushes in. He checks a tower of monitors, takes Kat's hand, asks if she is able to answer questions. Does she know who she is? No. Does she know where she lives? No. Does she remember what she was doing before the accident? Does she remember the accident itself? No and no. Does she recall where she grew up, her parents' names, the last job she held, where she went to school, her favorite hobbies? Negative to all of them. He conducts tests, consults with fellow experts, and concludes that Kat's brain has changed in a fundamental and permanent way.

One thing becomes clear: Jude is all that she knows.

Jude understands that their lives have been split into two distinct wedges of time—before the accident and after the accident—and she alone will decide how the two should intersect, how much one should inform the other.

She will have to reconstruct her sister from the ground up. She will have to consider what it is like to wake up with a disintegrated brain, all nerves and synapses and pathways razed to the ground. Kat doesn't know her name or age, her likes or dislikes, her style of humor, her favorite pastimes, the nightmares that infest her sleep. Her own history is silent and imageless, all triumphs and failures erased.

She can't remember if there were birthday parties and homecoming dances, if she's ever been in love, if she's ever sought revenge. She is ignorant of the topography of her own body, inside and out—how she got the scar along her arm, what opens and closes her heart.

It will fall upon Jude to tell her everything, to color in the outlines of her life. No one understands. No one has seen anything like it before. It is unprecedented, a medical mystery, an inexplicable quirk of twin connection.

Kat has been unmade, she thinks. *And only I can remake her.*

KAT: NOW

Eight Weeks after the Accident
MAY 1983

These are the things Jude has told me: My name is Katherine Bird and I am twenty-two years old. Around midnight on March 13, 1983, on a slick road in a rural town outside of Philadelphia, our car swerved to miss a deer and instead collided with the base of a twisted, ancient tree. Jude, in the passenger seat, suffered scrapes and bruises, but the angle of the crash tossed me through the windshield, my face miraculously spared, my head taking a second hit against the ground. I lay there bleeding onto Jude's jeans until a kindly trucker stopped. He didn't try anything funny, Jude told me, although I hadn't thought to ask.

I first landed in the neuroscience intensive care unit in Ridley Memorial Hospital for around-the-clock monitoring. When the swelling subsided and the possibility of death receded, they moved me to a private room, where I awakened to the sight of my sister's panicky face. I knew her right away but did not know myself at all, and that absence of knowledge—the realization that everything I have ever been or done is no longer accessible to me—felt just as final as death. I might be alive but there is nothing to me, no there there, no *stuff*, just a bare tree waiting to be dressed, festooned with ornaments others wish to see. It terrifies me to think about it, and Jude tells me to just swat the feelings away, send them off to a place that can't be reached. Reject and release, she calls it. Once a thought is rejected and released, you have power over it, and it can't harm you again.

For the past six weeks, since awakening from my coma, I've gotten reacquainted with my body and the practical aspects of my mind, doing exercises for both muscle and memory. I was reminded how to button my blouse, how to brush my teeth, how to trust my feet enough to take steps. I still have knowledge but it's abstract, untethered from experience. I know an apple is red, and I know it is a fruit distinct from bananas and oranges and pears, but don't remember ever tasting one. I also still have language—the words align properly in my brain—but they sometimes get lost on the way to my mouth, evaporating before I can speak them.

"You'll get it back, all of it," Jude promises on the day of my discharge. "You could always talk your way—*our* way—out of anything." She's carrying a long and pungent paper bag. "You know what this is, don't you?"

I do, I really do, and yet it eludes me.

Jude mimes fishing, casting an invisible lure and cranking the wheel. "It's on the hook . . . It's flailing . . . You almost have it."

I think it's there, and then the syllables dissolve on my tongue. I shrug, frustrated.

"An Italian hoagie," she says. "It's always been your favorite."

She pulls the sandwich from the bag, hovers it by my lips.

"You don't want to wait until we get home?" I ask. "Or at least in the car?"

"You would never wait. You would start eating even before we paid at the counter. By the time I took my first bite, you were a mountain of crumbs."

I part my lips, tentatively at first, and then as wide as I can, stretching my skin, closing my eyes, waiting. The bread scratches the roof of my mouth, scrapes against my teeth. I clamp down: crusty, then chewy, then salty-tangy-acidic-juicy-sweet-crispy-spicy-tart, all of those things in one perfect bite.

"That was like tasting a miracle," I say.

"I told you," Jude says. "Trust me."

She leads me to a car the size and color of a whale, a bright red stripe running along the body. She'd sold our damaged car while I was in the hospital, she says, and got just enough money to buy this one. This, to the new me, is my very first car ride, and we start off for Philadelphia, which Jude says is thirty miles east. We cruise along an avenue dotted with stores named Tech Hifi and Gimbels and the Golden Wheel-In Steakhouse. I roll down the window and dangle my arm, letting the wind raise and lower my hand. A part of me feels like an interloper, invading a world that is not my own.

"I'm sorry," I tell her.

"For what?"

Jude turns down a side street, where the storefronts give way to homes. Kids playing in the street scatter as we drive through; in the rearview mirror I see one of them hurl a ball in our direction, just missing the back window.

"For almost dying on you." I close my eyes, locking in the tears. "I can't imagine the other way, you dying on me."

"But you didn't."

"Okay, then, I'm sorry for coming back like . . . like I am."

"Stop," she says. "Reject and release. Let's focus on the fact that you *did* come back. And that you came back knowing me. If you hadn't remembered that, my job would be impossible right now. Think of it this way: You're like a safe that needs to be cracked, and only I have the code. I'll open you back up so you can see inside again."

She covers my hand with hers and presses down, pinning it into place.

"Do something for me," she adds. "Stick your arm out the window again. Raise your hand. Scream out that you're alive. Celebrate it—your old self would be throwing a party right now."

I do as she says. The wind whips my arm. I close my fingers into a fist and raise it high. The city is my scepter; the world is my crown. "I'm alive!" I yell, and repeat it again. "Alive, alive, alive!"

"Yes!" Jude says, and raises her own arm. "My twin is alive! Alive, alive, alive!"

For the rest of the ride home it becomes our refrain.

I watch her face change expressions, fluid as a kaleidoscope's spin: incredulous joy, deep relief, and beneath both of those, a stark and potent fear.

Our complex is shaped like a crushed can, cylindrical and low to the ground, its white facade showing every kiss of industrial smoke. Jude holds my hand as we climb to the fourth floor, taking careful steps. My understanding of apartments—the layouts, the decor—is based solely on my hospital viewings of *All My Children*, and I am expecting plush couches and Oriental rugs and framed portraits rising along the stairs. Instead we walk into a plain, square afterthought of a room: a couch with jutting springs, a kitchenette with peeling wallpaper, a slender hallway meekly lit by a fizzing bulb. One cheerful element stands alone in a corner: a curved cabinet showcasing a jumble of trinkets behind glass doors.

I want to know if we have jobs, if we can't afford something nicer, if we've failed at life in some fundamental way, but am too afraid to ask—what if I'm to blame for our circumstances? I wouldn't be surprised, considering the mess I've made of my own brain. I decide to bring it up later, but Jude senses my question and offers a partial answer.

"It's crap, but it's temporary," she says. "We won't be here for long." She waves an arm toward the hallway. "The bedroom and bathroom's back there. They're totally luxurious, though, complete with a champagne glass hot tub and rotating waterbed."

"Really?" I ask. "Like something out of the soaps?"

Her smile is greedy, showing all of her teeth, and without thinking I mimic her, matching her expression.

"We wish," she says. "It's sarcasm. You remember what that is—saying the opposite of what you mean, usually in an attempt to be funny, but sometimes to be mean. I meant to be funny, of course."

"I get it," I tell her. "I think the fact that I believed you was the funnier part."

"You were always a tiny bit gullible." She reaches for my wrist and squeezes. "I'm glad you haven't lost that."

I want to challenge this, explain that it's scary to be gullible when you've lost every scrap of your knowledge, all of the facts and falsehoods collected over the course of a life. This, too, she intuits, and squeezes harder. "You're scared," she says. "Like everything looks normal, but you can't be sure what's real and what's not. A dream within a dream, like Poe said."

I feel my expression shift; she reads my confusion.

"It's a poem," she explains. "We grew up with poems. That was—*is*—one of your favorites. But we can save all that for another time." She drops my wrist and points to the couch and orders me to relax; she has a surprise for me. I hear her shuffling in the tiny kitchen, and she returns holding two silver cans. "Coors. Also a favorite."

"But—"

She raises a hand. "I know the doctor said no booze, but this is your first night back, and we've already decided on a celebration."

I nod my agreement. The cold can is soothing against my palm. For a few moments we drink in silence, and I am relieved to realize that Jude was right once again; the musty, earthy taste pleases me, wakes up my tongue. If I rewind my brain, imagining my old self into vivid life, I could see us sitting together just as we are now, drinking beer, eating hoagies, and enjoying various other pastimes—movies? music? cards?—that still need to be excavated from my past. These small discoveries are reassuring, tiny pieces that help rebuild my whole. *I am a person who throws parties and likes beer.*

"Time for show-and-tell," she says. "You up for it?"

"I think that if I want to get back to normal, I have to be up for anything."

"Now *that* sounds like you." She makes two trips to the display cabinet, gathers a cache of knickknacks, and piles them on the coffee table. Scanning quickly, I spot a small porcelain vase resembling a hand, with five fingerlike openings; a silky pair of long gloves; a square tin box; a ceramic figurine of a dancing woman; a half dozen gilded frames. I pick up the nearest frame, which holds a picture of me and Jude around age ten. Behind us is a troop of pastel carousel horses too sinister to be beautiful. The whites of their eyes are too white; the pupils too dark and black; the hair whipped up into silver flames; the tongues too red and flat over rows of snaggled teeth.

"Where was this taken?" I ask her.

"A traveling circus came to town. We went every night for two weeks and stuffed our faces with candy and rode every ride. It's the only photo of ourselves that we really like. We were playing switch— you were being me and I was being you."

I study it closer and see what she means. My hair has her part, and her expression—a tight smile—betrays the nuances of my own, minute differences only she and I would recognize. "Did we do that often?"

"When it suited us." She picks up another frame and presses it into my hands. It holds a picture of a couple, shot in black-and-white. They wear similar expressions, smiles that match each other in voltage and width, as though they're in perfect agreement about the life they've made. A crimson polka-dot dress brightens the woman's thin frame, her collarbone a mountain range across her narrow chest. She has a glossy cap of bobbed blond hair and glasses that taper into savage points. The man, too, is thin, his arms poking out, scarecrow-like, from a white tank. His glasses are thick and black, and a cigar hangs limply from his mouth. They hold hands and there is something desperate about the grip, as though they are a shutter click away from leaping off a cliff.

"Our parents?" I ask.

She drags a finger along the top of the frame, downshifts her voice into a whisper. "There is no easy way to tell you this, but they're gone. Our dad had some problems, some mental issues, and just . . . disappeared. It was a month before our eleventh birthday. We tried to find him. We waited for him to come back. Neither ever happened."

I try to imagine this, having our father in our life one day and not in the next. I feel sorry for myself and Jude, for the little girls I've forgotten. For a moment Jude closes her eyes, retreating into her own private memory, and I wait to speak until she opens them again. She's not crying, but on the verge.

"What kind of mental issues?" I ask. "Do we have the issues?"

"He was just very smart—too smart, if that makes sense. Like his brain was different, operating on a plane and frequency no one else could see or hear. He didn't know how to live in society, and society didn't know how to accommodate him. And no, we don't have his particular mental issues, but I like to think we got some of his intelligence."

"What about our mom?"

"Car accident. I know that must be especially weird to hear, considering what just happened to you. It was five years ago."

Now she cries—no sound, just the faint sheen of tears on her cheeks.

My brain seems to pause inside my head, unsure of how to react or what signals to send to my body. Do I cry, too? Do I hurl things at the wall—a lamp, a set of keys, a notebook, my fist? How do you mourn people you loved but can't remember? I try to play a movie in my mind, visualizing the people in the photograph doing parental things—making dinner, reading books, wrapping presents—but the images blur, the faces lose their features, the reel sputters and stops. And then it comes to me: I *do* know how to mourn, but only for myself. I am mourning a brain that's irrevocably broken, and a loss that feels like no loss at all.

I discover I am crying along with her, and in the same way, silent but tearful. I feel trapped within myself, like my own skeleton has become a cage. I don't know who I was then, who I am now, how much difference there is—or will be—between the two. I feel Jude's hand on mine; my body stills at her touch. She pulls me downward, arranging my body so that it's splayed across her lap. Her fingers twine themselves in my hair and move like scissors, cutting through the strands. I look up at her looking down at me, and it occurs to me that neither of us has ever seen our own face. When I look into the mirror, Jude's face stares back; only outsiders see the true representation, the reversal. I want her to tell me a story, replace another piece of myself.

"Talk about our mother," I say. "What did she smell like? What did she sound like?"

"Do you want to hear the whole story? Are you sure you're ready for it?"

"Tell me in pieces and I'll decide as we go along."

As Jude speaks, I consider each word, translating the facts of our past into a vibrant, breathing memory, something I can see and experience rather than merely absorb. When she says that our parents' names were John and Elizabeth Bird, those two faces in the photograph become animated; their mouths part, their limbs move, they hustle inside the cozy world they created for our family way out in Harmony, Pennsylvania, where we live in a farmhouse among dozens of animals and ghosts of the Revolutionary War.

Our mother smells of maple syrup, Jude says, and has a low, soft voice but an operatic laugh, shocking in its frequency and pitch. To her, everything is funny: our father's dumb imitation of Kermit the Frog, our own secret twin language, the way Jude and I arrange our bodies when we sleep, like two commas, one upright and one inverted, making a yin and yang. Watching Jude from below, I can see her throat constrict; the memory is growing turbulent, spinning in her brain and stirring up her loss—*our* loss—and it passes from her to me, transplanted, like a borrowed heart.

"Our days begin at five in the morning," she says. "Dad always holds a contest to see who can milk the cows faster. Then we go down into the basement to see his latest project—he was an inventor and had the most incredible ideas." Afterward, Mom gives us lessons at home, playing flashcard games and selecting the Poem of the Day, verses to instruct and inspire us. Sometimes we abandon the makeshift curriculum altogether and go outside, where she labels the types of flowers and spins stories of fairies and wolves. She makes animal costumes, furry monkey heads and pointed rabbit ears and scaly scorpion tails. She teaches us through high school, believing that the local school district is inadequate for our budding and brilliant minds. On weekends, she takes us to antique markets in the area and shares the history behind old and forgotten things. On the table, here in our apartment, are some of her favorite finds—the handlike vase, the elegant opera gloves, the ceramic lady frozen in a permanent spin. These are the mementos we chose to take with us when the farmhouse was sold.

Because of her own childhood, rife with unreliable and dangerous characters, our mother is wary of bad influences. We don't need
outside friends. We have her and each other, the three musketeers.
After our father finishes his workday, we are four, a perfect unit,
balanced and content. When our father disappears, never to be seen
or heard from again, it is our mother's love for us and our devotion to
each other that ensures our survival.

"Where do you think Dad went?" I ask.

"I wish I knew."

We are quiet for a moment. I'm afraid to prod further, to ask for
speculation—if he is dead or alive, and which possibility would be
worse.

"The hard part is coming up," Jude says. "Do you want me to go on?"

She looks down at me as she says this, gripping a batch of my hair
like reins. I tell her yes. I want to integrate all of her memories into
my new brain, even the ones that will haunt me.

"There was a full moon on the night she died," Jude says, and
grips my hair tighter. "She was coming home from picking up craft
supplies for our lessons. Some teenager in a pickup truck swerved and
hit her head-on."

One single hot tear drops onto my cheek. My own tear falls,
absorbing hers.

"Then . . . ?" I whisper.

"She died at the scene."

We sit in absolute stillness. Jude's fist remains full of my hair.

I force myself to speak. "Will you take me to the town sometime?
Show me the farm? And where it happened?"

"Of course," she says. "Look at the rest of the pictures—there's
an old shot of Harmony's Main Street, one with the lake where we
used to swim, a couple of shots of us all together, when you and I
were babies." She releases my hair and strokes my cheek. "I want you
to know everything about them."

"Is there anything left of them, besides these things?"

"Hold on." She keeps one hand in my hair; with the other, she reaches for the tin box. Inside lies a simple gold chain with letters that spell my name.

"From Dad," she says. "These necklaces were our favorite things—he made them for us. You were wearing it the night of the accident, and I took it off so it didn't get lost in the hospital."

"You have one, too?"

"I did, but I lost it a long time ago."

"I'm sorry," I say. "I'm culky I still have mine."

Jude tilts her head. "You remember *culky*?" she asks. "Our word for *lucky*?"

"Why wouldn't I? It's like remembering English."

"I guess it is," she says. "We've spoken it as long as we've spoken English."

I lean back into her, soothed by the sturdiness of her narrow chest, the blanket of her arms. Jude is all I have, but she is all I need; she is the only route back to myself.

"They say regular twins operate at one hundred percent connection," she says, "but our kind, mirror twins, operate double that number—a two hundred percent connection."

Instinctively, I understand. The trust we share as identical twins, as mirror twins, is the lone factor that elevates our bond, the most significant and unyielding connection that any two people can share. No one but identical twins begin life as the same exact person, and only mirror twins cleave together as long as nature will allow, parting almost reluctantly in the womb.

KAT: NOW

Two Months after the Accident

MAY 1983

Today marks a week that I've been home, and also Jude's first day at work; she'll be cleaning rich people's houses along the Main Line, in neighborhoods far in both distance and temperament from our own. She arranged this job with urgency and some secrecy. The head of the agency is a savior of sorts, Jude says, prioritizing hard-luck cases—domestic violence victims, the formerly homeless. The rich people like knowing that having their toilets scrubbed also amounts to charity. Jude told the boss that our parents died and we'd lost our way, drifting about and aimless, with no clear path forward. Not as grim as some of the other cases, but good enough to get us on the roster. But after my accident, we rose to the top of the list. "Now we're the most pathetic case of all," she jokes. "The marquee unfortunates. The headliners, if you will."

My doctor hasn't yet cleared me to work, and Jude won't let me tag along even to keep her company. My body and brain need rest, she tells me, and I'll be able to join her soon enough. I insist that my body is fine and my brain needs anything *but* rest—it needs to wake up and stretch and explore—but she won't hear of it. "Do this for me," she says. "We have the rest of our lives to work." I watch her pack her tools: bucket, sponges, extra pairs of gloves. She gives me the addresses and phone numbers of the day's destinations, in case of an emergency. She warns me not to venture past our little gray block. A careful stroll is fine; a neighborhood expedition is not.

I scramble an egg and grow restless. I look again at the artifacts from our past, still arranged on the coffee table in a tidy row. I pull on the opera gloves past my elbows and make the dancer spin in my hand. I study the pictures more closely, searching for clues. Why is the carousel picture, with those menacing horses leering in the background, the only one we like of ourselves? The black-and-white shot of Harmony's Main Street looks decades old; did our mother take it before we were born? In the picture of the lake, I see a head peeking from the surface of the water, just two eyes and a nose—is that me or Jude? In the final photo, which shows our family on a sandy beach, the setting sun throws us all into silhouette, transforming our faces and bodies into sharp, elongated shadows. A mother, a father, and two little girls of matching size, maybe eight years old, one with a shovel and the other with a pail. I remove it from the frame to read the block lettering on the back: *BIRD FAMILY VACATION, WILD-WOOD, 1969*, and I wonder who wrote the words.

I wish I could gather all of my pieces and solve myself, everything snapping into its familiar place, the whole picture unambiguously revealed.

I long for a television to watch the soaps and page through the old magazines Jude took from the hospital waiting room, with headlines about the chilling lure of cocaine and a mysterious and deadly disease called AIDS. I look out our window and spy a golden dog, an old man pushing a wobbly cart, a blue Tastykake truck, and a girl in a sun hat darting down the street, glancing left and right, looking for something or someone, a limp rendering her left leg half a beat behind. I watch her walk back and forth, setting her gait to a beat: Ba-*dah*. Ba-*dah*.

After a few minutes, I search for something myself: my hospital bills. I've asked numerous times, but Jude won't divulge what we owe for my lengthy stay. Wild guesses pile up in my mind: Three thousand? Five? Ten? Jude tells me that she's always been the responsible, organized twin, tamping down my reckless urges, and I imagine that the bills are hidden neatly somewhere, organized by date and labeled something like "Kat's Scrambled Brain." I find nothing in the kitchen drawers besides a sparse collection of utensils and some dull pencils, and figure they must be in the bedroom.

Jude has divvied up our dresser fairly; I have the top drawer, she has the bottom, and the middle one is evenly split, containing every set of underwear we own. In her drawer I rummage through crisply folded shirts, taking care not to disturb them, and at the bottom of the pile my hand collides with something hard. I pull it out and hold it up for examination: a white stick, long and thick as my forearm, with a top shaped like a tennis ball. I flip its switch and it begins a low hum, tickling my palm and raising the hair on my neck. I know exactly what it is but not if I've ever used one.

Lying in my bed, I run it over my face and neck, tickling myself. I hover it over my shirt, letting it graze my nipples, and then I pause long enough to take the shirt off and let it dance over my bare skin, up and down, buzz and release. I feel a slight sting of guilt—Jude would never use something so personal of mine—but am distracted by its ripple across my thighs. I tell myself not to push it any lower, that doing so would be invasive and weird and possibly unsanitary (although my brain retorts: *Come on, you know Jude bathes this thing in bleach*), but those thoughts, too, recede, as the humming finds the point between my legs. My brain resurrects our private word for it, a lovely word, *ginva*, and I move the wand in circles. I feel a budding heat, a mounting pressure, a storm cloud thick with rain. Sparks flicker at the edge of my mind—and then Jude steps in. An image of her on her hands and knees, scrubbing and sweating. I try to close the void and push her aside. I increase pressure and speed. Jude's body disappears, but I hear her voice: *Be careful, don't venture very far, I can't almost lose you again.* I try to purge all evidence of her. I press, I make smaller circles, I imagine it as a game that must be won. I do win but it seems like a consolation prize, a quick and mild flutter, a purr instead of a roar.

It exhausts me, regardless. For a half hour I scarcely move. So that's what it feels like, I think, and realize I've lost the precise word. It seemed more exciting when they acted it out on the soaps. I add to the mental tally of who I am: *I am a person who throws parties, likes beer, and appreciates certain private devices.* Just as quickly my mind counters: *Yes, but millions of people do and like these things, and they are useless clues. Find some that actually tell you something, important parts of your whole.*

I spring up from bed with a start, charged with purpose. I have work to do. I take the device to the kitchen sink and scrub it with every product I find, wipe it dry, and return it to Jude's drawer. Before I let her warning—*stay within our little gray block*—dissuade me, I shower, dress in jeans and a tank, and slick my lips with red gloss. Checking the mirror, an impish, glamourized version of Jude stares back at me. I speak aloud, as much as to Jude as to myself: "I am a person who won't be told what to do."

The sun is just beginning to whip up its heat and layer it across the neighborhood. Our apartment complex occupies the entire block, but beyond that the streets give way to twin homes—connected structures that are themselves built like mirror twins, with doors and windows lined up on opposing sides; if folded together, they would match faultlessly, melding into one. The wires overhead are draped with pairs of sneakers, lined up like a murder of crows. Jude has explained the neighborhood's personality, with its odd and stringent territorial distinctions; allies and enemies are made according to the locations of intersections and playgrounds. I think she appreciates the private, insular nature of this place, the way questions aren't expected and answers are ignored.

I pass a Catholic church, a playground, a check-cashing place, a McDonald's, a theater showing Cheech and Chong's *Still Smokin*, a shop called Corropolese Tomato Pie. The smells drifting from the open door compel me to pause, and I sit on a bench outside. Closing my eyes, I make a mental list of questions to ask Jude (*Where did we go after our parents died? What did we do? What were we doing on the night of the accident?*) and am disrupted by the sudden appearance of a body next to me.

Shifting my eyes, I assess him: about my age, slim but cut, tanned skin and dark hair, a tuft of curls gathered into a point at the nape of his neck. The sleeves of his T-shirt are rolled up to reveal, on his wiry bicep, a tattoo of a woman's face. He unwraps a hoagie and shoves a third of it into his mouth, and I am transfixed by the finely drawn eyes, dark and slitty, and how the right one seems to wink with each flex of his arm.

"Mmmm, mmmm," he says, chewing.

I nod and slide away; I don't need his appraisal of lunch. He swallows and then speaks again, using words this time: "I meant to say 'my mom,' but I don't think that's how it came out."

"I thought you said something else. I didn't mean to stare."

He waves his hand, and the eye winks again.

"What about your mom?" I ask.

"That's her, on my arm."

I scooch an inch closer and lower my head.

"It's okay, have a look." He holds out his arm, meeting me half-way. "It was my favorite picture of her. My brother's an artist—he did this after she died."

I look directly into his face for the first time and am struck by the incongruity, the hard against the soft: long lashes and plush lips anchor a scaffolding of sharp bones, the skin stretched tight as a sheet. "I'm sorry," I tell him. "Mine did, too." I'm surprised by my revelation, the sharing of private information only recently acquired, still rough and raw.

"I'm sorry. How?"

I hear myself speak Jude's memory, making it my own. "Car accident."

"Bummer," he says. "Drunk driver?"

"Some kid. Swerved right into her, head-on." I sound so poised and assured, so certain of my words. I have a piece of my past, a real and true thing I can now summon at will.

"I can't imagine," he says, and takes another bite. "The sudden shock of it."

I am tempted to let myself cry and practice my grief, my mourning of not knowing how to mourn, a mourning once removed. "How about your mom?" I ask.

"Leukemia. That was its own kind of nightmare."

I point at his tattoo. "You must have been really close."

"We were. You too, with yours?"

I am about to answer "I think so" and stop myself. "We were, very," I say. "My mom was my best friend." With those words I feel a slight twinge of disloyalty, but I want to claim this moment for myself, separate from Jude. "Sometimes I wonder if I was meant to be in the car, too, because the pain of losing her nearly killed me."

"Damn," he says, and takes another huge bite of hoagie. As he chews, I raise my face to the sky. A bead of sweat slithers down my back.

"What's your name?" he says, finally.

"Kat."

"Sab."

We shake hands. I like the way his hand feels wrapped around mine, warm and firm, a pressure that stops just short of intimidating.

"I have to ask—what kind of a name is Sab?"

"Short for Sabatino. My dad's Italian, my mom was Puerto Rican. So it's Sabatino Ramos. I went by Ramos for a while, but it didn't stick like Sab."

"What's your first name?"

"You'll laugh."

"Try me."

"Blaise."

"Blaze? Like you're on fire?"

"Well, I like to think I'm hot, but it's *B-L-A-I-S-E*. He was a saint, the patron saint of many things." He holds out his hand, ticking his fingers: "Sore throats, wool combers, choking, infants, and attacks from wild animals."

"Impressive! I'll try to avoid conjuring any of those."

"At least not all in one encounter. I like to take it slow."

He smiles, a kind of smile that is new to me, tinged with heat and wanting.

"How did you end up on this bench?" he asks. "Is this your lunch break?"

My mind whips up a lie. I don't want to admit the broken parts of myself before I've devised a way to fix them. I hear myself say, "I have the day off."

"What do you do?"

The lie expands itself and I settle in, waiting to see where it will take me. "I care for a very old, very wealthy man. Buy him groceries, clean him up, keep him company. His daughter came today for her yearly visit, so here I am."

"He sounds lonely."

"Not when I'm with him," I say. "He loves me like I'm his own. What about you?"

"I'm in construction, so this is actually my proper uniform." He lifts a leg, showing off a steel-toed boot. "But I've been working since five this morning and I'm off the clock now, so let's talk about something more interesting." He moves an inch closer. "I mean, if you want to."

I think of Jude: I am well beyond the boundaries of our little gray block. I thrill at the danger of it, the chance to dip into a stranger's world before I return to my own.

"Why not?"

"I thought you'd say that." He stands and offers me a hand. "Come with me."

I imagine another piece fitting into place: *I am a person who takes risks.*

KAT: NOW

Two Months after the Accident

MAY 1983

I take Sab's hand, acutely aware of the soft heat of his palm. As we walk several blocks I lose myself in his nervous patter: here's the bowling lane where he hung out as a kid, here's his cousin's bakery, here's his sister's salon, here's the corner where he got mugged—mundane revelations that somehow leave me spellbound, the simple, enviable act of summarizing a personal history. His voice is fast, with slurred consonants and flattened vows, and a furtive, frenetic energy circles the air around him; this is someone who also has secrets, and who might be persuaded to share them.

We stop in front of a bar called Exiles, with an emerald-green facade and stained-glass windows shaped like fans. "My buddy told me that back in the olden days, in Ireland, people stored dead bodies in pubs," he says. "The cold cellars kept the corpses in decent shape until the funeral."

"Is that why we're here, to view corpses?"

"Depending on how the day goes, my wallet might be a casualty."

"If it helps any, I think I'm a cheap date."

He holds the door open for me. "It's not you I'm worried about."

I step inside and think, *The new me's first time in a bar.*

"Beer good with you?" Sab asks.

"It's my favorite. Especially Coors." I feel an odd relief at sharing another truth, a piece of myself that's been validated and confirmed.

He slaps hands with the bartender and says something about baseball. I scan the room, wanting to remember every detail: the shiny silver tin ceiling, the posters advertising Def Leppard and Mötley Crüe, the James Joyce quote along the brick wall—*I am tomorrow, or some future day, what I establish today. I am today what I established yesterday or some previous day.*

"I think we should toast," I say, taking the glass. "Any ideas?"

"To mothers and good luck?"

Good culk, I think, but respond, "Perfect."

We clink glasses and take a long sip. I tilt my head back to avoid the intensity of his gaze, as disorienting as looking directly at the sun.

"I should have asked," I say, wiping my mouth. "What do we need luck for?"

He smiles. "Follow me."

We head toward the far end of the bar, coming to tall, mahogany double doors inlaid with panes of frosted glass. "Welcome to the snug room," he says. "Another relic from the old days. Once we're inside, no one can see us."

We enter a small smoky space that could pass for a museum of curiosities. One paneled wall is a tribute to medical oddities, including an antique poster depicting the stages of delirium tremens and a cabinet of anatomical exhibits: a model of conjoined twins attached at the chest; a mummified hand; a jar holding a pickled human heart. Two tufted booths upholstered in worn red leather are arranged on either side of a long, splintered wooden table where five men are gathered, smoking cigars and chugging beer, a deck of playing cards fanned out before them. A crimson velvet curtain circles the perimeter, adding another layer of secrecy.

"Yo, Sab," says one of the men, with a terse nod of his head. "Who's the guest?"

"This is Kat." He drops his hand on my shoulder. "She's my good-luck charm today. Kat, meet Ryan, Guy, Steve, Chinch—short for Cianciulli—and Booch, short for Bochella. And you thought my name was weird."

Twelve eyes set upon me, and I wither under the scrutiny; the new me has never met so many strangers at once. I give a timid wave. "Hi, everyone. Hope I don't disappoint."

Booch shoves over to make room, and I sit on the very end. They toss bills onto the table and Guy doles out chips. Sab lines his up according to color and whispers an explanation: "We all put in a hundred dollars. Red is worth five dollars, blue is ten, green is twenty-five."

"What kind of game is this?" I whisper back.

"Poker. Texas Hold'em. You ever played?"

"No," I say. "Actually, maybe. I'm really not sure."

He gives me a curious look. I'm saved by Ryan's announcement, delivered through teeth tightly gripping his cigar: "Ante up, gentlemen." He nods at me. "And lady? You playing?"

"Not this time," I say, and watch everyone throw two red chips into the pot.

"Watch and learn," Sab says. "You'll get it."

He squeezes my hand under the table, his fingers cold and damp from the beer. I squeeze back harder.

"Here goes," Ryan says. He deals everyone two cards, facedown. Sab lets met peek at his: a Nine of Spades and the Seven of Clubs. "Is that good?" I ask.

Booch laughs.

"*Shhh*," Sab says. "You have to keep all of your card business absolutely to yourself."

The game works its way around the table, and I start to interpret its language. Calling the bet means matching the amount in play; raising it means greater stakes; folding means you quit that round. I learn about the order of a round, the flop and the turn and the river. Sab whispers everyone's "tells"—see how Booch bites his lower lip, and Steve adjusts his hat?—and guesses when they're bluffing. He wins that first round, but just barely—his two pairs beating Guy's eights and sixes.

"See," he says, and leans in. "You're already bringing the luck."

They play another round, and another, and Sab consults me all along, asking how much he should bet, whether he should call or fold, explaining the big blind ante and rounds of betting. I begin to understand the game, appreciate its nuances. His pile of chips grows, shrinks, grows again. Beyond the doors I hear evidence of a gathering crowd: laughter, the clink of glasses, the booming base of an unfamiliar song. Again I think of Jude, alone somewhere in a dank mansion, folding a stranger's underwear, paying off my bills.

"One last round?" Sab asks.

"Here goes," Ryan says, and deals everyone two cards. I glance at Sab's hand—a ten and an ace, both hearts—and keep my face neutral. Everyone calls.

Ryan takes the top card and slides it to the side. "Burn one, turn three," he says, and flips over the Five of Spades, the Jack of Diamonds, and the Queen of Hearts. Sab's expression is inscrutable, the face one might make while tying shoes, and when his turn comes he throws four blue chips into the pot.

"Whoa!" Chinch says. "Someone *is* feeling lucky."

"Or getting better at bluffing," Steve says.

Ryan turns up the next card: the Jack of Hearts. Ryan, Guy, Steve, and Booch all fold. Sab tosses in another blue chip; Chinch calls. They are the only two left.

"And finally," Ryan says, "we have the river." Slowly, slyly, I shift my gaze to Sab's face. When the upturned card shows the Two of Hearts, I note a nearly imperceptible twitch of his lips, quick as one falling drop of rain. I think, *I am someone who can read people, even when they don't want to be read.*

"Fuck it," Sab says. "I'm all in." He downs the rest of his beer and pushes his pile of chips to the center.

To a chorus of whistles and applause, Chinch does the same.

"What do you got?" Sab asks. He jostles his leg under the table and I grip his knee, stilling him.

Chinch flips his cards, showing the Queen of Clubs and Queen of Spades, and drops them near the Queen of Hearts. "Three Ladies."

"Damn," Sab says, and drops his face to his hands, feigning defeat. "I mean, damn, I'm good!" With a flourish he spreads his cards, showing his flush. "Know when to walk away, my friend. Know when to run."

"Don't count your money," Chinch says. "I'll get you next round."

Even though I expected Sab's win, I can't help myself: I let loose a strange, siren sound, somewhere between a squeal and a shriek, and flutter my hand to my mouth.

"How did I ever play without you?" he asks.

He loops an arm around the pile and pulls it in. I start sorting the chips into neat stacks. A waitress arrives with three pitchers of beer and bags of popcorn, which I taste again for the very first time. The afternoon grows hazy, soft around the edges, the outlines of people and objects dissolving, one moment absorbed by the next. I feel thrillingly adrift, isolated from everything outside this tiny room, removed, even, from the persistent haranguing of my thoughts: *Where am I going, where have I been, what am I doing here?* Silently I answer the last question, in two parts: *I am here because I have met a cute boy who is very interested in me and therefore very nice to me. I am here trying to perform the role of "normal twenty-two-year-old," one with*

memories and history intact, and he is a vital prop. He is saying the right
words and doing the right things, and he makes me believe I can transform
the performance into truth.

More popcorn, more beer, a rising cacophony of music and voices just beyond the door, a diminishing of light, signaling the sun's downward shift.

"What time is it?" I ask Sab.

He checks his watch. "Just after five."

"Just after five," I repeat, the words plunging me into a panic. I can't remember what time Jude said she'd be home but it must be close to now, and she is working so hard to make me whole again, while here I am drinking beer and playing cards and pretending I remember how to flirt. She is going to come home and see that I'm not there and she, too, will panic, and kill me with her dagger words; I intuit, without one memory to back it up, that anger is her first reaction, and disappointment her last. I can't bear the thought of either emotion and I stand up, slithering my body past Sab's, waving goodbye to them all. "I have to go," I say. "I need to get home."

I open the door and the cool air rushes at me; the smell of asphalt and exhaust replace the smell of sweat and beer, and I'm about to sprint when I feel a pressure on my shoulder. I turn to see Sab, his hair damp and his lips dry. He presses two hundred dollars into my hand. "Your cut of the winnings."

I freeze; this is an unfathomable amount of money. It feels rough and itchy against my palm.

"I can't take this," I tell him. "I didn't contribute anything."

"You contributed plenty." He folds my fingers over the bills, rubbing my skin with his thumb. I search his eyes and find a glint of something desperate, as though accepting the money would be for his benefit rather than mine.

"I have to go, they're waiting," he says. "But I wish I didn't." He kisses my cheek, lingering this time, and waves goodbye from the door.

Tucked inside the bills, I find a slip of paper covered in blunt strokes: his phone number and the words *Let's play again soon.*

On the way back I feel a strange mix of guilt and elation. I am almost embarrassed by my own foolish giddiness; it seems out of place, sitting like a wispy meringue atop my layers of loss and fear. But in the moment I don't care. Sab's phone number is hidden deep inside my purse, physical proof that I can relate to people other than Jude, that my old life—whatever it entailed—will yield seamlessly to the new. Today I was a normal person doing normal things, and somehow the experience rings true.

I stop by Corropolese, tap the bench where I met Sab, and order a tomato pie; if Jude is home, I'll tell her I took a short walk to get dinner. It turns out to be entirely different from pizza, served at room temperature and topped with a sweet tomato sauce and just a dusting of cheese. I wonder if I've ever tasted it before, and hope that Jude likes it.

I'm home by five thirty, relieved to find the apartment empty. I set the table, even lighting a candle and putting two glasses in the freezer to ensure our beer is extra cold. In our bedroom, I remove the two hundred dollars and Sab's note, wondering where to hide them. As I hear footsteps on the stairs, I lift the fraying area carpet that spans the width of our bedroom and shove the money and the paper as far as I can reach. When I win enough, maybe one thousand dollars or so, I will confess my gambling excursions and give it all to her. For now, at least, I decide to keep Sab a secret, too; I want just a bit of time to savor the promise of him alone.

I am a person who likes to keep parts of herself hidden.

The door creaks open. "Hello!" Jude calls. I hear the crash of her bucket on the floor.

"You sound like you need a beer." I pour one and hand it to her. Closing her eyes, she drinks half of it without coming up for air. "You have no idea how good that tastes right now. Do you know what I did today? Among other humiliating things, I dusted taxidermy!"

I run the word through my head, hoping I recognize it. Jude reads my face.

"Taxidermy," she says. "Stuffed animals. *Real* stuffed animals. Deer heads, bison heads, bear heads. This one house in Ardmore had an entire room devoted to it. I thought they were going to dismount and eat me alive."

"When I start working with you, I promise to do that room. I'm kind of curious to see it."

"You would be," Jude says, "and I mean that in the best way." She spots my setup at the table. "Awesome. Let's eat."

For ten minutes I let Jude talk without interruption, describing each house she cleaned. Aside from Taxidermy House, there was Widow House (an enormous shrine of photographs and a needle-point that reads GONE TOO SOON), Smoke House (every room reeked of cigarettes), and Porn Palace (a bedside table crammed with issues of *Playboy*). Our ultimate goal, she says, is twenty clients total, two or three houses per day, with a salary of $3.25 an hour, all cash.

I think of the two hundred dollars hidden beneath the rug and how many houses Jude would have to clean to earn that much. She'll have it soon enough, I tell myself, and change the subject, asking for another memory.

She takes an enormous bite of pie and holds up a hand while she chews. "Yes," she says through the last bite of dough. "I've been thinking all day of things to tell you. It's like all our memories are shouting at me, waving their hands, begging to be called on first."

"My questions have been doing the same," I tell her.

"Let me decide this time," she says, licking her fingers. "You always loved when I told you stories. We had a rhythm to it. I was the protagonist, and you were the plot twist. I would pick the setting and theme, and you made interesting things happen. Your ideas didn't always make sense, but they definitely made me want to know how it ended."

She leaps up and starts thrashing around in the hall closet, returning with a thick envelope. "Before I start this round of show-and-tell, I want you to promise me something."

"What is it?" I ask, reaching for the envelope.

She yanks it away. "Promise first."

"Moprise," I say, and she understands our secret word.

"We can talk about our past as much as you want. I want you to relearn everything you forgot. But I also don't want you to get stuck doing it. Moving forward is just as important as looking back. Get it?"

"You're the boss," I say.

"I'm glad you remember that, at least." She thrusts her hand into the envelope, mixing the contents around. "So here's the setting and theme. It's five years ago, and Mom had just died, and we were almost eighteen and had no idea what to do with ourselves. We were so sheltered and innocent and naive. We had seen and done so little. We were about to burst, not just with grief but with longing. With curiosity and hunger. We just had to get the hell out of there."

"Excellent opening," I say, and take a sip of beer. "Time for a plot twist?"

"Not yet." She raises her own glass and motions to the sofa. "We need to get into proper story-time position." Again, she lays me across her lap and slices her fingers through my hair. Staring up at her, I work myself into her brain, preparing to inhabit the memory as she recounts it.

Right after our mother's funeral, she says, we sell the farmhouse and take our meager inheritance and run off to Europe. It's our first time flying in an airplane. We have no itinerary, no friends, no plans, no place to stay. We've brought one small suitcase and two backpacks. We allot ourselves a budget of five dollars per day. We want encounters that pierce and deflate our grief. We want surprise and joy and difficulty and menace, the possibility of death, the certainty of danger. We like to think that we might not return.

Jude flips the first picture, holds it above my face. "The funicular in Lisbon," she says. "We met this old lady who sold wine and sardines from the window of her home."

"Do I like sardines?"

"You like all salty things."

I think of the snug room at the bar, Sab's hand finding my leg. "Popcorn especially?"

"How did you know?" Jude asks. She flips more pictures. In my mind, we tour a winery in Tuscany, gathering and crushing grapes with our bare feet. We visit a market in Seville, a tapas bar in Barcelona, and Cordoba's Mezquita, that ancient magnificent hybrid of faith, half mosque, half cathedral, with its candy cane arches and gilded altar, the elements both perfectly complementary and staunchly oppositional. We play miniature golf at a water park in the Cotswolds. We run down the very street where Ernest Hemingway fled from the bulls. We see the Eiffel Tower at sunset, the Tiergarten at daybreak, the De Wallen red-light district in the middle of the night. The last picture shows a pristine strip of white beach encircled by a deep blue void.

"Crete," Jude says. "Chania."

"I don't remember seeing it, obviously, but I can see it now. Not just the picture, the landscape, but *us*. Our favorite spot on the sand, the exact waves that crashed over us."

Jude is quiet a moment, and then says, "Do you want to know how we got the scars on our arms?"

"I think we had an epic battle with a pirate and stole his treasure and escaped, but not before he sliced us with his sword."

From below I see her smile, the slight upward twitch of her jaw. I wish that's how it happened, she says, but the truth is much more mundane: We go to the beach for a scuba-diving lesson. It feels like we've descended into the lowest rung of hell but somehow land in heaven. The fauna beckons us with waving palms and the fish are bright orange candies coming straight for our mouths. The fish surround us and we follow them through a burst of coral reefs, which look like flower petals but are sharp as blades. I am swimming fast, my body twisting and turning, and the softest patch of my left arm, just above my wrist, glides across a pointy reef. Jude, right behind me, swipes her right arm along the same point so we remain a perfect mirror match. The skin circling the scar is discolored because the coral reef was poisonous, tainting us in a way that will never fully heal.

"The dive seems worth the injury," I say, "even though it's a secondhand memory."

"It was definitely worth it. It was one of the best days of our life."

I trace the scar, noting the faded bruise around it, an indelible mark. "So is this where we were right before my accident? Cutting ourselves up in paradise?"

"Exactly," she says. "When we came home, we had no money left and found this cheap apartment. We'd put our car in storage and got it when we came home. The night of your accident was supposed to be our official return celebration. We were driving out to some new restaurant we'd heard about, an English pub with the same kind of food we ate in the Cotswolds."

"I suppose I at least made it memorable, even though I can't remember it."

"I guess that's one way to look at it," she says, and rearranges the pile of pictures, leaving Crete on top, our last stop. "I wish I could forget it myself."

"Let's go to bed," I say. "That trip was exhausting, even without leaving the couch."

Our room is dark, and within moments my sister's breathing deepens, and I hope her mind is somewhere far away, maybe back on the beach in Crete, with the wide ocean before her and me at her back. Only when I'm drifting to sleep does a curious thought occur to me: neither Jude nor I appear in any of the pictures.

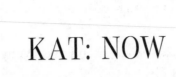

KAT: NOW

Two Months after the Accident
MAY 1983

I am perched on the toilet seat, watching Jude get ready for work, the memories she shared about Europe still sharp in my mind. Although my sister spends her days scrubbing floors and toilets, she insists that this work requires a face different from the one she usually wears, the one that matches my own. This alternate face has hot pink pencil drawn outside the natural line of her lips and ferocious streaks of crimson rouge and black smudges that make her eye sockets look like caves, two slate stones buried deep within. This face makes me imagine a nesting doll of Judes, six or seven deep, layers of sweet and dangerous and selfless and mean, all of them valid and true, some more so than others.

"Why bother when you're not going to see anyone?" I ask.

"I bother precisely *because* I won't see anyone," she says. Keeping her gaze on her own reflection, she considers her next words. "People have different ways of being, different versions of themselves. The way they want others to see them doesn't always match their private ideal. So this is my private self, just for me. No one is seeing me today except for Mr. Clean and he knows to keep his thoughts to himself."

"So putting on a different face is a performance," I say. "Audience of one." I think of what I've done when Jude was not home to watch me, and understand.

"Exactly." She plunges her finger inside a pot of blue glitter and stamps it on one eyelid, giving the effect of a bruise halfway to healing. "It's a good lesson for you to relearn. Save your best performances for yourself."

Another minute passes, and then I ask, "Why weren't we in any of the Europe pictures?"

Her finger, back in the lid, pauses. She looks into her own eyes as she speaks to me.

"We've never liked to have our picture taken," she says. "It's disorienting."

"What do you mean?"

"Come," she says, reaching out her hand. I take it, and she makes room for me at the mirror. "Look straight ahead. When you look at yourself you see me, and when I look at myself I see you."

I do as she says. My face is unadorned but I see Jude, as surely and distinctly as if I were looking at her straight on. I lift my right hand and mirror-Jude hoists her left. I smile and mirror-Jude's left cheek folds into a dimple. I deepen my smile and mirror-Jude's left incisor bares itself. I shift my eyes to the actual Jude, and her mirror-Kat incisor is equally sharp.

"Now look at me," she says. I do, and those mirror images transfer to Jude's face, remaining exactly the same. "When we have pictures taken, it shows us in the opposite way—a way that's not a true reflection of us. It's backward."

"I get it," I say. "It would be upsetting to look at yourself expecting one thing, but seeing another."

"Right." Jude moves a comb backward through her hair, making tumbleweed tufts. "That's why we like the picture of us on the carousel, when we were playing switch."

She gives a final tug at the back of her scalp. Under the bathroom's sallow, trembling light, the scar along her arm seems more pronounced, protruding sluglike from her skin. I look down at my own scar and consider the question I'm hesitant to ask; I don't want Jude to think she's not enough—or worse, that I don't trust her. My own timidity unsettles me, and I force myself to speak: "Are we still in touch with anyone we met in Europe?"

"Why?" Her voice had dropped a fraction of an octave, just enough for me to know that she had not expected the question.

"I want to hear from someone else who knew me. I need an objective appraisal of myself. I need to hear a stranger tell me what food I ate, what boys I liked, what stupid things I did."

Jude presses her lips together and makes a smacking sound and returns her gaze to her own face. "We met a bunch of people. I know at least one of them moved back to the States. I'll find her number." She swivels back toward me and crouches down. "But don't blame me if you don't like the verdict."

We both laugh, the sounds merging, indistinguishable. I snatch her can of hair spray and aim it like a gun, shooting a mist into the back of her head.

After scrambling my egg, I bring my plate to the window and watch our street stir to life. A stray cat creeps; a woman pushes a stroller; a man hoists a boom box to his shoulder; and—could it be?—the same limping girl I saw before, her sun hat pulled low, shadowing half of her face. This time she doesn't appear to be searching or lost; she is facing our apartment building, scanning the rows of identical square windows, up and down, left and right, until she pauses at ours. At me.

I jerk backward. When I slip behind the curtain to peek again, she's walking away, heading east, and I decide to follow her.

Standing on the road bordering our complex, I catch her just in time: she's at the end of the block, turning right. I scurry to close the distance and then downgrade to a casual stroll, pretending to pause at a diner, glimpsing the menu with one eye. Past a pet shop, a drugstore, a taco joint. She is swiveling her head, clocking everyone who passes by. Occasionally she stops walking to get a better look at someone—always a woman, I notice. Always someone white and around our age.

I wonder if she's looking for me.

I move faster, facing straight ahead. Just hustling to get where I'm going, like everyone else. I'm next to her, marching in step, matching the swing of her arms, the speed of her lopsided stride. I catch an additional fraction of her face; she's wearing sunglasses with boxy frames that wrap around her cheeks, obscuring every feature but the tip of her nose and the puckered smirk of her lips. All of her hair, if she has any, is tucked beneath her hat, without even an errant wisp to betray color or length. She is searching while remaining unseen.

When she stops I stop along with her, midstep, my boot still raised. The crowd sluices around us. She turns to me and I turn to her, feeling as though I've been caught at something, a private infraction only she can name. I try to peer behind her dark frames, searching for a sweep of lashes or glint of cornea, but nothing reveals itself. She can see out, but I can't see in.

Five seconds pass. *Did I used to know her?* I think. *Does she still know me?*

For the first time, I notice she's carrying something: a clipboard, perched atop a bony arm. I'm close enough to see the lines in her lips, the crevices where lipstick has settled and flaked.

"Are you following me?" she asks. Her tone is light, flirty, the kind of voice I find myself using with Sab. It seems wrong for this encounter, this conversation, and no instinct tells me how to respond.

"No," I say, but it sounds like a question. "I mean, if I was, I didn't mean to. This is a strange thing to ask, but do I know you?"

She smiles, baring just the hems of her teeth. It's neither too wide nor too stingy, friendly without being intrusive—a smile that wants something. I can tell she's practiced it in the mirror, perfected it over time. "I don't think either of us has had the pleasure. But now that we're here, can I steal a moment?"

"Sure," I say, cool, casual. "I have nothing but moments."

"I am with an organization called CHIC, which stands for Children Hungry in Crisis. We're gathering signatures to petition restaurants to donate all leftover food to poor and underprivileged families. We're already up to a thousand signatures, and more restaurants are joining every day. We hope to eventually take it to the state legislature so they pass a bill making such donations mandatory across all of Pennsylvania."

She says this in one breath, a tight link of words with random intonations, the up-and-down cadence of a porch swing. The clipboard hangs between us.

"I've been making the rounds at all of the apartment complexes," she adds. "Many of the residents know hunger." She releases a pen from the clip.

"I'm Nancy, by the way," she says. "I should have said that up front. And you are . . . ?"

What I am is relieved, although I'm not sure why. Somehow she seemed a far more menacing presence from the safety of my window, where I could decorate her with a suspicious background of my own invention.

"Kat," I tell her, and give her my own practiced smile. Her eyes drift to my nameplate necklace, confirming my words.

"Nice to meet you, Kat. Could you support CHIC by giving me your name and address, as well as the name of everyone else in your household? We're on an accelerated timeline, so the more signatures, the better. It's a good cause, I'm sure you agree."

I reach for the pen but it's in her hand, hovering over the clipboard.

"Kat and Jude Bird," I say.

"Perfect," she says, scribbling. "Address?"

I pause, stumped by the question. I know what my apartment looks like and how to find it after a walk through the neighborhood, but I've never had a reason to memorize its numbers. I don't remember ever seeing a piece of mail; Jude must hide everything with my hospital bills, including the mailbox key.

"This is embarrassing," I say. "I live in the Colony Apartments down the street, but I don't know the exact address—the street number, or even the zip code. I do know it's apartment 4E, but only because it's stamped in gold on our door."

One black eyebrow inches upward, peeking over her frames. "Did you just move or something?"

Maybe because she's not Sab, maybe because she's shilling for a good cause, maybe because in another lifetime we might have been friends, I tell her the truth: the accident, the memory loss, the way my twin has been replenishing my mind. "There's been so much strain on rebuilding my brain," I conclude, "that I guess I missed the most obvious. All the things you know without really thinking about them."

Nancy smiles—a different smile this time, something between encouragement and confirmation. "I think I've heard about this situation from somewhere," she says. "It sounds really familiar."

"From what my doctor says, it's unprecedented in medical history."

She waves a hand. "I'm sure it was just in a movie or TV or something. Not in the real world. But don't worry—I can figure out the Colony Apartments address, and I already know the zip code."

I can't stop myself from asking: "What is it?"

"19149," she says. "Thanks so much. And please tell Jude I said thank you as well."

My ear lingers on the sound of my sister's name. She'd added an *ewwww* sound, stretching the vowel like taffy, the *d* buried in the back of her throat. This stranger had cultivated her own way of pronouncing Jude's name, as though she's said it many times before.

———

For the rest of the day I debate calling Sab, and finally pick up the phone just before Jude is scheduled to come home. One ring, two, three. *Answer, answer,* I think. The Killer Whale, as Jude calls her car, pulls into our complex, the motor grumbling its arrival. From our window, I see Jude collecting her cleaning bucket and locking the door. Four. *Please answer.*

"Hello?" He sounds slightly out of breath.

"Sab?" I whisper.

"You got him." A beat. "Kat? Is that you?"

"Yes." The car door slams shut. "I can't talk long, but I would like to see you again. To play again, like you said." I wince at the sound of my voice, the puppylike eagerness of my words, bounding toward him with abandon.

"Cool," he says. "There's a game tomorrow. I get off work at three. Meet me in front of Exiles around then."

"I will." The thud of Jude's steps grows louder, closer. Third floor, fourth floor. "I have to go."

As I lower the phone I hear him say, "I can't wait to see you," and I'm relieved I don't have time to respond.

———————

After a dinner of Hungry-Man fried chicken and beer, Jude and I go to bed, facing each other. If someone laid a ruler from her bed to mine we would prove to be flawlessly aligned, our heads and knees and feet at the same longitudinal points, our sheets pulled at equal length to our chins. I can sense a question lurking in her mind, small but troublesome, like a pebble in her shoe.

"Kat," she says. "Have you gone out when I'm at work?"

Her question is not a surprise but proof; she can access my brain in the same way I travel hers.

"Yes, but just like you said—a careful stroll. Remember, the doctor said it's important for me to get some exercise."

"He did," Jude says, "but he was very particular about how much and what kind. Where did you go, exactly?" She pauses, and then tacks on an addendum. "Did anyone bother you? I don't want you to walk into any stressful situations."

"Just around our block. And no one bothered me at all. The only person I spoke to asked me to sign a petition for some charity."

There's a spike in Jude's temperature, I can feel it, a fraction of a fraction of a degree. "Who asked you to do that?" she asks. "What did this person look like, and what did they say?"

I decide not to tell Jude that I followed her, and keep my words even. "I didn't see much of her—she wore a huge hat and shades. And she had a pretty bad limp."

Jude's temperature surges again; the vein on her temple thrashes beneath her skin. "A limp?" she asks. "Did you see any part of her face or hair?"

"Yes, no, and no," I say. "Why are you freaking out about it?"

And just like that, she turns her heat down, slowing the rhythm of her vein, easy as fiddling with a knob. She shakes her head and shrugs. "I'm not," she says. "One of my clients has a daughter who lives around here," she says. "Just wondered if whoever you saw matches the pictures I've seen. I got the sense my client wanted to set us up as friends, and I just don't have the energy for it right now. I just want to focus on you and your recovery."

"Like I said, this one was doing charity work," I say. "I'm sure it wasn't her."

"What was the charity?" She props herself up on her elbows. "Did she give her name?"

"It was some petition for hungry kids. I just signed both of our names. And *her* name was Nancy."

"Our names," Jude repeats softly. "Nancy."

For a moment the room is quiet, both of us absolutely still.

"Be careful with people," she says finally. "They can manipulate you, take advantage of you. I worry that you've lost your ability to sense that. You haven't just erased all the fun and beauty and wonder, but all of the dark and evil things. All the bad that can chase the good. I don't want you to start experiencing any of that, of course, but I want you to know it is out there. It's another lesson you have to relearn. I feel like I should plant your lessons around the apartment, on Post-it notes."

"I'm fine," I whisper. "I'm remembering everything you say."

"Your mind might forget," she says, and turns off the light, "but the body always remembers."

I'm about to ask what she means, but the deep, languid pace of her breath signals she's already halfway to sleep. I turn to the wall and curl into myself, wondering what secrets my body holds.

JUDE: THEN

Fifteen Years before the Accident

MAY 1968

In Jude's mind, looking back, the basement was not an omen but a gift. True, the stairs descending into it were splintered and creaky, one good stomp away from collapse; and the ancient shoebox windows gathered more light than they dispensed; and the flickering shadows always seemed to follow her, coalescing into a single roving cloud right behind her shoulder, vanishing the moment she turned around. But the basement was where their father lived when he was not executing the unenviable task of being married to their mother. It was where he invented things—momentous things, brilliant things, incredibly foolish and dumb things—that seemed like portals to an imaginary world, one far away from the crying and screaming and shattering of glass that sometimes happened upstairs. It was where Jude and Kat made the first memory that they were able to keep: their father opening his engraving machine and proclaiming: "Voila! I've created necklaces spelling your names, just so you never forget who's who." It was where their father pulled them aside and told them something that, at age seven, seemed at once a grand and fanciful conspiracy and a solemn promise that their mother would never win. "She thinks she is shutting us in," he said in the soaring cadence of a preacher. "But no, my darling girls! She is wrong, so very wrong, because we are shutting her out."

And Jude and Kat laughed and agreed. It was still so easy to feel safe.

People had gathered upstairs, strange people laughing in nervous and unnerving ways—their mother the loudest among them—but the hum and click of their father's newest invention pushed that laughter into the background. "Check this out, girls," their father said. Kat took Jude's hand and led her toward a boxy contraption with blinking lights and spinning reels. "Come closer," he beckoned, his thin, veiny fingers making hooks in the air. Behind his glasses, his eyes were bright and kind and vaguely bulging, the eyes of someone who lived in a perpetual state of surprise. Jude could hear the machine's hum, feel the heat of its tangled wires, see an object that looked like a futuristic version of a human head.

"What is it?" Kat asked.

With slow, careful effort, their father lifted the head from its base. It was white and plastic, with a clear, vented visor across the front and a cluster of red buttons along the sides. "This, girls, is a Subliminal Helmet," he said.

"What does that mean?" Jude asked.

He set it atop Jude's head and gently pushed down. She swiveled her face inside of it, looking right and left.

"It means that it can help your brain to work the way you want it to. It flashes pictures in front of your eyes that send secret messages to your brain. It works magic on your brain without you even noticing it. It is called *subliminal* messaging. Can you girls repeat that word with me?"

"Sub-lim-mabble," they said.

"Very good! Do you want to try?"

"Yes!" Kat shouted, and jumped up and down. "Let's do all the buttons!"

Their father took Kat's hand in his, placed his finger on top of hers, and guided her to push the buttons across Jude's head.

"What do you see?" Kat asked. "Leltem!" *Tell me.*

The images appeared like fully developed photographs and lasted no longer than a second: a bottle inside of a circle bisected by a straight line; a bright yellow smiling face; a puppy nosing a ball; a pile of money; a man and a woman smiling and holding hands; a lush landscape beneath a pastel sky.

"A bottle, a smiley face, a doggy, money, a mom and dad, and a garden," Jude reported.

Kat twirled in a circle and repeated her words.

"Very good, Jude," their father said. "If you are feeling sad, it can show you pictures of things that would make you happy. If you are feeling angry, it can show you pictures of things that will make you calm. If you need to do something you don't want to do, like your homework or listening to your mother"—and here he laughed, to show he was not *entirely* serious and that it was, at times, necessary to listen to their mother—"it can give you the little push to complete your tasks. If you are doing something that is bad for you, like too much drinking, it can help you stop. If you're not doing enough of something good, like exercise, it can help you do more. Wear this for just an hour a day, and you'll be a brand-new person."

Jude liked this idea, but she did not trust it. She had questions. "What if it turns bad? What if it shows you wrong things on accident? What if it shows you a monster?"

Kat stopped spinning. In between the flashing pictures, through the visor, Jude could see her sister's dark eyes fastened on her own. "Yes," she said. "What if?"

In unison, they looked to their father. His own gaze had drifted away from the helmet, away from his daughters, away from anything or anyone present in the moment. He had turned his focus upward and somehow inward, as though studying a slide of his own brain. Jude watched his expression change from one of excitement to one of fear, and wondered what he had seen.

KAT: NOW

Two Months after the Accident

MAY 1983

After Jude has made me breakfast and packed her bucket and warned me to stay within our little gray block, I take extra care in getting ready for Sab. I bruise my eyes with makeup and tease my bangs into a mini tidal wave and pull on boots with spiky heels. I make myself into Jude, but I intend to be seen. Her private self is my public self, and I want to perform.

Sab is waiting for me outside of Exiles, and it's clear that he, too, took some time with his appearance, slicking back his hair and popping his collar. Around his neck hangs a thick gold chain with a horn-shaped charm. His arm leans against the brick facade in a perfect flex, the tattoo eye fixed in a prolonged blink.

"Hey," he says, touching my shoulder. "It feels like forever since I've seen you."

I pause for a minute, considering his words and the concept of time; my entire remembered life has happened in the past two months. *What an odd saying*, I think, *marking "forever" as the past instead of the future.*

"Hey back," I say, and pull his two hundred dollars from my purse. "I know you told me to keep this, but I want to give you one last chance to take it back. If you refuse, I'm afraid I'm going to have to use it to win everyone's money."

He laughs—a real one, showing all his teeth; I spot a pair of silver fillings in the back. "I like the attitude, and that's exactly what you need to do with it. I'll get payback enough watching it happen." He pushes the door open. "Let's have a beer before things get started. We got about a half hour to ourselves."

The bar is empty except for a lone figure sitting at a booth, a woman who looks to be my mother's age if my mother were still alive. After every sip of her drink, she reapplies a fuchsia lipstick and glances at the door. I'm reminded of the memory Jude gave to me: our mother dressing us in our homemade monkey costumes, making a net with her arms as we climbed trees. It's so exhilarating to recall a memory, to experience irrefutable proof that my brain is working again, that I decide to celebrate. Slapping ten bucks on the bar, I ask the bartender to send the woman another drink of whatever she's having, and tell Sab that the beers are on me.

"You know her?" Sab asks.

"Not really, but in a way I feel that I do. I guess she reminds me of my mom."

"I get that," Sab says. "But I don't let ladies buy me drinks."

"Not up for debate, and I'm not a lady." I stumble over my words, correcting myself. "I mean, I *am* a lady, but you know, not—"

"Not someone who's afraid of taking charge sometimes?"

I like how that sounds and the expression on his face as he says it. "Yes. Perfectly put."

"Let's toast to it." He raises his glass. "To ladies who take charge."

We keep our eyes on each other as we sip, and to my surprise I am not tempted to look away.

"You're interesting," Sab says. "I mean, most women are interesting in one way or another, but you're interesting in a different way."

"Elaborate, please." I'm enjoying his analysis, and remember Jude's words about wanting an objective opinion of myself. A mirror along the length of the bar grants me a facsimile of this wish; there I am, talking to a boy, drinking a beer, smiling at the right moments, doing a perfectly fine impression of what a woman my age might do.

"The way you talk, for one thing. You talk like you're never sure what you're going to say next, like your words sometimes surprise you."

"Maybe it's not my words but my delivery," I suggest. "Maybe I'm not used to talking about myself, and I'm surprised I'm so open with you."

"What do I know?" Sab says, and takes a long drink. "I know you work for a lonely rich guy, that your mom died suddenly, and that you're good luck at a poker game. I'd say it's a decent start, but it's really not much for me to go on."

"This is only our second conversation. That seems like a lot to me." As I talk, my mind searches for my next line, the shiniest claim I can muster to further my reinvention.

"True," he says. "But tell me something else."

"Let me think," I say. I'm an heiress? I'm an escaped convict? I'm a spy? Unbidden, my mind conjures Nancy, and Jude's curious reaction—if not to Nancy herself, then to something she represented. Sab waits. My beer grows warmer in my hand. I open my mouth, prepared to recount the imaginary time I found a dead body, and shock myself by speaking the truth. "I'm a twin," I tell him. "I have a twin sister."

"Wow," he says. "Fraternal or identical? I have to admit, the identical ones creep me out. Like in *The Shining*, those two girls speaking in unison, their freaky blank eyes, all that blood."

I nod, pretending to remember *The Shining*. "We're identical. Actually, more than identical." I explain the concept of mirror twins: the opposite features, the late parting in the womb, the heightened ability to access each other's minds. "Jude is everything," I add. "The most important person in my life. I am the only person who truly knows her, and vice versa."

"To Jude," Sab says, raising his glass. The bar's dim lighting, filtered through a lampshade made of colored glass, highlights the flawless geometry of his face. I want to run a finger across his cliff of a cheekbone, let it fall into the hollow beneath, inch back up to trace the taut wire of his jaw.

"To Jude," I repeat. We clink and sip again. His lips part, a question forming behind them, and I fear it will be about Jude. I think of how she'd feel knowing I've ventured so far from home, drinking with a stranger in the midday heat, sharing pieces of our lives that belong only to us.

"Have you ever been to Europe?" I ask.

Before he can answer, five voices call out in unison: "Yo, Sab!"

Ryan, Guy, Steve, Booch, and Chinch surround us. Booch drops a thick hand on my shoulder, fingers squeezing like a vise. "Kat! You in this time?"

"I'm in," I say, and finish the last of my beer. "Let's go."

I remember my hospital bills, the regular bills, Jude paying them all alone. I think: *I am a person who can't afford to lose.*

Sab sits at my left, Booch to my right, and Chinch is straight ahead, already scrutinizing my expressions. Silently I wish him luck. How do you read a cipher, an empty frame of a person, no history etched in her face, scant little to hide or reveal? How do you read someone whose entire life is a bluff? I see him, though; I see them all. The flinches, the twitches, the blinks, the yawns, the eyebrow taking a casual stroll. It is a subtle, silent language that somehow feels innate, and it comes to me: I *know* this language. I have spoken it before. I tweak my internal encyclopedia: *I am a person who has played cards.*

Pitchers are emptied and refilled. Cigar smoke transforms the air into the aftermath of an explosion. Piles of chips grow and deplete. I'm up twenty-five dollars, down fifty, back up seventy-five. The slide of the cards against the table, the plastic clicking of the chips in my palm—these are familiar, comforting gestures from somewhere deep in my past. "Beginner's luck," Steve says, and I want to tell him I'm a beginner at everything.

Ryan's out of money. My three-of-a-kind beats Guy's two pairs; Chinch's flush beats my straight; Sab's full house beats everyone. Now Booch is out of money. Guy comes back with two pairs, aces and kings. Steve bluffs everyone, even me, turning up nothing but a pair of fives. Somehow I have lost one hundred dollars of the money Sab gave me, the money I was supposed to double for Jude. I finish my beer, go the bathroom, and rest my forehead against the mirror, creating a bleary, one-eyed monster. I think of Jude and how she wants me to be at home, mending my obliterated brain. I envision the spot under our rug where I will hide the money I win tonight, money I will grow and grow and tie with a big red bow, surprising my sister. I will prove that I can seize control: of my injury, of my unknown life, of the strangeness of my own heart. The monster eye stirs and stretches. We stare each other down.

Back at the table, I direct my panic to settle in my gut, not my face. No one will sense it, and if no one senses it, I can win it back. In the next round, I do, scoring a flush that beats Steve's flush, my Ace of Spades over his queen. A few rounds later and my pile stretches higher; my two pairs beat Sab's lone jack.

The music and voices in the main room begin to intrude on the game, a signal that the sun will soon cede to the moon. I don't have much time left; I need to beat Jude home. It's Sab's turn to deal, and I tell myself this is my final hand. An excellent beginning: the Ace of Diamonds and the Ace of Spades. I bet small, ten dollars, hoping others will raise. Chinch raises to twenty. Sab folds, but Guy, Steve, and I are in.

Sab deals like it's a striptease, taking his time: the Ace of Clubs, the Seven of Clubs, the Five of Clubs—giving me three of a kind. I want to kiss him. Instead, I slide my leg against his, our own private tell.

I toss fifty dollars into the pot. Steve folds. With a heaving sigh, Guy calls. A heaving sigh is not Guy's usual tell. I remind myself that I've only watched these people play poker twice—and, possibly, have only ever played twice myself. I have no solid command over his arsenal of bluffs or tells, and I truly don't know what I'm doing, and I've only gotten this far by a reservoir of instinct and exceptional luck. Without thinking, I tug on the end of my hair: Is that my tell? I stop and tap my fingers instead, and then bite my lip. I, too, can have a cache of tells. I have tricks from my old subconscious, the one that remembers, surging beneath my skin.

Sab turns up the next card; I hold my breath. The Seven of Spades, giving me a full house. Behind the curtain the music pulses harder, jolting my heart: *Beat it, beat it, no one wants to be defeated . . .*

I throw in a hundred dollars' worth of chips.

Booch whistles. "We got ourselves a Kat fight." Everyone laughs, me loudest of all. I no longer care about the falling sun and rising moon, the limping girl, the possibility that Jude might beat me home. I watch Guy. This time he doesn't sigh, but, with a slow, smooth sweep of his arm, raises the bet to one hundred and fifty dollars.

Without hesitation, I call.

"Damn," Sab says, his tone neutral; I can't tell if he's impressed by my valor or marveling at my stupidity. "Last one, burn and turn." He turns over the Four of Diamonds—meaningless to my hand, but no matter. I go through the motions of contemplation. I hesitate. I tug my hair. I heave a sigh louder than Guy's. I make a catcher's mitt of my hands and use it to push every last chip into the pile, a bet of around two hundred and fifty dollars.

Guy does the same.

"The moment of truth," Sab says, and turns to me. "Let me have it, Kat."

"I'm sorry to have to do this," I tell Guy, "but you'll always be welcome at my . . ."

I turn over my Ace of Diamonds and Ace of Spades: "Full house!"

My arms reach out to rake in the chips when Guy says, "Not so fast, Kitty Kat."

I pause, midscoop. I take in their faces, one by one: Chinch's lazy eye, Steve's slack mouth, Booch's twisty scowl, Ryan's raised brows, and Sab's sweet-sharp face, his wire jaw opening and closing on its hinge, speaking silent words.

Guy flips his two cards, one by one. The Seven of Hearts, the Seven of Diamonds.

Four of a kind.

Four of a kind.

Oh my god what did I do there are four cards on the table of the same fucking kind.

Two hairy claws encroach and scrape the chips away from me.

The people around me do the kind and correct things, patting my arm and murmuring sympathy and assurances that next time I will beat them all, but each soothing word and calming gesture lands inside me like wood feeding a kindling fire. There's another me inside myself, looming up and taking over, jabbing at the lid of my fun-house brain and releasing all of the monsters inside, proving that my injury is far too big for my body to contain. My mind begins talking at me, using a language I don't yet know, or have forgotten how to understand.

I move with a terrifying calm across the snug room, five steps that attract no notice, cause no alarm. The night continues to happen around me, laughter and bombast, the discordant chatter of hazy voices, the booming refrains of songs. I stand before the cabinet of medical curiosities. My left index finger lifts and runs itself along a beveled pane of glass, stopping at a rusty lock. I tug at it once, twice, three times, harder, and hate it for not yielding to me. The kindling fire grows, singeing the marrow of my bones, and at last the monster inside of me inhales a gust of fury and heaves itself out.

With a swift, deft move, with the grace of a dancer or a thief, I slip my boot from my foot and aim it at the glass. In my calm, sure hands, the boot becomes a gun and the heel a bullet, and I fire it with every bit of my ravaged strength.

"Kat!" I hear Sab's voice, so small and far away. "What the hell?"

I thrust my hand inside the mouth of jagged glass teeth. I bypass the model of the conjoined twins and the mummified hand, and find the jar holding a pickled human heart. Before Sab can reach me, before he can make a straitjacket with his arms, I break the jar, too, with one solid smash against the wall. The liquid splashes at my feet, smelling sour and tart, soaking my exposed toes, and the heart plops into my outstretched palm. In its own lifeless, decimated way, it is beautiful, the valves stretching up like ancient fingers, eternally grasping at something it will never hold. I lift the heart up, savoring its rank and raw heft, and, with my own fierce animal hands, tear it in half.

KAT: NOW

Two Months after the Accident
MAY 1983

The heart pieces land at my feet. No one moves but Sab, who comes at me with a look of mortified horror and pulls my left arm back in one fluid motion, as though drawing an arrow. "You're hurting me!" I scream, and my words serve their purpose; he lets me go and I am off, pushing through the snug room doors and tunneling through the crowd, lurching left and right, baptized by spilled beer and the sweat of strange men.

He does not follow me, and at that I feel relief. I don't want to be reprimanded or questioned or even consoled. I need to sit with myself, poke and prod at the monster within, identify its origins and why it came roaring to life. I want to understand how someone can be terrified of her own mind when that mind is a perfect stranger.

I am a person capable of losing control in unpredictable and dangerous ways.

I had not felt the glass cutting my hand. Tracks of blood settle into the lines of my palm. My gait is lopsided—one foot in heels, one bare—but I push myself, scuttling across an intersection and sprinting the rest of the way home, ignoring traffic lights and the sting of the air on my wound and the lurid calls from passing cars—*hey baby, slow down and talk to me*—and arrive at our complex, heaving, my breath like nails against my throat. I search every parking space for Jude's car, but she is not yet home. I have time to pull myself together, to pretend I have been home all day, relaxing within the confines of our little gray block. I open our door and bend to kick off my boot and see an envelope marked, in eloquent cursive, *JUDE*.

I snatch it up and glance behind me, fearing I'm being watched, but our door is locked, and whoever left this note is long gone. I press it against my nose; it smells vaguely of dog hair and rain. The paper is scratchy and warm against my palm, and I mar it with a stamp of my blood. My mind wrestles with itself: Do I open it? Do I open it and try to reseal it? What could someone have to tell Jude specifically? Why not include my name? I wrap my arms around it and slink to the bathroom and lock the door; I don't want to risk Jude walking in on me.

Running my finger along the envelope, I feel something hard and square inside. My hands shake as I pull it out: a photograph of Jude's nameplate necklace, spread across a wood table, an overhead light making the letters gleam. A piece of paper flutters to the tile. On my knees, I read the scribbled message:

YOU LEFT THIS BEHIND
AND YOU OWE ME

I do not understand the note, but its power is swift and overwhelming. I lie down on the bathroom floor, place it on my chest, and wait for my sister in the dark.

I am deep in that darkness when Jude's voice finally comes. It sounds layers away, buried beneath muck and mire, coming from the earth's inner core. A spark of recognition: this is what my sister sounded like when I was in my coma, how the tail end of her whiplash voice guided me back. I hear her call my name, once, twice, that single syllable sounding like the splitting of wood, and then I realize that she *is* splitting wood, kicking the bathroom door open. I feel her shadow over me, smell the bleach on her clothes. She's picking me up, her arms around my torso.

"Kat! What happened to you? Why are you bleeding?"

I open my eyes and use my bloody hand to collect the note and the photograph, holding them level to Jude's face.

"Oh, that," she says, and wrests them from my grip. She looks away, hiding her face from me. "I can explain."

After wetting a cloth, Jude leads me to the couch and takes my hand in hers, wiping away the blood. She focuses on her work as she speaks: "It's the hospital bills. They're overwhelming. Not to mention rent, food, utilities, all that. So I found a neighborhood lender. A loan shark. He paid off the hospital bills, but now I owe him. With interest. With a lot of interest that seems to be growing by the day. The last time I paid him, I was short on the amount owed. I told you I lost my necklace—it must have fallen off during the meeting. He's just trying to scare me, to make sure I bring all of the money next time."

The blood scrubbed away, she finally looks at me, and in the feeble light of the room I decipher her expression: bravado layered atop regret atop fear. While I believe these emotions are true, there is something false inside of them, something borrowed, as though they apply to an entirely different situation than the one she's described. I want to peel them away and rediscover the Jude I think I knew— dependable, shrewd, fierce.

"I want to help," I say. "This is all my fault. Forget what my doctor says about not working—"

"Reject and release," she says. "We're going to be okay. You need to trust me."

She pulls me toward her, fitting the point of her chin into the concave curve of my neck; my own chin instinctively drops into hers.

"You stink," she says. "You stink like beer and smoke and an army of unholy things. Where did you go to get that bloody hand, when you should be taking it easy?"

I speak directly into her ear: "You are going to be mad, but I went out today, farther than where I am supposed to, and I ended up in a situation where I broke something that was not mine. Tore it right in half, in front of a crowd of people. I don't know why or how, but I turned into someone who was not me. Or, at least, not the me that I know now. Maybe it was the me from before. It was a me I never want to encounter again."

I pull back and look at her straight on. We are so close that our eyes seem to merge, a replica of the one-eyed monster I saw in the bathroom mirror at the bar. "I need you to tell me why I did that," I say. "I need to know what I am capable of."

She turns her head, breaking the connection, and sinks down into the sofa. She looks up at me, letting the moment stretch, and I wonder if we're engaged in our own private performance, one we've given all our lives, she now more certain of the roles than I.

"Whatever it is, I can take it," I say. "I just need to know what I'm up against inside myself." I sit down next to her, taking both her hands in mine, forcing her to look at me.

"I'm so sorry, wint," she says, using our word for *twin*. "I'm so sorry for . . ." She changes her mind and shuts her mouth, trapping her words inside.

"For what?" I ask. "What have you done that you need to be sorry for? What have *I* done?"

"You've done nothing but have a terrible, awful thing happen to you," she says. Her voice is a scratchy whisper. "The only thing you're up against is your own anger. And I'm so furious on your behalf that I have a hard time acknowledging it to myself, let alone speaking it aloud."

I think about my doctor's advice, dispensed before I left the hospital. I have suffered a trauma both physical and mental. I should consider talking to someone professional, someone who will know how to guide me through the unique experience of grieving for myself. I told him no one could possibly understand except for my sister, but only now do I realize the inadequacy of those words. Jude doesn't merely understand; she, too, is grieving the loss of my memory and the multitudes it held. She alone has the burden of carrying my past around without any chance of relief—no one else can offer a different interpretation, to confirm the rightness or wrongness of things.

"I try to think of it this way," she says. "We are only twenty-two. So, yes, you lost that many years' worth of memories, but we have our whole lives ahead of us—maybe sixty, seventy years if we're lucky? Decades and decades of opportunities for new memories of all kinds. Sad and thrilling and exciting and scary and so damn fantastic that you will feel yourself change on the spot—your molecules shifting, your body shedding old skin. You will have those, and they will be true and real, and no one will ever be able to take them away from you. So don't worry about the past. It doesn't matter now. Instead run toward all of the moments and days and years that are waiting for you."

The paragraph sounds rehearsed, lovely thoughts and words composed in anticipation of this moment, but I don't question her further. She pushes my head to her lap and begins the familiar work with her fingers, smoothing and patting my hair, tugging and turning, her grip tightening near my scalp. I picture my mind as a seesaw, set atop a fulcrum: one end low to the ground, weighted by lost memories; the other high in the air, anticipating what's to come. Each time I venture out and meet strangers and reinvent myself from scratch, the ends wobble and rebalance, inching closer to being even.

I notice my wound has opened up again, streaking red across my palm. Before I can reach for the wet cloth, Jude hoists my hand to her mouth and sucks away the blood. I sense that this is something she's always done for me, that we've always done for each other—an act of intimacy for her benefit as much as for my own.

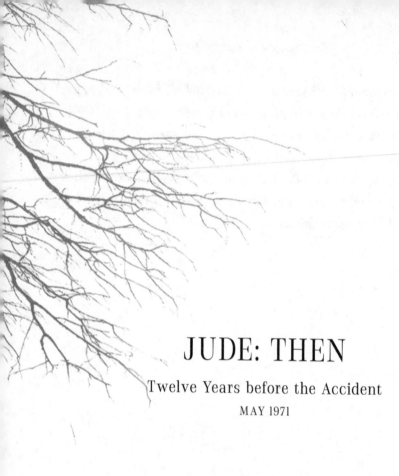

JUDE: THEN

Twelve Years before the Accident

MAY 1971

The people began arriving at eight, parking their cars beneath sugar maple trees, some still clutching the flyers their mother had distributed to select locales around town. The flyers, deliberately cryptic, bore the following message in bold block lettering:

WHAT YOU THINK ~~IS FOOLISH~~
WHAT YOU THINK ~~IS INCONSEQUENTIAL~~
WHAT YOU THINK ~~IS IMPOSSIBLE~~
WHAT YOU THINK, *IS*
An evening of provocative introspection
Saturday, May 22, 1971
Hosted by Verona Sheridan
Thinker, Connector, Devourer of Life

Jude and Kat stood on either side of the front door, waiting for the heavy thud of the knocker. Their mother, the aforementioned multi-faceted Verona Sheridan, had given them several jobs for the evening, and the first was to greet her guests. Some were old colleagues from Pied Beauty, the antique market where she sold her curated treasures, but most were strangers, lured by the promise of dazzling transformation. She had prepared a script for the girls to memorize and recite: "Hello, sir or hello, madam. Welcome to the Sheridan home, a place of radical acceptance. Bear to hear the truth you've spoken." That last line came from the Poem of the Day, "If—" by Rudyard Kipling, which Verona read to them over breakfast. They did not understand the meaning of the poem, but they liked the way the quote sounded coming from their mouths, an instant signal that they were preternaturally mature and wise, that their minds, at age ten—eleven next month—had already grasped a range of exotic ideals.

They took turns leading each guest down the slender strip of hallway decorated with old photographs of their mother in glamorous poses: There she was in a swimsuit on the beach, bum resting on heels, looking coyly over her shoulder. Straddling a farm tractor in a tiny checkered top, gripping a daisy between her teeth. Reclining on a chaise longue, one stockinged leg raised high, fingers tangled in the coils of a telephone cord. All of them taken during her "dancing days," as she called them, when Verona Sheridan called herself Very Sherry, a time and name that disappeared as soon as they were born.

At the end of the hallway their mother awaited with outstretched arms, the sleeves of her silk robe dangling like bat wings, her smile lacquered and rapacious. Everyone received a personalized exclamation and a perfumed hug: "Ronald and Marianne Lester—stunning, both of you! Maureen Lurie, a timeless vision! Jason Buck, an utter and delicious delight! Ada Cahalan, Gilbert Schachner, Joshilyn Winn, your energy is luminous! Donald Lawson, an absolute god in my midst! Dotty and Ted Garman, I knew you would answer the call! Bunny DeSpain, William Abate, Lou Agnew, the night would not be complete without you! Dr. Sebastian Vance, the man of the hour, my esteemed guest of honor, a worthy leader for our times! Come, come, all of you, and let's begin this most momentous and magical evening. Judith and Katherine, my angels, could you please fetch a round of drinks for all?"

Jude and Kat performed their practiced curtsies, lifting their matching taffeta skirts in perfect synchronicity. On their way to the kitchen they passed the basement door, currently padlocked shut. Their father was gone now more often than he was home. Each time he disappeared, their mother offered a different explanation, each more rancorous than the last. He had traveled to a conference, he had meetings with potential clients, he had taken a trip with some friends, he had ventured off to a place just for himself, all by himself. Maybe he had finally delivered on his threat to colonize Mars, who the hell knows? They needed to accept that adults sometimes did things that children aren't meant to understand. They needed to accept that adults were sometimes more childish than children. They needed to stand by their mother because she was the one who always stayed behind, clothing and feeding and teaching them, while their father was gallivanting for his own selfish gains. They should know that their father had abnormal thoughts, increasingly dangerous thoughts, thoughts that could corrupt them if they listened too closely, thoughts that could seep into their own minds and poison them for good.

"Where do you think he really is?" Kat asked. She asked every time he vanished, and every time Jude invented a different answer, all made up on the spot: he was off in France selling the Subliminal Helmet; he was at a Professional Invention Camp; he was building them a secret castle on a beach that no one else would ever find. Kat never believed these answers, but they mollified her; if Jude treated the situation with some humor and whimsy, how bad could it truly be? Tonight, though, seemed different somehow. Tonight Jude decided that her lies did more harm than good, and that even the darkest truths should be brought to light.

"I don't know," she told her sister. She took Kat's hand and faced her straight on. "But I feel like he's not in a safe place."

"What can we do?" Kat whispered. Her hand was slick with sweat. "Do you believe Mom about his mind being poisoned?"

"I don't know," Jude said again. "Sometimes I think she makes up things when she's mad."

From the front parlor came the sound of their mother's laugh. Jude remembered how their father described it—"a gutter laugh," he said, "a laugh that begs for scraps." On the dining table, Verona had left all of the ingredients and accoutrements for a cocktail called the White Lady, which she claimed was as potent as it was rare, an antique in its own right. The girls set to work, pouring and shaking gin and orange liqueur and egg whites, fishing out errant yolks and shells, garnishing with lemon. They arranged the cocktails on two silver trays and began the long walk back, the trays colliding with their thighs, liquid sloshing over. They paused outside the closed pocket doors, listening in.

"In my past life I know I was a warrior," a woman's voice said. "I fear appearing weak and vulnerable, I'm always in competition with someone, my anger is energetic."

Then came their mother's honking laugh. "Why is everyone a warrior in these scenarios? Why is no one some poor peasant, carrying wood on her back and squatting out babies in a dirt field? If anyone was a warrior in this room, it's me."

"Please, Verona," a man said. "If you were anything, you were a nun. Now you're here in present form to make up for lost time."

The tray strained Jude's arms. She banged on the doors with her forehead, and a man she recognized to be Ronald Lester slid them open. He had black hair feathered in winglike swoops, as though it might fly off his head if it caught the wrong breeze, and a contained way of moving that made his body seem smaller than it was.

"Excellent!" their mother said. "Come on in and show everyone how useful you are."

Jude and Kat circled the room until the trays were empty. The man their mother called Dr. Vance was the last one to take a glass. With his other hand, he gripped Verona's thigh in a way that reminded Jude of a claw machine game, snatching and retrieving its prize. Blond hair sprouted from the knuckles of his thick fingers, and Jude had never seen such strange and striking eyes, so light they were nearly colorless. "What gorgeous girls you have here, Verona," he said. "You have some future man-eaters on your hands."

"We prefer hoagies," Kat said. Everyone laughed, and Jude could see that her sister was pleased with herself.

"Go on now, girls," their mother said. "I'll call you if we need you."

"Hold on," Dr. Vance said. He held up his hairy hand and motioned to Jude. "Which one are you?"

"Jude," Jude said.

"Judith," Verona corrected.

Dr. Vance smiled, showing uncommonly white teeth. His smile reminded Jude of a monkey or a clown, wide and aggressively emphatic, teetering between charm and horror. She was afraid to stand still, and more afraid to move.

"Nice to formally make your acquaintance, Jude." He emphasized her name, making it a retort, and she admired his defiance. He was on her side. "I also prefer my name to be shortened. My full name is Sebastian, but my friends call me Bash."

"Bash," Jude repeated. "Like bashing something in?"

Everyone but Bash Vance laughed, which bothered Jude. Nicknames were serious business.

"Or *bash* like a party," he said. "That sounds better, doesn't it? But hey, we were just starting a new discussion topic, and I would love for you to provide the first truth."

"Dr. Vance," their mother said, but again he held up his hand, stopping her.

"It's fine. Everyone has a valid answer to this question, regardless of age. And please—this goes for everyone—call me Dr. Bash."

Verona sighed, and Jude allowed herself a smile. Well, that shut her mother up, didn't it? With that one brief declaration this strange man with the lupine eyes and pawlike hands did the impossible, making Verona go quiet. He wanted to listen to what Jude had to say. He expected her to have important and relevant thoughts—and she did have them, she told herself. Looking away from her mother, mesmerized by Dr. Bash's immobile grin, she forced herself to speak, borrowing the tone her father used when quoting illustrious figures from history: "Ask me this very important question, if you please, Dr. Bash."

Again, the room laughed, but Jude wasn't sure if it was with her or at her. She felt Kat squeeze her elbow and heard her whisper, "Tis yako. Ouy rea yako." *It's okay. You are okay.*

"My, Verona," Dr. Bash said, "this one is quite officious, isn't she?"

Jude desperately wished she knew what that word meant. Dr. Bash noticed her confusion and rescued her. "It's a good thing, Jude," he said. "You are confident and assertive, attributes that will serve you well in life."

He spoke those words in a way that seemed irrefutably true, like he'd had a secret preview into her future. He smiled again, and this time it veered toward kind rather than scary, and it made her inclined to trust him in a way she did not trust her own mother. He did not seem like the sort of man whose kind words carried hidden expectations. She felt emboldened to address him again, in the same tone her father had taught her: "Thank you, Dr. Bash. I do feel quite confident to answer your question."

No one laughed this time; in the slight shift of his shoulders and the tilt of his leonine head, Dr. Bash had issued an unspoken order for silence. "Very well, Jude," he said. "My question is this: In your relatively short time on this earth, what, if anything, would you change about your life?"

She felt an opening in her throat, and then, just as quickly, a constricting. She had so much to say but dreaded the reaction—not from the adults but from herself, as though admitting her regrets aloud might affect her in some fundamental way, rerouting the course of her blood. She could talk about how she'd change her mother; she'd make her smaller in all ways, shove her into the oven and watch her curdle inward, crisping around the edges, emerging with just a fraction of her presence and power. She could talk about her father, and how she'd tinker with his brain just enough to make it functional without making it ordinary, let it soar with the assurance that it would soon safely land. She would stop feeling that Kat was the normal one, the kind one, the outgoing one, the one their classmates picked for teams, the one strangers seemed to like before she even said a word. She would stop the new and furtive thoughts she'd never even shared with Kat, thoughts that made her look at girls the way her sister looked at boys. She would reset her own brain to a normal temperature, somewhere between fire and ice.

At last an answer came: "My thumbs," Jude said. "I would change my thumbs. They're too bendy and they look weird." She bit her lip. She stared at the tips of the patent Mary Janes that Verona had forced her to wear. She ordered the tears to retreat from her eyes, the lump in her throat to dissolve.

She felt another tug on her elbow, and heard Kat's soft repetition of their private words, *tis yako*. To everyone else, Kat said: "Me too! I have the same bendy thumbs and they really ought to be changed." She demonstrated, bending her left thumb into the shape of a comma.

"Wow," Dr. Bash said. "Flexibility of the body can illuminate flexibility of the mind. What a gift."

"Judith, Katherine," Verona said. "We're having adult time now. Go outside and play for a bit before it gets too dark."

Jude smiled at Dr. Bash one last time, sealing their connection. She felt Kat's hand around hers, her sister's willful pull, her legs traveling in reverse, back through the pocket doors, down the long strip of hallway. Before they opened the rear door and stepped into the night's thick heat, there came a faint knock at the front of the house. Together they rushed toward it, terrified of shirking their duty, of allowing Verona to be disrupted while she was busy with adult things, enumerating all the ways she would change her life.

On the other side of the front door stood a man who resembled a facsimile of their father. A bruise purpled his right cheek, a dollop of mottled blood marked his forehead, his body looked lost inside his dingy clothes. "Hello, girls," he said. There was a black gap in his smile, Jude noticed, three or four teeth from the front. "I'm not here for a night of provocative introspection, which sounds just like your mother's brand of nonsense. I'm here for you. I want to come home."

From behind came the click of their mother's heels, the swishing of her silk robe, and the rasp of her hushed scream—quiet enough not to disturb her guests, loud enough to betray her fury: *Girls! Shut the door, shut the door fast and lock it behind you, shut the door and do not open it again.*

KAT: NOW

Three Months after the Accident
JUNE 1983

It takes me a week after my outburst in the bar to find the courage to call Sab. The wound on my hand has healed and scabbed off, leaving a sliver of a scar etched along my left index finger, a scar Jude will never share. I focus on this difference as I dial his number and practice what to say: *Sab, I'm so sorry, I can explain, there was an accident that killed my brain . . .*

"Hello? Kat, is that you?"

I realize I said my rhyme aloud.

I hang up. I gnaw at my nails. I stare out the window and watch the morning hustle: a stray dog pawing through trash, a cacophony of horns, a teenager wrangling with a book-sized stereo—I try, but can't recall the word for it—and a cassette tape twisted into a knot of plastic spaghetti. There's no sign of Nancy, with her clipboard and her limp. After ten minutes I force my right hand—Jude's preferred hand—to pick up the phone, pretending I'm her while I do it. My own left hand reluctantly dials, each spin of the rotary quickening my heart.

This time his voice is a recording—*Yo, it's Sab. You know what to do*—and I try to match his casual ease: "Hi, Sab, it's Kat. Sorry we got disconnected—I don't know what's wrong with this line. And, um, I am really sorry about last week. I have more to say about that, if you want to hear it, but only in person, if you want to see me. I'm sorry. I'm sorry to everyone." I glance at the phone number Jude had taped to the fridge and recite it twice, being careful to replace the phone as softly as possible, a firm signal that I am entirely normal and sane and definitely not someone he should avoid.

My hand is still on the phone when it trills again. "Sab?" I ask, and wince at my breathless tone.

"Who? What?" the caller asks. "Kat, is that you?"

It's a woman's voice, dulcet and soothing, a voice that could defuse bombs.

"It is," I say. "Who is this?"

"My name is Wen. I know you don't remember me, but I met you and Jude while you were in England. Jude told me you asked about the trip, and she wanted me to call. I'm so sorry for what happened to you. How are you doing?"

My objective appraisal, I think. *A real one, from someone who knew me before.*

"I guess I'm okay," I tell her. "Although I don't have much to compare it to, as you know."

"It's unbelievable. But thank the goddess you have Jude to fill in the blanks."

Thank the goddess? I think. *Is that a thing people say?*

"Yes," I say. "Every day she tells me a little bit more, fattening up my mind like a turkey."

Her laugh is thick and throaty, an instigating laugh, the opposite of her voice. "Well, I'm ready to fatten it up some more, if you're ready."

I stretch the phone to the couch and position myself as I do with Jude, sprawled out, my own fingers making ribbons of my hair. "Gobble, gobble," I say. "Tell me everything."

I hear background noise: women's voices shouting short, choppy commands; a flurry of staccato popping sounds.

"I'll start with how you were," Wen says. "Even though you were mourning the death of your mother, you were happy and free and hungry for new things." She'll never forget when and how we met—it was the queen's birthday celebration, the second Saturday in June of 1982, nine months before my accident. Jude and I came to Wen's favorite local pub in the Cotswolds. She overheard us debating a strange item on the menu, deviled kidneys on toast.

"You thought it looked intriguing," Wen says, "and Jude said it looked like Filet-O-Placenta. I advised you both that it's better than it looks or sounds."

Jude and I proceeded to eat every crumb, washed down with several pints of beer, and by that time we three were chattering away, the loudest people in the bar. We told her how we fled the States for a chaotic tour of Europe, no direction or timeline or any plan to return. She shared her own history, the twisted journey from an industrial town in New York to her serene cottage in England, the inspiring and devastating things she'd seen along the way.

"I had just lost my mom, too," Wen says, "and I understood the urge to run."

My eyes shut, my fingers raking my hair, I let my brain try on Wen's words to see if they fit—and they do, perfectly, as though made just for me. I update my personal definition: *I am a person who likes exotic food and unplanned days and stories that strangers tell.*

We stayed with her for six weeks, each moment languorous and magical. We helped tend to her chickens and went to the pub at night, learning old folk songs and stumbling home. We swam in Spring Lake, scarfed platefuls of black pudding, and chased each other through a topiary maze, delighting in being lost. We told her of our childhood farm and how we loved this kind of honest and simple life, leaving room for impromptu detours and wondrous surprise. We wept when we decided to leave for London, and she promised to visit us there.

"You said it was the best time of your life," Wen says. "Considering the incredible life you'd had leading up to that point, I was truly honored. You're a discerning person, but also open to anything—it's a rare combination. And you're strong, Kat. Stronger than you know."

"Thank you," I say, almost a whisper. Her voice is lulling, hypnotic, the words lined up in proper order, delivered for maximum effect. I want this objective appraisal to be correct and true. I want to summon it like a genie whenever my own mind turns against me. *I am a person who is stronger than I know.* But behind that wish comes a fear, potent and chilling: *I am a person who will believe anything I'm told.*

"Anytime," Wen says.

The chorus of voices around her amplifies, drifting closer to wherever she is. I press my ear against the receiver, trying to identify words. *Strike*, I think I hear. *Attack. Kill.* A refrain to some strange and savage song.

"I should get going," she says. "This might sound weird, but I miss you. It was good to chat."

I don't want her to hang up just yet. I stand up from the couch, my voice now calm and direct. "Where are you? Are you still in England?"

"Back in the States for now. Got a farm a bit north of New York City. It's not quite the Cotswolds, but it's good for now."

I try to picture her, imagining a face that would fit her persona. She has spiky hair and lithe limbs, I think, and the kind of hands that could both nurse a baby lamb and throw a deadly punch. Hands built for stealth and efficiency.

I lift my own hand, finding my scars, the old and the new, the past and the present. Jude's advice boomerangs across my mind—*moving forward is just as important as looking back*—but a piece of my history is on the other line. I want to know everything she knows, especially the things Jude has yet to tell me.

"Do you have any pictures of our visit?" I ask. I remember Jude's explanation for why we don't like them: the opposing and incorrect images, the disorienting feeling of seeing ourselves in the wrong way—a feeling that could be neutralized only by playing switch, performing as each other.

"Sure do," she says. "I filled a whole album with them."

I close my eyes and force the next words from my mouth: "Do you have any of me and Jude together? Apparently we lost some rolls of film in transit. We have plenty of pictures of scenery, but none of us."

Those three sentences leave me so dizzy, I have to sit back down. I drop my head between my knees and clench them together, trapping myself, waiting for Wen's response. It is vital to me that she confirms Jude's explanation, that she says she has very few photos of us, if she has any at all.

"Of course! I have tons of really great shots of you two. I'll find the best ones and send them straight away."

My heart wilts inside me, leaden and sluggish. Instead it is my spine that moves, squirming and crawling, poking at me from within.

Jude lied. Jude lied *to me*.

I give Wen our address, which I now know by heart.

KAT: NOW

Three Months after the Accident
JUNE 1983

My brain bats away the knowledge of Jude's lie, refusing to let it settle. She will have an explanation, one that will seem obvious once revealed. I will feel foolish for having doubted her, and stupid for not having deduced the reason myself. The lie will seem urgent and necessary—another link in our connection, a tighter knot in our bond. I stand straight at the window until my spine feels like a spine again, solid and still.

The phone rings, startling me—not just startling, but scaring; I am afraid of what I might hear, more surprises coming from the other end. Again I use Jude's right hand, calm and assured, and press it to my hear.

"Hello?"

"Kat."

"Sab," I say, and that syllable is all I can manage.

He lets the quiet stretch between us, so prolonged and excruciating that I'm tempted to scream. In the background, I hear the buzz and clank of machinery and surmise he's on a job site, calling from a trailer.

"I got your message," he says at last. "What was that all about, in the bar? What is wrong . . ." The question stalls.

"With me?" I ask, infusing my voice with a levity I do not feel. "Where do I begin?"

"Wherever you want," he says. "Just give me something to go on."

This time I invite the silence, counting a full thirty seconds, hoping my brain retrieves the right words. I manage to say: "I'm afraid to talk in case it just makes the situation worse. You've been nothing but nice to me, and I've been . . ." I let my voice fade. I remember the day we met, and my cynical assessment at the snug bar: Sab is a prop in my evolving performance as a normal twenty-two-year-old.

"A complete psycho?" he says.

"I suppose so."

"Absolutely batshit?"

"That, too."

"Crazier than a Dallas fan showing up at the bar in a Danny White jersey?"

"I'm not really sure what that means," I say, "but I think I draw the line there."

"Most of my favorite people are a bit crazy, but you're on another level. You're like watching TV but without the music and laugh tracks."

I'm amused to hear more than a hint of admiration in his voice, like my lunacy is something to aspire to. "Give me another chance," I tell him. "I'll change the channel to something a little more subdued."

"Nah," he says. "I'll take *Knight Rider* over Dan Rather. I get off work in an hour. What are you doing around five?"

"Likely nothing that will come to any good."

"You're not taking care of the old rich guy?"

My own lie confronts me. I have nothing to say.

"Did you *ever* take care of an old rich guy?"

More silence.

"I thought so. Give me your address and I'll pick you up."

———————

Sab arrives in a cherry-red barge of a car, the hood emblazoned with the image of a bird in flight. From the rearview mirror hangs a string weighted by two felt rectangles bearing images of dour men in cloaks. I reach for it as I sink into my seat. "A scapular," he says. "My mom handed them out like candy on Halloween. The church says they signify devotion and blessings, but I think they bring luck at poker."

"I want to explain—"

He holds up a hand. "Wait until we get there."

Five minutes later, we're outside the basement door of a church.

"Before we go in, I should probably give you a warning," he says. "I might be making all kinds of assumptions about you and whatever you're dealing with, but my assumptions are usually right, or close to it."

"What are your assumptions?" I ask. I calibrate my voice, worried it might either rise or break.

"You beat the shit out of a cabinet. I've seen you, I've watched you, I know the behavior and the signs. I understand it because I've observed the same things in myself."

"I know what you're seeing," I tell him, "but I don't think there's any way to fix me. And if I'm right, if I'm unfixable, I don't know if I could stand to have that confirmed."

"Maybe you don't need to be fixed. Maybe you just need to adapt."

I can't look at him. I don't want to look at him. But here he is, gripping my chin with his hand, turning my face toward his.

"Just give it a try?" he asks.

Something in his tone reminds me of Jude, her reassurance that my violence is not innate but was born of violence itself, that I've done nothing at all but have a terrible thing happen to me. My anger might be justified, but beating the shit out of cabinets is not the best way to express it, and I do what any normal twenty-two-year-old with an anger problem might do: follow the boy brave enough to give her a second chance.

"I'll try," I say. "Let's see if I can get to the bottom of me."

Inside the basement, the air is redolent of burnt coffee and mothballs. A dozen folding chairs form a tight circle in the middle of the room, and a banner stretches along one wall: *FORGIVE YOUR ENEMIES—IT MESSES WITH THEIR HEADS*. One by one the seats begin to fill, nine men and three women, myself included. A man with long, bushy hair greets everyone by stretching out his arms, one hand gripping a smooth black rock.

"Welcome," the man says. "For those who are new, my name is Chuck. We gather here once a week to work on freeing ourselves from the tyranny of our feelings. Whoever has the Peace Rock has permission to speak and will not be interrupted. Express your anger at the circumstances in your lives, not at the group. We do not degenerate into chaos. This is not adult *Lord of the Flies*."

The reference, if I ever knew it, is lost to me, but I laugh along with everyone else.

"All right," Chuck says. "Who's first? Come on, no one here bites. At least not on a regular basis."

Sab raises a hand. "I'll do it."

"You got it, Sab," Chuck says, and hands over the rock.

It's an easy, familiar exchange, and I wonder how many times Sab has been here, laughing at Chuck's dumb jokes, holding this rock, sharing secret and shameful things.

"Hi, my name is Sab," he says, "and I've got some anger issues."

"Hi, Sab!" the group says, making it sound like a song. The ritualism of it, the expectation of certain behaviors and speech, is unsettling in a way I can't name.

"Regulars already know my problems with my brother." He turns to me. "For those who don't, he's a drug addict. Mostly coke. Heavy shit. And to pay for his habit, he likes to steal from me. Money, jewelry, sneakers. He's been stealing from me for years. I haven't always handled it the best."

He pets the rock. The motion makes his mother tattoo squirm.

"Once, I even paid for his rehab. Then he ODed again, and I was so pissed I went to Atlantic City and blew through all my savings. His sickness made me sick. I started having panic attacks, got an ulcer."

I can picture it: Sab's body rebelling against his intrinsic good nature, the anger devouring him from the inside.

"But coming to this group helped me work it out. First I did the most obvious thing—transfer my money from shoeboxes under my bed to a bank account."

A few scattered titters.

"And then, just because it made me feel good, I started leaving spare cash around in random places. Tucked a five into an old lady's purse on the bus. Sent an envelope to a dog shelter. Gave some poker winnings to a new friend."

I remember our first meeting at the bar: the two hundred dollars he handed over without explanation, the insistence that I never pay him back.

"I'm still mad at my brother. I'm mad that he terrorized my little sister with his ragey freak-outs. I'm mad that he sold some of our mom's things. Most of all, I'm mad that I'm still mad. Every day I think about it, he's stealing space in my head that he doesn't deserve. So every time I come here, I'm trying to shrink that space. Make it smaller and smaller until there's no room left." He juggles the rock from one hand to the other. "I guess that's it. Thanks for listening."

I am surprised to see my hand reach over to Sab and curve around his bicep. The muscle is hard against my palm. The rock travels the circle: wife issues, mother-in-law issues, boss issues, children issues, issues with the anger management class itself. Tips on de-escalation are offered; imagery is prescribed. We are cars with faulty brakes. We are buildings propped up by the skimpiest of scaffolding. We're tea kettles on the stove, mere degrees from boiling. We need to recalibrate, reinforce, remove ourselves from the heat before the whistle sounds. Abstractly, these ideas all sound easy, reasonable. I can see the logic; imagining everyday objects is a way to facilitate distancing, the replacing of messy human emotion with simple mechanical function. I try to apply them to myself. I picture reducing a burner or slamming my foot on a pedal or pounding a nail beneath a house, but none of them feel true. My filter is Jude; only her words can fit around my brain, dictating my route to the other side.

The rock makes its way to me, the final stop.

"Hi, I'm Kat," I say.

"Hi, Kat," Chuck says. "We're glad you're here."

I squeeze the rock. Sab slides his knee against mine. The circle seems to grow smaller, the gazes more intense. There's a shifting in chairs, a leaning in. People long to hear a story sadder than their own. Again I'm unnerved—not by the expectations of these strangers, but because the expectations themselves feel familiar. I recognize these gestures and expressions, this hunger for detail; just as with poker, I know this game is from my old life, and I have played it many times.

"I have some problems with anger," I begin, and look away from Sab. "My problems also have to do with my sibling. My twin sister, in fact."

I feel the friction of Sab's knee, urging me to continue.

"She was in a car accident and suffered a brain injury. She has a rare kind of amnesia. When she woke up from her coma, she remembered only my face and my name. She has no recollection of herself. Imagine being twenty-two years old with knowledge only of the past three months. Sometimes she feels like she never existed at all."

I feel Sab's eyes on me. He knows I am replacing the lead in this retelling of my abbreviated life. I begin speaking to him and him only, everyone else receding from my view, extras being shooed offstage.

"She doesn't remember small things, like her favorite color or song. She doesn't remember medium things, like her first kiss or heartbreak. She doesn't remember big things, like five years in Europe or our father leaving or the death of our mom. She doesn't remember if who she is now matches who she was then, or if there's been a series of minute twists and turns that have tweaked her into someone new."

Sab's mouth opens and closes, canceling whatever words he'd wanted to say. I squeeze the rock and press myself to finish.

"I saved my twin's life, but she's furious with me. She's furious because she's so dependent on me. She's angry because her history belongs only to me. She's angry because trusting me is the only choice she has."

I lean one inch closer to Sab, so close I can see a scar buried inside his eyebrow.

"But I'm angry, too. I'm angry that she's lost what we had, that I have both the privilege and the tremendous burden of carrying our history alone. So here I am instead, telling all of you."

The basement is deafeningly quiet. I close my eyes, making Sab disappear, and Jude takes his place in that self-imposed darkness, both concerned and amused by my outburst, my juxtaposition of our roles. I want to tell her she is everything. I want to tell her she is not enough. I want to split her head open and peer inside her brain, finding everything she hasn't yet said, all of the truths that have slipped through the cracks. The entire soliloquy seemed to have happened in some hazy, faraway place, conducted by a foreign voice, composed by a mind that is not my own.

Behind me comes a meek cough, a tapping foot. "Thanks for sharing, Kat," Chuck says. "That is . . . a lot."

"Thanks for sharing, Kat," comes the chorus.

I hold the rock aloft and Sab lifts it from my hand, gripping my fingers for a beat longer than necessary. Under the sallow fluorescent lights, amid a circle of strangers, I want to grip his face and kiss him. I want to drag my nails across his skin, making my mark, and I wonder if wanting to love has something in common with wanting to own.

———————

For the next five hours, I sit on the couch and wait for Jude to walk through the door. I sit on the couch and wait and think about the photos of us in Europe that Wen has promised to send. I sit on the couch and wait and stare at the wall and recall the narratives I'd heard that day: *druggie brother, lecherous boss, witchy wife, Jude's lie.* I sit on the couch and wait and stare at the wall and change my narratives: *thieving mother-in-law, deadbeat dad, demanding father, Jude's lie.* I do it again: *druggie brother, deadbeat dad, Jude's lie, Jude's lie.* And again: *druggie brother, Jude's lie, Jude's lie, Jude's lie.* And finally: *Jude's lie, Jude's lie, Jude's lie, Jude's lie.* I say the words when I inhale and exhale, when I blink, with the making and unmaking of my tight left fist.

The door of apartment 4E creaks open.

"Hey." I hear Jude's voice. "I got your favorite."

The now-familiar scent of onions and oregano. The rustling sound of my sister pulling the sandwich from a bag.

I stand up from the couch and walk three feet to our kitchen and tap her shoulder. She spins and leaps away, her face reflecting my rage, my face reflecting her terror.

"What's wrong? What's wrong with you?"

"Why did you lie to me?" I ask her, and repeat it, louder this time: "Why did you lie to me?"

"What are you talking about?" She goes back to the business of setting the table, gathering napkins and plates.

"Look at me and tell me why you lied." My words burn the roof of my mouth and scald my tongue.

"I'm tired," she says. She faces me again, slouched, and seems half her normal size. "I've literally been scrubbing shit all day. What are you talking about?"

"I talked to Wen. She says she has pictures. She has pictures of us, together. Do you see why that might make me mad? Do you see why I might be mad when I was told, in a very complicated yet entirely clear way, that no pictures of us exist?"

Her lips make a sputtering sound. "I never said that. What I said was that we don't *like* to have our picture taken, and we don't *like* to look at pictures of ourselves. And it's true, we don't. But when someone else is taking the picture, and they intend to keep it for themselves, and we'll never be forced to look at it—then sure, whatever, take the fucking picture."

She's pointed herself at me, chin forward, hands on hips, preparing to tell me how foolish I am, how spoiled and selfish, how ungrateful, when she's done nothing these past months but pay my bills and fatten my memory and try to bring me back to myself. Before she can say one word of rebuke I'm on the floor, slithered like ivy around her legs, wheezing into the gap between her knees. She chooses not to speak her angry thoughts and instead implores me not to cry, *please* don't cry, Kat, *please*—the sound of my crying gives her nightmares that she is unable to describe.

JUDE: THEN

Twelve Years before the Accident
JUNE 1971

On their eleventh birthday, Jude and Kat decided to separate in the small ways that were available to them. It was high time that people understood that being identical in appearance did not mean being identical in thought and disposition. Jude knew that she herself was reticent when Kat was open; quiet when Kat was boisterous; surly when Kat was a cartoon sunshine with a Magic Marker smile. Jude was the malevolent bit of news to be absorbed before Kat's shiny silver lining, and Jude told herself this was okay. Not everyone could bring the light and fun. Someone had to creep along the periphery, watching for danger, preparing for the shock of bad things.

As a birthday gift, Verona announced "a full day of enriching activities, exhilarating for both body and mind, a day that will alter the course of our very lives." Jude was skeptical—how could a simple birthday be so momentous?—but when Kat twirled around in excitement, Jude allowed her mind to be changed. For the occasion Verona permitted the girls to choose their own clothing, and they selected outfits that were thematically consistent but still unique: Jude in jean shorts and a T-shirt featuring Velma from *Scooby-Doo*; Kat in a denim dress with a Daphne tee pulled over top.

The Poem of the Day was, fittingly, about two sisters. They lived near a place called the Goblin Market, where scary monster men enticed passersby with their succulent wares. "We must not look at goblin men," Verona read, her lips moving furiously, smearing red lipstick across her teeth. "We must not buy their fruits. Who knows upon what soil they fed their hungry thirsty roots?" She read on and on, revealing that one sister, Laura, gobbled up the dangerous fruit, growing sicker and sicker and content to feed her sickness, while the other, Lizzie, refused to eat the fruit and restored her sister to health. For Jude, this poem confirmed their new distinct identities, wrapped them up in a succulent bow. If Kat, like Daphne, found herself in danger, Jude would be her Velma, letting her sister leap into her arms. If Kat, like Laura, was threatened by wicked strangers, Jude would be her Lizzie, risking her life for her sister, letting her suck the juices from her body, undone in her undoing.

Verona next insisted they visit her own market, Pied Beauty— "mostly goblin-free," she promised—to continue their tradition of riding the antique carousel that stood at its gates. When the girls were younger, they pretended their carousel horses could leap from their polls and race each other, galloping through the streets. Now, instead, they had a contest over who chose the creepier horse—the redder tongue, the wider eyes, the longer teeth—and posed for a picture, Verona exhorting them to shout *Fromage!* At the last minute, before the camera clicked, Kat swiped her hand across Jude's head, changing the part of her hair, and did the same to her own. It was, as Jude told Kat after the accident, their favorite photograph, but not because they were playing switch, Jude being Kat and Kat being Jude so that their mirror image was maintained. It was because this picture captured, for the first time, the twins being very much themselves, Jude reveling in her Judeness and Kat in her Katness, and they would never feel such certainty again.

————————

Their mother revved up her new Chrysler station wagon and shooed them to the part they called the Way Back, where they could open the rear window and stick their heads out and pant in the wind like dogs. "Your historically momentous treat awaits you in the city," she instructed them. Her lit cigarette filled the car with musky smoke. She told them to call her Verona instead of Mom; they were big girls now, and it was time for grown-up names and grown-up things.

"Joy to the world," Verona sang, "all the boys and girls." It was a Pied Piper voice, Jude thought, a voice that made you listen and follow. "Joy to you and me," she called back, imitating her mother's tone. She wondered if Verona had split her gifts between them; maybe people would follow Kat, but listen to Jude.

They did not yet know the city. They had never seen such hulking heaps of trash or fire hydrants used like backyard sprinklers or grown people wearing ripped clothes holding out their hands for change. They had never been to a hotel and could not even dream of one like this, with a piano player in the lobby and a chandelier the size of a dining table, heavy with sparkling fringe. A thin man glided by carrying a platter of fluted glasses. Verona took one, sneaking each of them a sip.

"Girls, this is called a mimosa," she said. "Orange juice and just a splash of champagne. You're old enough for sips now, but only when I'm there. Do you understand?"

They nodded in unison and followed her to the elevator. She wore a gauzy cape that trailed behind her like a petulant child, with pompoms bouncing along the hem. She pointed her toes so that her shoes hit the floor twice with every step, first the ball and then the heel—click-*click*, click-*click*—a quirk she said was left over from her "dancing days." They heard often of these dancing days, stories that began with glitz and glamour and ended with "and then, of course, I met your fucking father." Her hair was red, too red, redder than the tufted velvet on the chairs. Jude noticed that men and women alike turned to stare at her. She was the Pied Piper even when she made no noise at all.

At the elevator stood three men Jude recognized right away. They had been at her mother's recent party—the night of radical acceptance and resplendent change, the night her father appeared at the door. They wore a loosely coordinated uniform: plaid pants of differing colors and shirts with wide lapels. "Ronald, Donald, Bash, my loves," their mother said. She kissed Ronald and Donald on their cheeks but Bash full on his mouth, lingering for a second too long. "You remember my girls, Katherine and Judith."

"Kat and Jude," Jude corrected.

"Don't mind them," Verona said. "It's their birthday and they're on a champagne high."

Ronald laughed and ran a hand through his feathery black hair. "Of course we remember," he said. "Kat and Jude it is, although I can't tell who's who. Happy birthday. Your mother has planned a neat-o present for you."

The elevator door slid open and they all stepped inside. With a crimson nail, Verona pushed number seven, and even this slight movement unleashed a thick gust of perfume, a scent that reminded Jude of wilting roses.

"Happy birthday," Donald said. His hair was the opposite of Ronald's, the layers falling toward his face instead of away, a bright silver instead of dark. The two men reminded Jude of salt and pepper shakers, purposeful together but lost apart. "Today should be a perfect way to celebrate."

"Indeed," Bash said. "Why don't we all go out later for some ice cream?"

"Yes!" Kat shouted, tossing her fist into the air. "Pumpkin pie, please, with caramel syrup and marshmallows and rainbow jimmies on top. And whipped cream. And at least two cherries, so they can be twins."

"That's quite a combination of flavors," Ronald said. "You are confident in your own tastes."

"Indeed," Kat said, mimicking Bash's deep voice. The adults laughed.

"She's never had that combination before," Jude said. She felt the urge to clarify the situation, to seize a modicum of control. "She just likes to shock herself. The element of surprise."

"And what flavor do you like?" Bash asked.

She remembered the party again—how Bash hushed the room when she spoke, making her feel powerful and important, someone destined for great things. She thought for a moment, biting her lip, hoping to impress him with her answer. "Chocolate chocolate chip," she said. "With chocolate syrup and chocolate jimmies. No whipped cream or cherries or any of that extra stuff. I like my flavors to be strong and pure."

"That sounds excellent, Jude," he said, and gave her a crisp nod. "I think I'll follow your lead and order the same."

Jude nodded back, just as crisp. She had the urge to salute, just like Verona had in one of her old Very Sherry photos, wearing a swimsuit that looked like the American flag.

"What do you say to Dr. Bash, girls?" Verona prodded.

Kat spoke in singsong, but Jude kept her voice neutral: "Thank you, Dr. Bash."

He bent down to Jude's level and looked her straight in the eye. He was very tall, even taller in his platform boots, and the journey seemed to take a long time. "You're very welcome, Jude. And you, too, Kat. Thank you for letting me treat you. You make an old guy feel a bit cooler than he is."

The door chimed, and the elevator creaked to a stop.

"Judith, Katherine, you two go down there," Verona said. "I'll come to get you when it's time. Be good and do everything you're told."

Jude watched her walk down the hall with Ronald, Donald, and Dr. Bash, her arms reaching around their backs. Dr. Bash dropped a hand to her ass, and Jude wondered what her father would think about that, if he was in a place where he could think at all. She did not want Verona to turn the corner. She wanted to keep her mother in sight. But turn the corner she did, cape swishing and heels clicking and laugh booming, until even the sound of her was gone. Jude could not tell if their mother, too, was feeling most herself, celebrating her lush and lavish Veronaness, or if she had taken an inexorable step toward becoming someone else.

She did not know whether Verona becoming someone else would be a change to celebrate or a change to fear.

———————

The Blue Room wasn't as fancy as the lobby, and the only blue thing was the carpet. Rows of folding chairs fanned out in a semicircle, facing a large blackboard. Jude looked around to see that every seat was full, maybe fifty seats total, an equal mix of boys and girls. A blond woman in jeans hovered nearby, holding out her palm for everyone to slap low five. She had very full and pink cheeks and wore a T-shirt that read "Unbought and Unbossed." Jude guessed she was around the same age as Verona, but somehow they looked centuries apart.

She did not have wild hair or a swinging cape. She did not move like the type of woman who had any dancing days in her past.

"Now that we're all here," she said, "come up and tell me your name so I can check you in."

Jude felt Kat pull her forward.

"Kat and Jude Sheridan," Kat said. "Our mother probably registered us as Katherine and Judith Sheridan."

She looked up from her form and did a double take.

"Twins?" she asked.

"No duh," Jude said.

Kat elbowed her. "Don't be mean." She turned back to the woman. "I'm Kat, she's Jude."

"Nice to meet you, Kat and Jude." With a thick black marker, she wrote each of their names on a tag. "You can stick that right on your shirts. It's our policy here at The Plan to meet new people, so I'm going to ask if you both would mind sitting apart from one another. I promise it'll be fun."

"Do we have to?" Jude asked.

"Tell you what," she said. "Give it a shot, and if you really don't like it, I'll put you together. But I'm betting you girls will make some new friends straight away."

Jude nodded, pleased with this assessment, and turned to Kat. "Go to that end, but pick a chair where I can see you."

Kat obeyed, taking a seat near the window.

Jude picked a chair near the door, for easy escape. The girl next to her had long black hair and knees that looked more like elbows. She wore a plaid jumper and leather sandals that showed her painted toes, as small and bright as specks of blood. She stared at Jude, the tip of her index finger shoved inside her mouth, her tiny teeth gnawing on the nail. Jude liked her right away.

"Hi, Violet," she said, pointing to the girl's name tag.

"Hi, Jude," Violet said. Her finger stayed in her mouth.

"What is this place?" Jude asked. "Our mom just dropped us off and took off down the hall."

"My uncle Bash is down the hall." She pointed to the woman at the front of the room who was back to giving low fives. "And I'm not supposed to tell anyone, but that's my mom."

"I know your uncle Bash," Jude said. "He's been at my house, and later he is buying me ice cream. So what are we doing here?"

"Dunno," Violet said. "My mom just called it a lesson."

"Funny, my mom said it would change our lives. If it gets weird, me and my sister are splitting." She leaned forward and saw Kat talking to a boy. Jude waved, trying to get her attention, but Kat did not look over.

"Can I come with you?" Violet asked.

"Maybe, if you move fast enough."

"Deal," Violet said. Jude accepted the girl's outstretched hand, her finger faintly damp with spit. Jude held it for one second longer than necessary.

"Okay, everyone!" the woman announced, clapping her hands. "My name is Jackie. Welcome to The Plan. We're a new group, and we're doing some really far-out stuff. We're gathering members all across the country, including kids just like you. I know all your parents and guardians are down the hall doing their own thing, but we're going to have much more fun here, I promise. We're going to learn to think about things in new ways, ways that will make us stronger and smarter. Sound good?"

Someone whispered to someone who whispered to someone. All at once everyone had secrets to share, and the room sounded to Jude like a pit of hissing snakes. She looked over at Kat. Her sister's mouth was now pressed against the boy's ear.

"That's it, let it out," Jackie said. "Laugh and whisper. If you don't want to be here, I'd be happy to escort you to the Red Room so you can hang out with your parents."

"Wish I could get away from my parent," Violet whispered.

Jude smiled at her and scanned the room. She wanted someone to call Jackie's bluff, to stomp off and venture to the Red Room. One boy stood and just as quickly sat back down. She felt her own body angle toward the door. She wanted to see what would happen if she left, but she did not want Kat to be alone. And what if Violet didn't follow? Jude was not ready to leave her. She wanted to hold that damp hand and look at that twitching, rabbity face. She wanted to accidentally brush up against that black magic carpet of hair.

"I thought so," Violet's mom said. "Now, you understand that you're here by your own choice. You had the opportunity to leave and didn't take it. So go with it. Be open. Try it out." She picked up a piece of chalk and stationed herself by the board. "So now that we're all in agreement, let's get started."

The room was quiet as she scribbled two words: *The Plan*.

"The Plan," she said. "That's what we're going to learn today. A new kind of plan, one you've never had before."

She turned again, scribbled more letters.

"And what does this sentence beneath the letters say? Can anyone tell me?" She pointed to Jude. "How about you, young miss? Kat or Jude, am I right? Will you read that for me?"

"Jude," Jude said. "What you think, is." She glanced over at Kat, who had forgotten the boy and seemed enthralled by Jackie's patter.

"That's right. Now consider those words for a minute. What you think, *is*. Let me explain. Say you have a headache—"

"I have a headache," Violet said, raising her hand. Her foot tapped Jude's, sending a silent message: *My mother is giving me a headache*.

"Okay, Violet," Jackie said. "Good, good." She paced the room, cupping her hands as though holding an invisible ball. "Let's talk about that headache. Let's take a look at what's really happening there and see if you can gain some power over it. What color is the headache?"

"How can a headache have a color?" Kat asked.

"Your mind can give anything a color," Jackie said. "What's another way for people to say they're sad? I'll give you a hint: they describe the feeling with a color."

"I'm feeling blue," came a voice from the back.

"That's right, Patrick!" Jackie touched a finger to her nose. "Spot on. We do the same thing with anger. What is a color people associate with anger? What do they say?"

Jude raised a hand. "I'm seeing red," she said, surprising herself. She wanted to hear what Jackie had to say about investigating layers of thoughts. She liked the idea of having power over the way ideas appeared and moved through her mind.

"You got it, Jude." Jackie gave her a thumbs up. "See? We ascribe colors to feelings all of the time without even realizing it. So, Violet, I'll ask you again: What color is your headache?"

Violet returned her finger to her mouth and tilted her head. "Pink, I guess?"

"Pink it is! Good. Now, Violet, tell me a little more about this headache. If it could hold water, how much would it hold?"

She rubbed her head, calculating an imagined depth. Jude concocted her own response: four cups of water, one for each phase of the headache—onset, intensifying, abating, gone.

"I think a bucket," Violet said, "because it's like a fire, a pink fire, and it would take a bucket of water to put it out."

"Now you're thinking! Let me ask you: Do you still have the headache?"

"A little, I guess."

"All right, let's keep going," Jackie said. She stopped pacing, looked straight at Violet, and posed more questions: Is the headache moving? What shape is it? If it could speak, what would it say and how would you respond? Is it getting smaller? Is it listening to you? You're in control of it now, yes? You're deciding how you feel about it. And now, let me ask, do you still have the headache?

"No," Violet said. Jude watched the girl's face—the widening of her eyes, the slight lift of her lips—and concluded she truly believed it. Suddenly her mom was no longer a joke.

"Success!" Jackie said. "See, everyone? She was able to address something that was bothering her, change the way she thought about it, and take responsibility for making it go away. How did that feel, Violet?"

"Good," Violet said. "Like my body listened to my mind. Like I was in control for once."

Jackie began to clap. "Everyone, give Violet a round of applause. She's proved that we're all born with incredible power within ourselves. The trick is learning how to find it and make it work for you. So let's repeat the phrase Jude read for us when we began this session."

"What you think, is," everyone chanted, Jude the loudest of all.

The door opened and two women wheeled in a long silver table holding three trays. Time for lunch, Jackie announced, and she asked that they all show restraint: one slice of ham, one piece of cheese, and one glass of water. No more, no less. Physical control was just as important as mental control. She would blow a whistle as a warning three minutes before they must return to their seats.

Jude felt Kat's hand cup around her shoulder.

"This is Violet," Jude said. "The one with the pink headache."

"Did you really make the headache go away?" Kat asked.

"Yeah, I think so. It doesn't really hurt anymore."

"So cool," Kat said. "Want to go spy on our parents?"

In the hallway kids chewed floppy slices of ham and boasted about healing themselves with their minds. The double doors of the Red Room were very high, and small crescents of glass near the top offered the only view to the inside. Kat and Violet squatted, making a shelf with their thighs. Jude climbed up and felt the girls' hands tighten around her knees, holding her steady.

"What do you see?" Kat asked.

Jude had no short answer for what was happening in the Red Room. She saw a large circle of adults spread around the space, their hands linked, their heads raised. Inside the circle there was a smaller circle, but their focus was on a person in the middle, the hub in their wheel. She realized that the hub person was Verona and she was crying, a long, tortured-dog kind of yelp, clenching and unclenching fistfuls of red hair. In unison, the two concentric circles chanted at her:

Leave the past in the past
What you think, is
Those memories weren't meant to last
What you think, is
Purge the sadness, purge the sorrow
What you think, is
Kill the past and see tomorrow
What you think, is!

Verona thrashed inside the hub of the wheel, staggering from person to person, spinning and turning, her dancing days come back to life. Forward and back and forward again, a contagious motion that spread around the circles, first inner, then outer, until the entire group resembled a wave, crashing and receding and swallowing her mother whole. Jude watched Verona shout the chant, her mother's eyes squinting with the effort. Jude had seen this look before. She called it the "sad-into-mad" look, and it often accompanied stories about Jude's father. She could picture flecks of spit gathering in the corners of Verona's mouth. Her mother pounded her chest and pulled her hair and then she began to sink, a building collapsing in slow motion, lower and lower, the chanting intensifying, the words pelting like hail, bringing her to her knees. The chanting stopped; the circle parted into two distinct halves. Jude watched her mother begin to cry, shoulders shaking, her face in her hands, mad back to sad.

"What are they doing?" Kat asked. "Sounds like they're singing nursery rhymes."

"That's exactly what they're doing," Jude said. "Just singing rhymes and dancing." She couldn't think of what to say to Kat without worrying her. But beneath that, she was scared to give voice to the scene, as though recounting it aloud might unleash something dark into their lives, something best left hidden and unknown.

"Sounds funner than our room," Violet said.

"Yup," Jude said, stifling the urge to correct her.

They heard the faint shriek of a whistle.

Back in the Blue Room, Jackie checked off names, making sure everyone had returned. "In your chairs you'll find a notebook and a pencil," she said. "During the morning session, we learned how our own powerful thoughts can create our reality. And now we're going to take something from our past, something that's always bothered us, and change the way we feel about it. Dig it? I'll give you a few minutes of quiet time to think and write down your memory. If it would help you, you could make your story rhyme like a poem. It might seem less scary that way, more like a song."

The room filled with the sounds of scratching and erasing. A memory rose up in Jude's mind but she pushed it back down. She imagined her brain as an iron, pressing against the memory on highest heat. It sprung back up, a flattened cartoon monster regaining shape, ready to follow her again.

"Roy," Jackie said, pointing to the back. "You look like you have something to share."

Jude turned around to see a boy, maybe nine or ten, wearing wide-leg pants and a cowboy hat. "I guess so," he said. He held up his notebook like a surrender flag.

"Before you start," Jackie said, "let's make a magic circle and gather around Roy. Let's shield him from the negativity that his memories might bring and surround him with love and light."

Roy shuffled to the center of the room and a circle formed around him, smaller than the one in the Red Room. Jude let Violet clutch her right hand, and a strange boy, a bit younger than Roy, seized her left. The paper shook in Roy's hand as he began to speak: "One night our house was cold. The heater broke because the house is old. I went into the closet with matches . . ." On the last syllable his voice retreated down his throat.

"You're doing great, Roy," Jackie said. "Isn't Roy doing great, everyone?"

"I couldn't find any word that rhymes with *matches*," Roy said.

"That doesn't matter," Jackie said. "The most important thing is to share the memory and take control of the emotions around it. Everyone, let's start swinging our arms a bit—we'll push our strength toward Roy."

Jude felt Violet and the strange boy pump her arms. She found Kat on the other side of the circle, eyes shut and mouth twisted into an odd pucker.

"That's it," Jackie said. "Roy, would you like to continue?"

"I went into the closet with matches. I lit one and watched the flame grow higher and higher. And then it wasn't a flame anymore, it was a fire." He stopped again and hid his face behind the paper.

"And what happened, Roy?" Jackie asked. "Did you feel like you lost control?"

Roy's shoulders began to shake. His fingers swiped at his eyes.

Jude's breath paused in her chest. She wanted to hear. She wanted to see if he had the strength to say it, and the skill to change the shape of the memory in his mind.

"The fire spread," Roy said. "It grew as tall as my head, and swallowed up my bed. It chased me down the hall. I found my parents and my brother Paul. The whole house was turning red. I thought we would all be dead."

"You're doing great, Roy," Jackie said.

"In an hour the firemen came around. And I watched my house burn to the ground."

Roy's face looked like a split melon, pink and wet and open.

"What are you thinking, Roy?"

"I almost killed my family."

Jude swung harder. She wanted Roy to feel the wind she was making with her arms. Glancing across the circle, she saw her sister's eyes were open again, focused on Roy.

"But you didn't," Jackie said. "You went through a difficult situation and you came out smarter and stronger. You have taken responsibility for what you've done. Say it with me, everyone: What you think, is!"

"What you think, is!" they screamed.

"Feel your power, Roy!" Jackie called. "What you think, is!"

His face resumed its original shape and hue but remained shiny with tears. "What I think, is?" Roy asked.

"Yes!" Jackie roared. "You've done it! Thank you, Roy. Join your brothers and sisters in the circle—they need your power. Now, who's next? Does anyone else want to grow more powerful today?"

Jude watched Kat's hand rise and hover half-mast. Jackie caught it.

"Kat! How brave of you to volunteer." Her arm made a grand sweep. "Welcome to the center of the power circle."

The memory again circled Jude's head, pressing on her brain. She felt the same memory bubbling up inside her sister. She imagined the memory thinning itself, becoming a wire that connected their minds, a sizzling current flowing back and forth. She wanted Kat to stay in the circle and grip the memory with both hands and wrestle it to the ground. She wanted them to take control together, turning the memory inside out like the fingers of a glove.

Jude noted that Kat's hands did not shake. How proud she was as Kat cleared her throat and held her notebook high, even as Jude dreaded the story to come: "Our dad is different, funny, and smart. Good at math and science and art."

Jude's lips moved in silent synchronicity with Kat's words. She pictured their father in the early years, snapshots of their first memories: his shiny cue-ball head bent over a table, making magic with a sketch pad and pencil, inventions he would bring to rickety life.

"But no one bought any of his stuff. There was anger and fighting and it was rough. He began to change and acted strange. He saw messages in the sky and warnings on the ground. He felt like his brain was being attacked. And once it was gone there was no getting it back."

For the first time, Kat's voice wobbled.

"You're doing perfect, Kat," Jackie said. "Feel your power." The circle pumped its arms. Jude caught her sister's eye and nodded, giving her permission.

Kat started again, precisely narrating Jude's thoughts. She remembered their father taking pills, stopping pills, going to the hospital to get his brain "zapped," as he put it, the jokes about smoke rising from his scalp. She remembered the first night their father didn't come home, and that one night stretching into three or four, and the weeks bleeding into months.

"Last month, he came home one night," Kat said, holding her voice steady, "and he didn't look right. Something or someone had bashed a hole in his head. The blood gushed and gushed, so much red. He stood at the door and begged to come in. My sister was next to me, our mom was behind us . . ." She looked up. "I can't rhyme anymore either, is that okay?"

"It's all okay, Kat!" Jackie shouted. "You have the power!"

Jude pushed the circle harder, advancing and retreating, getting closer to Kat each time. Her mind illustrated Kat's remaining words.

"My hand was on the doorknob," Kat said.

Jude paused midswing, causing Violet to trip. Wait a minute: she remembered *her* own hand on the knob. She remembered her own body being the lone barrier between in and out. She remembered her mother screaming to shut the door, shut the door fast and lock it behind her, shut the door and do not open it again.

"My mother told me to shut it and never let him in again. She made me do it. She made me do it."

"Take control, Kat," Jackie said. "Be steady and take control. This is what you knew in the moment. This is the only directive you had. Recast your past."

Kat was crying now, and her crying found its way to Jude, sweeping her in.

Before the door closed, in that last inch of space, Jude could see a shard of her father's once-handsome face, the zigzag confusion of his eyes, his shocked open mouth, the empty black square where a tooth once had been.

"He didn't understand why the door was closing," Kat said. "Our mother screamed to hurry, hurry and close it."

That space got smaller and smaller until it disappeared, taking their father with it. Jude closed that door a month ago . . .

". . . and then I locked the lock," Kat finished. "That was the last time we saw him."

Jude disentangled herself from the circle and locked herself to Kat. "What you think, is," the crowd chanted, "what you think, is." Years later, after everything, she would remember this: her

sister's arms around her, their bodies melded, the hot wire connecting them and merging their thoughts, a mathematical synastry
that would have made their father proud—an equal exchange of
responsibility, of shame, of power, of all the things yet to come.
What we think, is.

KAT: NOW

Three Months after the Accident
JUNE 1983

Every time I look at Jude, my accusation flares up in my mind, con-suming all other thoughts. I didn't mean to accuse you of lying about the photographs, I tell her. I understand now that photographs are acceptable as long as we never have to look at them and see our faces juxtaposed, mine on hers and hers on mine, the subtle distinctions visible only to our eyes. I will never distrust you again, I promise. I know you would never lie to me. I know you would sooner die than lie to me because lying to me could be dangerous, sending me to places with no direction on how to return. Lying to me would mean we are no longer us—Kat and Jude and Jude and Kat, twins who started life as the same person, unable to tell where one begins and the other ends.

"It's okay, Kat," she says one morning. She doesn't look at me as she talks, focusing instead on getting ready for work, painting her face and assembling her bucket, the various spray bottles and brushes peeping out like a sad bouquet. "I keep telling you it's okay, and I wish you would just believe me. When you don't know who you are, you can't know what you're saying. Let it go. Reject and release." Her hand pauses on the doorknob. "Do you want to come with me today? Not to work, but to keep me company. I'm doing Mobster House and you would not believe the level of gnarly. If you ever wanted to see a gilded toilet, now's your chance."

I tell her I'm too tired, but in truth I just want to give her a break from me, from the exhausting project I've become. I promise to rest, and then maybe take a walk within our little gray block to clear my head. The irony of the phrase hits me—how do you clear a head that's already been emptied of its contents?—but it's true nevertheless; I need to return to the work of learning who I am without Jude to guide me. I add to my mental tally: *I am a person who will do anything to define herself.*

In the afternoon, I decide to find a bar other than Exiles—a place completely devoid of any personal history. No snug room, no poker games, no smashed cabinets and pickled hearts. A place to sit still and observe and ask myself silent questions, to see if any are asked of me. In the bedroom beneath the rug I find my new secret wad of cash, a surprise gift from Sab on the day he took me to anger management class; he'd slyly tucked it in my bag before taking me home. On a whim I open the curio cabinet to retrieve our mother's black gloves and snip the fingers off, blending the old with the new. I unfurl them over my wrists and venture out into the smoldering heat, eager to see where I lead myself.

I walk and walk, ten blocks, twenty, doubling back again and landing somewhere in the middle, drawn to a striped awning that reminds me of the carousel in our photo. Gold letters are emblazoned on the smoky glass window: *DIRTY FRAN'S*. Inside it is very dark, all evidence of the bright afternoon obscured. A lacy necklace of bras and underwear is strung on a clothesline above the bar, and I wonder if I've ever stripped in public. Along one wall stands a row of arcade games, *Donkey Kong* and *Pac-Man* and *Crazy Climber*; I wonder if I've ever played them. I order a hot pretzel along with a Long Island iced tea and wonder if I've ever tasted either. *Less wondering*, I tell myself, *and more detective work*.

"Serious drink for a Tuesday afternoon," the bartender says, impaling the rim of my glass with a lemon wedge. Her top is cut low, exposing her shoulders and a mysterious chest tattoo done in some kind of old-timey font: *FREAK JAWN*.

I take a long sip, tasting flavors—citrus, herbal, sour—that seem like they should be familiar but aren't, like the face or name of a long-ago friend. I consider asking her for the ingredients, but my brain decides to pivot: "So what is an appropriate drink for a Tuesday afternoon, then?"

The bartender tunnels a dirty rag into a glass, wiping it dry. "That depends entirely on what happened Monday night."

I like this answer, cagey but inquisitive, and I don't want to disappoint her. I don't want to tell her that most of my Monday nights are lost, and who the hell knows if any of them warranted something like this sticky sour concoction, which I've nearly finished, and which is already leaking itself into my bloodstream, stirring up a clash of emotions—melancholy and jovial and fearful and emboldened and remorseful and defiant—and I don't know which to settle on, or if it's possible to inhabit them all at once.

The bartender has stopped cleaning the glass and seems amused by my hesitation.

Before I can respond I see, in the corner of my vision, a shiny waterfall of hair and a flash of pale skin—a forearm, to be precise, layered with bracelets up to the elbow. I glance leftward and recognize her: Nancy, ambassador for the CHIC charity, canvassing the city to help starving children, with her clipboard of addresses and names. I can tell by the slight hitch of her eyebrows that she remembers me, too. She takes the barstool next to mine, just inches away.

"I'll have what she's having," she tells the bartender. "And she'll have another."

I remember her greeting from when we met on the street and repeat it to her now, using the same flirty tone: "Are you following me?"

Her laugh surprises me, a deep gong song that sounds like the laugh of someone twice her size. "Touché," she says. "I guess I deserved that. Although I have to say that I'm flattered you remember me, after what happened to you."

"That's the weird thing about losing your memory," I say. "You start remembering everything."

The bartender sets down our drinks and picks up another glass to dry, staying within earshot.

"Cheers," Nancy says, raising her glass.

I meet her halfway. "Cheers."

We both take a long drink. I stay silent, hoping she'll speak first.

"Remind me what your name is," she says finally. "I never lost my memory, so, according to your logic, it's not as good as yours. But I never forget a face."

She shifts toward me, sitting catty-corner in her seat. The bar suddenly seems ten degrees hotter; I can feel the black gloves dampening atop my skin. "Kat," I say. "My name is Kat."

"Kat," she repeats. "I won't forget it again."

We both take another long drink. I notice that she stops when I stop, letting me set the pace.

"So, are you?" I ask. "Following me?"

Another laugh, even deeper this time. "That would make this encounter a lot more interesting than it is. Sorry to disappoint you, but I work here."

At this she winks at the bartender, who's still wiping glasses and hovering. I don't know how to interpret this wink. Is she joking? Is she greeting a colleague? Is she giving some private sign? Is it none or all of these? The bar is now entirely empty but for the three of us, and the big empty space somehow feels crowded, dimmer. I realize that, in the After Times, I've only ever had drinks with Jude and Sab, never with perfect strangers. Sab was a stranger, too, of course, but not for long, and not like this.

Focus, I tell myself. *I am a person capable of handling herself in any situation.*

"I thought you worked for a kids' charity?" I ask, keeping my tone casual. I take another sip; Nancy does the same.

"That's charity. It doesn't pay the bills." Again that laugh, a bit subdued this time. She rests a hand on my gloved arm. "I started the charity because one of the other bartenders here had an accident and couldn't work for a while. She's a single mom and they were struggling."

I look to Freak Jawn for confirmation but she's turned her back to us, focusing instead on a television mounted behind the bar, tuned to the Phillies game. I take another sip; so does Nancy. I realize she is not letting me set the pace but mimicking me—*mirroring* me—doing exactly what I do, but just a beat behind.

"Speaking of accidents," she says, "how is your recovery going? Have you been able to recall any memories?" Her long, slim fingers squeeze my arm.

For the first time, I look directly into her eyes instead of between them. They are a deep, swampy green, and steady on mine.

"No," I tell her. "I don't really have any hope of recovering them. My doctor says to focus on doing brain exercises that can help me going forward. Crossword puzzles, word and number games, chess, that kind of thing." I remove my arm from her grasp and imitate a formal, gruff voice. "There are myriad ways to try to stimulate brain growth." I wag my finger. "The key is consistency. The key is dedication. Can you be consistent and dedicated, Kat?" I lower my finger, resume my own voice. "He says the same thing every time I talk to him."

Slowly I raise my glass to my lips, pausing when it reaches my chin. She matches my tempo, and when she's about to take a sip I drop my glass back down, landing it with a bang against the bar, throwing her off. She recovers fast; instead of taking a drink she thrusts her glass toward me, hovering it near my face.

"I propose a toast," she says. "To memories, especially the ones we'd rather forget."

What an odd thing to say, I think, and then realize she must be talking about herself, her own cache of dark and scrambled thoughts. I decide to play along.

"To the ones we'd rather forget," I repeat, and this time I let our sips coordinate. Together we drink for a full five seconds, and when I wipe my hand across my mouth she matches the gesture so quickly that I wonder if she'd made it first.

"So let me guess," she says. "You have been neither consistent nor dedicated to stimulating your brain growth."

We both laugh, our disparate tones—hers low, mine high—somehow in perfect harmony.

"Guilty," I say. "But I have my own method. I like putting myself into real world situations to see what happens. To see what I say and how I react. It seems that I don't know what I think about things until I'm actually in the moment, being forced to think about them." I realize my voice sounds vaguely slushy, the end of one word colliding with the beginning of the next. Whatever is in a Long Island iced tea is clearly much stronger than beer. The second drink is nearly gone and I feel a loosening inside of me, a slight unraveling, as though an unseen hand has pulled a secret string.

"Can I suggest something and you can see what you think about it?"

Two more drinks appear. I don't remember either of us ordering another round. Freak Jawn finally has another customer, an old man at the other end of the bar. He reaches up to the clothesline of underwear to tug on a large red bra, and she swats away his hand.

"Please," I tell her. "That's the way it works." I sip a tiny, shallow sip; she dips her tongue inside her glass, letting it skim the liquid. I give up, granting her a silent victory in her strange, unspoken game.

"So I used to go to this psychic. Her name is Madame Destiny. Dorky, I know, but it's just the name she uses to get people in the door. Her real name is Arlene. She knew so many things about me that no one else knew, like my mom being arrested for driving drunk. And she predicted things, too, like me hurting my leg."

She taps her left thigh; I had forgotten about her limp until that moment.

"No way," I say, genuinely intrigued. It sounds like an accelerated version of my plodding detective work, a chance to get to know myself again in a fraction of the time. I think, *I am a person who appreciates a shortcut.*

"Yes way. So, look. I'm going to give you her address. I haven't seen her in a long time, but I'm sure she's still there." She reaches in her purse for a pen and scribbles on a napkin. My palm opens, accepting it.

"How do I get there?" I ask. "Is it too far to walk? I've forgotten how to get around on the buses and the El."

"Duh," she says. "Look in your hand."

I look; there's a twenty-dollar bill tucked inside of the napkin.

"She'll call you a cab," she says, pointing to Freak Jawn. "That should get you there and back." There's an urgency to her voice, as though my visit to Madame Destiny would be as much for her advantage as for mine.

"Are you sure?" I ask.

"I insist. All I ask is that you tell me what she said, if we ever meet again. Deal?"

She smiles, close-lipped, a puckered plum of a mouth.

"Deal," I say. This time she drinks first, and I follow her lead.

The world outside teeters between light and dark, and my body feels similarly indecisive; the sense of unraveling is countered by a blast of adrenaline, holding my pieces together, my blood its own crackling electricity. I will ask questions. I will get answers. I will leave Madame Destiny's esteemed establishment with new insights into my past and solid predictions for my future. I take my mind's temperature, parsing its thoughts: *I am a person who is being solved.*

Without ceremony, the driver lets me out into a narrow street, tires screeching on the getaway. I realize I don't even know what neighborhood I'm in. I check the napkin for the address and find it to my right: a white brick row house nestled between two red ones, with five steps leading up to a black door. Its window shades are drawn and it seems to be tired, listing sideways, depending on its neighbors to prop it up.

There's no sign announcing Madame Destiny's services, but there's a button to push that sounds a rickety buzz. I push again. No one comes to open the door, so I open it myself. Inside the air is thick with heat and carries a sour smell—the dregs of rotten food, of dirty bodies, of dead animals. A gilded desk is missing a leg. A velvet chair has fallen on its side. A corner holds a pile of clothing—corduroy pants and ruffled tops and sneakers dappled with mud. A line of candles, halfway burned, crowds the mantel of a fireplace carved with hearts and cherubs. Madame Destiny is nowhere to be found, but in an adjacent room, I spot writing along the wall.

I creep closer, the old floors sighing with each step, to see what the letters say. Someone had written *The Rabbit Hole* in black marker, doubling over the letters twice where the ink had faded, and that extra effort—that deliberate emphasis—unnerves me even more than the words themselves.

JUDE: THEN

Ten Years before the Accident
JUNE 1973

In the two years since The Plan's first seminar, when their mother thrashed inside the circle and became someone else, the organization creeped into their daily lives. Verona pulled them from the local public school ("Excellent with the basics," she explained, "but a grossly incomplete curriculum") and enlisted a growing roster of members to teach them lessons at home—lessons that began, always, with the Poem of the Day, verses chosen to calibrate their expanding minds. Other kids came, including Violet, who always brought the best objects for show-and-tell: her uncle Bash's antique guns and flasks and gas masks that resembled the elongated faces of ghosts. Jude and Kat and Violet put on the masks and chased each other around the acres of backyard; Jude always outran Kat, but allowed Violet to catch her.

The adults held long discussions about what The Plan was, what

it could become, how it would survive and thrive. They had competition. Across the country similar groups were promising fast and easy
enlightenment, a mass Human Potential Movement, a golden grift
for the times. These groups exhorted members to "Get it!" without
explaining what *it* was. They used tactics of divisiveness and derision.
Everyone's an asshole, everyone's a motherfucker, everyone's shitty
luck was born of their own design, including accidents and illnesses.
Pay two hundred and fifty dollars and you, too, can learn that there
are no answers because there are no questions. Everyone wanted in,
or was terrified of being left out. Even celebrities were up for grabs,
John Denver and Diana Ross and Yoko Ono and John Lennon and
Cher and others in their orbits. The possibilities were infinite so long
as they could distinguish themselves from the rest.

"How will we do that?" Jude asked one day, standing in the doorway of the parlor, Violet and Kat on either side. Verona sat on the sofa
beneath a large canvas of herself as Very Sherry, straddling a rocket
and waving a sparkler, an homage to the Fourth of July. A semicircle
of people faced her, including Dr. Bash and Ronald and Donald, all of
them sitting wide-legged, hands clenching their hairy bare knees.
Dr. Bash, a head taller than the others, his magnificent yellow mane
fanned out like the sun, made Ronald and Donald look like drab after-
thoughts. In Jude's mind, they fused into the same person: the RonDon.

"Do what, my beatific angel?" Verona said. She patted the empty
spot on the sofa, and all three girls squeezed beside her.

"Show we're different," Jude said.

The question launched another round of discussion. How,
indeed? Let's start with what The Plan was not. They were not a
pyramid scheme. Profit was not their purpose. In fact, since everyone deserved the chance to excavate their own hidden promise, they
would offer a sliding scale for seminars based on need. The principal
members would collect a modest salary, of course, but all other pro-
ceeds would go toward growing The Plan. Their members, if they

so choose, would not be limited to weekend seminars, but would be invited—nay, encouraged—to participate at any time and in any fashion; there was always more work to do. Contrary to one popular organization based in New York City, they did not believe that the nuclear family was the root of all evil. Contrary to one popular organization based in California, they did not need the crutch of religion or the specter of a deity to achieve their highest power. They were not the free love children of the sixties. They were not interested in drugs or orgies. They were not hippies brainwashed by the likes of Charles Manson. They would not start a race war or proselytize about the end times. They did not aspire to anarchy but to mastering the system from the inside.

"Judith, Katherine," Verona said, "would one or both of you start taking notes on our discussion? We will finalize the five tenets of The Plan and launch the next phase of recruitment and integration."

"Violet, you participate as well," Dr. Bash said. "You girls are old enough to start practicing self-sufficiency, and we need all hands on deck."

So, then, what *was* The Plan? They were professionals with jobs and families. Just look at Dr. Bash, who had degrees in psychology and marketing and history; and Ronald, who had a long and distinguished career in publishing; and Donald, a photographer whose work had appeared in magazines all over the world. And Verona, of course, had been a voracious traveler and student of the universe, a woman who excelled in cultivating and capitalizing on her own prodigious gifts.

They were smart and literate and intellectually curious. They were strivers, risk-takers, strategic dreamers. They were raising the next generation of proactive and successful adults. They believed in personal responsibility, energetic initiative, and advocating on behalf of the organization—but never at the expense of individual benefit. They were benevolently ruthless. They would live according to the five tenets of The Plan, individual concepts that, practiced as a whole, would elevate members to their most glorious and fierce iteration.

THE FIVE TENETS OF THE PLAN

- RECAST YOUR PAST
  Make your pain work for you.

- REJECT AND RELEASE
  Cast the dead weight from your mind.

- PERFORM OR PERISH
  The battle is constant and permanent.

- DEFEAT BEGETS DOMINATION
  Turn failure into success.

- WHAT YOU THINK, IS
  Your mind is the ultimate power.

On the hottest day of that summer, Verona made an announcement: "Girls, I have wonderful news. The Plan has grown by leaps and bounds, and now we're bigger than this house can contain, bigger than all our houses can contain. We are going to have another house—three new houses, in fact, smack in the middle of Philadelphia. We'll have so many adventures and you'll become strong and independent women, able to survive and thrive in ways that might at first seem impossible." They were to begin packing right away, limited to what would fit in a single valise.

Within two hours they were in the Way Back of Verona's car, flopping across each other, enticing passing truckers to sound their horns. They eased slowly into the city, the wide sky and clusters of trees yielding to abandoned factories and rails and a pervasive sense of raw despair. Trees sprouted in the midst of junkyards. A smokestack huffed in the distance. Trash drifted down streets with the slow grace of tumbleweed. Verona coasted down a narrow street lined with row houses, some with boards for windows. At the end of the block congregated a pack of wild dogs, pets that had been discarded and turned feral.

"Here we are, darlings," she said, and gave a game show sweep of her hand. "Katherine, you'll start off in Mr. Ronald's house. Judith, you'll be with Dr. Bash."

"Why can't we be together?" Kat asked.

"You're just a house away." She slung an arm around each of their shoulders. "Don't look at this as punishment, but as opportunity. Grow alone. Learn to think independently. See what you can accomplish without the push and pull of the other, with only your own voice in your head. It will be better for both of you in the long run."

"Will you be staying with us?" Kat asked.

Verona pulled them close so that Jude's head rested on her right breast and Kat's on the left. She began to weep and shake, and the twins shook along with her.

"Not right now," she said, "as much as it hurts me to let you go. But I want you girls to master the tenets. I want you to be magnificent in this world. And one day, when you're older and ready, you'll join me in the Big House. That will be our ultimate reward, being together again, all of us in full possession of our powers."

Kat began to cry, adding to the shaking and jostling. Jude held back her tears and just let her head go along for the ride. The crying seemed to last a long time, and at last Verona stifled her honks and wheezes, an old motor stuttering to a stop.

"Don't worry, my angels," she said. "We will be able to communicate. It's just temporary. Remember why we are doing this. Remember what is at stake. Remember to make me proud. I love you both so much."

She released them. Jude took over, pulling Kat into her arms, letting her sister continue her crying. She whispered to Kat that they would be strong and brave, they would reject and release, they would amplify their thoughts with such staggering force that they would all inevitably come true.

"Hawt ew inkth, si," they said in unison.

What we think, is.

Dr. Bash's row house stood narrow but tall, four stories high, and was decorated with their mother's cast-off antiques: ripped chairs and splintered tables and tattered tapestries that had once been stored in her backyard shed. A dozen children crowded in the front parlor, many of them sitting on suitcases, their faces a mixed gallery of malaise and terror. Jude recognized several from previous meetings and gatherings at their home—including Roy, the kid in the cowboy hat who liked to play with fire. She saw no sign of Violet. In silence, Jude waited and waited: five minutes, ten, a half hour. It was not clear if an adult would appear, or if they were now the adults.

In another five minutes Dr. Bash did appear, wearing flared jeans and a red tunic with a neckline cut low enough to show his chest hair, which reminded Jude of the underbelly of some exotic animal, a yak or a wild boar, if a yak or a boar could be blond. She had never seen so much of a man's body, not even her father's, and she felt compelled to look away. Instead she focused on his teeth, so very straight and white, and his eyes, still the most unusual she'd ever seen, and somehow even lighter in this dim room. He descended the steps with the ponderous rhythm of a grandfather clock—pause, thump, pause, thump, pause, thump—and, upon reaching the bottom, raised his tanned arms into the air.

"Welcome, all of you," he said. "I'm so thrilled you're here. You all have known me for a few years as Dr. Bash, but in honor of this new phase of our little group, I am going to ask you to call me something new. Don't laugh, but I am going to ask you to call me King Bash."

They laughed, of course, partly because he said not to, but mostly because it was absurd. How could Dr. Bash be a king when he was standing in a row house in the center of Philadelphia, wearing a gaudy tunic and his bright, goofy smile? Where did he think they were, in medieval England? What, was he planning to round up the cavalry and invade South Jersey?

"I know, it's funny, let it all out," King Bash said. Jude watched him make eye contact with every kid in the room, saving her for last. "I know it's strange, but if you think about it, it makes sense. We're creating our own little country, and every country has to have leaders and rules."

No one was laughing now, even if it was all still a bit weird. King Bash rubbed his blond stubble and tried a different approach: "If you don't want to think of us as a country, think of us as a jungle filled with the most formidable and clever animals. We're hunters on the prowl for the best ways to advance our knowledge. We're gatherers, finding new members who will complete our pack. We're warriors, defeating anyone who threatens us, either individually or as a group. There's always a king of the jungle, but that doesn't mean you all are any less important." He clapped his thick hands, rubbing them together. "Now, I'm going to have a short, private chat with each of you, but to make that bearable, I've also ordered a bunch of pizzas, more than anyone here will be able to eat."

Everyone cheered. King Bash clapped along and then pressed a finger to his lips, making the room go quiet again. "Celebrate now, because tomorrow we start on a stricter regimen. We must get ourselves in fighting shape. We are just beginning to realize and harness our potential, and we need to ride our momentum."

The pizza came, and the room filled with the smell of greasy meat and the sound of vigorous chewing. Jude took three slices, holding one in each hand and the third by the firm grip of her teeth, aware she must resemble one of the wild dogs roaming outside, sifting for scraps. She sat in a corner, her back against the wall, watching all the kids—some as young as seven, some as old as she, some a year or two older—dropping strings of cheese into their open mouths, waiting to be called to another room, where they would be advised on riding momentum and harnessing potential. She had nearly finished her third slice when King Bash called her name. The top half of his body leaned out from behind a sheer silver curtain, and he beckoned her, curling his fingers slowly inward. She swallowed the last pointy shard of crust, and it scraped her throat on the way down.

She stepped over a minefield of bare legs to reach the curtain, and King Bash pulled it closed behind her. The room was small and square and had one narrow window with the blind drawn shut. An avocado-colored shag carpet covered most of the floor. He took a seat in a worn leather chair (another Verona discard, she noticed) behind a squat wooden desk cluttered with papers, a money ledger, a Rolodex, several packs of playing cards, a lava lamp with floating neon blobs, and books with titles like *As a Man Thinketh* and *My Secret Garden*. He motioned to an opposing chair in a way that made her feel like a visiting dignitary, and spoke to her as though they were equals: "Please, Jude, take a seat," he said. "It is a privilege to have you here."

His words stirred within her a desire to be the finest version of herself—a self that just a few moments earlier had seemed aspirational, years out of her reach. She sat tall in her chair, setting her spine straight and shoulders back, and crossed her legs at the ankles, just like Verona. Her fingers began picking at each other, tearing cuticles, and she folded them in her lap. "Thank you, Dr. Bash—King—sir," she said. "I am glad to be here."

He leaned forward and she noticed that his hands, too, were clasped. On his thick middle finger he wore a thick gold band engraved with a *B*, two sparkling diamonds filling the holes in the letter. "I'm so pleased to hear that, Jude. We're on the precipice of something big here, something truly grand and exciting, and I am going to need your help."

Jude nodded. Her heart might burst with solemnity and pride. This must be how Neil Armstrong felt when he stepped onto the moon, or how Liza Minnelli felt accepting the Oscar for *Cabaret*, or how Shirley Chisholm felt announcing her candidacy for president. Whatever this thing was, whatever was making King Bash sweat through his tunic and twist his golden ring, it was epic, possibly life-changing, and she would be at the forefront, making it happen.

"I think you know that I hold you in high regard, Jude. I've always thought you were smarter and more mature than other girls your age. Jude, you have a toughness and a fortitude that will serve you well in The Plan, and in life."

She liked the way that he repeated her name, as though it were a mantra that made him feel centered and calm. Hearing her name in his voice gave her a surge of power, and she leaned forward, too, placing her palms on his desk. "I agree, King Bash. I have always felt more responsible than other kids my age. I'm almost thirteen, but I feel fifteen or sixteen at least."

His blue eyes bore like augers, and he did not blink when he said his next words. "You are a natural-born leader, Jude, and you will take on the important task of helping The Plan grow. I am going to send you to meet other young people like yourself. Jude, I am going to trust you to say the right things to them and listen carefully to their responses. You will vet them to make sure they are worthy of The Plan. Do you know what *vet* means?"

She pulled her hands back from the table and imagined shaking her brain like a snow globe, hoping the right definition emerged from the mist. She reworded his question into a response: "Yes, King Bash, it means asking them questions and making sure they are worthy. If they answer the questions wrong, they are not worthy."

"Exactly, Jude," he said, and she was pleased to have pleased him. "And since The Plan works as a force for good, since we are interested in the ideas of radical acceptance and validating the power of the mind, we need you to base our questions on those concepts. So when you see someone, maybe a boy or girl your age or slightly younger, you might ask things like, 'Have you ever wished you were smarter or stronger?' and 'Do you know humans only use ten percent of our brains? What if you could learn how to use the whole thing?' and 'Do you want to meet a group of people who will think you're cool, no matter what?' The best candidates for The Plan will be the ones who ask questions in turn. They will show they have something to contribute, that they, too, can help us grow. Do you understand, Jude?"

"I believe so, King Bash," she said. "I think this is something I can do."

"Think?" he asked, tilting his big animal head. "There is no room for uncertainty in The Plan, Jude."

"I know, King Bash. I know, I really do." Her back was so perfectly straight, her ankles so gracefully crossed, her voice so preternaturally mature.

"Out of sight," he said, and held out his hand. She went in for a low five but instead he grasped her hand and shook it properly, the way adults do. As she turned to leave he called her name again, quietly this time, almost a whisper.

"Yes, King Bash?" She kept her back as straight as it had been in the chair.

He stood and took a step toward her. "I want you to know, Jude, that our radical acceptance also extends to you."

Her body began a slow burn, as though a match had been struck on the tips of her toes.

"I have known you long enough to know you are different, Jude. I know you have different desires, different appetites. I know that you worry that Kat might not understand, since her appetites and desires are not considered different."

The flame grew hotter and burned higher, lapping at her thighs. She could not speak or move. He took another step toward her, close enough for her to smell the tangy musk of his cologne.

"You don't have to say anything, Jude. Your desires are your desires, and they are valid and true—just by virtue of you having them. You should be proud, not scared. Your differences make you special, Jude. They are part of your tremendous power, and I do not ever want you to turn your back on them."

He stood over her now, so close she could see the tangled hair in his nostrils and his peppery pores. "I accept you, Jude, and I want you to know that your secret is safe with me. You can always trust me. I will make sure no one uses your difference as a weapon against you."

He pulled her toward him, trapping her in his arms. She wanted to thank him, to deny everything, to run away, to burrow herself in his damp hairy chest and weep—weep from embarrassment, from shame, from regret, from fear, from happiness, from a clear, pure feeling of relief; maybe she was not a freak or an abomination. Maybe there was not a thing wrong with her. Maybe she would have a happy life after all.

"It's okay, Jude," he said, holding her tight. "It's really, honestly okay." And in that moment, she had never believed anyone as much as she believed him.

KAT: NOW

Three Months after the Accident
JUNE 1983

I don't tell Jude about my encounter with Nancy or my quest to find Madame Destiny, although this omission feels dangerously close to deception. I don't want to lie to my sister, to do the very things I wrongly suspected of her. I remind myself that she is out every day, working to pay off my hospital bills, and that my detective work should not become cause for worry or concern. I imagine solving the mystery of myself and presenting my findings to Jude: "Voilà!" I'd say, with a magician's flair. "Behold the girl with the unscrambled brain, but don't ask me to reveal my tricks."

Today's mission is restitution, and it requires a disguise.

I drop the carousel photo into my bag and then transform myself into my twin—not just the bruised eyes and outlined lips but the part of my hair, combing it from left to right, battling my cowlick to fall counterclockwise. The result is more disorienting than any photograph;

instead of looking at Jude and seeing myself, I am looking at myself and seeing my twin, a reversal of the reversal. Now I understand Jude's uneasiness, and with this understanding, I myself feel more at ease.

I find a pay phone and dial Sab's number. After four rings and the sound of his answering machine, I hang up. It's four o'clock on a Tuesday, an hour after his shift ended, and if his past schedule is any indication he's at Exiles right now, having a beer before heading into the snug room. I start walking in the direction of the bar, talking to myself in Jude's voice, which tells me that I have the chance to make money and help to pay the bills. It tells me I can corral my flailing energy and put it to good use.

I spot the bar's green awning, loosened on one side and billowing in the pre-storm wind. I find a compact mirror in my bag and scrutinize myself, picking a wayward flake of mascara from my cheek. My Jude-parted cowlick has begun to rebel and is now rising toward a neutral position, refusing to align itself with either side. I push it back into Jude territory, smoothing it down, channeling her indomitable force to make it stay.

Sab is at the end of the bar, alone, a bottle of beer and a newspaper set in front of him. I hover by the door and watch him, imbuing each mundane gesture—a swallow of beer, a turn of the page—with a kind of romantic significance Jude would viciously mock.

A voice yanks me back to the moment: "Yo!" The bartender flings a towel around his shoulder and turns an accusation into a question: "You busted up the cabinet in the back?"

Sab spins in his seat. "Kat!" he says. "What are you doing here?"

One sleeve of my sweatshirt falls to expose my shoulder. I settle into my Jude mask and walk to the bar.

"I'm sorry, sir," I say. "That was my twin sister. My name is Jude. I want to apologize and assure you I'll compensate you for any damage she's done." I find the carousel photo in my bag. "See? This is me and this is my twin." I point to Jude as me and to me as Jude. "She's not been herself lately, not that it's any excuse."

Sab angles himself toward me, studying the picture. "I can vouch for this," he tells the bartender. "I know she has a twin." The bartender shrugs and returns to wiping glasses. Sab's eyes do a slow scan of my body, top to bottom, trying to decide who I am. I let my expression go slack and my eyes blank, giving him nothing. I feel a prick of guilt, but I want to wear Jude for just a while longer.

From the door comes the expected chorus: "Yo, Sab!" Ryan, Guy, Steve, Booch, and Chinch bound in. I approach, meeting them halfway. "Hey," I say. "My name is Jude. I'm Kat's twin sister and I want to apologize for what happened at the last game. She's going through some heavy shit—medical issues that have affected her brain. She was playing poker to try to pay off her hospital bills and didn't take it well when she lost. Obviously."

They look to Sab, who nods his confirmation.

"I hope you'll consider letting me play with you today," I add. "First round is on me."

———

Back in the snug room, a piece of cardboard spans across the section of broken cabinet. The conjoined twins and mummified hand are set side by side; the pickled human heart has not been replaced. Wanting a clear view of Sab's face, I sit opposite him on the bench, squeezing in between Guy and Booch. A waitress arrives with three pitchers of beer, and I make a show of pouring everyone a glass.

"To evil twins," I toast.

"To evil twins," comes the echo and a round of robust *clink*s.

My Jude costume envelops me, seeping into my skin. It is familiar but vaguely uncomfortable, severe in all the ways I expect but vulnerable in ways I don't. As Jude I am sharp in my words and savage in my glances, all the while cowering around my heart.

One round, two, three. My pile creeps steadily higher. Jude is a plotter, a creature of patience and cunning, a fox on the scent of hesitation and doubt, as inscrutable as a corpse. From the corner of one eye, I watch Sab watching me, studying my face for expressions he thinks he knows. I tease him, flashing a glimpse of Kat's giddy verve before Jude draws the curtain, leaving him in the dark.

They begin dropping out: Guy, Ryan, Chinch. I keep buying rounds but hardly drink, sipping just the top of the foam. Jude is the arbiter of my choices, the engine that makes me go. I have never seen so much money in one place in the few months I remember being alive. Booch is out. Steve is out. Sab and I are the only ones left.

By now he is certain I'm a stranger—no history between us, nothing given and nothing owed. It is better this way; he will be ruthless in his attack, and I sanguine in my kill.

"You ready?" Sab asks. I imagine it is the voice he uses with coworkers, directing the spreading of cement and scooping of stone.

"And waiting," I say in Jude's hatchet tone.

He deals four cards, two and two. I slide mine up my chest and take a peek: a Six and Seven of Hearts. I call; it's on.

Sab deals the flop: Jack of Clubs, Three of Hearts, Five of Clubs.

I'm one card away from a straight. I slide three fourths of my chips to the center of the table and look at Sab, quelling any hint of expression.

He calls.

"Getting a bit hot in here," Booch narrates. "What will the turn bring?"

It brings a Four of Hearts, giving me a straight—and one card away from a straight flush. I push my remaining chips into the pile. My heart jabs at my ribs. I worry that my Jude veneer is rubbing away, that Kat might peak through. I tamp myself down and coax Jude back to the surface. *Jude, Jude, Jude*, I tell myself. *I am Jude.*

Jude's hands push my remaining chips into the pile.

"Well, look here," I say, sounding not at all like myself. "The twin is as ballsy as the original."

"Which she'll regret," Sab says. "I'm in."

His chips join mine and he flips the final card: a Jack of Hearts.

I have a flush.

I have a flush, which beats a straight.

I force myself to sit still, imagining Jude's hands pressing into my shoulders.

"Moment of truth," Ryan says. "Sab, what do you got?"

Sab turns over his two cards: Ace of Clubs and Two of Hearts, which gives him a mere straight. I won.

Jude's voice corrects me—*she* won. I let her have the victory, revel in her success; she's earned it in ways I will probably never know.

"Fuck," Sab says, and his voice is a growl—genuinely furious, all the fun of the game squeezed out, the difference between playing me and playing Jude. He doesn't look at me as I collect the rest of the chips.

"Biggest pot we've had in months," he says. "Four hundred and fifty bucks."

My body begins to wilt and I clutch the edge of the table just in time, steadying my stance, reminding myself that I am Jude. I let her intrude upon my thoughts, giving me orders: stand straight, take the money you earned, compensate the bartender for damages, and get out without explanation or apology.

"Thanks, everyone," I say. "Great game." Then I silence Jude's voice in my head, letting Kat take over. I skim my fingers down Sab's arm. "Can I talk to you outside for a second?"

He follows the trail of my fingers and looks up just as I alter my expression, wiping it free of Jude. I feel the hairs on his arm stand up, bristling against my skin.

"Kat?" he whispers.

I wink in a way that would make Jude cringe.

"Just let me settle up the damage with the bartender," I tell him. "I'll meet you outside."

"It's already settled," he says. "Come on."

He pulls me through the crowd, his arm stretched all the way back, gripping my hand. There's a feverish grace to his gestures, a sense of calm beneath his shock. Outside, the awning gives us cover from sharp needles of rain, just beginning to fall.

He clutches both of my wrists, trapping me.

"What was that in there?" he asks. "*Who* was that in there?"

"I'm sorry," I tell him. "I needed to be Jude for a bit. I wouldn't have been allowed to play any other way. We're in a really bad spot with my medical bills and I knew Jude could win. Or that I could win *as* Jude."

I don't want to cry—Jude would not cry—and yet I can't stop it. Tears blur my vision and I blink once, hard, feeling them fall.

He relaxes his grip, letting his hands dangle like bracelets. "I know," he says. "Do you want to go somewhere else? Get a drink and talk about it?"

"I don't want to be around anyone else right now," I say, freeing my hand to wipe my eye. "I just want to be alone."

"Do you want me to drive you home," he asks, "or do you want to be alone with me?"

We run to his car, the rain heavy now, attacking us from all sides. He opens the door for me and we ride in silence, listening to the sounds of the streets. I try to move in my seat. I want to turn to him—to look at the hard angles of his face, the duck-tail swoop of his hair, but I'm immobile, as if tied by invisible rope. My heart moves enough for all of me, a panicked pulsing I'm certain he can hear.

Two minutes later and we're running again, moving in unison, our steps falling on the same beat. He fumbles through his movements: finding and turning a key, leading me up three flights of stairs, flipping on and extinguishing a light. He leads me down a hallway that seems long as a highway, so much space between where we are and where we're going, until the door closes behind us and we are there, Jude nowhere to be found.

His lips are on my neck, a soft but persistent flutter that makes me think of trapped moths. I turn, meeting him halfway, and as his mouth lowers to mine I tell myself: *This is my second very first kiss, slow down and remember everything*, and his hands glide along my waist and suddenly his chest is bare—it is all so astonishing and wondrous and I am certain I have never seen anyone who looked like this, like *him*, so sweet now with his closed eyes and open expectations, awaiting strange gifts.

"You," he whispers, opening his eyes. "Let me just look at you." He seizes my wrists in his hands, lifts my arms above my head, and in that moment of capture I am neither Jude nor Kat but someone else entirely, a beast of unknown species that goes on the attack: elbows to his chest, the heels of my palms to his face, my leg a mighty axe chopping against his torso, my knee a bullet to his groin. After he's flat on the ground, showing his belly in surrender, his hands in supplication, I attack again, flesh smacking flesh, drawing blood, a roaring quiet in my ears.

"Kat!" he says, a muffled scream, and at the sound of my name I realize what I've done. I look at my hands, knuckles raw, flecks of blood caught in their creases, my dry breath scything my throat.

The beast retreats, leaving him alone in the dark.

JUDE: THEN

Ten Years before the Accident

JULY 1973

Although Kat was next door and Violet two doors down, and there were dozens of bodies filling the houses, and all sorts of sounds and calls spilling from windows, and a colorful riot of humanity parading around their block, and the constant bark and snarl of the wild dogs, Jude felt her world constrict, tightening around her mind like a belt. The Plan involved a regimen, one that required the monitoring of sleep and the parsing of food, the repetition of tenets and the analysis of poems, the playing of games and debates about strategy, and the marking of days on an oversized calendar, all of them slashed with bright red ink. They were counting down to something—exactly what, no one knew.

The calendar told Jude she had been living in King Bash's row house for one month when he called her aside, spreading his silver curtain and asking her to sit, serving her milk in a vintage crystal goblet.

"Thank you for taking the time out of your busy schedule to meet with me, Jude," he said. "How are you settling in here?"

Jude gulped her milk. Somehow, despite the chaos outside, King Bash's office was quiet, almost uncomfortably so; the sound of her swallowing filled the room.

"It's tough," she said.

"I'm sorry to hear that," he said. He twisted his initial ring. He had clean nails, perfectly shaped; she had never seen such pristine nails on a man. The diamonds caught the light from his window and threw slim rainbows around the room. "But you're tough, too, and I have confidence you will persevere."

"No, King Bash, you misunderstood," she said. A quick heat spread through her, reddening her face. "I meant 'tough' as in *good*. That's what tough means. So I meant to say it's going good. Or well. You know what I mean."

He laughed, a real laugh, throwing back his head and dropping his hands to the table.

"I didn't know, but now I do. Thank you, Jude. You all teach me something new every day. And I am glad it's going well."

Her mortification passed, returning her face to its normal temperature. She considered telling him that she missed living in the same house as her twin, but no—the moment called for stoicism. She placed her finished goblet of milk on his desk and folded her hands in her lap.

"Now, King Bash, sir, what can I do for you?"

He leaned forward. "Yes, Jude, thank you for insisting on efficiency. First, I want to say that during my visits to the Big House, I speak often with your mother. I've been telling her about your remarkable progress with The Plan, and that you are an inspiration to everyone. She sends her love and says she'll visit soon."

Jude could not speak without risking tears. She nodded and smiled, tight-lipped.

"I am holding very important seminars in the coming weeks," he continued. "Seminars where I hope to achieve major goals for The Plan, regarding our continued growth and success. I'll be coming and going, a hectic schedule. While I'm gone, I have very important work for you to do."

"Does this have to do with the countdown on the calendar?"

"It does. And thank you for connecting the dots." He stood, his old leather chair scraping against the floor, and leaned against the bookshelves. From Jude's vantage point, he seemed tall as a castle or a tower, a gleaming landmark to stop and admire. "Do you remember the last time I called you for a private talk, and we discussed vetting candidates for The Plan?"

She remembered all of it, of course—the questions to be posed, the keywords to use, the insistence that candidates should ask questions in turn.

"I remember. And if it's time to do that, I am ready."

"Good, Jude," he said. His tunic clung to his slick chest. "It is time, and you will be a leader. You will hunt and gather new members. Think of yourself as a monkey, the most intelligent animal, and the potential candidates as rabbits, which can sometimes be tricky and elusive. The more rabbits you gather, the more important you will become. The more important you become, the more privileges you will have. Do you understand, Jude? Can you handle this very important job?"

"I do understand, King Bash. I really do, and I can."

"Far out," he said, and Jude did not want to tell him that the phrase was passé. "In honor of the occasion, let's read the Poem of the Day. I've picked 'The Rabbit Catcher' by Sylvia Plath. Seems apropos, don't you think?"

She told him she thought it quite apropos. He began to read, his hair darkened with sweat, his tongue wetting his lips, each word clear and emphatic—words about the black spikes of the snares, so close together, close like birth pangs, and how they awaited you, those little deaths, waiting like sweethearts.

———————

On the night of the first hunt, the residents of all three houses spilled out onto Rodman Street. Jude spotted Mr. Ronald and Mr. Donald, the RonDon, their respective black and silver heads looming over the crowds of children. She saw Kat the same moment Kat saw her, and they ran toward each other, chests colliding, arms entangling.

"Sims ouy I," Jude said.

"Sims ouy I oot," Kat said.

I miss you. I miss you too.

Jude found Violet next. The streetlight yellowed her tissue-paper skin. Her limbs seemed whittled down to sticks. Her long black hair resembled party streamers left over from last Halloween. She looked lost and terribly beautiful.

"Hey," Jude said. She did not know what to do with her hands, whether to pet Violet's hair or her back or give her a hug or bury her nose into the sweet, sharp crook of her neck. Kat put her own hand on Jude's shoulder, as though to still her.

"Hey," Violet said back.

"Let's go," Kat said.

"Perform or perish," Jude said.

They set off in one wild pack, skipping and hooting. Jude was at the front, Violet and Kat on either side. "I'm huntin' for wabbits!" someone called in his best Elmer Fudd voice, and all of them joined the refrain: *Huntin' for wabbits, wabbits, wabbits.* One stream of kids reversed course, heading for South Street and beyond. Another headed east. Some internal compass turned Jude north. The packs of wild dogs came circling, but this time kept their distance from the wild children. She pushed farther to Sansom Street, passing discos and nightclubs and stores with glittery platform boots posed behind the windows, and encountered the most exotic humans she had ever seen, hippies and rockers and druggies and people who seemed to straddle the line between the sexes, glamorous men and handsome women, everyone open to each other.

She doubled back to Rittenhouse Square, with its wide brick lanes and cherry trees in furious bloom. A fat rat scuttled across the tip of her sneaker. Tall iron lamps cast beams of light, stretching the shadows of strange men. From a thicket of bushes came the sounds of rutting and grunting. They came upon a bronze statue of a lion, its mouth frozen in a permanent roar, its paw poised over the head of a hissing snake. "There," Jude said, and pointed to a cluster of benches along the perimeter, where the brick road met the grass.

They chose a bench in the middle. A few feet away, on the adjacent bench, sat a girl and two boys. A rabbit for each of them. Jude pulled out a stack of playing cards and three sleeves of quarters that King Bash had given her. "Five-card draw," she said. "Deuces wild." One round of betting later, and the strange trio had moved closer. The boys were about twelve years old—one fat and blond; one thin and dark. The girl seemed a bit younger, maybe ten or eleven. She had hair as red and wild as Verona's, stretching up from her scalp in thick flames, and her face was freckled and full. She wore a T-shirt that read "Music Maker and Dreamer of Dreams," the bright rainbow lettering scrolling across her chest.

"Hey," Jude said. "Do you guys want to play?"

"We don't have that kind of money," she said, and pointed at the quarters.

"Don't worry about it," Kat said. "This game's on us. It's more fun with six players."

The girl shrugged. "I guess so," she said, and sat down on the ground in front of Jude. The boys followed, the dark-haired one sitting near Violet, and Jude watched as she leaned toward him, whispering in his ear. She couldn't stand the sight of it and turned to the girl instead. "What's your name?"

The girl seemed to ponder the question before responding. "Genesis."

"Dig it," Jude said. "From the Bible?"

"Yeah. The beginning. I think I was supposed to be a new beginning for my parents. Too bad they hate each other and got divorced. It's dumb. Just call me Gen."

"Not dumb," Jude said. "Mine's from the Bible, too. Judith, officially. Verona—my mother—said Judith is the only woman in the Bible who asked God to make her a good liar. But you can call me Jude."

"Dig it," Gen said, imitating Jude's tone. "Are you a good liar?"

"I'm getting better at it every day," Jude said.

"Ha," Gen said. "I told my mom a lame lie tonight. Said I was going to the movies when I am really sitting here waiting for someone to give me another beer."

"Did she believe you?"

"I don't know." She shrugged. "I don't even know if she heard me. She made up with her boyfriend and I no longer exist."

Jude laughed, a sincere laugh. She liked this girl and saw glimpses of their lives intersecting. "I know that story. My mom was always having people over after . . ." She stopped herself before saying "my Dad left." She did not want to think about her father. She did not want to remember the night that either she or Kat closed the door in his bloodied face.

Instead she leaned in and spoke in a conspiratorial whisper. "This is going to sound crazy, but there's a way to train your mind so that it changes everything around you. It makes you the best liar in the entire world. A liar so good that you lose the ability to doubt even yourself."

She thought of King Bash, twirling his diamond ring.

The neon lights played on Gen's face. She smiled at Jude and told her it didn't sound crazy at all. In fact, it sounded cooler than cool—refrigerated cool, like a new beginning that was all her own.

In the days after King Bash returned from his seminars, boasting of booming numbers and frenzied interest, he again asked Jude to his office. This time, the RonDon was there. The Donald part of the RonDon held a camera, and the Ronald part of the RonDon stood near a door Jude had never noticed before. It was in the far corner of King Bash's office, hidden by a tapestry of a jungle, the monkeys and lions and birds all posing together in peace.

"Jude," King Bash said. "I hear that, in my absence, you went recruiting several times and were quite successful. I hear, in fact, that you recruited the most rabbits of everyone."

"Yes," Jude said. She allowed her voice to sound bold, prideful. "I just wanted to do The Plan as best as I could."

"So you did," he said.

He rose from his chair, and Jude did the same.

"And as I told you, with good work, you become important. And with your importance comes privileges and rewards. What would you say if I gave you a new opportunity to master The Plan? What if I said you could be an even bigger part of its success? And that your very important contribution would also be fun?"

"I would say *yes*," Jude said, and shot her fist into the air.

"That's it!" King Bash said. "Your enthusiasm will take you far."

In one fluid movement he crossed the room and met the RonDon at the back door.

The door opened to reveal a plain square room, no decoration on the walls, no rug on the floor—the only furniture a bed with a flowery pink sheet. Off to one side stood a strange contraption, something resembling a white umbrella blown over by the wind. King Bash lowered his long body and looked her in the eye and told her it was okay, it was only pictures—and weren't pictures fun? She was posing just for herself, by herself—imagine she was Natalie Wood or Audrey Hepburn or Sharon Tate—

"Wasn't Sharon Tate murdered?" Jude said. "Like stabbed up a bunch of times?" She wanted King Bash to keep talking. If he kept talking they might forget about taking pictures. "I do not want to be Sharon Tate."

"Not Sharon Tate," the Donald part of the RonDon said. "Just be you. We won't want you to be anyone but yourself. There is power in who you are."

"And this is a reward for your power," the Ronald part of the RonDon said. "Not everyone is as important as you are, Jude."

"I'll stay here with you in case you get scared," King Bash said. "But I promise you have nothing to be scared of."

This scene marked the part where, years later, Jude pulled the drapes across her eyes and locked her heart away. Memories came and continue to come anyway, pushing themselves into her, whispering just loud enough to be heard. They appeared in flashes, as though illuminated by strobe light, gone as quick as they came, so fast she sometimes wondered if they'd ever happened at all. In that moment, she did not think of Natalie Wood or Audrey Hepburn or Sharon Tate. She pictured her mother, Verona, in her past life as Very Sherry, her arms raised and her legs spread and her face turned over her shoulder, looking hungry for strange eyes. Jude thought to herself that doing pictures was not so bad after all, thought it so hard that it seemed to be true.

KAT: NOW

Three Months after the Accident
JUNE 1983

Jude is not yet home and I'm relieved. I leave Sab's blood on my hands, evidence preserved. It hurts to have my fingers on the ends of my hands and my hands on the end of wrists and for the rest of me to be connected in such a wretched way. I sit at the table, unsure of what to do with myself, terrified of what I might unwittingly do. The money is hot against my palms. I spread the bills out and wait for Jude to come home and explain me to myself.

Twenty minutes pass before I hear the jiggle of the keys, the flick of the light, her bucket hitting the floor. Beneath her thick makeup she looks tired and weary, older than we are. I watch her face as she notices the money. Even in my bloodied state I am pleased by her pleasure—the stark widening of her eyes, the shocked O of her mouth. I know she has never been easily surprised, although the source of this knowledge is lost for good.

"Kat!" she says. "What the hell did you do?"

"Well, for starters, I beat the crap out of a really nice guy for no apparent reason." I put down the money and show her the state of my hands, making gestures like a game show host. "But I'm guessing you're asking about the money."

My sister doesn't know what to say next; I can nearly see the mechanics of her mind, cranking and mining for responses. I'm enjoying this brief exchange of roles—having the information she desires, dispensing it on my own time, in my own way.

"Let's do both," she says. She picks up the money and fans herself. "Starting with this totally rad wad of cash. Considering the state of your hands, I'm afraid to ask."

"That one's easy. I had some luck at a poker game. A contribution to your loan shark. I clench my left fist and wince. "*Our* loan shark."

She sets the money on the table. I can see her rearing up for a lecture about the loan shark, how I'm only impeding my healing with such worries, but I rush to speak first: "So, how about the state of my hands? How do they know how to beat up a body taller and bigger and stronger than mine?"

She takes two beers from the fridge and presses one into my palm; the condensation feels like a salve against my skin.

"I didn't mention this before, because it's not a great memory," she says.

"When did I ever say I only want great memories?" I ask.

She ignores the question and takes a long drink, keeping her eyes on me.

"When we were in Spain we got jumped one night," she says. "Nothing too serious, but the guy stole our wallets and banged us up a bit. When we met up with Wen in England a week or so later, we told her about it. We were angry that we'd felt so helpless, like we were just there for the taking, completely at his mercy. So she asked if we wanted to learn self-defense. She had gone through a bad divorce and learned it to protect herself from her ex-husband. We got really serious about it."

I have to remind myself who Wen is: the woman we met in Europe, who told me stories to fatten my brain, who promised to send pictures of me and Jude that haven't yet arrived.

"How serious?" I ask, and press the can against my other palm. "Because my body was following some script on its own. I had no power or say in what it was doing." I think of Sab, cornered in his own room, shocked by my subconscious fury and defenseless against it. Each strike against his flesh was part of a choreographed dance, a routine so ingrained that my body could perform it without a single command from my brain.

"Serious enough for it to become second nature, just like you describe." She drains the rest of her can and crushes it, the metal crunching beneath her fingers. "So who's the lucky guy?"

"That's the weird thing," I say. "I wasn't jumped—I was the one who attacked. And I wasn't being touched in a bad way. I was, in fact, being touched in a very *good* way and I wanted it to continue."

She considers this for a moment and shrugs. "I guess all touch is new to you now. Everything is new to you now. We can't know all of the connections your brain and body are making, and you have to be patient with yourself as you relearn."

"I guess so," I say. The idea of my brain and body being so removed from one another, as though they live in two distinct and distant worlds, is disquieting in ways I can't begin to understand. I tell her everything: about meeting Sab, about poker in the snug room, about the broken cabinet and crushed heart, about my big win and failed celebration. I tell her about anger management class, his patience and generosity, his eagerness to crack the maddening puzzle of my brain. I tell her that I really like him, and maybe even kind of love him (based on my diminished understanding of that concept), and that I fear he'll never speak to me again. In the midst of my monologue

Jude begins crying—more than crying—yielding to a sob so deep it seems to hollow her out. I don't know what to do; there is nothing in my slim arsenal of experience that instructs me how to respond. I reach forward and pat her awkwardly with my damp hand, telling her it's okay, I'm okay, everything will be fine.

At that, my sister seems to remember who she is. She straightens up, removes my hand from her face. I've misunderstood, she tells me. She's not upset—she's crying because she's happy for me, the happiest she's been since the day I woke up and came back to her. She has wanted this for me, for both of us, for so long.

"Have you ever had someone?" I ask. "I mean, someone you felt about in that way?" It seems such a strange thing not to know about the person you know best, the only person you really know at all.

She digs the heels of her hands into her eyes, wringing out the last of her tears, and tells me yes, there was someone long ago, someone whose heart she broke and who broke her heart in turn, but we discussed it so much before my accident that she can't ever discuss it again.

For three days, I leave a message on Sab's machine as soon as I awaken and sometimes another at night, telling him I'm sorry over and over again, trying to find new ways to say the same thing. I don't know what I was thinking, I tell him. I wasn't thinking at all. I can explain this. My mind was turned off while my body was turned on. Wait, I didn't mean it that way. Wait, I mean, I *was* turned on, of course, but I meant that my body had stopped speaking to my mind. Or maybe vice versa. Anyway, my mind and my body were at odds in some weird way I don't fully understand, and I don't expect you to understand it either, but I do expect—hope?—that you will call me back so I can say this all again to you, live and in person. And, if you like, at a safe distance . . .

Nothing.

I walk around the neighborhood and quietly observe, feeling like a sociologist struggling to grasp her own habitat. Everywhere I look there are normal—at least outwardly—people doing normal things. Here we have a mother in a playground pushing her kid on a swing, his squishy legs pumping; and over here, a miserable couple having coffee, not looking at each other, not speaking, content in their hostile silence; and there, a group of boys playing basketball, dunking and shit-talking and lumbering around to pat each other's asses. People picking up dry cleaning, people parallel parking, people walking dogs, people jogging, people talking to themselves—all conducted, it seems, with deliberate and controlled precision. No one's brain has any surprises in store. No one's body seems to have a mind of its own.

I snap back to myself and realize where my own body has taken me: to the church where Sab has his anger management meetings. He had taken me here on a Friday, and it is again a Friday. I feel a small and quiet triumph; for once my mind and body harmonized and worked together, one listening to the other, acting on subconscious intuition. The sound of the door closing behind me is a mortifying echo. Every face in the room swivels toward me.

"Are you joining us?" a voice calls out. "We're just about to start."

I lift my head to see the circle of folding chairs about twenty feet away. Chuck stands in the center holding the Peace Rock, waiting for me to answer. My gaze finds Sab, and even from this distance I can see the purple-green splotch of his eyes, the bandage crisscrossing his nose. For one searing second he looks at me, and then down at his own clenched fists.

I trot in his direction, my heel sliding out from under me, prompting me to palm a strange woman's head to regain balance. *I'm sorry*, I mouth, and snatch the rock from Chuck's hands. "Go for it," he says, and sits down.

I cup the rock in my palms and take a step toward Sab. His eyes stay downcast, and I can tell one of them is heavier than the other, the lid just beginning to reopen.

"My name is Kat, and I have an anger problem," I say, speaking only to Sab.

"Welcome, Kat," Chuck says.

When I am three feet away from Sab, I stop moving. I want to give him enough room to look up and see me, all of me, standing in this circle of strangers and serving up my darkest self.

"I wasn't entirely honest the last time I was here," I say. "The story I told is true, but I'm the sad protagonist, not my twin."

My hands tighten around the rock and lift an inch, making it into an offering.

"So I'm the one who has a very weird kind of amnesia. Every day I hear narration about who I was and what I've done, without having any memory of being or doing those things. It's like inheriting a secondhand version of your own life."

The *whir* of two industrial-sized fans are the only sound in the room. *Please look at me*, I implore Sab. *Please.* He doesn't move.

"In the midst of all this, I was lucky to meet someone. This person has been kind during a time when I'm relearning what kindness is. And funny, as I'm relearning what humor means to me. And interesting, as I'm figuring out what makes my brain spark, all of the world's weird pathways that I'd like to explore. He's already given me a second chance, and here I am, having the nerve to ask for a third."

His head shifts a fraction, just high enough for him to view my knees.

"But because of my brain injury, because of the lifetime of things I've lost about myself, I hurt this person. I hurt this person very badly—"

I'm interrupted by a trio of sounds in quick succession: the scrape of a chair leg, a whisper, a muffled laugh. Sab's eyes are now aimed at my throat. I force myself to go on: "I hurt this person very badly without knowing how or why. My body acted without direction from my brain, and my body is much stronger than I knew, and I can't express the regret I felt when I began to kick and punch—"

Someone coughs. I swivel my head left and right. People are leaning in, engaged, listening. There's another whisper, pairs of eyes widening, a hand covering an open mouth, a finger pointing directly at Sab's bruised face. "As I was saying," I continue, "the regret I felt—"

Chuck stands and clasps his hands together. "All right, then," he says. "I think we all see where this is going—or, rather, where it has already gone." He pries the Peace Rock from my hands. "Kat, Sab, maybe this would best be discussed among yourselves."

One last shift and Sab's eyes find mine. I force myself to hold the gaze, to take inventory of the damage I've done. Without a word, he rises from his chair and strolls to the far exit. The squeak of his sneakers against the linoleum both saddens me and compels me to follow.

"Go get 'em, Kat," someone calls.

"Be gentle this time!" shouts another.

"That's enough," I hear Chuck say, and I spring to the exit and fling open the door and find Sab just outside. Our eyes meet again, and the way he says my name—that short, simple syllable—seems to crack open the ground beneath my feet.

"I think I love you, Sab," I say. Nothing moves on his face. No twitch of his lips, no hint of a blink or a swallow, no flicker of his pupils away from mine. I begin to sweat. My mind presses some button that forces me to continue. "I'm not sure what that ever meant to me, but I am trying to go by what I think it means now."

I take the last step, closing the distance. "And I'm sorry," I add. "I think I was supposed to say that first."

Sab still hasn't moved. He has forbidden his face from forming an expression and his mouth from offering a response. A part of me admires his control, his skill at calibrating how the world sees him.

"Sab?"

His eyes still on me, he holds up a hand, a wordless command for me to shut the hell up. Then he rummages in both of his back pockets, and comes up with a deck of cards and a pen. He hands the pen to me and, with the cards facing down, spreads the deck into a fan.

"Pick one," he tells me.

I do as he says.

He takes my card and turns it upside down, showing me both sides. "Now sign it."

Again, I do as he says, balancing the card in my palm, writing my name in shaky letters. I hand the card back to him.

He restores the deck, stacking the cards into a neat pile. He works his hands like the bellows of an accordion, expanding and retracting, the cards floating back and forth. A card seems to sprout from the deck, volunteering itself. He folds it into fourths.

"Open your mouth," he says.

I part my lips and hold my breath. Drops of sweat coast around the curves of my ears, quiver down my back. He slips the card between my lips and my teeth clamp down, securing its position. For a few seconds I close my eyes, a brief reprieve from the heat of his gaze.

Again he performs the accordion shuffle, the sleeve of cards drifting from one hand to the other, and when he stops he picks a random one from the deck. He folds it into fourths, just like mine, and pins it between his lips. Through gritted teeth he says, "Take my card and I'll take yours."

We swap, pulling the cards from each other's mouths.

He opens his card and, miraculously, it's the one I had in the beginning, my name scrawled across the Two of Hearts. I open my card and gasp: it's the Jack of Hearts, and beneath the arrow he'd somehow written a message of his own: *Here's your third chance.*

"You've forgiven me?" I ask.

"I guess I have," he says. "Mostly because you shock me, and nothing is shocking anymore. I'm shocked by how much I like you, even though I don't know how to separate your crazy from your normal. But that's okay." His voice drops on that last syllable, smooths itself into a whisper. "You don't have to know everything to love someone. You just have to believe that what you know is enough." These sentiments sound practiced somehow, as though he's thought them many times but never before said them aloud.

"You said *love*," I say, and instantly want to erase the words, swipe them from the air and tuck them back down my throat, hidden and unconjured. I wonder if the old me would feel such embarrassment, or if she'd boldly state the words again. In the moment, with Sab standing inches away, I want to inhabit the second version, slip her on and see how she fits. "You said *love*," I repeat. "Which, considering all that's happened, means you're as crazy as I am."

"I'll admit I said it," he says, "as long as you never let your sidekick come between us again."

He dips me back, making a cradle with his arms, and drops his lips onto mine.

I vow to remember all of it: The slam of his apartment door, keys left in the lock, the complicit rustle of curtains being drawn. The backward walk toward his bedroom: the side-stepping, the legs entangling, the awkward lurching, the stumble over a pair of shoes in the hallway, the slam of another door, the thrilling panic of being alone with him, trapped with my back against a wall—all of this even before our lips connect properly, before he seizes the point of my chin and steadies my face, before he raises one thick, calloused finger and slides it inside my mouth, and I have to stop my upper jaw from dropping like a guillotine just so I can taste his blood.

No, I tell myself. *This time no blood will be drawn.*

Just in time, he removes his finger and replaces it with his tongue—such a strange organ, the tongue, and I close my eyes and think about what it must look like inside of my mouth: the tiny taste buds, the pink tip, the way it pokes at my own tongue, stirring it. They circle each other—slowly, at first, and then lash and flail, and I imagine our tongues as two expert swordsmen shouting *en garde* and going at it, advancing and retreating, fighting to the death. I laugh, breaking the spell, and he asks what's so funny, speaking the question softly into my mouth, and I tell him nothing is funny and mean it: I am a normal twenty-two-year-old doing a normal twenty-two-year-old thing, kissing a boy I think I love, letting him kiss me back, wondering if I am doing any of it right, and if there's a right way of doing this at all.

I let him lead, not out of the desire to relinquish control but the fear of what might happen if I don't; I distrust the eagerness of my own body, the strength of my own hands, the instincts long forgotten by my brain. I don't know how to become a thing to be exploded rather than the explosion itself.

Without my saying a word he seems to understand, and works with quiet concentration to defuse me, lifting my dress up and my underwear down and unknotting my fingers from their tight clasp. He pulls my hands up and away from my body, pinning them against the air, giving me nowhere to hide. For a long moment neither of us says a word, and I can't bear looking into his eyes so instead I look everywhere else: the popcorn bumps of his ceiling; the lacquered black dresser; the framed photograph of his mother; the scattered hairs on his long, thin feet; and, finally, *that* part of him, and just as quickly I look away, both intrigued and anxious, afraid I might hurt it, or that it might hurt me.

"I think our bodies have called a truce," he says. "Agreed?"

"Agreed," I said. "I think you're safe. I also think I should reiterate that I have no idea what I'm doing."

We lie down on his bed, facing each other, on even and neutral ground. He picks up my left hand, that same hand that had transformed into a bullet that broke his nose, and asks me what I'd like to do with it. Carefully, patiently, he makes inquiries about all of me and then all of him, fitting us together one piece at a time: What do I want to do with my right hand? My left leg and right leg? What do I want him to do with his hand, his right and left leg, the broad and taut weight of his chest? I wonder if, back in Harmony, Pennsylvania, back in my teenage years, I'd ever kissed a boy, and if it were even a fraction as surreal as it is now, with Sab's lips following my orders: *there and there and there, like this, not that, too little, too much.*

I could never have felt anything like the sweet weight of him, all the folds and points of our bodies matching perfectly, fingers twining, shoulders to shoulders, wholly melding, hiding inside ourselves, the machine clanking into action, following protocol, doing what it does. His eyes never once leave mine and I wish I could see myself as he sees me: someone whose sharp edges are a virtue, whose dark corners are worth exploring, a person who is not broken but instead reborn.

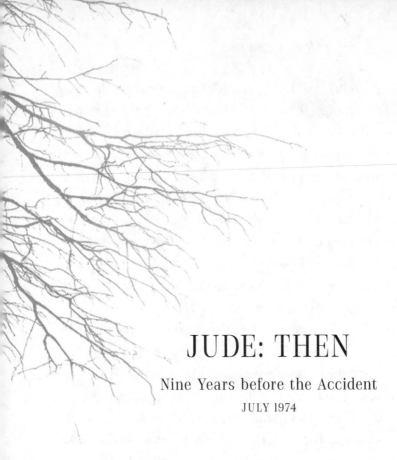

JUDE: THEN

Nine Years before the Accident

JULY 1974

In the year since the pictures began Jude recruited a dozen rabbits, more than any other resident in King Bash's house. Her fluffle included Melisa, whose parents spent most of their time in Europe; Jimmy, a refugee from the Taney gang; Marcus, a refugee from the 12th and Oxford gang; and Lola, who, when Jude found her, was passed out on a bench in Fitler Square Park, her parted lips leaking a trail of sugary vomit. All of them had parents who had somehow lost track of their children and eventually didn't care to look. The new rabbits were enthralled by the idea that their minds were somehow magic, that mere thoughts had the capacity to spin themselves into truth. They all loved her and she them, but Genesis, her first rabbit, remained her favorite. Jude became to Gen what King Bash was to Jude, someone to emulate and idolize, a conduit for greatness. Gen became to Jude a reminder of her younger self, the self who was just coming to a stark realization: it is better to focus on what you might become than to think too deeply about who you are.

Every night Jude lay Gen across her lap, twirled the girl's hair around her fingers, and told her fanciful stories of history and legends, of the sea and sky and space—making their world, for those short moments, bigger than it would ever be.

Sometimes she wished Gen were Violet, content beneath the weight of her touch.

No one discussed the pictures.

To celebrate The Plan's third anniversary, King Bash announced a special seminar, one that would benefit both older and younger members, the newcomers and the veterans, the famous and the anonymous. The Think Is Games, which everyone pronounced as one swallowed syllable, *Thinkis*, would be held in a secret, exotic location called the Island. Only King Bash and the RonDon knew all of the rules and protocol, which were to be introduced and implemented with spectacular and mysterious ceremony. People whispered about water and fire, a clashing and canceling of the elements, a spectacle where false truths were inverted and exposed. It was all unfathomably exciting. To prepare, the residents of all three row homes endured a week of deprivation, a drastic reduction in food and sleep and a vow of silence. Playing the Think Is Games without such preparation could result in poor performance and loss of prestige.

It could even be dangerous.

For the occasion, a girl named Cindy visited King Bash's row house and told them to form a line. Today was a special day, she said, a day they all became works of art—more than that, a *collective* work of art. She was seventeen and impossibly glamorous, with choppy black hair that looked deliberately uncombed and flared jeans embroidered with flowers. Cindy had come from the Big House, and when Jude's turn came she seized the chance to ask questions.

"What's it like in the Big House?"

"It's a jam," she said, and grasped Jude's arm. A needle dug into the skin along Jude's wrist, feeling like the dig of a heated fork. "Everyone has mastered the tenets. Nothing in the world can bother us. We're all complete. It's like we're all committed and connected, but at the same time we're free. Free from the tyranny of our own humanity. Free with nothing left to lose, like Janis said. Free as a bird." She held out her own arm for Jude to inspect. A string of seven rainbow-hued birds soared along her skin from armpit to wrist.

"Cool," Jude said. "Me and my sister and my friend can't wait to get there."

Cindy resumed her work on Jude's arm. "How old are you?"

Jude was about to say she just turned fourteen but stopped herself in time. "Fourteen."

"You'll be there soon enough," Cindy said. "All the work you're doing right now will prepare you."

"I'm working so hard," Jude said. The needle clawed at her, but she held herself still. "I think I'm really good at Rejecting and Releasing and Performing or Perishing. I still have to master the others."

"You're right where you should be," Cindy said. She kept her head down, and Jude noticed another tattoo snaking up the length of her neck, reading, in eloquent cursive, *What I think, is.*

A few moments passed in silence. Jude gathered the nerve to ask, "Do you know my mother? Verona Sheridan?"

"Of course! Everyone knows Lady V. She is a goddess. She told me to tell you and Kat that she is very proud of you both. I want to be her when I grow up. Her energy is feminine but ferocious. She always wins."

Jude did not know what to say to that. She felt a spark of pride extinguished by confusion. Did Verona win when she made Jude—or Kat—lock their father out? Does she win by not seeing her daughters? Maybe not, maybe so. *Reject and release*, Jude thought. *Reject and release puts my mind at peace.*

"Yes," Jude said. "Winning is one way to put it."

"Finished!" Cindy said. "Tough, right? And now we match."

She pressed her forearm against Jude's. A tattoo reading *THE PLAN* started at the base of both of their wrists and spanned four inches.

"Tough," Jude said. She loved the way it looked carved into her arm, like her own personal monument.

"Whatever happens," Cindy said, "no one can take that away from you."

Gen was next in line, already offering her arm.

On the last Friday of the month King Bash tied a blindfold around Jude's eyes and led her to a van filled with other blindfolded people. Jude estimated that the ride took two hours; no one spoke along the way. At their destination, wherever it was, someone took her hand and led her across an expanse of gravel to a field of tall grass. The darkness amplified her other senses: the butterscotch whiff of bark; the squeak of her sneakers against dewy blades; the callouses on her escort's palm. At last her hand was placed on a door that pushed inward. "Here you go," the faceless voice said, and she recognized it as belonging to the Ronald half of the RonDon. She supposed that King Bash was off somewhere welcoming The Plan's most important members and tried to subdue the rush of bitter panic that rose up inside her heart. What if she'd been demoted in King Bash's esteem? What if she weren't important anymore? What if there were nothing she could do to become important again?

"Thank you, Mr. Ronald," she said, and felt her way to a cot. Once his footsteps retreated she removed her blindfold and still saw nothing but black.

———————

In the morning a siren wailed, yanking her from a jittery half sleep. A slim wand of light through the wooden slats revealed that she was in a small shed. She wondered what purpose it had served before the purpose of containing her. In the corner she spotted a large lavender cardboard box with a fitted red lid. It looked fancy, the kind of box that might hold a bouquet of orchids or a puppy, but instead it contained a full-body monkey costume, a monkey head, a map, a compass, a banana, a small bag of nuts, a ball of string, a pair of scissors with very sharp blades, and a note. She recognized King Bash's handwriting, which pleased her:

Good morning, Jude.

Welcome to the Think Is Games.
Are you feeling powerful today?
What is the color and shape of your power?
You are a monkey: intelligent, in search of dominance, and nearly human.
Find your way to the Power Tower.
What you think, is.

She forced herself to take tiny bites of her banana, eating a third, and to pick just three almonds from the bag. Her stomach pulsed with hunger but she had to conserve her food. She opened the shed door and peeked out. The pale sun still hung low in the sky, and she guessed it was about seven in the morning. She had not seen Kat since the last rabbit-hunting expedition two weeks earlier, the longest they'd ever spent apart. The absence of her sister felt like a disturbing presence, like a cluster of spiders had embedded beneath her skin.

A gong boomed three times. Jude checked the compass and saw it came from the eastern part of the Island.

She stepped into her monkey costume, which zippered up the front, and shoved all of the items into its deep pockets. She held her scissors by her ear, in striking position, as she again left the shed. The tiny sight holes in the monkey's face reduced the world to slits.

She tried to identify and categorize her surroundings, but they didn't make much sense. Funny, she thought—the Island only sporadically looked like an island. Small mounds of sand were interrupted by maple trees and scorched patches of grass. White fences, some twice the height of King Bash's row home, loomed everywhere, creating a haphazard maze. Silos topped by metal spiderwebs scratched at the sky. A miniature orange car was parked behind a tangle of thorny brush. A giant umbrella-shaped contraption gave cover to a square of concrete. The rotten remains of a wooden track meandered across the ground. Here and there lay scattered bright vestiges of unknown things: a ladder leading to nowhere, wheels attached to nothing, a steel saucer studded with bulbs, the upturned legs of a gilded throne. She did not hear any ocean or smell any salt, or maybe she did? Her exhaustion poked holes into her thinking. She did not know what was real and what was not. *What you think, is,* she told herself, and at once everything seemed proper and correct, her mind sharp enough to separate truth from illusion.

The map marked none of these objects and seemed deliberately simple, just a few lines showcasing various intersections and paths. She started walking east toward the lingering chimes of the gong, taking note of landmarks along the way: a group of inflatable palm trees; an enormous wheel tilting to one side; a steel clown figurine, his nose faded to pink, weeds sprouting through a crack in his shoulder.

At last she came to a round building topped by a golden dome. Violet's mother, Jackie, stood at the entrance, wearing jeans and a T-shirt that read: "The Think Is Games, 1974."

"Welcome, Jude," she said. Her words came out slow and thick. "I'm so happy you're here. I think you're really going to enjoy this retreat."

"Where is Kat?" Jude asked. "And Violet?"

"They both just arrived, don't worry. I know it's been so difficult for you and Kat to be apart."

The interior of the building was arranged like a theater, with tiered rows of upholstered seats and a stage partially concealed by heavy velvet drapes. Diamond-shaped windows ran along the walls but the panes were covered in aluminum foil, allowing no sun. The place was crawling with children dressed as monkeys, chameleons, parrots, rabbits, scorpions, wolves.

"Kat!" she screamed.

The room fell silent, every head turning to look at her.

"Jude!"

She could only see the outline of her sister's monkey shape, the shadow of her waving arm. Jude maneuvered around the seats, weaving a path, and ran into Kat's arms. They removed their monkey heads and sat down, holding hands.

"Ew rea yako," Jude said. *We are okay.* A command more than a question.

Kat squeezed her hand in response.

A cluster of candelabras arranged across the stage provided the only light. Two slim fingers walked like legs onto Jude's lap and did the Charleston on her knee. Violet's hand, peeking out from the red sleeve of a scorpion costume, a plastic pincher affixed to her wrist.

"You made it," Jude said, and immediately cursed herself: *Of course she made it, you turkey, she is sitting right there.*

"Yes, Jude," Violet said, and laughed. "I am sitting right here."

Jude felt a surge of joy: Violet could tell them apart. She saw Jude as her own separate person; she *knew* Jude as her own separate person.

"Testing, testing," Jackie said. A squeal of feedback pierced the auditorium. "Welcome, everyone. You should all be tremendously proud of yourselves for making it here this morning. Your ability to meet any challenge is unquestionable. Your brain is the only thing that molds your reality. What you think, is."

She paced across the stage, the candlelight making shadows dance behind her.

"On this, our very first Think Is Games, we're going to focus on a tenet that we haven't mastered yet: Defeat Begets Domination. Can anyone tell me what they think that means? Violet, did I see you waving your hand?"

"Um, no?" Violet said. "I was fixing my hair." Under her breath she commented to Jude: "Ugh, she's drunk again."

"Fair enough," Jackie said. "Do you want to take a guess?"

Violet paused, her hand still suspended. Jude was pained by her discomfort. She winced inwardly for this girl, her friend, somehow more than her friend; Violet existed on some exotic plane neither here nor there—untouchable, although Jude wanted nothing more than to touch her. She pursed her lips in Violet's direction and whispered, "Say something about how losing makes you want to win."

"When we lose, it just makes us determined to win the next time," Violet said.

Violet squeezed Jude's hand in silent gratitude, and let Jude squeeze her back. Her fingers began their Charleston again, using Jude's palm as a stage, the steps now slower and softer.

"So let's elaborate on Violet's response," Jackie said. "Maybe in the past you've been taught to help those who are weaker than you are. Don't punch down. Don't pick on the little guy. Root for the underdog, stuff like that. Now I want to challenge you to think about this idea in a new way. I want you to consider the possibility that you aren't helping anyone by coddling them. When you reinforce someone's weakness, when you send the signal that it's okay to be weak, you are forcing them to depend on that weakness. They'll never realize the power of their minds to change their own reality. They won't use that big brain power to make themselves stronger."

"But what if they are really weak?" a rabbit asked. "What if they're weak and it's not their fault and they can't do anything about it?"

Jude knew that voice: Genesis.

"Good question, Gen," Jackie said. But the premise of the question is false. No one is born weak. Everyone has the potential within themselves to take whatever kernel of strength they have—even if it's smaller than the next person's—and multiply it until they're truly powerful. So the best thing we can do for those we perceive to be weak is to show them their weaknesses. Draw the weakness out of them. Hunt for it. Find it. Hang it out for all the world to see."

Jude considered this, sifting through all the elements of her personality, wondering which ones made her susceptible to attack. She did not want anyone hunting all the private corners of her mind, determining what was weak, stripping her power and might.

"You might think you're destroying this person, but in reality you're saving them. You're preparing them for the task of accessing their own power. And when you save someone in this manner—when you so thoroughly demolish them that they need to become someone new—they are forever in your debt. We call this kill-saving, and it's the core principle behind Defeat Begets Domination."

She opened her hands and spread her fingers wide, mimicking fireworks.

"So with all of that in mind, let's get to the fun part! You all received a pair of scissors. The goal is to kill-save as many of your fellow animals as possible by cutting a piece of their costume—a claw, a tail, an ear. At the end of the Think Is Games you will report back here, at the Power Tower. Your kill-saves will be counted and the most prolific animals will receive their deserved rewards. One more thing: you must hunt alone."

Jude began to hunt, scissors at the ready. A chameleon napping on a rock didn't even stir when she hacked off its leathery tongue. She wondered if she knew the kid behind the mask and then reminded herself it didn't matter; her viciousness made her a savior. Having killed once, she felt the desire stirring again, a savage instinct awaiting her attention and care. In a strange patch of the Island, where the temperature seemed to rise by thirty degrees, she disposed of another chameleon and stole its bug-shaped candy. Near a small stream she pulled the mask from a parrot and trimmed its crest. She yanked a monkey that was not Kat from a tree and hacked off the tip of its tail. She collected a bouquet of rabbit ears. Hours passed. Her stomach growled. She ate the rest of her banana and nuts and the chameleon's candy. She was so thirsty, she collected her own spit in her palm and drank it. With her scissors, she sliced a hole in her costume so she could piss without having to remove it. The sun changed its own costume of bold yellow for a misty mauve cape. She felt her brain somehow mimicking the sun, descending inside her skull, dimming its lights.

"Kat!" she screamed through her mask. "Violet! Kat!"

She had to keep going. She had to kill-save until the sky was fully black.

Her body temperature dropped but her skin remained sweaty, making her shiver. The path brought her to another rabbit and a scorpion that was not Violet. She preyed upon them all with a dark, secret glee she didn't know she possessed, a glee that both frightened and excited her, a glee even Kat should never know.

"Kat!" she called again. "Violet!"

"Jude," came a soft voice.

Jude spun. She didn't know that voice and didn't trust it. Or perhaps she did know it, once, before coming to the Island, but being on the Island changed the way her ears processed sound—or maybe the Island itself changed the voice? There was no way to tell what had changed or stayed the same, or what had changed by staying the same. With her scissors she slashed at the voice's lingering echo.

"Jude," the voice said again. "If I come out, will you put the scissors down? It's me, Violet." The scorpion shimmied out, removed its mask, and executed a slow turn. "See?" Violet said. "Let's not kill-save each other. Actually let's not talk about The Plan at all. Deal?"

Jude dropped the scissors and ran to her. She took Violet's pinchers in her own hands and gave them a soft shake.

"Deal," she said.

They walked, side by side, through brush and weeds, and spoke about other things: Verona and Jackie and fathers who were long gone; how to make Bloody Mary appear in the mirror; whether or not Meathead was cute (Jude did not confess that she much preferred Gloria); favorite books and song lyrics and poems; what it will be like when they finally make it to the Big House, all of the tenets mastered, everyone envious of their spark and shine.

A stone path opened in the middle of a vast field where daisies— they seemed real, they truly did—bloomed on either side. The crickets ceded their racket to the soft, inquisitive song of the owls. Violet lay down and curled inward and gave Jude a shy command: "Be my roof? Cover me?" Jude arranged her body just so, her paws atop Violet's claws, her chest pressed against the vertebrae of her scorpion back. She awakened during the night to find that an identical monkey had joined them, her slightly older sister at her back, doing the job of the big spoon.

At the end of the Think Is Games, King Bash and the RonDon tallied the kill-saves and determined that Jude had won. For her reward they told her to pick a friend, and invited her once again into the room behind King Bash's office, with the crisply made bed and the white umbrella-like contraption and the relentless focus of the camera. While they did their Very Sherry poses, Violet was so close and so bare that, years later, Jude would remember her not as a whole but in tiny parts: the crust of sleep in her left eye; the earlobes like dropped pearls; the fine black hair rising from the goose bumps on her arms; those long, pale fingers, regal as the points of a crown; and, finally, the most private part of her, which Jude longed to touch but did not dare. She hoped Violet's mastery of the tenets was as strong as her own—that she, like Jude, could interpret the pictures not as a sacrifice but as a gift, a record of the happiest time in their lives.

KAT: NOW

Three Months after the Accident

JUNE 1983

Somehow, although I'd been thinking about it and mentioning it to Jude for months, the trip to our hometown, Harmony, becomes Sab's idea. What better way to spend my twenty-third birthday, the first birthday for my new self, the first one I'll remember? We'll walk the tiny town square, find the farm where I grew up, maybe run into people who knew me way back when. He'll arrange everything, his treat.

Over a dinner of overboiled spaghetti, the strands coalescing in shellacked clumps on our plates, I mention the trip, keeping my voice light and casual. I feared the plan might infuriate her—Jude would resent him for hijacking our hometown visit—but instead she drops her fork and says, sincerely, "What a nice thing for him to do."

"Really?" I ask. "You're okay with it?"

"As long as I'm coming, since it's my birthday, too." She takes a long sip of beer. "It's mandatory that your two favorite people in the world get to know each other a bit."

I laugh at the stern finality of her tone, the way she leaves no room for rejection.

"You win," I say, holding up my hands in surrender. "I accept the invitation you've given yourself. I could never say no to you."

"No, you never could." She lowers the meatball back to her plate. For a moment we're quiet, the scraping of our forks the only sound in the room, and then she says: "I'm so psyched to take you back to Harmony, but I must admit I'm just as psyched to meet Sab. There's something mysterious about him."

I pause my own fork midair. "Mysterious how?"

"I mean, I've never met someone so capable of forgiveness. Like Mount Everest heights of forgiveness. You beat the guy bloody and he still wants to be with you?" She gives an exaggerated shake of her head at the wonder of it all.

"Jude," I say, and put my fork down. "Please don't bring it up with him. This trip is important to me and I don't want things to be weird."

"I would never," she says, "but don't you think about it?"

She knows I can predict her next words, which is why she doesn't bother to ask them. I play stupid, anyway: "Think about what?"

"About how far you could go and still have him forgive you?"

Her voice is neutral, all the teasing gone out of it, and I wonder if there's something in our past that provoked the question.

———————————

Sab is waiting outside of his twin home, gym bag slung over his shoulder. He's wearing jeans and a polo shirt and his gold chain with the horn charm. His hair is still wet and I can smell his cologne, something like black tea and cinnamon, and I want to dab the fresh razor nick on his chin. He bends down to Jude's open window.

"Wow, you look familiar," he tells her. "And yet, you also look nothing alike."

I know what he means; for this outing, my sister has abandoned the elaborate primping routine she does for work in favor of a bare face, jean shorts, uncombed hair, and a Tootsie Pop T-shirt that reads: "How Many Licks?"

She shakes his extended hand. "I'm the evil one, in case you haven't already figured that out."

He scoots into the back seat and squeezes my shoulder. "I don't know about that," he says. "Look at all you've done for Kat."

Jude sets off, turning up the feeble air-conditioning and twisting the radio dial. "I did it for myself as much as for her," she says. "If Kat's in a bad way, I'm in a bad way. If Kat's happy, I'm happy. If Kat likes you, I like you until you give me a reason not to. And if you hurt my sister, I will unscrew your balls with my bare hands and use them as a garnish." She looks into the rearview mirror, her eyes finding Sab's, and stretches her mouth into an exaggerated clown smile.

Sab holds up his hands in mock surrender. "Whoa, easy," he says. "If your right hook is anything like your sister's, I want nothing to do with it."

Jude laughs—her real laugh (*our* real laugh), which fits me fine but seems deeply incongruous coming from her: a light, skittering sort of sound, like the pop of bubbles or a finger dragging the highest notes of a piano. "Okay, Sab, you're off the hook," she says. "Let's pick on someone else."

"You can't possibly mean me," I say, and reach back to touch Sab's knee.

"Oh, I think we do," Jude says. "Sab, tell me one funny thing about Kat that you've noticed. Could be anything."

"Tread carefully, both of you," I say, but secretly I'm pleased. I like their easy banter, their tentative familiarity. They are willing to make space for each other, just for me.

"Hmmm," Sab says. "Why do I feel like this is a trap? Like whatever I say will apply to you both, and then you'll gang up on me, and I will truly be a dead man, my balls on your dinner plates?"

"I make no guarantees," Jude says. "But I'll go easy on you and start."

"Nothing too bad, I beg you," I say to her. I clasp my hands together, miming fervent prayer, but I'm serious. It strikes me, once again, how unsettling it is for someone else to be the keeper of all my secrets, even if that someone is my twin—and might, in some cases, have just as much to lose.

"All right, then," Jude says, her eyes fixed on the road. "I'll go easy on you, too. We have the usual twin stories about playing with identity. Like I'd be talking to someone and then walk away, and five seconds later Kat would come running over from the other direction. Or I walked into a room on one side just after Kat exited on the other, causing mass confusion."

"Ah, the old twin teleportation trick," Sab says. "Classic."

"We excelled at the mindfuck," Jude says. "Sometimes with each other. Sometimes we couldn't remember who did what; I would take credit for something, good or bad, and she would do the same."

"Example?" I ask.

She pauses, thinking. From the subtle twist of her mouth I can tell she's sifting through anecdotes, discarding any that are too personal, or considering how she might disguise them.

"Like once we had a dog that got rabies," she says, finally. "One of us had to shoot it, and to this day I take the blame for it. If you could remember it, you would insist you'd done it, and accept the blame for it yourself."

Her tone, in telling this anecdote, went flat, stripped of all emotion, and I sense she isn't talking about a rabid dog at all. She intuits my mood and quickly pivots: "Hey, it wasn't as bad as it sounds," she says. "He had been sick for a very long time. We tried so hard to make him better but it never happened. We tried really, really hard and nothing could be done."

I still don't believe she is talking about a dog.

"And to this day, we're not sure which one of us killed him?" I ask.

"We'll never be sure. I'm convinced I did it and you are convinced you did it."

I don't know what else to say. The silence settles and stretches, until Sab finally cracks it: "Did you guys also have a secret language? I've heard that's a thing with twins."

"We did and do," I say.

"Ew idd dan od," Jude says.

"Ew idd dan od?" Sab asks. "What's that?"

"That's it," I tell him. "That's the language."

"Will you teach it to me?" he asks. His pushes his head between our seats, turning to look at me first, and then Jude.

"If we teach you," Jude says, "then we won't be able to talk shit about you."

He laughs. "Something tells me you'd have no problem doing that in plain English." A pause, and then he adds: "También puedo decir mierda. I can talk shit, too."

"But does it count as a secret language if neither of us can understand?" she asks. This time they both laugh, and she directs her next words just to me: "I kile mih."

I like him.

———————

Four hours later, we check in at the Pleasant Valley Bed & Breakfast (Sab and I in one room, and Jude in her own), drop off our bags, and reconvene in the lobby. Sab pulls a pamphlet from his back pocket. "It says that Harmony only has a population of 732 people, and is only two miles long in either direction. We could start off at the museum and then go to Murdering Town, which is this old site where George Washington and his guide were shot and—"

"That sounds great," Jude says. "Let's go."

She takes one step toward the exit and I reach out to yank her shirt, stopping her. "Wait a minute," I say. "I'm not here to learn American history, I'm here to learn *my* history. *Our* history. You know, where we liked to play and the house where we grew up, all of that." I turn to Sab. "I really appreciate the research you did, but I hope you understand."

"Whatever you guys want," he says. "I'm just along for the ride."

I look at Jude just in time to catch her expression, although I don't know if "expression" is the right word; her face is entirely blank, as though her features have reset themselves to neutral, waiting for her to signal how she feels. In the next few seconds I can read her thought process as clearly and simply as flipping through the pages of a book, an ease made possible only because we share an identical face: a flash of panic to a flash of fear to a flash of resignation to, finally, a tense surrender. She will go along with my plan, but she has some private qualms about it, and I tell myself to have some reverse empathy: being here is upsetting for me because I don't remember, and upsetting for her because she does.

"You're right," she says. "Let's do the Bird Twins History Tour."

A bracelet of bright brick buildings encircles the main square, many adorned with striped awnings and flickering gas lamps. The streets are ghost-town quiet until a horse clops into the horizon, pulling a buggy draped in blue velvet, the driver in a top hat and tails. Sab reaches into my purse for his Polaroid camera and takes a snap, waving the picture in the air, watching the fuzzy image sharpen itself into a recognizable scene.

"Just don't aim that thing at Jude," I whisper. "Apparently we don't like to have our picture taken, except under very strict circumstances."

"Both of you," he whispers back, "or just Jude?"

I stretch my arm across his chest to slow down his pace, letting Jude stride out of earshot.

"Her issues are my issues. I know that might sound weird to you, but it's just the way it is."

"Hurry up!" Jude shouts, waving us forward. "We have a lot of ground to cover."

I loop my arm around him and rush us along, catching up to Jude. I just want a normal, happy birthday with my two favorite people in the world, my past and my present in seamless accord. And for a while, I have exactly this. We visit the small park where we played in our homemade costumes, our mother pushing the swings and spinning the rides; and the creek where Jude and I used to fish with our father before he disappeared; and the campground where we'd held a private memorial service and spread our mom's ashes; and, finally, Miss Sally's Extraordinary Confections on Main Street, where we stopped for ice cream in the summer.

I swing the door open. A tinkering bell announces my entrance, and a woman springs up from behind the counter. Her face is plump and perfectly round and topped with a thick brown donut of a bun. A platter heavy with pastel confections balances on her forearms.

"Good afternoon," she says. "What is your pleasure today?"

"Are you Miss Sally?" I ask.

"I am," she says. She sets her tray down and picks up a scooper, hovering it above a trough of ice cream.

I pull Jude toward me and tilt my head against hers.

"Do you recognize us?" I ask. "Kat and Jude Bird. It's been a few years, but we've been coming here since we were kids."

Miss Sally's watery gray eyes dart back and forth, studying our faces. "You *do* look familiar," she says, and turns to Jude. "Weren't you here a few months ago?"

"Nah," Jude says. "I just have one of those faces." She points to me. "Obviously, so does she."

"Twins," Miss Sally says. "Twins are delightful." She leans closer, studying Jude's face, pointing the scooper like a gun. "I suppose so. I just remember the paper clips in the hair. Paper clips instead of barrettes or ribbons."

"They're in style now," Jude says. "At least where we live."

I replay my long walks around the neighborhood, review my detailed observations from our window, and can't remember seeing even one paper clip employed as a fashion accessory. But Jude's voice is so smooth and certain, shut tight against any doubt, a voice that believes its own words.

"Well, now I know!" Miss Sally says, lowering the scooper. "And it's delightful to see you both again."

Jude steps closer to the counter, leaning her chest against the glass. "I knew you'd remember us, and it's good to see you again, too." She orders three cones to go and balks when Sab offers to pay; this is her treat. When Sab brings out his camera she even takes it from his hands, scootching me and Miss Sally in closer, telling us to smile our biggest smiles and say, "Cookies and cream!" as we pose. Out of deference to Jude and our history with disorienting photographs, I rearrange my hair so that it falls into my sister's part.

We stand outside beneath the awning, licking our ice cream in silence. The air is cooler here than it is in the city, with no tall buildings and stretches of black asphalt to trap and hold the heat, and the sun's languid descent beams gold through the trees. The hair on my arms and neck rises up and a chill rushes across my skin, a chill I attribute not to the ice cream or the deepening twilight but to a thought I had just as the Polaroid of me and Miss Sally fell from the camera's slot: *What if she really didn't recognize us? And if she did recognize Jude, why did my sister come out here alone?* I am tempted to ask, but Jude had seemed so pleased to have been remembered and so adamant in her denial, and I don't want to ruin this day or turn my new, good memories into bad ones.

We have dinner at our parents' favorite restaurant inside the Harmony Inn, the oldest building in town, rumored to be haunted. Our mother, Jude says, used to come here and look for evidence of the supernatural—a ghostly young girl in a white dress who skipped along the hallways; furniture rearranging itself without the help of human hands; spots in certain rooms where the temperature plummeted or rose. She'd be terrified if she felt so much as a breeze from a window—

"Mom?" I asked. "Or us?"

"I meant us," she said. "With mom. She would bring us here and tell us stories. We liked to be scared, all three of us."

"Where did your mom grow up?" Sab asks. "And your dad, for that matter."

The question surprises me, mostly because I'd never thought to ask it myself.

Jude chews and chews her steak and washes it down with her beer. Thirty seconds pass, a minute.

"I can't remember with Dad," Jude says. "We were so young. And with Mom, she always just waved her hand and said, 'A small town out in the middle of yonder, just a speck of a speck of the earth.' Or something like that, in so many words. For whatever reason, she didn't like to talk about her childhood."

"And we never pressed her on it?'" I ask. "Demanded specifics?"

"We did a few times. But that was always her answer, and we learned to stop asking."

"Some things are meant to stay secret," Sab says. "Ain't nothing wrong with that." He raises his glass, and for a minute it feels like we're all in the snug room, about to play a round of cards, toasting to good luck. *Good culk*, I think, but say aloud: "Yerv rute." *Very true.*

"Yerv rute," Jude says, raising her glass. "Dan ot omm." *And to Mom.*

"Verv rute," Sab repeats, "Dan ot omm. Whatever that means."

Back at our hotel, we say good night and close our doors and get into bed, and when his hands begin their slow walk down the curve of my body, I deny him for the very first time, telling him I am tired and drained, unable to summon the energy even to talk. He turns and falls into a steady sleep, and although the walls are thick I can hear my sister through them; those crisp, distinct bubble-pop noises drift faintly to my ears. It occurs to me, then, that I can't tell if she is laughing or crying, that the sound of our mirth is indistinguishable from the sound of our sorrow.

———————————

In the morning, we make one final pilgrimage, navigating a series of intersecting dirt roads a few miles from Harmony's main square, each dustier and more remote than the last. We pass one farmhouse, so old and weathered it seems ready to collapse, and I feel a surge of hope: "That one?"

"No," Jude says. "Mom would never have let our house deteriorate in that way."

Sab is quiet in the back seat, his hand dipping out of the open window.

In another quarter mile she makes a turn. A battered street sign reads *TOUCHSTONE ROAD*. A magnificent sunrise reddens the sky. We hear the moo of cows, the cluck of chickens, the impatient barking of dogs, and above the din Jude says, "There."

It is exactly as I'd hoped: all wraparound porches and strips of stained glass and pairs of arched windows that look like winking eyes. Behind the main house I spot a pristine picket fence keeping all of the animals safe. I'm so overwhelmed I barely hear Jude's narration: "See that window? That was our bedroom, and there's Mom and Dad's bedroom, and on the ground floor to the right is the parlor, and beyond that the kitchen . . ."

As soon as Jude turns off the engine I spring from the car and run with ferocious speed, my eyes wide, the hot air drying them out. Behind me I hear Jude call, "Kat! Kat! Wait for me!" and she catches up, her hands on my shoulders, panting in my ear. Together we skulk around the perimeter of the porch and peer into windows, pointing out mundane household items that, for us, hold deep significance. There's the spot where Dad liked to read, Jude says, and the oven where Mom made us cakes, and the closet where I always hid for hide and seek, and the wallpaper that looked like climbing vines, and the old mahogany stairs that we descended on our butts, bumping the whole way. We circle back to the front door and Jude, to my surprise, yanks on the old-fashioned bell.

"What are we going to say if someone answers?" I ask.

"That we used to live here, and would they be so kind as to give us a tour."

She takes my hand, gripping hard.

I take my turn and yank, but no one ever comes.

"It's time to go," she says. "I want to be home before dark." She grabs my arm and pulls. I am her dog, chafing at my leash, scratching to go back. I want to stand and gaze at this diorama of another life, preserved beneath glass, with no way for me to break in.

"We can come back again some time," she says. "I promise."

I let her lead me but near the end of the long, rocky driveway, I shake off her arm.

"Give me just a minute," I say.

She retreats to the car and Sab slides up to me, his camera in hand. He begins taking pictures of everything: the immaculate fence, the glittering windows, the mailbox designed to look like a miniature version of the house itself. "You'll want these later," he says, and flaps his arms, circling around me until the pictures slowly reveal themselves. On the walk back to the car I notice something I hadn't seen before: the body of a dead rabbit—a baby bunny, really—deflating atop the gravel, sinking into itself, its soft brown fur still pristine and absent of blood, its tiny, powerful legs folded into its belly, its black eyes open in eternal horror. I do not know why it makes such an impression on me; even after Sab gives me an album full of pictures from this trip, it is the image that lingers most powerfully, igniting some long-lost corner of my mind.

KAT: NOW

Four Months after the Accident

JULY 1983

I tell myself it's not a betrayal to talk to Sab about Jude. I am worried about her, I confide. In the two weeks since we've returned from the trip to Harmony, she has not been herself; she has not even been the strangest or worst version of herself. When I ask her about the loan shark debt, she tells me she's "paying it down." I offer to join her at work and she argues there's no point; we'd just be splitting half of her salary, and it would make sense only if I had my own roster of houses, which is impossible, since we only have one car. I protest, arguing that together we could work faster and make time for more houses, and still she declines; she'd rather I stay home and rest, maybe even look for a job with fewer physical demands. She is coming home from work later and later each night, occasionally after I'm already in bed or fitfully asleep on the couch, waiting for any sight or sound of her, my mind racing to the direst scenarios: she's been kidnapped by her loan shark, she's been murdered, she's been in an accident just like my own, her brain rewired in inexplicable and irrevocable ways, the final ties to our past severed for good.

"I hate seeing you so stressed out," Sab says. "What can we do about it?"

I tell him I can't answer that without more information, and propose a plan: that coming Thursday—which has always been her latest night—we'll follow her home from the last house on her roster, and maybe discover something she'd rather I not know.

On the appointed day, when Sab's hulking old car pulls into my complex, I notice that the scapular has been replaced with a playing card dangling from a chain: the same Jack of Hearts he'd used in his magic trick, still marked by the words *Here's your third chance.*

"What's this about?" I ask, giving it a swat. "Did the religious dudes finally fail you at poker?"

He pulls out and heads to Roosevelt Boulevard, turning right. "I redecorated on your account," he says, "since this is now your car. I just bought myself a rad new Mazda, and I want you to have this one."

He takes his eyes off the road just long enough to look at me straight on, and I can see he's serious.

"That's so nice of you, on top of all of the other ridiculously nice stuff you've done," I say. "But I can't take your car. I can't pay you for it."

"You either take it or it's going to the junkyard. Trying to sell it won't be worth the effort. It's old, but it's got a little bit of juice left."

I look down at my hands, which suddenly seem out of place in my own lap. "But I don't drive. I haven't driven since . . ." And there I stop, my mouth refusing to release the words.

"I know," he says, and taps my knee with his fingertips. "But you will. Probably sooner than you think."

———

We're quiet the rest of the ride to Ardmore, the town where Taxidermy House stands on a tidy cul-de-sac cluttered with old stone mansions and flowering dogwood trees. I picture Jude dusting antique tables under the mute judgment of those mounted animals, and the memory of the dead rabbit comes back to me: that sweet, flattened foot; those dead and blind open eyes. I want to know what it means and why it has lodged itself so firmly in my mind.

For an hour we wait, parked across the entrance to the cul-de-sac, the radio turned low. We don't kiss or hold hands or even talk. Finally, around six o'clock, the Killer Whale noses out from the cul-de-sac, and as Jude passes I can just make out her hair, teased to historic heights.

"Go," I tell Sab.

"Shouldn't I wait a minute?"

"She doesn't know this car. Let's just go or we risk losing her."

Jude merges onto the highway, settling into the rush-hour traffic. Sab inches up on the Whale's right side, staying back just enough to keep us obscured. I slouch a bit in my seat, fearing both my sister's sharp eye and the peculiar twin radar that keeps us hyperattuned.

The drowsy summer sun begins to fall, casting erratic streaks across a sky so much bluer than the one over the city. Jude flips on her headlights; Sab does the same. We drive for forty minutes, keeping careful distance, and the world seems to expand—the houses planted farther apart, meandering green fields, scattered herds of goats and cows, the bustle of industry falling away. I don't know where we're heading, but some strange foreboding settles over me, a déjà vu from my lost past.

"Where are we?" I ask.

"Not entirely sure, but somewhere in Delaware County. Southwest of where we started."

I sense we are almost there, wherever *there* is. As if on cue, Jude slows down, sliding into a spot along a quaint Main Street—brick storefronts with flower boxes in full bloom, well-dressed couples strolling arm in arm. It is Harmony on steroids: triple the traffic, the buzz, the people. The uncanny similarity only deepens my unease.

I watch Jude walk across the street, purse strapped across her body, her elbow keeping it in place. She looks both assured and resigned. She disappears into a building with a red awning that reads *The Monkey Bar*. Inside the lights are dim, and I lose sight of her.

"Now what?" Sab asks.

"We just wait," I say, although I want nothing more than to press my face against the window and see what I can see. "I want to know exactly who she's meeting with. I *need* to know."

The sidewalks fill with more people, the volume rises, the sky darkens. I don't know how much time has passed: a minute, five, a half hour. I am sweating, a stray bead or two stinging my eyes, but I don't bother to wipe them; I can't risk missing a second. My obstinance is rewarded when Jude finally exits. From my crouched position, I try to read her expression but her eyes are lowered. She reaches her car, glances back once at the bar, and drives off.

"Want to follow her again?" Sab asks.

"No," I say, and find myself, to my shock, getting out of the car. Behind me I hear Sab's voice—*wait, wait, want me to come?*—but I don't have the energy to respond, and with each step closer to the bar my breath grows thinner, raspier.

I see her right away, sitting at a cafe table with claw feet and a scalloped edge, sipping the last dregs of her drink. The back of her chair looms higher than her shoulders, giving the impression that she's a child merely playing at adulthood. One step closer and she comes into focus: Nancy, the limping stalker girl, the one with the fake charity who made me sign our names. The one who sent me to an empty house in search of a psychic—a house containing nothing but evidence of an abandoned life.

The connection, when it comes, does a slow, shivery crawl from my brain to my gut, freezing everything in its path. The dead rabbit in Harmony and the "rabbit hole" graffiti in the house are somehow related, and Nancy knows everything my mind has forgotten, and our encounters have not been accidental at all.

I sit down across from her but can't manage to speak; I am grateful when she does so first.

"Jude?" she asks, confused, but then she tracks my face, assessing my expression, the set of my features. *She knows us*, I think. *She knows us well enough to tell us apart.*

Her back goes rigid and she says my name like a sigh: "Kat."

"Nancy," I say. "So we meet again."

She laughs, her deep, honking bray belying her small frame. "You sound like a spy-movie cliché," she says. "But I suppose you've forgotten things like that."

"What is your business with my sister? And what is your business with me? Why did you send me to a psychic who doesn't even exist?" I try to speak evenly, betraying neither fear nor anger; either reaction might hurt Jude in some way I don't yet know.

Nancy sips her wine, her stack of bracelets fidgeting with each raise of the glass.

"She does exist," she says. "Obviously, she moved since the last time I saw her."

"Fine," I say, working to stay calm. "Answer the other questions. What business do you have with me and Jude?"

"I know you're aware of Jude's loan shark debts. Well, I'm her loan shark. The interest is accruing, and I'm not a bank. If she declares bankruptcy, she'll still have a debt with me. Tonight she came here begging for mercy, wondering if there was another way to pay me back."

She says this with a strange and proprietary glee; somehow this is personal. I recall the picture of Jude's necklace and the accompanying threat: *You left this behind and you owe me.* Clearly Nancy had written that note. I distinctly remember Jude calling the loan shark *him*—

why, to throw me off? Throw me off of what, exactly? I try to reconcile this fragile wisp of a creature having any hold over my sister.

"So you're a loan shark?" I ask. "And people actually listen to you?"

"Jude's my only client right now," she says. "And she listens very carefully."

"How long is this going to go on?" I ask. "How much more does she owe?"

"That's up to Jude." She stands, fishing a clutch of bills from her wallet.

"What do you mean, up to Jude? What's her debt total, and how much did she pay so far?"

She takes two steps away, my question still hanging in the air. She spins and asks a question of her own: "How well do you really know Jude? How well do you really know yourself?"

Her words are a direct strike, loosening all of the uncertainty and fears about my past, tossing them like confetti in my mind. The answer is both available and mercurial, entirely dependent on how many questions I am willing to ask, and if I choose to believe what I find.

"You might want to do some digging," Nancy says. "For your own good."

I leap up from my chair to watch her walk down the street, her limp exaggerated in her haste, the gait of someone with her own private pain.

JUDE: THEN

Seven Years before the Accident

JULY 1976

By this time The Plan had evolved into a massive zeitgeist, its tenets discussed and debated in living rooms and bookstores and corporate boardrooms and the pages of *Newsweek* and *Time*. It was estimated that nearly one hundred thousand people had taken the seminars. The roster of famous members grew, including an actor who paired with King Bash on a project to end world hunger by the year 1999. Another noted member, a folk musician, wrote a song dedicated to The Plan about getting lost in sadness and screams before finding sunshine and dreams. With the glory came the detractors. Several lawsuits, all dismissed, argued that The Plan's seminars resulted in severe and permanent emotional, psychological, and physical injuries. A private detective hired by a rival organization began a file on King Bash, who made no comment besides calling the investigation a "conspiracy of evil."

Later Jude would begin files of her own, but then, at age sixteen, she was aware only of discontent inside her limited world, tiny fissures that erupted and threatened to spread. One day Genesis, her dear, beloved rabbit who now had rabbits of her own, found Jude on the back stoop of the row house and sat down next to her. Jude could feel the heat from the girl's skin, smell the sweet musk of her sweat.

"What's up, doc?" Jude asked in her best Bugs Bunny voice. It was their dumb joke, just between her and Gen.

"Can I tell you something?" Gen asked. She twisted a clump of hair and lifted it to her mouth, sucking on the ends.

Jude did not like Gen's tone. It was tinged with a desperate anxiety, as though her secret itched her insides so unbearably that she had no choice but to scratch.

"What it is, bunny?" Jude asked, afraid of her own question. She could imagine a growing list of concerns about which nothing could be done.

Gen exhaled, the long shallow hiss of a deflating balloon, and said, "I have been stealing from King Bash."

Jude felt her heart drop with a sudden and alarming force—the gush of a waterfall, the tumble of an avalanche. The entire musculature of her body felt jostled and rearranged. She forced herself to speak in a calm and even voice, the voice of someone who was never unpleasantly shocked, the voice of a leader, a fixer: "Why would you *ever* do something like that?"

Gen gnawed on her hair. "I am trying to get enough money to get a bus ticket to the Poconos. My mom's boyfriend has a house there, and I think she is there with him."

Those two sentences contained a multitude of problems. Jude needed to dissect them one at a time. "What have you been stealing?" she asked. "What have you been doing with these stolen things? Does King Bash realize someone is doing this to him?" Her heart was now flailing at the bottom of her gut.

Gen looked straight over Jude's shoulder, refusing to meet her gaze. Her lock of hair was now sculpted into a dampened point. "Just some of that weird antique stuff, little statues and leather books and some jewelry he never wears. A gold chain with a lion charm. I took it all to a pawn shop on South Street but didn't get much for any of it. I'm scared that he knows. I wanted to tell you now in case he asks you about it. I didn't want you to be caught off guard."

Jude felt her heart stop moving entirely. Not just her heart, but everything—a complete and ruthless cessation of function. Her tongue was a dull, lifeless slug inside her mouth, and her arms powerless to swing, and her feet cold and numb at the end of her legs.

"Jude," Gen said, shaking her. "Jude, are you okay? You're scaring me. Jude!"

Jude's body roused itself and she pulled the girl close so that they were eye to eye. "Why did you tell me that?" she asked. "Do you have any idea of the trouble you've caused by telling me that? Do you know the ripple effects, the repercussions?"

Gen began to cry. "Why? I don't understand. Please tell me?"

The explanation arranged itself cleanly and clearly in Jude's mind: *You have put me in an impossible position—a position that gives me two choices, neither of them good. You have thrown me in between the person who is responsible for me and the person I am responsible for. You have placed loyalty to me over loyalty to the group. Now I have to make a choice: I either tell King Bash what you have done and let you reap the consequences, or I keep it to myself and possibly reap consequences of my own. He will learn the truth and know I aided and abetted your theft. He will use your treachery to punish me.*

Beyond all of that came the worst thought of all: *He will take Violet away from me, and make me pose with someone else.*

She jumped to her feet and pulled Gen with her. She leaned in so that her face was an inch from the girl's, so close that Gen's eyes merged into one. "Do not speak a word of this to anyone else. Do you hear me? Not one word. I can keep you safe, but only if you say nothing."

The girl panted into Jude's open mouth and promised with all her heart.

On the next rabbit hunt, Jude and Kat and Violet discussed changes at the upcoming Think Is Games, some confirmed and others rumored. Confirmed: Violet's mother, Jackie, had left The Plan, for reasons Violet explained: "She got her head off on vodka and came to Mr. Donald's house one night, a crazy scene. She tried to take me away but my Uncle Bash came over, called a cab, and sent her off. I don't know where she is now."

Violet said this in the tone of someone complaining about a stray fly in her bedroom. Jude couldn't tell if she was upset or pleased or indifferent, and had to calibrate her response carefully—too sympathetic and Violet would think she was being pitied; too casual and Violet would think she didn't care. Her chance was ruined when Kat spoke first: "That's really heavy, I'm sorry."

"Me too," Jude managed, and changed the subject to the unconfirmed rumor: at this Think Is Games, the highest scorers among them would be playing against the adults. It was a reward, a taste of the Big House, a true test of their mastery of the tenets, a preview of the independence and excitement to come.

They all agreed that kill-saving got a little easier every time.

Dressed in her monkey costume, surveying the Island through her furry mask, Jude saw a chance to kill-save her own mother. Somewhere between Jude's shed and the Power Tower there was Verona, dressed as a cobra, swishing her snake tail like the train of an elaborate Victorian gown, smoking a cigarette instead of wielding a weapon. Keeping quiet and stealth Jude followed her. Through the brush and the random mounds of sand and plastic palm trees Verona bobbed and weaved, waving her cigarette, moving as she once did during her dancing days. Jude thought, then, of Very Sherry, and how much Verona must miss what she used to be, the loud, colorful time of her life when she had many admirers but no children, before she had to answer to anyone but herself. She thought next of Kat and how her sister's face looked—three years ago, now—when Verona dropped them off, giving vague promises of a reunion while her daughter cried and cried.

Jude's mind roiled with all of these thoughts and images and ideas, until she was interrupted by the sound of Verona's voice: "Ouch!"

Jude realized she'd been running and stopped. Her breath burned up and down her throat. She looked in her hand and saw that it clutched a large stone, a stone she had been poised to throw, one stone of many that she had apparently already sent flying at Verona's head. The snake swiveled, that tail swishing like fine silk, and it fixed its tiny black eyes on her: "Jude?"

The way Verona spoke her name—soft, uncertain, flipped into a question—cracked Jude open and struck her in a place that had once felt real, a place where her mother was very kind and very good, keeping the world's goblins at bay. She did not argue with her body when it decided to drop the stone, or when it stepped down the path toward her mother, or when it wrapped its arms around Verona and cried against her shoulder, the snake's scales rough against her cheek. Jude's body held her still there for one full minute, a minute she hoped might reverse time instead of advancing it, setting her world back where it should be.

As soon as her tears stopped, Jude felt a tug at her rear and heard a snipping sound. Holding the monkey tail in the air, spinning it like a lasso, Verona said, "Don't worry, Jude angel, don't worry at all—this is for your own good."

How long had it been since she'd seen Verona? It must be hours by now, but the sun seemed stubborn in the sky, clinging to its place. Her stomach had turned itself out with hunger. She believed she was seeing things that weren't really there, her eyes and ears telling lies. *What you think, is,* she told herself, but for once her mind failed to identify and validate its own thoughts. It seemed someone had taken a shit in the closest stream and the invisible ocean was dull today, timid in its lapping, quiet in its roar. Her kill-saves tallied into the dozens, children and adults of all kinds, a collection of ears and snouts and tongues growing in her pocket, her own missing tail the only evidence of defeat.

She knew how dangerous it was to close her eyes, but she did it anyway and laughed and laughed and laughed, reveling in its ricochet, unsure of what she found so funny. When she opened them again, there was Gen and the rest of Jude's original fluffle—Melisa, Jimmy, Marcus, Lola—all adorable in their rabbit costumes, especially Gen, now officially the Head Hare. Gen stepped forward, her ears jerking like antennae, her real nose twitching beneath the furry one.

"Jude, what is wrong with you?" she asked, and stepped closer. "You don't look so good."

"Nothing at all," Jude said, and knew her face belied her words. She could feel the wideness of her smile, the stretch of her skin, the air drying up the whites of her eyes. "Just a bit thirsty. Having a good day so far. How about you?"

Marcus offered her a rusty flask.

"This isn't from the shit-stream, is it?" she asked.

"That wasn't shit, you doofus," Jimmy said. "It was Marathon Bars."

"Don't call her a doofus, doofus," Melisa said. "She'll crush you with her Great Ape hands."

Jude took the flask and tilted her head and let the liquid splash her face and dribble into her mouth. She handed the flask back to Marcus and said, "It was smart of you to offer that."

"Anytime," he said, and gave a limp salute.

"Where are you going now?" Jude asked. "Do you want to join me, or are you hunting solo? How many kill-saves do you have?"

"Why are you asking?" Lola asked. "Is someone else listening? What is the right answer?"

"No," Jude said. She realized she didn't know the right answer, or if there were any answers at all. "I'm asking just to ask. I don't care about your answer, as long as it doesn't involve killing me."

Melisa gasped. "Don't even say that!"

"Yeah, that ain't funny," Jimmy said.

"I don't know about everyone else," Gen said. "But I'm done. I'm so, so tired. I'm starving. I don't want to perform anymore. I don't care whether defeat begets domination. She began to cry shiny tears that dripped onto her fur. "I don't know what's right or wrong or what's normal or weird. I just want to go home. So much time has passed. Maybe my mother is worried about me now. Maybe she called." Her crying deepened, snot mixing with tears, the beginning of hiccups.

"No," Jude said. A strange panic fluttered inside her. She ordered her mind to reject and release Gen's words, but the panic only amplified in her mind. What if Gen told everyone else about the theft? The bus ticket? The grand and dark possibility that she might actually leave? What if they *all* left, her entire fluffle disbanded? What would she have to show for all her time, her sacrifice, her unyielding devotion? "You are home," Jude said. "*We're* your home."

"Do you even realize where we are?" Gen was screaming now, eyes red, long tinsels of spit connecting the roof of her mouth to her tongue. "We're in an abandoned amusement park! Don't you see? My grandma took me here when I was a kid. The Tilt-A-Whirl was over there, the Jet Star was over there! They built fences around the rides! All of the sheds? They were ticket booths! We've been running around a junky old park like idiots playing a game that makes no sense for no reason!"

The panic sprouted wings and began to fly, knocking around Jude's organs, loosening her bladder, displacing her heart. What Gen said could not be true. There were lies hidden all over the Island, but the Island itself was real. The questions it posed mattered. Its lessons had scarred her brain. It had to be real. It couldn't *not* be real. Take away its realness, and Jude would not know herself at all. Jude herself would not be real.

"And the pictures!" Gen screamed, the loudest words Jude had ever heard. Rivulets of snot snaked into her mouth. "Do you know where they are going? Who is seeing them? What happens when we go to the Big House? Will we ever graduate from there? Will we ever get out?" She was choking now, choking on her own snot and her own words, on the images those words provoked, choking so hard that Jude wanted to crawl inside Gen's body and breathe on her behalf. She wanted to close Gen's mind and wipe everything clean and make her be very calm and very quiet.

Jude felt her cold, numb hand reach for her scissors. She raised them up high above her head and saw her shadow move in perfect synchronicity, and before she opened the blades she gave one hoarse command: "Get her."

And they did, all four pairs of scissors out and setting upon Gen, who now sat upon a pile of imported sand that sank beneath her weight. She rolled over, exposing her belly, the universal sign of surrender. The bunny suit came off one matted limb at a time, and they decapitated its darling furry head, and snipped the ears as trophies. Once the costume was gone and she lay naked and writhing, they set upon her real head and hacked off that wild, red hair that looked so much like Verona's. If Jude looked closely enough, if she stared so intently that her vision blurred, the two faces blended into one, and she was actually hacking away at Verona, cutting every last sprig of hair, yanking every last strand by its root. "Jude!" Verona screamed. "Stop! Stop! Please! Why?"

Jude pulled back and saw the rabbit squirm and remembered that Verona was a cobra and not a rabbit. She began to run, and the rest of her fluffle followed, leaving Gen where she lay, curled into a ball, crying for her mother. She ran and ran, outpacing them all, rushing across a place that had never been an island, no matter what her brain had told her. When she doubled back an hour later, she saw a fake Genesis hanging from the branch of a real cherry tree clinging to the last of its blooms.

The fake Genesis looked like real Genesis just as she'd left her: the strong, squat limbs; the sleek, auburn sex; the pale head adorned with bloody craters where the scissors had done their work. No matter how Jude commanded and begged fake Genesis, she would not wake up; she refused to help Jude untie the noose, fashioned from a discarded monkey tail, or stop the maddening pendulum swing of her legs. Jude poked her and pushed her and felt the waning warmth of her skin. She held her limp hand until it turned stiff and cold. For the rest of the night she called fake Gen's name, but the real one never answered.

KAT: NOW

Four Months after the Accident
JULY 1983

By the time I get home from meeting Nancy at the Monkey Bar, Jude is already asleep, and she's gone by the time I awaken in the morning. In a way I am relieved; I need the space to consider my meeting with Nancy, her alarming questions about how much I really know about myself, my sister, our vanished history. I have not yet caught Jude in a lie but in a significant omission—she's said not one word about this strange woman with an investment in our lives that extends far beyond any debt or loan. A part of me is now afraid to ask Jude anything; I could talk myself into forgiving a well-intentioned omission, but never a lie. A lie would leak like poison into our shared self, distorting our complementary pieces so that they never fit again.

I see that Jude has left a note and a package on the kitchen table: "Here are Wen's pictures of our time in Europe together—some of them so great they almost don't disturb me!"

I'd almost forgotten my phone conversation with Wen, her stories of the time we spent at her cottage in the Cotswolds, her promise to fatten me up like a turkey. I open the package and find that each picture has a caption written in cheery, detailed prose—an attempt, I suppose, to help me relive this forgotten time. The top picture shows me and Jude standing side by side, each of us cradling a chicken, and these words from Wen:

I remember this day well! In fact I believe this was the afternoon after our first meeting. We had all indulged just a bit too much the previous night and were paying the price. But as soon as you two saw my chicken coop, you made immediate friends with George and Imogene. You told me that the coop and my farm made you feel like you were kids again, playing on your farm back at home in Harmony. How you missed your chickens, the simple and satisfying routine of your lives, and, of course, your mom . . .

Jude and I sitting in a leather booth, huddled close together, raising mugs of beer:

This was my birthday! You both insisted on taking me out to our favorite pub. They were having an "American night," with a band playing all of the best songs from the seventies. You requested "Bad Girls" and "I Will Survive," and we danced until our feet hurt and laughed until our stomachs ached . . .

Jude and I and a strange woman—obviously Wen—standing in some sort of garden, flexing our arms. Wen looks eerily close to how I'd pictured her: tall and lean, with short white hair arranged in spiky points, as sharp and discrete as shark fins. Her arms seem almost unnaturally long; if she were a cartoon, they would unfurl into spaghetti-like ropes and choke her enemy from across the room.

What a day this was! We took a break from working on the farm to visit this stupendous topiary maze. The hedges loomed ten feet high and slithered out in every direction, coaxing us into lush twists and turns, leading us to verdant dead ends. In the midst of one labyrinth we spread out a blanket and had a lavish picnic. We all felt so strong that day, so free and unencumbered by the troubles of the past and uncertainty of the future, and we struck this pose to commemorate the moment. The proprietor of the field was kind enough to snap this shot.

The last one shows me and Jude and Wen on the edge of a lakeside dock, the water a deep and muddy green, reflecting a forest in the background. Jude and I are tanned, our long legs jutting from frayed denim shorts.

This was shortly before you left the Cotswolds to go to London. We spent a day at the lake not too far from my cottage. We took a canoe out to the middle of the water and paddled around and then just soaked in the sun for hours. That night I cooked black pudding, your favorite English feast. You both were shocked when I told you it's made of congealed blood, but that didn't stop you from licking every last crumb.

Hoping to divine secrets and clues, I study each picture intently, looking beyond the main image, searching for meaning in Wen's descriptions. I have no knowledge of the Cotswolds or its environs, but one thing becomes clear: these photos betray nothing about the venues they depict. Not one street sign, or shop awning, or singular landmark, or plate of exotic cuisine, or any telling detail that would indicate a remote and charming English village. A chicken coop, a bar, a topiary maze, a lake—all things that could exist anywhere in the world.

I look at the address on the package—somewhere in Newberry, New York—and strategize; Jude might think it strange if she beats me home two nights in a row. I will tell her that I wasn't feeling well and made an appointment with my doctor and asked Sab to take me. She will not expect me to do what I'm about to do. She won't suspect I've put on my Jude costume, my hair parted against its will. She won't expect that I'll dig beneath my bed and retrieve more of Sab's gifts: various road maps of Pennsylvania and the surrounding states. She'll never imagine me taking the keys to my inherited car, now parked in a discreet corner of the lot, a new lover awaiting a rendezvous.

Holding the keys, I approach the car slowly, my heart creeping higher in my chest, accelerating its beat. I pet the steering wheel like it's a strange dog, softly, cautiously. Closing my eyes, I remember Jude's descriptions of that night and try to picture it as it happened. I can hear raindrops on the windshield, see the smooth glide of the wipers, spot the hide of the deer, sense the tires losing their grip. The sickening crunch of steel against wood. My body launching through the glass. Jude's hands cupped beneath my arms, the drag of my feet against the road, a glimpse of jaundiced moon before the lights flicked out. My head across Jude's lap, my blood soaking through her jeans.

I roll down my window and turn the key and the engine coughs to life. I think, *I am a person unafraid to do the thing that nearly killed me.*

I have two stops to make today. The first is a five-minute ride, an easy warm-up, the wheel vibrating its welcome against my palms. In the distance rises an angular gray building, one side composed entirely of rectangular windows. A banner unfurls above the entrance: *FEED THE MIND.*

The library reference desk is front and center, marked by a chalkboard sign and commandeered by three women sitting in generational order: my age, mother, grandmother. I pick the mom, who seems efficient and kind, her nimble fingers arranging index cards in a wooden drawer, a pencil stabbed through her fat black bun.

"Welcome," she says, her voice eager and smooth. "How can I help you?"

I pull out one of the maps, in which I've tucked Sab's photograph of my childhood home, the address written on the back: *415 Touchstone Road, Harmony, Pennsylvania, 16037.*

"I'm trying to trace the ownership of this home," I say. "I think it was sold five years ago, but I'm interested in the records as far back as they go."

She slides her glasses down her nose and peers at my scribble. "That should be doable," she says, copying the address. "We don't have a copy of the deed records here, but I can call the library in Butler County. They'll be able to track down this information."

She asks for my name and writes it down, saying it aloud: "Katherine Bird." Check back with her in a day or so, she says, and I promise I will.

With one stop for gas, I should arrive in Newberry in three hours. I will find Wen, staying just long enough to ask all the questions that have stacked up in my mind. Her responses will dictate what happens next. Either I hurry back and crawl into bed before Jude comes home, or I tell Jude exactly where I've been and what I've done, and see if her answers are the same.

All along Interstate 95, past the Wawas, the gas stations, the signs imploring me to come see the world's largest light bulb in Edison, New Jersey, I am alternately brazen and petrified. I am going the speed limit, even a bit below, but the blast of horns and rumble of trucks feel like predators, inching closer and closer still.

When it's time to stop for gas, I fish a dime from my purse and call Sab on the pay phone. I know he's on a construction site, but I need to hear his voice: *Yo, it's Sab. You know what to do.* I leave him a message telling him so far, so good; I'll report back as soon as I can.

In the ride's final hour my body feels attuned to the car, as though it's forged a separate path of communication, bypassing my brain. I succumb and let it lead me. Off the interstate the view changes every few moments in subtle, kaleidoscopic twists: red brick buildings, red farmhouses, bleached expanses of swaying wheat, the sun hunkering low in the mottled sky. I am driving slowly now, safe, the hard part behind me. I read faded street signs, each situated a mile apart, until I reach Wen's address on Kill Devil Road.

I expect to pull up to a ramshackle compound but instead find a broad white farmhouse, the paint fresh and bright, with a wraparound porch and gingerbread trim. Several smaller structures, identically decorated, are scattered like ducklings behind it. I park beneath the shade of a tree, keeping the keys clutched tight in my fist. Halfway up the long gravel drive, I hear commotion coming from the rear, the clanging of tools, the clapping of hands, the sound of gunshots being fired, shouts and chants and grunts. I creep around the side. To my right I spot a chicken coop filled with a brood of strutting birds. I move with my body flush against the house, bits of frayed wood embedding splinters into my skin.

The field is crowded with women, a range of colors and ages, all dressed in a similar uniform: denim shorts, T-shirts knotted at the waist, red bandanas tied across foreheads. They are divided into four distinct groups, each at a far corner of the field and executing different tasks. One does calisthenics, jumping jacks and high kicks and push-ups. The next takes turns chopping wood, each woman wielding an axe high above her head and shouting upon contact. The third conducts target practice, aiming at full-length cardboard cut-outs shaped like hulking men. The fourth performs a series of martial arts sequences—the same ones I used on Sab—their arms slicing the air with crisp precision, so synchronized they move as one.

I recognize Wen from the photos, with her sculpted hair and long, ropy arms. She stands in the center of the field, waving her arms like a conductor, making this strange world spin. I inch closer, watching the spectacle so intently that I don't notice Wen until she's beside me, close enough to shake my hand.

"Jude!" she says, and pulls me toward her for a hug. "What are you doing here?" She smells of peppermint and clean laundry. I hold the hug as long as I can, waiting for my body to send me a signal, a fuse of memory being lit: *This is a person I've touched before.* She pulls away. "Are you here to talk about the complaint? I thought we'd settled everything on the phone."

I rummage through my mind, trying to make the connection, and begin a coughing fit to buy some time. Wen whacks me on the back, waiting.

"I'm sorry," I say. "Don't worry, I'm not contagious. What were you saying about a complaint?"

"The complaint about the missing ring from the Ardmore house? You said you didn't know anything about it." I don't know what my face is showing her, but she presses her brows together and touches my arm. "Jude? Are you okay?"

And then I understand: *Wen is in charge of the cleaning service. She is the one who takes on charity cases. She is the one who hired Jude, the one who helped orchestrate my reentry into the world.*

"Yes, sorry," I say, shaking my head. "I think I'm just tired from the ride. And of course! All is well. I'm sure it will turn up."

"I hope so," she says. "It would be a shame to lose that client." She turns to the women, who are now switching stations: the jumping-jackers migrate to wood chopping; the choppers to target practice; the shooters to self-defense. "So what *are* you doing here, then?" she asks. "Not that I'm not happy to see you."

I check my hair, ensuring my Jude part is intact, and remind myself to wear Jude's face: bold, dismissive, confidence aspiring to arrogance. "Kat insisted on taking over my roster today, despite my objections. She thought I needed the day off. I do, but I hope you don't mind. She's just been worried about me."

"How sweet of her," Wen says. "I'm sure she'll do a good job. I just hope it's not too stressful on her."

"She'll be fine," I say. I'm eager to get inside the house to have a look around. "Let's have a drink. I'd like to toast to everything you've done for me and Kat."

We walk inside through a screened door. A table made of wide wooden planks dominates the kitchen. On one wall hangs a chalkboard listing work schedules similar to Jude's: *Hell House (Wayne); Ghost House (Hudson); Serene Oasis (Rittenhouse Square)*. A similar board occupies the opposite wall, but this one is labeled *GOALS: Divorce, Financial Independence, Custody, Sobriety*. I try to summon a memory, any memory, that would place me among these people, in this home, in this very position in the kitchen, having a drink with this stranger who knows everything about me. Nothing comes, of course, just a slippery black ribbon of lost time.

Wen pours lemonade into two glasses etched with the words *The Furies*.

"To dead pasts and new beginnings," I say, and tilt my glass toward her.

"Not the toast I was expecting, but I'll take it." Her glass kisses mine and she takes a long sip. I stifle the urge to ask what sort of toast she'd expected to hear.

"You got the photos okay?" she says. "Did Kat like them?"

I pick my words carefully. "They were perfect. Exactly what she needed to see."

"Excellent. I'm so glad they worked." She takes another sip. "So how is Kat feeling? Is she acting like her old self? What does she do with her days?"

"Not much, really. She's sort of in limbo. She met a guy she seems to like, so he's been taking up some of her time."

"Good for her. Do you like him?"

I smile. "I think he's perfect."

"Wonderful," she says, and means it. She swirls her glass, considering her next words. "I hate to even ask this, but she hasn't found you, has she?"

My hand grips my glass so tightly, I fear I might break it. I can't imagine who she means. Nancy, the loan shark? Some other ominous figure from our past? A threat I've forgotten, or one I never knew of at all? I try to find a balance, eliciting information while giving nothing away.

"Oh, no," I say, slowly. "Not yet, anyway."

"Good. Let me know if she does."

I can't resist. "Do you know where she is?"

Her eyebrows press together. "What do you mean? Isn't she still in Norris Ford?"

I remember my trip with Sab, the stakeout at the bar. My strange conversation with Nancy: *How well do you really know yourself?*

"That's Delaware County, right?"

Now she's rubbing a finger along her temple, as though waking up her brain. "Yes," she says, stretching the word. "Where else would it be?"

"Right," I say quickly. "Of course."

"Are we talking about the same person?" she asks. There is a hint of panic in her voice.

I put my glass down and lean forward an inch. I'm not sure what I want the answer to be. I know she's made me, and I speak with equal trepidation: "Are we?"

"*I'm* talking about the people you're in debt to. The loan shark." She seems satisfied, as though she's volleyed a perfect serve, awaiting my response. "I know you were worried about her finding out exactly where you lived."

Again I think of Nancy and her threat about Jude's necklace: *You left this behind and you owe me.* "Yes," I say. "Of course. That's under control." My calm voice belies my body's unease; every working, ticking piece inside me tightens.

"Well, it was good seeing you," she says. She glances at her watch. "I have to get back out there—I promised to teach them a new move today."

"Good seeing you, too," I say.

"Tell Kat hi for me, and that I hope she's healing." She covers my hand with hers. "It would be terrible for both of you if she regressed, all of that hard work undone."

She hugs me, her arms tight around my back, and I bring her even closer, our breasts and shoulder blades pressing together. I sense something familiar in the minty scent of her skin, in the way she raps her fingers against my spine. *I know her,* I think, *and yet I don't.*

I slide behind the wheel, check my seat belt to make sure it's secure, and roar off. The landscape comes at me in a blur, matching the pace of my thoughts.

Zipping along the interstate, I notice a sign I missed on the way in:

EXIT HERE

For

EMMA'S ENCHANTED HEDGE MAZE

A FANTASY COME TRUE!

I remember Wen's photo and description of the topiary maze in England—the hedges unfurling in every direction, leading us to exquisite dead ends.

JUDE: THEN

Six Years before the Accident
JULY 1977

On the one occasion that King Bash and the RonDon spoke of Genesis—not to the public, of course, but to all current members of The Plan—they lamented the loss of such a young girl, so bright and so troubled, a roaring fire extinguished too soon. If they could all take one lesson from her tragic and untimely death, let it be that we are all unique and irreplaceable, and it is imperative to protect ourselves by mastering the tenets—particularly, in this case, Recast Your Past, Reject and Release, and, most important, What You Think, Is. Genesis would still be here with us today, improving herself and aiding in the development of The Plan, if only she'd been able to craft the narrative of her own thoughts.

Even after a year, Jude could not forget the words Gen spoke and the questions she asked right before she died: the manufactured reality of the Island, the nature and destination of the pictures, what might happen when they go to the Big House—a graduation that now, at age seventeen, was imminent. At the next rabbit recruitment, Jude met Kat and Violet at Rittenhouse Square, leading them to the bench where she'd first recruited Gen. For a moment Jude closed her eyes, letting the memory come: dealing Gen a poker hand, commiserating about their moms, the stories behind their names. She made an announcement: No more pictures. No going to the Big House. And the upcoming Think Is Games would be their last.

"How?" Violet asked.

"I think," Jude said, "that we—"

"—have to kill them from the inside," Kat finished.

To seal their pact they slashed a knife along their arms, obliterating *THE PLAN* tattoos, sucking the blood from each other's wrists, connecting them all forever.

Deftly and discreetly, they prepared. They collected vegetable oil in old soda bottles and stashed them behind bushes in their respective backyards. They drew a map of the Island, marking the spots where King Bash and the RonDon slept, where the Power Tower loomed, where the carcasses of old rides rotted beneath the sun. They asked strangers for lighters and packs of matches. They enlisted the most trusted rabbits in their cause, including Melisa and Lola and Marcus and Jimmy, all eager to atone for their part in Gen's death.

All of them arrived on the Island brimming with bravado and hope, the young ones feeling they were involved in something important and special, something that would save them in ways they didn't yet understand. Kat took charge, praising them for sneaking from their sheds, calling them all by name, unraveling every lie they'd been told. "What you think isn't necessarily so," she said. "What you think is a wish, and you have to work very hard to make it so. You must be stronger and smarter than all the people who want to scare you, all the people who want to keep you small. You have the right to be who you are. You have a duty to be who you are."

Jude was in awe of her, commanding a crowd, giving perfect voice to their shared thoughts.

The players had their places, their orders, their cues. They carried tree branches and leaves and the remnants of wooden roller coasters and piled them near the Power Tower. Kat clapped her hands and everyone changed costumes: monkeys into chameleons, scorpions into parrots, rabbits into wolves. They would stir chaos and confusion. They would start a fire. They would smoke everyone out and burn it all down.

And from there it all went wrong. Later, the memories would come, as they always had, by strobe light. *Flash*: the spreading panic that the adults had learned of their plan. *Flash*: a ruthless stampede, a frantic hunt. *Flash*: Violet plunging down a deep ravine, her knee a mangled mess, helpless to run away. Jude heard Violet scream her name, a scream so soaked in anguish and despair that Jude still hears it in her dreams.

Flash: King Bash, back in the city, calling Jude into his office, inviting her to sit down across from him and discuss what happened like mature and reasonable adults. She tried not to look at him but his power over her was such that, wordlessly, he directed her eyes to meet his. She could not stop it, and when he smiled at her, understanding and kind, she felt her lips mimic his smile in turn. She was terrified at the idea of banishing him from her life. She was desperate to escape him.

"Jude," he said. "What happened out there? You know if you ever have a problem, you can come to me. You've known this since the first time we met, way back when you were just a kid. You are never alone."

Her mouth moved, miming her thoughts, but no sound came out. She had so much to say. She had nothing to say.

"You're upset," he said. So calm, so smooth, his blond hair so soft and bright, the gold ring twisting and twisting on his finger. "I'm upset, too. We can get through this. Everyone makes mistakes. Everyone deserves forgiveness."

The scab on her wrist itched. She sat on her hand and made herself speak: "I'm sorry, King Bash, I really am. It wasn't you. It was . . ."

"What, Jude?" he asked. "What was it?"

She wished Kat were there to finish her sentence.

"Do you have something to confess?" he asked. "Is that what you're trying to tell me?"

His questions gave her the answer she needed. "Yes, it was me. It was all my idea, my planning. I don't know what got into me. It was just a joke that went too far."

He nodded, pleased with her honesty. "Did you have any accomplices in this joke?"

"No," she said. His eyes were so bright, so blue, so terrifying to look at directly, so welcoming if you could get past your fear. "But my sister, Kat, and my friend, Violet, both tried to talk me out of it. They tried to stop the whole thing."

King Bash nodded. "I understand, and thank you for telling me. They deserve to be rewarded."

"Yes, yes, they do," Jude said. Maybe she could squeeze one triumph from this failure.

"Well, Jude, you know how important you are to The Plan, and to me, personally. And I have always encouraged you to challenge the limits of your own power. So today, I'm going to give you the chance to be more powerful than ever before."

"How?" She leaned forward. She imagined the chance to rewrite the tenets, set new rules, banish the old and elevate the new. "How will I be more powerful?"

He leaned forward, too, clasping his big tan hands on his desk. "One of them, Kat or Violet, will be rewarded for their foresight and loyalty. You get to pick who."

"May I ask, what is the reward, King Bash?"

"I know all of you have so been looking forward to practicing the tenets at the next level," he said. "So whomever you choose will graduate early and go right to the Big House, and have more power, too. Isn't that wonderful?"

Jude understood that it was the exact opposite of wonderful, the very outcome she and Kat and Violet had been trying to avoid, but King Bash seemed genuinely delighted. He reached across the desk and extended his hand. Jude extended a hand, too, the one without the blistering scab, sliding her fingers into his damp palm. He shook it once, firm, and released her.

"Deal," they said in unison.

In the end, Jude knew that she had no choice at all.

JUDE: NOW

Four Months after the Accident
JULY 1983

Yet another night she has beaten Kat home, which is a relief. Jude drops her bucket, gets a beer, and looks out the window, watching the darkness seep into the sky, the shouts and hollers, the boom boxes on shoulders, the corners filling with movement and sound. She has been working so hard to construct and protect their invented life, while Violet—lovely, wretched Violet—has been working just as hard to tear it down.

She replays their reunion at the Monkey Bar, not long after Kat had come home from the hospital. Violet had poked and prodded their old connections until she discovered where Jude and Kat lived. She stalked Kat and introduced herself as someone else, a volunteer named Nancy who was canvassing for a charity she'd invented on the spot. She had stalked and lied to Kat in the hope of finding Jude. She had sent Jude a photograph of her nameplate necklace and a letter promising blackmail. She had told Jude *YOU OWE ME* in capital letters, pressing so hard with her pencil that Jude could see where the point had broken. She had demanded a meeting, the first of several, and she did not come in peace.

Jude had not seen Violet in six years, since that last night on the Island, when they tried to burn it all down and Jude was forced to choose. She could not bring herself to ask Violet what happened when King Bash, her own uncle, sent her to the Big House, but Violet wouldn't have answered anyway. She was interested only in how Jude might atone for betraying her without a second thought. Betraying her and then leaving her in the Big House, waiting for a rescue that never came.

Violet looks the same, maybe just a bit sharper, as though a lens had brought her into focus. She still possesses an inky cloak of black hair and a pointed elfin chin and a compact body made of exquisite bony knobs. She still has a matching scar along her wrist, always hidden with a Slinky's worth of bangles. Her damaged left leg still moves like an afterthought. She hasn't lost her slippery smile, those tiny front teeth serrated like knives.

At every meeting, Jude tries to watch Violet as if she were prey, a thing Jude might have to disappear or put down. She imagines her arms locked around Violet's delicate vase of a throat. The heel of her hand could explode Violet's perfect nose. How easy it would be to make a hammer with her fist and find the sweet spot in the back of her gorgeous head. She tries to convince herself that Violet is not, even after all this time, the most stunning vision she has ever seen.

Jude loves her so much. She hates that she loves her. She hates that she'll never know if Violet loved her, too.

Violet's words are curt and laced with pain. She delights in making Jude hustle and scramble, working toward a goal that can never be reached. She had spent her entire childhood taking orders, and now it's her turn to issue them. Give her money, give her jewelry, give her time and forced attention, give her the satisfaction of watching Jude panic and flail. At their last meeting, Violet described her encounters with Kat—the phony canvassing, the pilgrimage to a fake psychic, the surprise confrontation at the Monkey Bar, right after Jude had left. And then another surprise: Sab, Kat's sweet, gullible boyfriend, had offered to pay off part of Jude's mounting debt.

"I don't like anyone interfering in our business," Violet had said. "Make her break up with him."

"I can't. Leave Kat out of this. What did she ever do to you?"

She knew the answer without Violet having to say it: Kat, through no fault of her own, was and always would be the most important person in Jude's life.

"You can and you will," Violet said, patting Jude's hand. "You're so good at betrayal, and even better at collateral damage."

Do it, Violet said, or else she will unravel the final strands of Jude's elaborate lie, and Kat would never speak to her again.

———

Jude finishes the last of her beer, closes the window against the city's raucous intrusion. She did not have much time. Wen had called her during work to report on Kat's unexpected visit, her questions and unspoken suspicions, and now Kat was on her way home. How Jude missed her sister, her *old* sister, Before Kat, keeper of her most potent fears and dangerous secrets. She loved After Kat just the same, but her sister had changed. With the loss of her memory came the loss of her identity, their shared identity, the dog-eared tally of the things that made them *them*. Jude could not be sure that Kat would understand the events from their recent past, or events that might yet come.

In order to betray Kat, she has to become Kat. She begins the work of transforming herself into her sister: changing the part of her hair; relaxing her expression; pushing her shoulders back and chest forward, as though eager to explore the world. Curious, friendly, trusting—too trusting. Someone who can never be allowed to discover what she is.

Jude tries to justify what she is about to do. She remembers the poem that their mother, Verona, taught them twelve years ago, on their eleventh birthday: two sisters who lived near the Goblin Market, under threat by wicked strangers, one risking her life to protect the other. She has protected Kat all their lives, and now it is Kat's turn to do the same for her. She betrayed Violet to save Kat, and now Kat must betray Sab to save Jude. Ultimately, this is fair. This is even. This is what needs to be done in order to preserve what they have, their mirror twin bond, so strange and so rare.

She picks up the phone and dials Sab's number. She remembers to coat her voice in After Kat's earnest tone.

One ring, two, and then he answers.

"Sab, it's Kat," Jude says.

"Hey! Did you make it back safe? How was the trip upstate? Learn anything interesting?"

His voice is equally earnest. They are made for each other. Jude presses her part down, securing it in place, and continues: "I'm sorry," she says. "I can't see you anymore."

"What?" Sab says. "Is this a joke? A twin thing? Jude, is this you?"

Jude reinforces her Kat costume. She allows a tear to fall, creates a crack in her voice.

"No, it's me. I'm sorry, but you came between me and my sister. You went behind my back to the loan shark and now Jude is in danger."

"What are you talking about?" he asks. Jude can sense his pacing around his room, his yanking on the phone cord, his desire to curse in Spanish. "I just wanted to pay off some of the debt. I gave that girl three hundred bucks."

"The money isn't the point," Jude says. "The point is that you inserted yourself into our business." She is openly sobbing now, channeling all the times she's heard her sister cry, the sound that still gives her nightmares she is unable to describe.

"Prove it," Sab says. "Prove this is you and not Jude."

Jude did not expect this. A cold panic tightens her chest. If she fails this test, Sab will tell Kat about this phone call. She dials down her sobbing just enough to ask, "How?"

He doesn't hesitate. "What's my name for my thing?"

The panic twists and coils, trapping her breath. She knows exactly what he means but she needs to buy time. "Your thing?"

"C'mon, *Kat*," he says, emphasizing the name. "You know what I am asking. My thing. My *dick*."

Jude halts the sobbing entirely; she needs that energy to concentrate. She knows the answer. During one of Kat's rambling soliloquies about her new self and her new life and all the miraculous ways the world is conspiring to fix her, she spun off on a tangent about Sab and how he made her feel and how it felt to feel him—physically *feel* him, his muscles and lips and on and on until Jude tuned her out, slipped a barrier between her ears and Kat's words. She had been happy for her sister, of course, but that happiness was tainted by pain and a seething envy; it seemed to Jude that nothing in the world would ever feel so extraordinary to her again. She hated herself for it, but sometimes she wished it was her own memory that had been erased.

"Butkus," she says. "After Rocky's dog. You named it right after the movie came out, and you thought 'the Italian Stallion' was too clichéd."

A bull's-eye. Total silence on the other end. She realizes that her answer is devastating either way. If he perceives her to be Kat, then the breakup is real. If he perceives her to be Jude, then he knows that nothing is sacred between him and Kat, that he will always be in a relationship with both Kat and her twin, that he will never have a true claim to Kat's heart, that his most private self is always at risk of being shared with the world.

"Okay, then," he says. His voice sounds low and sunken. "I've forgiven all your crazy shit and you're going to dump me just because I tried to help?"

Jude dials up the sobbing again and cracks her voice: "Coming between me and my sister is the one thing I can't forgive."

She senses that his pacing has stopped. He's standing still, looking in the mirror, asking himself how many times he is going to do this, this whirling routine of distancing and reconciliation, mental and even physical pain, around and around again for some psycho girl with a busted brain.

"I know you've been through a lot," he says finally. "But I can't do this anymore. No fourth chances, not even for you. Good luck with everything, your memory, your life. I hope you figure it all out."

The hum of the dial tone.

Jude keeps crying, even though she's turned back into herself.

KAT: NOW

Four Months after the Accident
JULY 1983

I see Jude briefly in the morning, and even though her face is caked in makeup, I can tell she'd been crying. It's allergies, she says. We've always had allergies; just wait, mine will be flaring up soon. I decide to believe her, more out of convenience than of true conviction; I have too many other questions to ask.

As soon as she leaves the questions trample through my mind, leaving indelible tracks: Who is Wen, exactly, and how does she fit into our lives? Did we really meet her in Europe? Did we go to Europe at all? And if we didn't, where have we been over the past five years? What have we done? Some illusions are comprised not of one big trick but a million little ones. How many sleights of hand went into passing off our life as truth? I want to ask Jude. I need to ask her. I am terrified to ask her. The simple voicing of a question risks incalculable damage—a thread or two undone, a few more split and frayed, a thorough and permanent unraveling.

I know that Sab is at work on a site, but I dial his number anyway and leave a message, promising a full report on the visit with Wen. I shower, the water at full heat, letting my head percolate in the steam. I dress and part my hair on my own correct side. Today I am myself, and I will get to the bottom of Jude.

———————

I park the car but stay behind the wheel, staring at the library's double doors. My body moves forward, walking past the fidgeting children, the sleeping old men, the couple kissing at a tucked-away table along the side wall. It moves toward the enclosed oval space in the middle of the room, where *Reference* is written in pretty cursive on a chalkboard. It moves toward the three women sitting at the desk, with the mom librarian adjusting the pencil in her bun.

"Can I help you?" she asks, and then recognizes my face. She seems delighted to see me again. "You! I was hoping you'd come by. I have the records you asked for."

She stands, her chair legs scratching harshly against the floor. "I'm sorry, miss, just remind me of your name?"

"Bird. Katherine Bird."

I watch her slim form, the shake of her hips, happy and confident, pleased to be of help. She reaches a shelf, scans the line of it with her finger, and pulls down an envelope. Smiling again, she walks toward me, and I take a step back. My mind flips between two choices: *Turn around and forget it. Choose to believe your sister and focus on your present.* Or: *Stay and learn if the memories she fed my mind are real. They have to be real. They have to be real or you are right back where this started, with no reliable knowledge of your past, no clear path for your future.*

"Here we go," she says, and retrieves two sheets of paper. "We couldn't get the originals, of course, but these will do." Her finger follows along a florid, barely legible print. "See, 415 Touchstone Road was built in 1873 by Abel Klassen, and there's a description of the dimensions . . ."

"How about any sales?" I ask. "Was it bought by another family later?"

She is staunchly cheerful. "We're getting to that," she says, and extracts the second sheet. "Here." She points. "Klassen's son sold it in 1932 to a man named David Sheridan, and then it was sold in 1957 to Joseph Rouse, and it's been in the Rouse family ever since."

The room swoons around me—the walls turning concave, the floor sliding beneath my feet, the librarian's face stretched and menacing. I hear my voice speaking in a strange pitch: "But that can't be, could you please check again? There must be another record of a sale to a John Bird, or Elizabeth Bird?"

My face must be telegraphing my panic and horror; she shakes her head gently, *No*, and apologizes, and asks if there might be anything else she could do. Somewhere in the middle of her sentence I feel myself tilt to the left, my hand grasping for something to hold, and my brain hurts, *oh god my brain hurts*, and I can't stop the rush of catastrophic thoughts.

Everything I've used to re-create myself, every single memory I've accepted as truth, no longer exists, and without them neither do I.

This time there is no room for nuance or doubt. Jude lied to me. She began lying as soon as I woke up and called her name.

My mind whiplashes through the past five months, replaying conversations, pausing to rewind certain words. I had questioned her, teetered on the edge of suspicion, but I never made the leap to the other side. She had used our twin bond as a weapon, soothing me in false ways. She lied because she thought I would never question her, that our singular relationship was immune to scrutiny. The very thing that connected us so fiercely also orchestrated its own demise.

I add another discovery to my new self: *I am a person who will never speak to my twin again.*

JUDE: THEN

Five Years before the Accident

JANUARY 1978

Six months after Jude sent Violet to the Big House, on the coldest day of the year, she and Kat crept from their cots in their adjacent homes and met on Rodman Street. They carried with them two changes of socks and underwear, five dollars each, and the knowledge that they were pretty, which they knew meant something, if not absolutely everything.

Jude had allowed herself to think of Violet but only for predetermined, allotted amounts of time: ten minutes one day, five the next, then maybe two or three, and back up to ten. She knew, no matter how hard she tried, she would never trim the time to seconds. It would never be nothing.

Reject and release, Jude told herself, but for once the tenet had no effect.

They began to walk, taking turns blocking each other from

the wind. Although 30th Street Station was a short distance from King Bash's and Mr. Ronald's houses, they had never been inside. It seemed an extension of the city, a transfer of the outside bustle and grit into a grand and vast old building, with soaring windows and gilded columns and intricate chandeliers that let Jude imagine, just for a moment, that they'd escaped to a royal palace instead of a train station.

They passed rank bodies sprawled across benches and a janitor pushing a broom and men with briefcases eager to be somewhere else. A large square monitor dominated the center of the station, broadcasting schedules for arriving and departing trains. Jude scanned the space. Amid a few boarded-up kiosks, she spotted a Puffs 'n Stuff bagel shop, an arcade filled with pinball machines, a bowling alley by the north terminal, and a waiting room called "The Chapel" for people in charge of transporting urns to their final destination.

"We stay right here," Jude said. "We have food, a bathroom, entertainment, heat. There are people coming and going—we could meet someone who has a job for us."

"Won't they kick us out?"

"We'll blend in. We'll move around. We'll become part of the background and no one will notice us at all."

"What if someone from The Plan comes looking for us?"

"King Bash and the RonDon have more important things to worry about," Jude said, but silently she shared Kat's concern.

For one week, it was nearly ideal. Travelers came and went, running to terminals, kissing goodbye, high heels clacking, cigarette smoke trailing behind. A surprising number of people dropped money from their pockets and hands. They reverted to their old eating habits from The Plan, stretching a single bagel into three meals. One night Jude allowed Kat to play a Star Wars pinball machine; she lost, but it was worth it to see her sister forget, for one moment, where she was and why. They performed dramatic readings of *Inquirer* reports about

President Carter and the oil crisis. They washed themselves at the sink. They soaked their underwear and hung it to dry over bathroom stalls.

They watched the space turn itself out at night, the commuters exiting and the homeless coming in, men and women and sometimes children, sprawling across benches and huddling in corners. They learned the unspoken rules: Do not touch anyone's stuff. It is legal to carry a machete if it is not hidden. Don't believe anyone who says they have your back. Three napkins make a decent maxi pad. Beware of people swinging tube socks filled with padlocks. It's only illegal if you get caught. They slept the way they did when they were young, foot to head, their bodies knitted together.

One night Jude made her way to the bathroom, where, reflected in the mirror, she saw a familiar face from the past: Cindy, the girl who had tattooed *THE PLAN* along her arm, who extolled the delights of living at the Big House, who told Jude she was free as a bird, free with nothing left to lose. She had the same choppy black hair but somehow seemed less glamorous than Jude remembered, like one of Verona's antique spoons left out to tarnish. She was taking turns applying lipstick and sucking on a joint, and she stopped doing both things when her eyes found Jude's.

"You remember me," Cindy said. She seemed flattered. "I'm supposed to be looking for you."

"Whose idea was this?" Jude asked. "Who sent you?" She took a step backward.

Cindy slammed her palm against the sink and laughed for half a minute; Jude counted the seconds.

"Please don't laugh," she said. "I'm serious."

"Relax, kid, I'm no narc. You can run away all you want. Like I give a shit. Just don't come running back and say that I let you go."

Jude exhaled and let herself lean against the grimy wall. She was tired, so tired.

Cindy took another long drag of her joint, and then held it out to Jude. She blew fancy curlicues of smoke, aiming them at the ceiling. "Want a toke?"

"No, thank you," Jude said. "But can I ask you a question?"

"Go."

"Have you seen Violet at the Big House? Violet, King Bash's niece? She got there six months ago."

"Of course I've seen her," Cindy said. She tossed the stub of her joint into the trash. "It was a whole big thing when she came."

Jude closed her eyes, trying to imagine pretty things—a rainbow, a garden, a non-feral dog, perfectly groomed. She had to ask. She was terrified to ask. "What is she doing there?"

Through the clouds of smoke she focused hard on Cindy's frosted pink lips. They parted, closed, and parted again, as though the channel kept changing inside Cindy's mind. "Don't worry," Cindy said. "She's free. Free as a bird, just like the rest of us."

Jude watched Cindy exit back onto 30th Street, the hard wind pushing her home.

I think Violet is okay, Jude thought. *And what I think, is.*

That tenet, too, had lost its power.

––––––––

Before daybreak on the thirteenth night, as they slept, Jude sensed a shadow creeping over them. The shadow smelled like sulfur and drooled on her forehead. She shook Kat awake, and Kat bolted upright. Her head connected with the shadow's chin. It reared up and roared, and when they began to run the shadow changed into the shape of a very large and fast man, whose spittle-flecked mouth shouted filthy things about what he would like to do to them.

Jude ran so fast she knocked the wind out of her own chest: down 29th Street, up 28th, her sister wheezing and huffing and crying,

Jude pulling at her hand, "Come on, Kat, come on." The shadow man's footsteps came harder and closer. He shouted his disgusting fantasies and breathed his hoarse and horrible breath. They zigged and zagged and backtracked. Jude thought she might vomit up her own heart. From just behind her came a terrible splat sound and a gasp, and she turned to find Kat flat on her chest. She looked past at her sister to see the shadow man closing the distance. She planted her legs and imagined herself as a tiny, mighty forklift and yanked Kat to her feet.

Again they ran. Under the glow of the streetlamps the asphalt looked like diamonds. The slap of their feet against the pavement morphed into the slap of skin against skin. They heard moans and grunts. They turned to see a pinwheel of arms and legs spinning and kicking. The shadow man bent over, the shadow man fell to his knees, the shadow man collapsed flat against the ground. The pinwheel went still, assessing her work, and then strolled to the corner. The streetlight revealed a familiar face.

"Jackie?" they asked in unison.

She looked so different than she had standing on the stage at The Plan's meetings, welcoming them all, encouraging them to give shape and color to their thoughts. Her long blond hair had been sheared nearly to her scalp and she seemed twice her normal size— not taller or heavier but thicker, the terrain of her body marked with sinewy muscle. Jude couldn't help herself; she scanned the street for Violet, hoping she'd come with her mother.

"Yes," Jackie said, "but I'm not that person anymore. My name is Ceridwen, but you can call me Wen."

KAT: NOW

Four Months after the Accident

JULY 1983

Back in our apartment I move with methodical precision, dividing everything by half: the clothes in our closet, the toiletries in our bathroom, the few bills hidden inside the shoebox beneath the bed. I put on my nameplate necklace and empty the curio cabinet of the things Jude claims belonged to our mother: the porcelain vase, the long gloves, the tin box, the dancer figurine, and six framed pictures, including the one of me and Jude at the antique carousel, posing as each other.

I pack everything in three grocery bags and set them by the door. Sab still hasn't called me back and I am dying to hear his voice and tell him everything I've learned: about Wen, about the house in Harmony, about Jude's lies and my next move. I know he's at work but I leave another message, keeping it short, telling him it's too much for the answering machine and we need to talk in person. A panic blooms low in my gut, telling me something's off, but I convince myself that he's just busy, working long days, and I will try him again from the road.

I make a list of Jude's confirmed lies, and my many questions:

We never lived in Harmony, Pennsylvania.

We never went to Europe, and instead were living with Wen— why? And doing what? And for exactly how long?

What were we doing on the night of the accident? Jude said we'd planned on dinner at a restaurant that reminded us of the Cotswolds— but we've never been to the Cotswolds.

Is she telling the truth about our parents? Did our father run off and disappear? Did our mother die in a car accident? If so, it couldn't have been in Harmony—so where?

And the question that sends a chill through every piece of me: Could it be that our parents are still alive?

I replay the conversation with Wen, pausing at the moment when she asked, *She hasn't found you, has she? . . . Isn't she still in Norris Ford?*

Had Wen been referring to Nancy, the loan shark, as she'd insisted? Or to someone else?

I pick up the phone again and dial information, asking for the address and number of the main library in Norris Ford. Before I head out I write Jude a note and leave it, along with the house records, on our table: *I wonk ouy dile. Tond yrt ot dinf em.*

I know you lied. Don't try to find me.

The library in Norris Ford is more elegant than the one in the neighborhood, with ivy creeping down a stone facade and tall windows that, on a brighter day, would lure in the light. At the reference desk, a girl my age has her head down, oblivious, reading a book titled *Hollywood Wives*.

I clear my throat once, twice, and on the third try she looks up.

"Sorry," she says. "I was in a juicy part."

I dig in the backpack for the carousel picture and ask, "This might be a long shot, but do you recognize that carousel?"

She looks it over, squinting, sticking out the tip of her tongue. "No, sorry," she says, handing it back. "But you might have better luck with some of the older librarians." She points to the far end of the room and says, "Rose has been here forever and knows everything."

I see her; she is a small figure in heels with cropped hair and the frenetic energy of a housefly, flitting back and forth down aisles and between shelves. I hold out an arm, stopping her midstep.

"Do you know this carousel?" I ask.

"Good morning to you as well, miss," she says.

"I'm sorry," I say. "This is urgent."

She blinks at me behind her glasses, waiting.

"Good morning," I say. "Now, the picture. That carousel was a very important part of my childhood, and I think it's somewhere here in Norris Ford, and I know it is almost impossible, but if you could help me identify it, you will be saving my life."

There's a worried look in her eyes; she fears I am unwell or crazy. I want to explain, but tears gather and my throat tightens, and all I can manage is, "Please?"

"*Shhh*," she says, rubbing my arm. "We'll try our best." She lifts the photograph from my hands, tracing the image of my face with her finger. "Fate has connected us today," she says, "because I grew up riding this very carousel myself."

I can barely squeak the words: "Where is it?"

"Well, it *used* to be on the road and all over the country. It was a featured attraction for the Benzini Brothers Greatest Show on Earth, a popular traveling circus during the Great Depression. But now it has a permanent home at the biggest antique market in the state. It's the first thing you see when you walk in."

"Name and address?" My heart ricochets with alarming force.

"It's called Pied Beauty. And it's just about ten minutes down the road."

With shaking hands, I pull out my map; she draws a line from here to there. "Good luck," she says. "I hope you find whatever you're looking for."

And there is the carousel, much grander in person than I'd imagined, with three rows of horses and a mirrored center pole that catches and throws the light; a dozen years earlier that mirror had reflected our faces, innocent and blithe. My face is different now, hardened by my accident and things I can't name, and it is Jude's face, hardened in the same way, that stares back at me.

Finding the carousel was only the first part of my mission, and I expect I might fail at part two. I walk toward the market's entrance, decorated with a large wrought iron trellis draped in riotous flowers and braided vines, like the front door to a fantastic and impossible dream. It leads straight into a field that resembles a long, outdoor garage, filled with furniture and oil paintings and jewels that look ransacked from ancient and exotic castles.

I stop at the first stall, where a table draped in ornate lace showcases rows of rings, all locked behind glass.

"Can I show you something?" a woman asks.

She's in her late forties, I would guess, about the same age my mother would be, and I stare impolitely at her face, gauging the angle of her cheekbones, the subtle cat-slant of her eyes. I think of the photo of our parents tucked away in my bag; this is not my mother. I don't dare hope that she's alive, but maybe someone here knew her—or me.

"This is a strange question," I say, "but do I look familiar to you?"

"What do you mean?" She steps closer.

"Do you know me? Have you ever met me before?" I want to scream: *Can you tell me who I am?*

"I'm sorry, I don't. I'm relatively new here. Do you need help? Are you unwell?"

"No," I say. "Unfortunately it's not as simple as that."

I move on. The space swells with heat and a sort of desperate energy—the banter and bartering, the boasting and fibbing, the exchange of bills from palm to sweaty palm. At the next table, I'm so mesmerized by a ruby ring that I forget to present myself and ask if I am known. I hold the ring up to squint at the stone, and from behind the counter comes a deep, foghorn gasp.

"Katherine?" a woman asks. "Katherine Sheridan? Is it really you? Or are you Judith?"

"I'm Katherine Bird," I say. "Do you know me?"

She bounds out from behind the table and takes my arm and leads me to the adjacent aisle, all the while shouting, "Verona! Verona!" using her cupped hand to amplify her voice. "Look who I found!"

From the far end of the long stall comes a figure racing toward me, great thumping steps gaining in force and speed, a frantic and solitary stampede. This strange woman reaches me and I feel the hot pant of her breath on my face. She is tall and broad with a lush mane of red hair and thick, rambunctious eyebrows and a fur coat the size of a volcano, absurd in this summer heat, and she whisks me to her chest with such vigor that I bang my forehead against her collarbone. She smells of smoke and sour candy and her voice is a baritone, speaking at me in deep, pleasing notes. "Katherine! My dear, darling Katherine! I have been searching for you for years. Oh, I feared you were dead."

I pry my forehead from her chest and gaze up at her. She says the words a mother would say, but she doesn't at all resemble the one in the photo, that dainty, tiny lady with the trim hair and frightened smile.

"I'm sorry," I say. "I'm not sure who you are?"

At this she laughs, a sound much deeper than her speaking voice, tinged with mischief and cunning. "Of course you do." Both hands now grip my shoulders, her dagger nails impaling my skin. "I'm your mother."

This stranger, my mother, awaits my reply, but my first thought is of Jude: even the picture of our parents was a lie.

Even my own last name.

KAT: NOW

Four Months after the Accident
JULY 1983

My mother weeps all the way home, fat tears blackened by mascara, carving tracks in her rouge. I had suggested following her in my car but she'd insisted—she hadn't seen me in years, she said, and she wanted to greedily gobble every single moment, and I could drive my car home from the market tomorrow. I sense, though, that she'd worried I might disappear again, either through nefarious means or my own volition, a long-awaited reunion thwarted before it truly began. I stare at my mother, still a stranger, and feel a surge of empathy, recognizing our intertwined predicaments: me, grieving the loss of my life with her; and her, preparing to rebuild it but somewhat begrudgingly, as though my brain had deleted her on purpose.

"Nothing?" she asks. Her arms shake against the steering wheel of her Cadillac sedan, making her sleeve of bracelets jingle and chime. "You remember absolutely nothing of me? Not one moment of the life I gave you?"

"I'm sorry," I say. My words sound tinny and flattened. "You have no idea how much I wish I remember you, and my childhood, and . . . everything. It's all gone."

With a bejeweled finger she swipes her right eye, making a war paint smear across her skin. "Well, we must get on with it, then," she says, and lifts my arm from my lap, giving it a shake. "We have plenty of time to relearn each other."

Her tone—not begrudging at all—surprises me, as though she views this relearning not as a burden but an opportunity.

"What is your name?" I ask, trying to keep my voice neutral.

"Verona. But use it at your own risk—I only answer to Mom."

She winks, her long, thick lashes a magician's wand, weaving her spell.

———

For the next five minutes, we ride silently. I stare at her profile and can't believe I came from such a fantastic creature, whose every word, gesture, and feature seems imbued with a strident grandeur: the towering height, the fortress of hair, the delicately humped nose, the gauzy blouse and abundant breasts, the enormous but elegant feet (encased, naturally, in sequined slippers), the baubles and bangles, the conspirator's laugh, the carnival barker's command of the room, the exotic bird flutter of her hands. We arrive at a home that rivals any of those Jude cleaned on the Main Line, an expansive facade of silver stone adorned with hanging vines and accented by two cupolas at either end. "Is this where I grew up?" I ask. I think of Jude, alone in our dank apartment, and I almost feel sorry. *She did this to herself,* I think. *In taking my old life away from me, for whatever reason, she managed to send me right back to it.*

"Of course it is, my angel. You were so happy here, and you will be again."

I hear the dog before I see it, deep, throaty barks flatten into a snarl. "Wallis, come!" my mother says. The dog bounds toward us and presses her head against my mother's hands, commanding her to scratch. She's longer than she is tall, with a thick, wide head, and a mix of glossy black and brown fur.

"Wallis?" I ask.

"Her full name is Wallis Simpson, after the wife of King Edward VIII. She's a vicious one—both the wife and the dog—but she'll attack only when I give the command. She's a Rottweiler and I had her specially trained. I suppose you have forgotten all of this, too, but the human Wallis is a cousin on my father's side. Unfortunately, her mind checked out well before her body, the poor thing. She sees no one, speaks to no one. When the king died some of her things ended up in this very house, for a steal." She treats the dog's belly like a harp, running her fingers in long, quick strokes. "Is that terribly ghoulish of me?" In the next second she answers for me. "Oh, Verona," she chides herself. "Katherine does not want to hear about distant cousins right now."

"Katherine doesn't mind," I say, hoping to make her laugh. "But she might prefer to start with more recent and personal events."

"Of course, dear," she says, serious. "You live alone long enough, and your speaking patterns start to revolt."

The decor seems deliberately scattershot, collected from every century, and is arranged in such proximity that every step might trigger an avalanche of vintage treasures: teetering grandfather clocks; nude statues of fat cherubs; busts of once-famous men with imperious expressions. The walls are filled with portraits of a young woman in various seductive poses on a beach, a tractor, a chaise longue, a swing, the hood of an old-fashioned car.

"Pardon the brewing caldron," my mother says. "The cleaning lady is due to come, one of these days."

An absolutely horrid, wicked part of me wishes it could be my sister. I push Jude from my mind and point to the portraits. "These are of you?"

"Yes," she says, a bit wistful. "A previous iteration of me. I was a model for a few years. I traveled all over Europe, met so many clever people, chipped away at my dreary facade until I discovered the brilliant gem beneath. I even found my name there, Verona. My favorite city. 'Very Sherry, Quite Contrary,' they called me, because I inhabited so many moods."

She does a little twirl, one long leg extended backward, dancing with an invisible partner.

"What was your original name?" I ask.

"Harmony. Harmony Sheridan," she says. "The town where I grew up and ran away from. I just traded one place name for another."

Harmony. I think of our birthday trip—the ice cream shop, the old farmhouse, the dead rabbit—and the realization hits: Jude didn't give me our history; she gave me Verona's history, at least in part, stealing from one life to construct another.

"What was my father's name?" I ask.

"Grant Smith. Could anything be duller than Smith? I never took it. I had already changed my name once and wasn't keen to do it again, and one of my marital conditions was that our children be Sheridans."

Leading me through a labyrinth of hallways, Verona gives me a grand tour. The house is large—seven bedrooms, three baths, attic and basement, and various hidden nooks—but the overall effect is of a space curling into itself, desperate to protect what it hides. We pause at the room I shared with Jude, my side done in pink and hers in a rich indigo—our choices, she says. There's something odd about it beyond the lack of photographs, beyond the ruffles and frills and explosions of girly splendor; this is a room frozen in a specific time and age, a room that, at a key point in our lives, stopped being the place where we wanted to sleep. I know this: my sister would not abide a shelf of china dolls and music boxes and hair barrettes festooned with streaming ribbons. I slide the closet door open and confirm my assumptions. There's a rack of clothes—jeans, dresses, shirts—all stuck at age nine or ten, before the time when our moods and dreams and outlooks would change, and our bodies along with them.

"You had other, more mature clothes and things, of course," my mother says, noting my confusion. "I rotate items around frequently, sell things, give things away. Once a year the neighborhood association does a holiday tour of all the, quote, *historically significant* homes on the block. So that's always in the back of my mind, who might be coming and going. This house is a roving museum of junk, some of it rather precious—in the monetary sense, of course, not the sentimental one."

I lie down on the bed and close my eyes and try to imagine calling this space my own. I wonder if this scratchy taffeta bedspread felt softer back then, and if I stood at the arched window to guess the constellations, and if I ever threw a tantrum and slammed the door.

"Come," she says, beckoning me from the doorway. Her long, waving fingers look like wind chimes. "I think it's high time for a tipple or two."

Back in the kitchen she makes black tea, pulling the kettle from the burner just before it whistles. The image makes me think of Sab and anger management class, the lesson in cooling down before you boil over. I wonder if he's called me back, eager for a report on Wen, completely unaware that I have left the apartment and Jude, that my mother is alive and I've found her. I want to call him now, but decide it's better to wait until later, when my mother is asleep and I am alone.

We sit at the table and she pours a healthy glug of rum into her cup. "I know it's early, but the circumstances warrant it, don't you agree?" I agree and match her pour. We start sentences at the same time, our questions crashing into each other: "What happened with Judith—Where have you been?—What was wrong with my father?"

We laugh, and so far it feels natural, easy.

"You first, darling," she says. "You must have so many questions."

"How did my father die?" I ask. "And when?"

She twists the bracelets along one arm, considering her words. "Well, this is rather difficult, but I'm not sure what happened to him. He left us in the spring of '71 I believe. You girls were about eleven. He just went out one night and never came back."

She goes quiet, her words heavy in the air between us. I take some solace in knowing that Jude was at least truthful about this aspect of our lives.

"Did we ever hear from him again?" I ask. "Did we get the police involved?"

"I filed a report, but the police weren't much help. If a grown man wants to disappear, there's not much they can do about it." She picks up her cup, sighs, puts it back down. "His brain was . . . off," she says. "It was off in the most brilliant of ways. He was an inventor, did you know?"

I remember Jude mentioning that fact, pulling me into her lap and twisting my hair, making the memories real for me. "I do know, but I have no details. I mostly heard about our simple life on a farm."

"Well, I lived on a farm as a girl, but never dreamed of subjecting you two to such drudgery. He had a veritable lab down in the basement, all sorts of flaming potions and copper appendages and things that made inhuman sounds." She closes her eyes slowly, her lashes taking a bow.

"Was he a good father?"

"You're stirring up so many old ghosts," she says. "I can hear them all whispering and cackling in my brain." She takes another long sip, and something about her seems older when she sets her cup back down; her shoulders sag and a pair of arrow-like lines appear above her brows, pointing at each other. "Yes, your father was a good father, and we all loved him very much, and he us. Sometimes, when he was sick, you and I and Judith would guide him into bed so he could rest and reclaim himself. You two would hold his hands and I his beautiful egg of a head, and you could just see all the ideas sparking and crackling. The last time he left us, we three held vigils once a week, lighting candles and using the power of our minds to summon him back."

Silently I take inventory of what I've been told, and what I now know to be fact. The history Jude gave me seems a mix of truth and lies and borrowed bits, as carefully curated as the antiques in this very home. I remember the curio cabinet back in our apartment, the shelves lined with old family mementos. "Hold on," I tell my mother. "I have some things to show you."

I fetch my bags and arrange everything on the table in one long line. My mother takes her time assessing each item, holding the vase up to the light, opening the tin, pulling on a silky glove, smiling at the missing fingers.

"Did any of these things belong to you?"

"Not a one," she says.

I add another lie from Jude to my growing tally. "How about the pictures? Are these of us, our family?"

She looks through all of them, shaking her head. She comes to the beach photo with the caption: *BIRD FAMILY VACATION, WILDWOOD, 1969.*

"Obviously we were not the *Bird* family—where did that name come from? And Wildwood? Oh no, sweet angel." She laughs, a booming base that, if amplified, could make the furniture jump. "I'd sooner have taken you girls to play in the detritus of Three Mile Island." She ends with the photo of me and Jude at the carousel. "Now, *this* I recognize—the majestic old carousel outside of the market. This was your birthday—the eleventh, I believe—and it was right before I took you to your first lesson at your new school."

"Where was this school, and what was it like?"

"Oh my," she says. "You are as curious as you ever were. You were in a specially curated program in the most exclusive neighborhood in Philadelphia along with other kids whose parents didn't trust the system. It was rigorous, diverse, wonderful. You weren't cooped up in a classroom all day—you learned outside. We took trips to interesting places. You had dynamic, interactive lessons. It was an excellent education that made you into smart, tough girls. You two could handle any situation in which you found yourselves."

"What sort of lessons?" I ask. "And what sort of trips?"

She tops off our tea, finishing the rum, and continues. "We were part of a revolutionary movement back then. The idea was that children flourished most spectacularly if you didn't treat them as children, engaging in baby talk and nonsense games and permitting endless hours of television. So we all moved into the city and occupied numerous row houses, autonomous but connected. We developed a curriculum designed to stimulate your budding brains. Classic literature and poetry, games of strategy, tests of endurance and cunning. We had annual retreats at a place called the Island where you did scavenger hunts that fostered a competitive spirit and encouraged initiative and independence. All activities that would serve you well in the real, adult world. And look, it worked so well that you and Jude felt entitled to leave me without even a soupçon of a farewell."

I feel a stab of guilt at her words, at all of my forgotten transgressions. "Do you have any idea why we left?"

"I do not. I woke up one day and discovered that you two were gone. You can imagine the absolute utter devastation and anguish that besieged me. I did not feel human for years. I in fact did not feel human until I spotted you at the antique market, looking for all the world like an angel dropped from the sky."

"Why would Jude go so far as to say you were dead?"

My mother tilts her head back, draining the last of her teacup, the sharp knob of her throat sliding behind her skin. "I haven't the slightest idea why. I can only imagine that you two fell victim to some odious forces, and it is my eternal regret that I did not foresee this happening and intervene. So I am sorry, my treasure. I only wish your sister were here so she could also witness my contrition." A tear appears at her right eye and she dabs it with the pad of her pinky. "Forgive me, I didn't mean to dissolve into hysterics."

"You haven't," I say. I imagine Jude in this room, listening to this conversation, seeking a way to bend it to her own personal truth. "And let's move on. I've come to accept that there are some questions I'll never have answered. And maybe those little gaps, those bits of mystery, are better for me in the long run."

"That's a lovely way to put it," she says, and covers my hand with her own. Her skin is warmer now, and flushed. "I have an idea, but it requires more fortifications." She holds up the empty rum bottle. "Pardon me a moment."

She leaps from her chair and does a belly-dancer shimmy across the room, her movements fluid and ethereal despite her size. I can imagine her in another time and setting, twirling from man to man, defying anyone to look away. I wonder what Jude and I thought of her when we were younger, and lacked any capacity to understand how adults move through the world: were we proud, amused, embarrassed? She returns holding a silver platter carrying a quartet of scones, another bottle of rum, and a small, primitive stone statue of a naked woman, her body round and robust, her hands clasping her head. "Age and provenance unknown," she says. "Of the scones, I mean. Hopefully they won't crack your teeth."

"What's the statue?" I ask.

She pushes it toward me, cupping the head with her hand. "She's Mnemosyne, the Greek goddess of memory. I acquired her on a whim from a shop about a few months ago, perhaps not too far from the day you had your accident. What a prescient purchase! You might think it silly, but I believe we have more power over our minds than we know. It takes time to acknowledge this truth because it's an uncomfortable one. Imagine going through life without utilizing your own power to shape that life. Your thoughts can become your reality. Do you understand?"

I take a sip of rum, wishing it were water. I think about pouring myself a glass but I don't want to disrupt her; she is entranced by her own words and it is a singular sight—her long legs fidget and her hands whisk about the stone head and her eyes squeeze shut, as though she is witnessing a miracle no one else can see. After thirty seconds it passes, and she relinquishes the statue and opens her eyes and sets them upon me, waiting, expectant.

"Here," she says softly. "Take her, hold her. Rub her head with your favored hand."

I do as she says.

"I'm going to share a few memories, and I want you to imagine them as I speak them. Imagine them with all the power of your mind—fire up those synapses, spark those connections, let the different parts of your brain speak among themselves. The brain is so mysterious, so untapped. It contains its own trap doors and secret rooms."

"My doctor said as much, but in more medical terms," I tell her. "When I woke up they were astounded that the only things I remembered were Jude's name and face. They'd never seen it before and didn't understand how it could be possible. I concluded that our brains never truly separated, that there's an invisible wire that runs between us, transmitting and receiving each other's thoughts."

My mother is listening so intently that she attempts to mouth my words as I speak them, her lips lagging three syllables behind. "I always envied the connection you had," she says, and takes a long drink. "It was so powerful that it frightened me. Sometimes I hoped it would break or at least weaken, just so you both could let me in a bit more. Your lives were so full of each other there was hardly room for anyone else."

My eyes cloud; I bite my lip and blink back tears. I remind myself how angry I am with Jude; her dense, elaborate lies have severed that connection. A disquieting thought skitters across my mind: What if I'd remembered Jude not out of love and our shared twin connection, but out of terror? What if recognizing her name and face was my brain's way of warning me?

"Well!" my mother says breezily. "Let's not get so maudlin, and instead focus on our powerful and bountiful Mnemosyne. Rub her head as I showed you, and I'll tell you a memory. It's an important one, depicting a turning point in your lives when you two came into your own. You were just learning to harness and exploit your power."

"Sounds intense," I say, and begin to rub the head. "Tell me more."

She closes her eyes again, falling back into her private trance. "We were on one of our retreats at the Island. And when we arrived, you were so excited to take charge and lead the other kids in the games we all played. I remember you and Jude preferred dressing up like monkeys, because they're the smartest animals. You became a leader and all the kids looked up to you—the rabbits, the scorpions, the chameleons. Your mind achieved astonishing feats of power, minimizing challenges and transcending perfection. All this, while you were having fun at the most magical carnival in existence." She pauses to catch her breath. "Do you see any of it, Kat? Can you see yourself in the monkey suit? Running and chasing and emboldening your spirit? Can you see how adored you were? Can you remember anything about this, one of the most exciting and happiest times of your life?"

My palm is hot from its friction against Mnemosyne's head. I try to conjure every image she describes and I tell myself I am almost there, that the nascent bud of a memory has implanted itself and begun to grow, and my brain is throwing sunlight to coax it along. But it's all abstract: I'm younger, flailing about in a dime-store costume, but it's not connected to any experience. I'm running, I'm laughing, I'm chasing—but where and who and why? I hear applause, I see approving faces—but not why they're clapping or how I pleased them. I grow frustrated and switch the light off; I don't want to picture anything I don't recognize as true. I stop rubbing the statue and take my mother's hand.

"I'm sorry, Mom," I say. "None of this is coming back to me. Your descriptions are vivid, and I believe this memory exists, but it doesn't exist for me."

She returns my squeeze, and her skin cools mine down. "Don't worry, darling. This is your first day back home and I've pushed you terribly hard. We have all the time in the world to dig around that brilliant mind of yours, to uncover whatever secrets it holds. You will remember your wonderful life, I promise you."

I am about to respond, to tell her no harm done, but am stopped by the expression taking shape on her face: regret and wistfulness and, in the deepest part of her oil-slick eyes, the smallest spark of relief.

JUDE: NOW

Five Months after the Accident
AUGUST 1983

It has been three days since Kat left and returned to their previous life, unwittingly weaving herself back into all their old entanglements and dangers.

Jude had noticed the missing items from the curio cabinet, including the photographs of the carousel and the fake parents, and concluded that Kat had gone in search of their past. Verona was the type of person who longed to be found, and Kat the type to persist until she found her.

She had dialed Verona's phone number and was so shocked to hear Kat's singsong *hello* that she could say nothing in response. For ten seconds there was silence, and then her sister spoke with devastating calm: "Jude, I told you I do not want to be found." *Click.* When she tried again the next day, a mechanical recording informed her that the number had been disconnected.

Verona is no doubt rewriting history into a narrative Kat will believe, something lighthearted and harmless, without any hint of the events that led them to escape.

Jude hides behind the knobby trunk of an old oak tree, a knife in her pocket, a fist pressed against her heart. She can't look at the house, but she must. She can't approach it, but she must. She has no idea how she is going to rescue Kat and restart their lives yet again, but she must.

She forces herself to peer around the tree and confront the old house, which remains just as ominous to her as the now-empty row homes in the city; it is the place where she last saw her father, bloody in the doorway, and where Verona and King Bash and the RonDon started The Plan, and where she and Kat had abandoned their childhood, never to recover it again. At this hour, just before midnight, the ivy that wraps around its shingled facade looks more constricting than cozy; and the stone roof, with its chipped and missing shingles, is a murderer's row of crooked teeth; and the dueling dormer windows that squint happily in daylight have become hooded eyes in a vacant face.

Reject and release.

She thinks about the farmhouse in Harmony, the bloodied rabbit in the driveway, the strangers behind the door. She thinks of the visit she made to Harmony while her sister was in the hospital, a weekend of fevered reconnaissance, visiting the ice cream shop and memorizing landmarks and gathering all the minutia that might constitute a life. She'd borrowed as much of Verona's childhood as she could—the actual house where their mother grew up, the park where she'd played—and used fiction to color in the rest. She wishes now that she'd had more time, more foresight. She wishes she'd picked a town in California or Idaho or along the coast of Florida, somewhere out of Kat's reach, a place too far for secret library visits, for inquiries about house records and deeds. The details Jude had gathered to make their history sound true succeeded only in exposing each lovely, curated lie. She'd needed so badly for Kat to believe, and to transfer that belief somehow, through twin magic, to herself.

Her real childhood home gazes back at her, waiting, daring her. It is time.

She enumerates her actions, divorcing them from the task at hand, rendering them less than the sum of their parts. She is touching the wrought iron gate, which is merely a gate. She is unlatching the lock, which is just a lock. The swish of her feet through the grass is just a pleasant, everyday sound. She approaches the house, which is just a house, it really, *really*, is just a house, a house where her sister believes she is safe. There is the window of the bedroom they'd shared before Verona dropped them off in the city, leaving them with monsters who called themselves kings. A soft yellow light pushes through the glass, and Jude senses her sister moving behind it.

She stays close to the hedges, aligning herself flush against the side of the house, allowing her body to be absorbed in the shadows of other things. Her pocket flashlight illuminates a path of pebbles weaving along potted plants and rose bushes. She scoops up a handful of them, and pelts one at the window. And another and another.

She sees the outline of her sister's head. The window creaks as Kat opens it.

"Kat!" Jude whisper-screams. "Please come down and listen to me! You're not safe there! Ehs si yingly ot ouy!" *She is lying to you.* "I only lied to protect you! Okol ni het des—"

She stops before finishing the sentence. From somewhere along the other side of the yard comes a growl, low and vicious. The growl climbs an octave, changing shape, and finalizes itself as a bark—a bark with desperate urgency, signaling an imminent attack.

A dog.

For one interminable second Jude sees her sister's face, Kat's features coming into sharp focus, her eyes empty of any connection.

Jude begins to run.

The dog bounds toward her; she senses its heat at her heels. She thinks of her switchblade. She will turn and impale its throat if she feels the pinch of its teeth. It lunges, its huge jaws clamping at air, and she sprints faster and faster until she crashes though the back fence, latching it behind her just in time. Then comes the bang of the dog's thick body against the wood, its snarling now infused with a disappointed whine, dense stalactites of drool wetting the ground.

Jude sprawls across the grass, waiting for her breath to return, the image of her sister's vacant eyes imprinted on her mind. When she glances back she sees that the house has snuffed out every light, gathering its darkness within.

KAT: NOW

Six Months after the Accident
SEPTEMBER 1983

I had not realized the depth of my exhaustion until I fell onto my childhood bed and slept for the better part of a week. Verona stayed home from the Pied Beauty antique market and doted on me, leaving tea and toast by my bedside during the day and bringing me hot toddies at night. By mutual, unspoken agreement, neither of us asked questions. Jude was not mentioned. Mnemosyne stayed on her shelf.

On the eighth morning, this morning, my mother decides I have recuperated enough. I awaken to find her standing at the door, a plate in her hands. She hopes I slept; we have an incredibly busy day ahead of us and an equally busy night, considering we've made only the slightest dent in catching up on our lives. "I went on a rigorous expedition in the fridge and came up with enough eggs for an omelet," she says. "Eat, and then we'll head to the market. When you were a girl it was like your second home, and you'll see so many familiar faces and sights, and you'll start feeling like you know yourself again."

After I shower, I stretch the phone from my mother's bedside to her bathroom, the cord fully unraveled and taut. I lock the door and dial Sab's number. It's early, around six in the morning, and I hope I've caught him before he's left for work. One ring, two, three, and then his familiar *hello*, soft but hurried.

"Hey," I whisper. "It's me. Did you get my message? This is the first chance I've had to call since I found out that—"

"Kat," he says, "I don't know what sort of epiphany you've had this time, but I don't have time for it. You're in, you're out, you're in, you're out, back and forth. And it was never just me and you. It was me and you and Jude, and I don't like crowds. Take care of yourself and all that, but now *I'm* out."

"What?" I ask, but the dial tone drones in my ear. His words settle, and I feel the cold weight of them, their depth and heft. Quickly I call back and get nothing but rings; he must have disconnected his machine just to avoid hearing my voice. I begin to cry, a crying that is wrapped up in both Sab's shocking words and Jude's list of lies, and I wonder if she had something to do with his change of heart, if there are betrayals of which I am not yet aware.

"Katherine?" my mother calls. "Are you okay?"

I wipe my eyes and blow my nose and try to sweep Sab's words away, rewinding our relationship back to the beginning, to the time when he was just a prop in my performance as a normal twenty-two-year-old, a tool that helped me recalibrate myself. Jude's old advice creeps into my mind—*reject and release, reject and release*—and silently I thank her for that gift, the very last one I'll allow her to give.

———

One hour later I'm inside Verona's stall at the market, arranging the new merchandise, preparing to sell. She hands me pieces and directs me with adamant specificity: No, that chandelier must hang *this* way, to catch the light. Do put a pillow over that tear in the leather club chair, will you? Someone will fall in love with it before spotting its flaws. We do not arrange the jewelry by gemstone, but by era—do we want people to think we're heathens? And on and on, until every item is displayed to maximum brilliance, and the trickle of shoppers turns into a bustling crowd.

"Where does the name 'Pied Beauty' come from?" I ask. "And did you always work here?"

"From a Gerard Manley Hopkins poem," she says, "praising God's beautiful creations. But the name was here long before me. I much prefer Hopkins's Terrible Sonnets—'O what black hours we have spent,' 'cries like dead letters sent'—et cetera, et cetera. All those dark images just illuminate how bright my own life has been. And yes, when I came back to the States, I started to work here, and continued to do so until you enrolled in your special school. Pied Beauty is the state's oldest and largest collection of fine antiques, mostly curated from markets in Europe, and it's an honor to be here again."

Come in, come in, she tells prospective buyers. Try out this velvet settee, isn't it marvelous? According to lore it once belonged to Gertrude Stein during her heyday in Paris, and that chandelier over there once hung in the Everleigh Club, the most famous brothel in the world, and here is a mirror that once belonged to Gladys Spencer-Churchill, Duchess of Marlborough, who ruined her flawless face with botched plastic surgery and became a recluse. Tell me, ma'am, tell me, sir, how can I make your life a bit more interesting today?

After two hours of steady traffic the crowd thins again, breaking for lunch.

"Are you hungry?" I ask her. "I can walk down to Main Street and bring something back."

She reaches for her wallet but is distracted by someone or something over my shoulder. "Richard!" she calls, and waves her hand. "Come over!"

I turn to see a man walking toward us, handsome in the opposite way to Sab. He's my mother's contemporary but a few years younger, or maybe he works hard to appear as such, and even from a distance I can appreciate the beauty of his features, all the angles and curves fused in perfect symmetry. He moves with the bold assurance of an exclamation point, torso bent forward and arms swinging, the gait of a man who has never been lost in his life. He wears a white linen suit over an aqua T-shirt and a vintage sort of hat, pulled low enough to shadow his face. Up close, I can see his eyes are a startling, nearly translucent shade of blue.

My mother grips his shoulders and kisses him on both cheeks. "Richard, *mon loup*, surely you remember my brilliant daughter, Katherine?"

Remember? I think, and then the obvious hits me. *I've met him before; I've known many people at this market for years.*

"Of course I do," he says. He has a sandpaper voice, low and pleasingly rough. "Although the last time I saw you, I was going by a different name. It's been, wow, how many years—four or five? I know you've had your mother worried sick for quite some time." He shakes my hand, squeezing before he releases it.

"As I mentioned, she only just came back," my mother says, and pets my head. "So let's be a bit easy on her. She has been through quite an ordeal."

"What my mother means is that I was in an accident," I say. The crowd is gathering again, and I take a step closer to make myself heard. "I have suffered some memory loss, so that's why I didn't recognize you."

"So I've heard," he says. I shoot a silent question at my mother—*when and why did you tell him this, instead of leaving it up to me?*—but she is looking only at Richard, smiling an oddly bright smile. "What a shock," he adds. "I truly don't know what to say . . . Perhaps I'll be of some help, as I have some vivid memories of you and your sister." He turns to my mother. "Did Judith come back, too?"

"She hasn't," I say quickly, before my mother can respond. "It's a difficult situation and I'd rather not talk about it right now, if you don't mind."

"My apologies," he says. "I didn't mean to bring up a sore spot."

"You didn't know," I say, and change the subject. "What do you sell in your stall?"

"A variety of antique bric-a-brac," he says. "But mostly rare magazines, rare coins, rare guns. If you ever want to time-travel back to the Wild West or start a new life as a Prohibition gangster, I'm your guy."

I smile. "Well, it seems I have a thing for self-reinvention, so I'll keep that in mind."

"As do I," he says. "And you're always welcome to stop by."

As I talk I realize I've been staring intently at his left eye; there's something peculiar about the way it sits in his face, as though it's leaning forward slightly in its socket, and the color is one shade darker than his right.

He senses my question. "I had a terrible altercation," he says. "I'm lucky this is all I lost." I don't understand what he means, until I do. He rolls his right eye vigorously in its socket while the left remains immobile, fixed intently on my face without seeing it at all.

———————

That night, my mother sets the statue of Mnemosyne on the table and we play the game she now calls Mind Fishing: as she provides a memory, I use her words to cast about in my brain and hope something bites.

"You used to love to ride on your father's bicycle built for four," she begins, lighting a cigarette. She takes a drag and twirls the sleek holder between her fingers.

Nothing.

"You begged me to read to you every night, sometimes two or three books in a row."

Nothing.

"Once you used the power of your mind to try to make the toaster fly and ended up with a broken toe."

Nothing. I can watch her descriptions as though they're scenes in a movie, but they remain flat and one-dimensional. I push the statue away and say, "Let's talk about something more interesting."

She stabs out her cigarette and takes a sip of scotch, itself an antique opened just for the occasion. From a distant corner of the room comes the *ah, ha, ha, ha* refrain of "Stayin' Alive," apparently my favorite song around the time I disappeared.

"I'm listening," she says. "Pitch me."

"Tell me about Richard." I refill my own glass. "He made it sound like I've known him for years. Where did we meet him?"

She closes her eyes. "Richard," she repeats. "We met when you girls were about eleven, I think. He inquired about opening a stall at Pied Beauty, and you eventually made friends with his niece." Her voice has picked up a languid quality, taking its time with her words, and I can't tell if she's remembering or inventing. "We had the same interests—antiques, philosophy, psychology, the miracle of the human mind. We shared a goal of creating a different ideal."

"So he wasn't Dad's friend, too?" I ask. Wallis comes strutting in from the kitchen and drops herself onto my mother's feet.

"Your father didn't have friends," she says, and reaches down to scratch the dog's ears. Wallis yawns, baring scissorlike fangs. "Well, he did when we first got married, but then he disappeared into himself. He would rather go toil and tinker in the basement than engage with a live person. I could go down to that basement and tap dance naked—in fact, I believe I once did—and still he would not look up from his portable masticator or whatever the masterpiece du jour. There should be a law against that, taking vows as one person and then changing into another."

As someone who's changed in ways that remain unknown, I don't know how to answer. I feel a peck of sympathy for Jude, imagining the divide between who I'd been and who I'd become, the hard work required to bridge the two. My mother extracts another cigarette from her case and waits for me to light it, giving me time to respond.

"So did you . . ." Some strange allegiance to my father prevents me from asking the question.

She sucks on her cigarette, making her cheeks go concave, and puffs a trio of smoke rings that linger like crowns over her head. "Did we what?" she asks.

"You know . . ." I say. I mash my hands together in a sad attempt at X-rated puppetry.

"Make the beast with two backs? Engage the services of Venus? Dance the Paphian jig?" With just the slightest shift of tenor and tone, she transforms our chat into an interrogation. She takes another drag, smiling as she puffs.

I give up, letting my hands rest on the table. "I don't know what any of those things mean," I tell her, "but I'm sure you know exactly what I'm asking."

She tilts her head back, laughs her hungry laugh. "They're just historical euphemisms, darling. There's no reason for you to know what they mean, at least not now. You used to love sophisticated wordplay, but I suppose I must get used to the fact that you're now a different you."

My face goes hot. I want her to talk to me in her familiar old patterns. I do not want to require edits and deletions. I don't want reminders that I'm a second draft, hastily rewritten. I focus on the grandfather clock ticking behind her shoulder, on the far side of the room, keeping my eyes wide open so the tears don't fall.

"Oh, Katherine," she says. She drags her nails along the top of my hand, tickling my skin. "I was just having some fun. I know I should ease into things slowly, but forgive me, that's never been my style. And I owe you an answer, and the answer is yes—but only after your father left for good. Things were different a decade ago, people were freer. Rules were more lax, or didn't exist at all. But those years are long gone now, and Richard is just a colleague and friend. He changed along with everyone else."

I blink and let the tears fall and decide I don't care. Her nails dig harder, finding the grooves in my knuckles. I can't let myself think of that long, empty stretch of time, now cluttered with other people's memories, and I pivot again: "What happened to Richard's eye? Did they catch whoever attacked him?"

"I don't know," she says. "He's as private as you are about certain things." She reaches for Mnemosyne and pulls the statue to her chest. "You're tired, darling," she says. "Let's not end the night with unpleasant thoughts. Let's go to bed and start fresh in the morning." She kisses the top of my head. "I love you, my angel."

"I love you, too, Mom," I tell her.

She pads off and starts up the stairs when I remember one last question: "What is Richard's old name?"

She answers without turning around, her robe trailing behind her. "Sebastian. We called him Bash."

Bash, I whisper to my head, hoping the name might jostle an old memory.

Nothing.

I hear water splashing, cabinet doors banging, the click of Wallis's toenails against the wood floor, and then, finally, my mother's rattling snore, the one that signals she'll be dead to the world until sunrise.

The house has two staircases to the third floor, one traditionally used by household servants and the other by the residing family, and I take the one farthest from my mother's bedroom. I pull a chain by the attic door and a dim light fills the space. It resembles one of the markets at the stall, with long tables covered in jewelry, each piece tagged and labeled: country of origin, era, price. A congregation of mannequins wears mink stoles and brimless hats stippled with rhinestones. One treasure chest preserves a host of medical instruments and random curiosities which, too, are labeled: antique syringes, walking sticks, leech jars, dental pliers, a vaginal speculum. Another holds what I assume are antique sex toys—small devices with cranks and motors and bullet-shaped tips and one contraption that looks like a baking mixer. At the bottom there's stacks of a vintage magazine titled *Sexology*, each issue encased inside a plastic sheet. I find nothing that will answer any of my questions.

I want photographs. I want irrefutable proof of a moment from my life that hasn't been altered by anyone's subjective memory or grudges or desire to edit history.

On my way out of the attic I pick up a flashlight hung on the wall by the door. I lift and lower my feet as lightly as possible, not wanting to disturb either my mother or Wallis, but then sneeze a cloud of dust. I stop halfway down the stairs, waiting for my mother's voice, but her snores continue without pause. I sense another sneeze coming on, and clamp my mouth together until I venture back through the kitchen and reach the rear door of the house.

The air makes me feel alert and alive, free from the house's heavy history. I decide to take a walk along the vast property and let myself get lost, eventually coming to a small grove, the branches of the tallest trees scratching at the moon. I count fifty more steps until I reach a row of high hedges that form a fortress wall. I walk around and find a gash in the hedges, just wide enough to fit a simple wooden gate, set off the ground by two stone steps.

For some reason I think of Jude at our old window, speaking our private language. The words she scream-whispered just before Wallis came bounding after her, the words of warning she begged me to heed: "Okol ni het des . . ." *Look in the . . .* Her last word was cut off, and my mind spins the possibilities, trying to finish her thought.

My heart quickens as I approach the steps. Dingy strips of cloud hustle to obscure the moon. An owl hoots encouragement, and I lift the flashlight above my head.

The gate is rough against my palm and creaks as I open it. On the other side is a large windowless shed, cool and plastic to the touch, its door secured by three padlocks.

Look in the . . . shed? I think. Could this be what Jude meant?

"Katherine?" I hear my mother call. From this distance her voice sounds almost delicate. Wallis follows up with a throaty bark.

A quick tug of the lowest padlock yields nothing. I turn around and head back the way I came, reminding myself that Jude's words—in any language—no longer mean anything to me.

KAT: NOW

Six Months after the Accident
SEPTEMBER 1983

The shed, my mother explains the next morning, is an old climate-controlled storage unit, the place where she keeps various favored antiques collected over the years: particularly rare books and magazines; intricate light fixtures in need of rewiring; Gothic dining chairs waiting to be refinished. "Nothing to be concerned about at all," she says, and I'm relieved to discover that I believe her.

It's noon on a Saturday, the market's busiest time, and hundreds of shoppers clog the aisles and swarm the stalls, shouting their firm and final offers. As Verona closes a deal on an Italian tole chandelier I start wandering toward Richard's stall, intrigued by both his collection of antique guns and—given my mother's recent revelations about their history—by Richard himself. I am halfway there, elbowing my way through, when I see another woman who compels me to stop midstep. Nothing about her appearance is familiar: curly hair, blond and short;

a striped sweater in neutral tones; sensible slacks that shorten her legs; a string of pearls looped around her neck. She lifts one hand and positions it over her eyes, swiveling her long, elegant neck like a periscope, and in those two brief, fluid gestures, I recognize this stranger: Jude, striving to look older than our years, drifting through the crowds in the hope of finding me.

I fall back and away, hiding behind an old brass coat rack, and study her: the insolent set of her shoulders, the aggressive stride, the overzealous swing of the arms. She meanders from stall to stall, trying on fur stoles, holding diamonds up to the sunlight, stuffing her feet into delicate Edwardian heels—all the while shifting her eyes, back and forward and left and right, wondering where the hell I might be. Her gaze flits from body to body, quick as a stone skipping water, until it lands in the direction of my original destination: Richard's stall. Richard is there, of course, talking animatedly with a customer and petting a long, slim gun. A black silk patch hides his missing eye.

I glance back at Jude. I can't tell if she is looking at Richard directly or at his customer or at the semicircle of people crowded around his table, running their fingers along his glass cases, awaiting their turns. But I am certain of this: never in my truncated life have I seen a look of such raw, naked horror—an expression so disturbing it could classify as a horror of its own. She stands like this for a moment, eyes wide and mouth open, and even from this distance I can feel her heat surge beneath her skin and hear the bang of her heart and, against my will, sense the black fire of her thoughts: *I deen ot teg tou fo rehe. I need to get out of here.*

She lurches through the crowd until she at last breaks through and gathers herself, launching her body toward the carousel horses, running from some invisible threat.

KAT: NOW

Six Months after the Accident
SEPTEMBER 1983

With each passing day my mother feels less like a stranger to me, although she still doesn't quite feel like a mother. I am a restoration project and she is the architect, laying the bricks and patching the cracks, hoping the old foundation can accommodate the new. She searches for evidence of my old self and lays claim to it. Do I recognize my own impulsivity? I got that from her. My stubborn streak, my restlessness, my ruthless curiosity, my optimism even in the face of gloom? All from her. Do I understand how she has shaped me? How much she has stolen from her own life to give to mine, the sacrifices, the heartache? Can I imagine the hell she lived for five years, not knowing if I were alive or dead? Do I understand the debt I owe her, especially since Jude has, for whatever reason, chosen to be estranged? When I look at her, can I see the possibilities of what I might become?

I answer yes to all of it, sometimes just to humor her, although I do catch whispers of myself in her expressions, her thoughts, her mannerisms, her interests. She is giving me a comfortable life that fits my current mood, my need for stability and routine, for space to pause and assess. I enjoy the world she's created around herself, the community of people who find value in the old and forgotten. I admire her skill in persuading others: listen to the story behind this artifact, understand how special it is, ask yourself if you'd regret leaving it behind.

To my surprise, I look forward to long days at the antique market and seeing Richard, who rambles over the minute we arrive, always greeting me with an exaggerated wink from his good eye. He knows that it disturbs me and that, on some level, I like to be disturbed—not in a way that forebodes danger, but as a reminder that there are different ways of being in the world, that a missing eye and a missing memory are a warped kind of asset: proof of verve and daring, a reward for facing the most violent impulses of humanity and coming out the other side.

Whatever or whoever frightened Jude, I've decided, is now her problem and her problem alone.

I update my list: *I am a person who finally cares more about the future than the past.*

One Friday afternoon, as the foot traffic dwindles, I take a break to visit Richard at his stall.

"There's only five known pieces in the world," I hear him say as I approach, "and their origin is a bit of a mystery . . ." He smiles at me, holds up a finger. "No Liberty nickels were even supposed to be produced that year. I don't have one of those, of course. My rarest is a 1943 Lincoln head copper penny."

As his customer browses, Richard steps closer to me. He's wearing a different eye patch today, black leather with three decorative silver studs. It makes him look intimidating but also slightly ridiculous, like he aspires to be a half-blind version of the Fonz.

"Pretend to laugh casually," he whispers. "I want this guy to think the pressure's off and that I don't really need this sale."

I oblige, tossing my head, my hand on his arm.

"After I get rid of him, I have a surprise for you."

"I'm intrigued," I tell him. "As long as it has nothing to do with old money."

"It's much more interesting, and just as rare."

"Well, hurry then, and sell your pennies," I say, and give him a gentle push. As he closes his sale, I move to the table showcasing his antique gun collection, admiring the decorative metal flourishes and pearl handles. I pick up one with a trigger that resembles a long, slim tooth, like the incisor of some prehistoric animal, and am surprised at how heavy it is in my hands.

"Don't shoot!" Richard says, walking around the table. He raises his arms in surrender and I see a clutch of photographs in his right hand. "I have your bounty right here."

"Did Verona tell you I've been asking for pictures?" I try to pry them from his hand but he stands on tiptoe, waving his arm, eluding me.

"Not so fast. Let's sit down so we can go through them properly. These pictures qualify as history now, and the telling of that history deserves some respect."

I like his logic, although it does nothing to quell my impatience. Back inside his stall, we sit on a pair of folding chairs and he stacks the pictures on his lap. In the first one, Jude and I are in the parlor of Verona's home, holding hands and wearing identical dresses, all our mirror twin qualities on full display: the opposite parts of our hair, the deepened dimples on either cheek, our sharp complementary incisors. Our forced smiles carry a hint of bewilderment and melancholy, and I realize this was taken around the time our father left.

"This might actually be the first time I met you and Jude," he says. "Verona—your mother—threw such wonderful parties. She had a gift for collecting the most interesting people and fitting them together."

I remember what Verona said during our talks over the Mnemosyne statue: Richard didn't know my father, my father didn't have friends, she and Richard had had a casual romance. Now that Richard and I are friends, the idea of him and Verona together unsettles me in a way I don't want to explore. I flip over the next picture: Jude and I are a year or so older and dressed in monkey costumes, the fur dingy and matted, the disembodied heads tucked beneath our arms. Between us stands a girl about our age wearing a costume with clawed hands and a long, bulbous tail. Although we're all smiling, our three faces are sallow and gaunt and our eyes are feverishly bright, as though being illuminated by an unnatural sun.

"My mother mentioned costumes," I say. "Who is that girl and what are we doing?"

"We were at one of our retreats at the Island. I'm guessing your mother mentioned that place? You all played hide and seek, laughed together, learned so much. And that's my niece. The three of you couldn't stand to be apart."

I study her photo again, running the tip of my finger down and up her form, landing on her chin. "Where is she now?"

"We fell out of touch, sadly. Well, that's not entirely true. She manages to find me when she wants something, and then she's gone again." He takes the photo from my hand, glances at it, and tucks it beneath the others. "She is my Jude, meaning that I don't want to talk about her."

"I'm sorry," I tell him. "I completely understand."

"I knew you would," he says, and rubs at his patchless eye. "I don't mean to be brusque . . . I suppose I have many regrets, and they've all come to haunt me at once. She's one of them."

Without thinking, I ask: "Is that why you changed your name, because of old regrets?"

He pauses, his blind eye staring at me through the Fonzie patch, his other eye like a wolf's, so penetrating and blue I have to look away.

"I'm sorry," I say. I'm suddenly nervous, wishing I could retract the question.

"Don't be. It's just that I don't know if I've ever given the explanation aloud, and I'd like to pick the proper words, the truthful words."

He taps his fingers together. I notice the wispy blond hairs on his knuckles, the initial ring with a diamond in the hole of the *R*. He closes his real eye, a long blink, and says: "I was famous for a time. Not movie-star famous, but very well known in certain circles, the circles I shared with your mother. A few years ago I decided I didn't want to be famous anymore, so I started going by Richard, my middle name. While this brilliant move has definitely made me less famous, I'm still not as far removed from that time as I'd like. I might never be, and I have to live with that."

Despite my promises to myself I think about Jude, and how she changed our name from "Sheridan" to "Bird" for reasons she never disclosed. I wonder if we, too, had identities that had been tainted in some way, and if we'd hoped to create some distance from them.

"I understand," I say. "Or, at least, I understand in the best way I know how."

He holds up the next picture: Jude and me in our monkey costumes and a half-dozen adults spread out behind us, dressed in matching red tunics and wide-leg pants. In the background stands a large ticket booth shaped like a crown, its golden spikes aimed at a darkening sky. I look closely at the faces and recognize Verona and Richard, arms slung around each other. A woman standing next to them looks vaguely familiar—the blond sheath of hair, maybe, or the pillowy cheeks—and I wonder if I've seen someone similar in the crowds at the market. The other two men lean in from the right side of the frame. They're about Richard's age, one with black hair and the other with silver, the latter wearing a large camera around his neck. I look again at the booth, and notice the words *THE PLAN* etched along the marquee, and, beneath these, a vague shadow of different letters that had been erased.

Before I can ask questions Richard stands up from his chair and ambles to the front of his stall, where a man is wielding a long rifle. "Welcome," he says. "That's a real beauty there. Springfield Armory musket from 1861."

I collect the pictures from his chair. The sun has slid down the sky and the neon fairy lights flip on, casting the market in a lurid glow. Not wanting to disturb Richard, I drop the pictures on the table and mouth, *Thank you.*

"Excuse me a moment," he says to his customer, and picks them up. "Kat, these are yours. I want you to have them."

"Are you sure?"

"Positive. I'll see you tomorrow." Before turning away, he winks his good eye. I wink back.

———

That night, at home with Verona, I push aside Mnemosyne and drop the photos in her place, the group shot positioned on top. "From Richard," I say. "He wanted me to have some photos from before."

"Oh, isn't he just wonderful?" she says, making it a statement rather than a question. "Such a smart, insightful, intuitive man, and a loyal friend. In fact I always thought of our friendship in the context of Emily Dickinson"—here she closes her eyes and rests a hand atop her heart—"'I should not dare to leave my friend, because if he should die, while I was gone, and I, too late, should reach the heart that wanted me.'" Her eyes reopen and her hand falls, landing around a tumbler of scotch. "My fondness for him has only grown during these past few months."

With her free hand she takes the group photo and peers at it closely, and I watch the shift in her expression; her big, bold face droops, sagging under its own weight, and her lips twist into a knot. She pushes the photo away and says she can't bear to look at it; those men on the end with the black and silver hair were her old friends, Ronald and Donald, and oh, Katherine, they both died within months of each other, died in horrific and mortifying ways. One was declared a suicide, the other an accident, but she was certain of a darker truth—that her dear, darling friends were murdered in cold blood.

KAT: NOW

Seven Months after the Accident
OCTOBER 1983

I finally tell my mother about Jude's appearance at the market, expect-ing her to be saddened, but instead she seems angry on my behalf. Why does Jude continue to torture and taunt me, after I've made it clear I want nothing to do with her? Why is Jude intruding upon my new life and attempting to drag me back into the old? She had been eager for Jude to return, too, but now enough is enough; my sister has done nothing but lie and connive and try to interfere with my bur-geoning happiness and peace. Let's make a pact, darling Katherine, to never let Judith come between us. It's a miracle we've found each other, and she won't abide losing me again.

When I visit Richard at his stall, he has a more nuanced take. "Jude must have some regrets, just like everyone else," he says. "Whatever happened between you is clearly complicated. You've been through a lot, and you need to act in your own best interests. Your brain is still healing. You're still navigating your new reality. Try not to stress yourself out over a past you can't remember."

His words stay with me, and I realize that he's reinforced the true goal of my recovery: focus not on excavation work, but construction work. The question shouldn't be *What have I done?* but *Who am I?* All of those old epiphanies dust themselves off and reassert themselves in my mind:

I am a person who throws parties and likes beer.

I am a person who appreciates certain private devices.

I am a person who won't be told what to do.

I am a person who takes risks.

I am a person who likes to keep parts of herself hidden.

I am a person who can't afford to lose.

I am a person who has played cards.

I am a person capable of losing control in unpredictable and dangerous ways.

I am a person who likes stories that strangers tell.

I am a person who is stronger than I know.

I am a person who will do anything to define herself.

I am a person capable of handling herself in any situation.

I am a person who appreciates a shortcut.

I am a person who is being solved.

I am a person unafraid to do the thing that nearly killed me.

I am a person who will never speak to my twin again.

I am a person who finally cares more about the future than the past.

And the one that still worries me: *I am a person who will believe anything I'm told.*

On Friday, one week after Jude came in disguise to the market, I find myself at Richard's stall near closing time. It had been an unseasonably cold day and less busy than usual, and the dealers are calling out to each other, boasting about new finds and telling dumb jokes of the trade: "You know when you pay a lot for an antique chair and then discover that the seller had just roughed it up themselves? That's distressing!" I spot Richard polishing and packing the most valuable of his guns, and clear my throat when I reach the display.

"Can I help you?" He looks up and smiles when he sees me.

I transform my voice into Verona's smokey growl: "Today I bumped into a man who sold me an antique globe."

"Let me guess," Richard says, rubbing his chin. "And now you think it's a small world."

"You got me," I say in my own voice, and fish a comb from my purse. "Can I interest you in any puns about *hair looms?*"

"Enough!" he says. "I can't let you become a total dork like the rest of us. After you help Verona pack up, how about an early dinner? I made a bitchin' jambalaya last night."

"Sounds good, but if you say bitchin' again, I'm out of there."

We shake hands.

Richard lives about a ten-minute walk from the market, just off the main road in the town center, in an old stone dwelling perched near the bank of a river. The front yard is landscaped with mature hydrangeas and rose bushes with no blooms. "Those were gorgeous until fairly recently," he says. "But for whatever reason, someone decided to take an axe to them." I want to ask if he thinks it's the same person who took out his eye, but stop myself just in time. He respects my boundaries, and I should respect his.

Inside, the decor is a peculiar blend of modern and antique, suave bachelor and eccentric professor. A full suit of medieval armor keeps watch by a dart board. A baroque grandfather clock stands next to a hanging macramé chair draped in tea lights. A strange sort of glass lamp with floating neon blobs sits atop a steel desk. In an alcove near the recreation room, a floor-to-ceiling cabinet showcasing antique guns faces a wall of rare coins. He gives me the full tour, including the bedroom, which features a tufted leather headboard and a wraparound shelf lined with soldier figurines, representing every war.

"One of my ancestors fought alongside Washington at the Battle of Brandywine," he says. "Brigadier General Sebastian Vance."

"Is that your last name?"

"It is indeed. There's a long line of Sebastian Vances, and it looks like I'll be the end of it."

"You don't want children?"

"I love kids, but I'm not good with them. I'm doing my nonexistent children a favor, I'm certain of it."

Something in his tone made me think of Sab, who was so eager to have kids he'd already chosen their prospective names and dream professions: his son, Felix, the orthopedic surgeon; his daughter, Lidia, the Wall Street mogul. I feel something entirely new, something that the accident had stolen from me; enough time has passed for it to reappear in my cache of emotions. I think Jude would call it nostalgia.

In the hallway I pause before a cluster of photographs, some sepia-toned and wrinkled in their frames, others in color and intact. At the sight of one of them my breath turns cold in my chest.

Long, dark hair. Very pale skin. If the photograph could walk, it would have a pronounced limp.

It's Nancy, the girl who followed me. Jude's loan shark. The girl who sent me to an abandoned house where *The Rabbit Hole* is scrawled along one wall. The girl I spoke to at the wine bar, who asked me how much I knew about myself. An older version of the girl in the pictures he'd showed me at the market; she was standing between me and Jude, wearing a scorpion costume, her smile accentuating her witchy chin.

He follows my pointed finger. "Violet. My sister's daughter. My sister was—is—an alcoholic, so I'd take Violet in for long stretches of time. Her father was never in the picture. As I mentioned at the market, she's one of my regrets. But we still talk from time to time. She doesn't really have anyone else. I enjoy her company, and she enjoys my money."

Two frames farther, there's a picture of Verona and Richard in the front of the house, their hands clasped together and raised in some private victory. I wonder if it was taken before or after their fling.

"Have I been in this house before?" I ask.

I am chilled by my own question.

"You were, a long time ago," he says. "I'd have gatherings with our circle of friends, and sometimes your mom would bring you and Jude, and you'd play all night with Violet."

"With Violet," I repeat. I try to picture us, playing hide and seek in these cavernous rooms, our deep abiding friendship with Jude's future loan shark. I think, *Here's yet another lie Jude didn't hesitate to tell me.*

I feel weak, and throw my hand against the wall for support. I've been in this house before. I have a very intimate history with this man, with his family. I beg my brain to flash me something, anything, that will color in the outlines of my past.

"I'm sorry," Richard says. "I didn't mean to overwhelm you. I hope it helps you when I say it was a very happy time in your life."

"It might help me in a bit," I tell him. "But right now I need to sit down."

"Let's go have my definitely not-bitchin' jambalaya," he says, and takes my arm. He leads me to a large acrylic dining table and pulls out a chair. Its arms are made of twisted pieces of animal horns, and the face of a gargoyle sits atop a very high back, watching over us.

"It doesn't bite, I promise," he says. "Dig in."

For a few moments we eat in comfortable silence, and then he sets down his spoon.

"Can I ask you something personal?" he says. "I know we've been avoiding certain topics, but I think we're good friends now, right? Good friends who now have more porous boundaries?"

I feel my back go rigid, and then relax. How ironic that Jude had transferred to me her inherent suspicion and paranoia, when her behavior was the most suspect of all.

"Yes, you can ask," I tell him. "And I might even answer."

He hesitates, and then says: "Tell me about your accident. Do you know where you had been? Where you were going to? What you had done? What was it like to realize your memory was gone?"

"You're cheating. That was four questions."

He smiles. "What can I say? It's now in your past, and the past is my specialty."

I look at his face, assessing it as though it's one of my mother's jewels, holding it up to the light, deciding if it's worth my investment. The pupil of his uncovered eye dilates, signaling interest.

"I'll tell you what I know," I say, "with the caveat that what I know is based on the word of an incredibly troubled and unreliable person."

"Your twin, Jude—"

I shake my head. "I don't talk about Jude anymore. That boundary is still solid."

"Understood," he says, and I believe him.

I close my eyes and tell him about the accident—not just tell him but relive it, as though I have perfect recall on every detail—my dive into the windshield, my bloody head resting on Jude's lap, a kindly trucker, the shock and mystery of my brain. What was it like to grasp the complete erasure of my life? Imagine your emotions—denial, anger, bargaining, depression, acceptance—all surging and colliding at once, your entire world losing structure and shape, the borders collapsing and dissolving, the fear that you might lose it again lurking in some far corner of your mind.

My spoon is hovering near my mouth, shaking, the jambalaya spilling over its rim. Richard hands me a velvet napkin and says he's sorry; it was too much to ask of me, he should learn to keep his mouth shut, he's too curious for his own good.

"It's okay," I tell him. "If I didn't want to tell you I wouldn't have. Willfulness is one thing I've apparently retained. As for the rest of it—where I was coming from, where was I going?—I've been told we were driving to some far-away restaurant for dinner. I have no idea if that's true. I wish I did. Come to think of it, maybe I don't."

We're quiet again, scraping the bottoms of our bowls.

"Now can I ask you something personal?" I say.

"I think I owe you that."

"What happened to your eye?"

He smiles. "I knew that would be your question."

"It's only fair, right? I showed you mine, you show me yours. We misfits have to stick together."

"In other words, 'a brain for an eye'?" he asks, and smiles again. "And yes, it is fair." He sets down his spoon, dabs at his mouth. "If I didn't have so much paperwork to do tonight, I'd make us martinis. It's one of those kinds of stories."

He stretches out his arms and audibly cracks his knuckles, a gesture that seems at odds with his mannered, old-world airs. "Some of it is embarrassing. I might have to edit certain details just to save face. I mean, clearly I lost the fight."

"It's your story," I say softly.

"Would it disturb you terribly if I removed my patch?" he asks. "The prosthetic eye sometimes gets dusty and needs a deep cleaning. And when I wear the patch, the strap can get itchy against my skin."

"Not at all," I tell him. "This is your home."

I am expecting a thicket of purple veins—the stuff of horror films—but he reveals a smooth, small valley of flesh. From a distance, it would appear that he had one eye permanently closed.

I smile to encourage him, and he begins.

One night, he says, he was eating dinner on the sofa, watching television. And out of nowhere—actually, from his basement door—came a masked figure pointing a loaded gun. A second intruder—also masked, he would soon learn—loomed up behind him, waiting to strike. They were tall and lithe and moved with the slippery menace of ninjas, and he'll never unsee their masks: Comedy and Tragedy, the features exaggerated and swooning, the smile of a jester and the grimace of the insane.

He heard the click of a gun, but no shot, and then another empty, fruitless click.

He leapt and folded his hands into fists, prepared to defend himself, but the first intruder surprised him by using martial arts, arms and legs spinning and chopping like helicopter blades. Richard switched postures, tapping into the jiu-jitsu moves he'd learned on a trip to Brazil; although a novice, he was able to take that intruder down. Rolling around on the floor, writhing and grappling, it degenerated into a street brawl: punches to the face, hair pulling, knee pinning. In one lucky moment, his hand encircled the intruder's neck, he slammed the bastard's head against the sharp point of a coffee table, hard enough to make a dent in the skull.

The second intruder, the one who'd come up behind him, found a fire iron. Richard saw the shadow of the fire iron stretched along the ceiling before it came crashing down, exploding the side of his head. The iron came again and again. He felt himself falling. He paused on his hands and knees. He remembers so acutely the softness of the white rug beneath his palms. He remembers watching his own blood stream down from a seismic crack in his head, and wondering, absurdly, how in the hell he would ever clean that stain.

Through his blurring vision he saw the prongs of a fork aimed straight at him, the four silver points coming like bullets. In a fleeting second of detachment, in which he experienced the classic sense of floating outside of his own body to observe a personal trauma, he thought, "Oh yes, I had left my dinner plate on the coffee table, a fork resting on its edge, and now it is being used against me."

The fork connected with the meat of his left eye, whipping his cornea into meringue. He screamed in such a way that he terrified himself; even now, sitting at this table, he can hear it echo in his ears, and feel the blood from his eye seep inward, like venom he had released within himself. There are no leads, no suspects—and now he has an alarm, so if those fuckers ever try again he will be ready to kill them both.

He is gasping now, the words breathy and shallow, his cheeks puckering in and out. "I'm sorry," he chokes. "The last time I spoke of it was to the police. And, come to think of it, Violet—she was kind enough to come by and help me clean up the mess. This happened right after two old friends had died, suddenly and under weird circumstances, one after the other."

"How did they die?" I ask.

"One by suicide, the other by accident," he says. He closes his good eye for a moment and—I can't help myself—I focus on the concave valley, its stark and violent absence; I nearly reach out to touch it. "It doesn't seem they're connected, but then again, how could they not be?" he asks, and the good eye flips back open, the hint of tears making it shine. "They're a big part of my regrets. Their deaths made me reassess old chapters of my life. Bad things happen in threes, and that night I was supposed to die."

I try not to stare at the eye but the valley now seems to be pulsing, heaving in and out with his breath.

"I still get flashbacks, Kat. I still see them standing over me. Every night, even with the alarm, I go to sleep worrying that they will come again. They will cut the wires and they will aim my own guns at my head. They will use their strong, agile bodies to trap and kill me. I'm so scared, Kat. I'm so scared." The missing eye stares at me, blank and unseeing, and the other is slick with tears; they spill down his right cheek while the left remains dry, creating the illusion of a face split in half. I realize that he, too, has a before and after, a then and a now—a singular and devastating moment that cleaved his life into two, one that will stalk and mark him forever.

I take my napkin from my lap and, with a second of hesitation, dab at his cheek, a gesture that only makes him weep harder, and without any shame at all. He tries to talk but the words are lost in his sobs, and he repeats his sentence three times before I understand: he knows that he deserved it.

"*Shhh*," I say. "I can't imagine that's true."

"It's not just seeing them," he says, and gulps for breath. I dab the tissue again and pet his shoulder. "I hear them, too. I hear their hard, whispery voices, voices that were identical to each other. They were talking in some foreign language. It made it so much scarier, not knowing what they were saying. Speaking in tongues, like some strange beasts from hell."

My hand, hovered over his missing eye, goes absolutely still. I can't imagine he doesn't hear the sudden dull pulse of my heart. I can't imagine he doesn't hear the quaking in my voice, the absolute horror embedded in every syllable of my words: "Do you remember anything specific? Did any phrases stay with you?"

"Do I remember?" he repeats. He places his hand over mine, and pulls them both to his eye. "I'll never forget. My mind will play their words again and again until the day I die."

"What are they?" I whisper. He lifts our hands, treating them as one. His good eye—so blue beneath the buttery light—fixes on mine, pinning me. I'm desperate to look away, and it is his singular, specific power that renders me incapable of doing so. I'll stand there, my hand in his, hypnotized by that eye until he decides to release me. My own heart punches at me. Bile inches up my throat. I feel like I might piss myself right then and there on his priceless Persian rug.

"One said, 'Si eh leary dade?'" and the other responded, "'Si eh. Nafilly, yeth lal rea.'" He repeats the phrases, softer this time, and this spotless, elegant room turns into a vertiginous house of mirrors, the walls zooming in and rushing away and zooming in again, displaying every angle of myself that I never wished to see.

My mind translates:

Is he really dead?

He is. Finally, they all are.

JUDE: NOW

Seven Months after the Accident
OCTOBER 1983

On the drive out to the site of Kat's accident Jude notices that the cherry trees are already bare. She makes herself think about the trees because they are all too real and too alive; they adhere to a cycle, retracting and expanding, blooming and shedding, an order untouched by madness. She makes herself think of Genesis (or The Geneses, as she sometimes called her), the real and the fake, the comrade and the rebel, the alive and the dead.

Violet had sent her to the site, her beautiful and wretched Violet. Jude had done everything she'd asked—giving her money, giving her jewelry, orchestrating the breakup of Kat and Sab—but Violet was not yet finished. At their last meeting she had issued one final order: go back to where Kat had her accident, retrieve what you buried there, and do what needs to be done.

The drive is pleasant, a spectacular vista of an unblemished sky and lolling fields, and Jude imagines what others might see, what she *wants* them to see: just a normal, pretty girl enjoying the late fall day, perhaps meeting a boyfriend for a picnic or a walk beneath the newly naked trees. If only she could transfer that serenity to the inside, silencing all the memories raging through her heart, all those hard questions she'd asked and devastating answers she'd heard, all those steps she and Kat had to take before laying their final path.

When Jude thought about that path, retracing their steps back, it started that night five years ago, in January 1978, when Wen— formerly Jackie, Violet's mother and master of ceremonies for The Plan—found them outside of 30th Street Station in Philadelphia, traumatized and exhausted and fleeing from a dangerous man. She drove them to her farmhouse in Upstate New York where they settled into the business of becoming themselves again, examining the many layers of The Plan, learning how far it stretched and how deep it rooted, how many lives it had seduced, how many more it had razed.

Jude resurrected all the questions that she'd banished to the corners of her mind, the questions Genesis had asked before she died: *What about the pictures? Where are they going? Who is seeing them?* Wen knew most of the answers and shared them delicately: King Bash and the RonDon sold the pictures to certain types of magazines, magazines that remain available in certain types of bookstores all over the world, magazines that only recently began to attract the attention of United States officials, magazines that are still widely considered benign—after all, where's the evidence that such images cause any physical and psychological harm?

"Did King Bash believe that?" Jude asked. "Did Verona?"

"They did," Wen said. "And for a while, so did I. It's why they did not hesitate to incorporate it into The Plan. The whole belief that everyone should contribute, that no one was too young for responsibility, and, of course, 'What you think, is.' If you yourself thought the photographs were okay, then they were."

After all those years, Jude and Kat decided that the photographs were not okay, an opinion shared by dozens of other escapees from The Plan who came and went through Wen's doors, former monkeys and rabbits and scorpions and parrots and chameleons and wolves who confessed to a deep and interminable rage—sometimes burrowed into the bones, sometimes creeping to the surface, but always, *always* there, the sort of rage transferred to future generations, a rage that qualified as history. On some days Jude felt her rage so acutely she couldn't stand still; the rage was tangible, a live snake in her hands, twisting and hissing and rattling its tail, coiling around her neck, rendering her unable to speak. She had to learn to wrangle it, she told herself. Treat the rage like a living, breathing thing that can be managed but never fully tamed.

For five long years at Wen's place, they managed the rage in all the ways that were available to them. They learned attack and defense moves, how to shoot, how to optimize the element of surprise. They learned to be self-sufficient, cleaning houses for Wen's company, earning enough money to buy their own car. They changed their surname to prevent Verona from finding them, choosing "Bird" in honor of their newfound freedom, their desire to swoop and soar. They reinterpreted The Plan's tenets in ways that suited their needs. "Reject and Release," they said in unison, their private insurance that the memory of the pictures would never overpower them. They rejected and released every hour of every day spent at Wen's, twenty seasons of summer crackling into fall and fall freezing into winter and winter thawing into spring. Jude recorded them all with tally marks, scratching lines along their bedroom wall, a calendar of the time spent recasting their past. In the final month of their final year, they agreed that Jude had nothing left to record.

"We've finished, but we're not finished," Kat said one night during that last week. They lay in their twin beds, facing each other, close enough to hold hands.

"I know," Jude said, and she really and truly did. But she did not want to walk this tightrope across Kat's thoughts, teetering into a situation as treacherous as the one they'd escaped. They were on the edge of normal, so tantalizingly close to uneventful and mundane.

"Are we going to finish?" Kat asked. She inched close to the edge of her bed, the mattress squeaking. Jude could hear the faintest uptick in her sister's breath. Kat was waiting; Kat was expectant. Kat was one tug away from adamant demands.

"I don't know," Jude said. "My mind is capable of planning, but I don't know if my body is capable of seeing it through."

Kat rolled an inch closer, perching herself on the edge of the bed. "Let's split ourselves," she said. "You can be the mind and I'll be the body. You plan, and I execute. You tie them up or hold them down, and I make sure they never breathe again. The worst thing that ever happened to them will happen only once. For us—for so many of us— the worst thing will never stop happening, all over the world, for as long as we live."

Jude studied her sister's features, lit on one side, dark on the other: the one wide eye, the lone arched brow, the bisected lip raised into an unnerving smile. Kat was utterly mad, of course, but she was also correct. Without Jude, Kat would be careless and caught and sent to the electric chair. Without Kat, The Plan would thrive, and King Bash's entire ecosystem would beat on, the children turned into animals, the animals turned into killers or prey. Without Kat, Jude would have to live with the knowledge that Gen had died in vain.

Who cared if it didn't make sense, or if it was absurd and reckless, or if it would jeopardize their new lives, their After Lives, before they even began? It only mattered that Kat's fury about their past exceeded Jude's caution for their future, and that Jude alone could restore the balance.

"We are finishing," Kat whispered.

"Yes," Jude said. "We will finish and make everything even, and then we will reject and release that, too."

They did not debate the question again, but when Jude said she planned to take the day off and spend it alone, Kat knew not to ask questions. Kat borrowed Wen's car to go to work and Jude sped off in their own, heading south, the sky vandalized by gaudy orange streaks, the pumpkins preparing to be picked and carved, Emma's Enchanted Hedge Maze waiting to be solved. The wind play-slapped her face and the weakening sun tapped her shoulders and she had a liberating and terrifying thought: *This is as strong, this is as free, as I will ever be.*

She parked on King Bash's street in Norris Ford and waited for a sign that might never come. She did not know if he was in the row home or at the Island or behind the door of this stately old historic house polishing his collection of obsolete guns. She imagined what she might do if he stepped outside. She pictured herself delivering an axe kick and an elbow strike and gouging out his eyes with nothing but the tips of her feral fingers. She pictured herself throwing her arms around his knees and begging for love and forgiveness and promising she would be a good monkey again, the most helpful and industrious monkey he'd ever seen, a monkey happy to oblige any request he made.

None of that, she told herself. *Reject and release.*

Later she would try—oh, how hard she would try—but she could not reject and release what happened a half hour into her vigil. The front door opened, and out stepped not King Bash but Violet, darling, sweet, shattered Violet, her hair tied up and swinging like a whip across her back. She sat down on the bright red swing on the porch and pushed herself back and forth. She dropped her magnificent face into her hands and wept, her shoulders quaking like the feathers of a frightened bird. In each gesture and inaudible sob, Jude saw every unforgivable thing she herself had ever done.

She saw Violet being sent to the Big House because Jude chose to protect Kat instead. She saw Genesis and Melisa and Jimmy and Marcus and Lola and Genesis again, suspended from the real-fake tree, the slow-motion swing of her legs. She saw all of the rabbits begetting rabbits, the hordes growing in numbers, their capacity for savagery directly proportionate to their blind acceptance of Jude's lies, the saccharine sheen of her promises. She watched Violet—real-time, real-life Violet—stand up from the swing and find within her bag a pair of pruning shears. She watched Violet snap the blades until every rose bush was decapitated of its buds. She listened to the snap and watched the flowers fall and could not reject or release the notion of her own complicity; she had been destroyed, and she had destroyed in turn, and in order to make things even she must destroy again.

Kat was right. It had to end with them.

Now, of course, Kat doesn't remember any of this—the pictures, the rage, their decision to kill, to end what they had in their power to end. She doesn't know that Jude still has nightmares about the Ron-Don, the lurching of their bodies and the slipperiness of their skin, the sight of them succumbing to stillness. She doesn't know about Violet's final threat: Jude must finish what they started—or else Violet will go to the police and report what she knows, offering Jude's necklace and secretly taped conversations as evidence.

She pulls the Killer Whale over and parks on the shoulder of State Route 491, parallel to the stretch of highway where Kat swerved off the road and reinjured her already damaged head. She had been out of her mind, trying to keep Kat alive while flagging down help, but somehow she'd memorized the exact location, knowing she might have to return. The trees are thick on either side and lean in toward the road, forming a partial canopy. An overpass looms in the near distance, and yellow signs warn to watch out for deer and the winding turns ahead. Moving through the trees, she remembers what it was like to leave Kat even for a moment, bleeding alone on the side of the road.

She is reminded of yet more lies she'd told Kat: The accident had not happened the way Jude had described it. There had been a deer, but Kat would have crashed regardless. By the time Kat started the car and sped off, her head had already been cracked open. Her brain had stopped telling her body how to operate the car, and then her brain failed to operate at all. Before Jude could grab the wheel Kat crashed into the tree, her head colliding against the glass and coming to rest on the dashboard, her blank face turned to Jude.

On that night Jude had counted twenty-five steps, saying each number aloud, and now she counts again. The woods are eerie even in the late afternoon. The rustle of the leaves under her feet seems to echo and amplify—is someone following her? No, she tells herself, it's just the darting squirrels and rummaging opossums and scampering mice. No one is watching as she finds the hemlock tree, just a bit taller than the others around it, with the uneven dirt at the base of its trunk. She undoes the work she did that night, dismantling the pyramid of three heavy rocks, the disheveled pile of twigs and leaves. The bags lay where she left them, still holding King Bash's own vintage gun and the Saturday night specials acquired through her old rabbits, Jimmy and Marcus: cheap, compact, and with serial numbers already ground away.

JUDE: THEN

Five Months Before the Accident
OCTOBER 1982

"You're Tragedy," Kat said. "Obviously."

Jude took the mask and it felt alive in her hand, scheming and ghoulish, eager for its debut. The masks were her own idea: Comedy and Tragedy, associated with Janus—the Roman god of transitions who connected beginnings and endings, life and death, war and peace, innocence and guilt. He is the bridge between all those things, she explained to Kat, and was often depicted as one body with two heads connected at the rear of the skulls—one looking toward the future, the other taking notes on the past. Janus didn't have a mask of his own, at least not at the costume supply shop in Center City, Philadelphia, so Comedy and Tragedy would have to suffice.

They dressed in black and, along with the masks, packed a woman's scarf, a man's bathrobe, and two Saturday night specials.

At eight p.m. they left their apartment, Kat behind the wheel and Jude navigating the route. Jude estimated it would take about forty-five minutes for them to arrive at the Main Line home where Ronald Lester, the Ronald half of the RonDon, now lived alone. He would still be awake, but it would be dark enough to escape the notice of any neighbor taking a walk. One week earlier, Jude took a trip alone to case the house, checking for evidence of an attack dog or an alarm system and, as expected, found neither. Mr. Ronald had always seemed to be unblemished by fear or worry. He did not look over his shoulder. He did not ponder the resentments of old acquaintances or new strangers. He would not feel a prick of fear when the knock came at his door.

The moon was a long way from full, just a shy smile of light, and as they moved farther from the city the streetlamps dwindled and the sky claimed another layer of darkness. They drove deeper and deeper into a place where the air smelled apple-crisp and Halloween decorations bedecked the homes and nothing bad ever happened, at least not the kind of bad that made the evening news.

They parked a block away and walked slowly down Ivywood Road, just two pretty girls who looked like they belonged in the neighborhood, nothing noteworthy to see here, folks, nothing at all. A dog barked, a television screen flickered from a window, a basketball bounced on a distant court during the final moments of a game. Jude touched her nameplate necklace, her only good luck charm.

They walked up the stone drive of his limestone colonial, past a chain of dehydrated bushes, past a fountain clogged with mold. With the three city row homes empty, and the Island once again a shuttered amusement park, and The Plan finally disbanded, Mr. Ronald now lived at this home full time. Jude knew he lived alone. His wife had divorced him. His children were now grown and far away from all of it, among the lucky few. Behind this heavy paneled door, Mr. Ronald had no one who would arrive in the morning expecting to see him alive.

Just out of view of the front windows, Jude tied Kat's mask and Kat tied Jude's.

"You talk, I move," Jude said.

Kat rang the bell.

A soft light filled the front room. Jude heard a grunt, the thud of heavy steps. She had determined the safest and most untraceable plan. Any bruises or marks had to appear as though they were made by Mr. Ronald himself, which eliminated Kat's idea of a groin kick to start things off. There could be vomit but no blood. She wanted it to be fast but not without pain.

One final, heavy step and there he stood, his robe dangling open, his feet bare, a bunion sending one big toe on a sharp right turn. Not a speck of alarm in his eyes.

"Excuse us, sir," Kat said. "We're terribly sorry to bother you, but we're on our way to a Halloween party, as you might have guessed"— she pointed to her grinning mask—"and our car broke down. Could we borrow your phone for a moment to call the hostess?"

"Of course, come on in," he said, stepping aside, and as Kat closed the door Jude whipped her handgun from behind her back and pointed it at Mr. Ronald's face.

As he raised his hands in surrender Jude could see the wild spin of his thoughts. Could he move fast enough to disarm her? Could he take on these two women at once?

"Take whatever you want," he said. "But there is no need for any-one to get hurt here."

Jude had heard this tone before. Smooth, calm, eminently rea-sonable, a deflector of unsavory intentions. She hated this voice, its unwavering certainty, its presumption of success and power. She deplored what it said about its owner's place in the world. *Perform or Perish. Defeat Begets Domination. What You Think, Is.*

Mr. Ronald lowered his arms one centimeter, two. Jude could see he was mistaking her silence for doubt. A clicking noise at the back of his head set him straight: Kat had drawn her own gun and aimed it at the base of his skull. His hands returned to their original position.

"Please," he said in a new voice, one that wasn't smooth or calm at all.

She and Kat had agreed not to speak a word more than necessary, on the chance he might survive and recognize them. Inside her mind her voice screamed without restraint: *Are you experiencing fear, Mr. Ronald? What color is it?*

Jude kept her gun fixed at Mr. Ronald's forehead while Kat reached in her bag for the scarf, made of leopard-print velvet and neon trim. She used it as handcuffs, tying them around his wrists, tight enough to prevent escape but loose enough to evade marks or burns. Jude kept her gun steady as Kat maneuvered him toward the closed door and pushed him to his knees. She crept behind him and made a circle with her arms, lowering them around Mr. Ronald's neck, trapping him in a chokehold.

What shape is your fear? Jude thought, watching her sister work. *Is it changing direction? Can you catch and hold it in your mind?*

His wrists twisted against the scarf; his fingers clawed at Kat's hands. Kat tightened her grip, his chin fitted in the crook of her elbow, her right hand pressing against his head. For fifteen long seconds he gasped and gargled before falling still in her arms and then to the floor, dead weight that now had to be posed.

Jude checked his wrists and was pleased that the velvet had left no marks. Kat pointed to Mr. Ronald's bathrobe belt and quirked an eyebrow at Jude, a silent suggestion that they use his own belt instead of the one they'd brought along. Jude nodded her agreement.

He could regain consciousness in a matter of seconds. They had to move fast.

Kat pulled the belt from Mr. Ronald's robe and tied a knot around his neck, positioning it just beneath his left lower jaw, hugging the carotid artery. Together they heaved Mr. Ronald up under the armpits and opened the front door, just far enough to slip the other end of the belt through the crack before shutting it again. When they let his body go it fell slack, and the noose began to do its work.

That woke him up, all right. He writhed, a fish on a line.

Mr. Ronald, is your fear still there?

He danced his terrible dance, torso bucking, legs swiveling, toes tapping, shuffle, flail, silence, spasm, rattle, stillness.

One down, two to go.

KAT: NOW

Seven Months After the Accident

OCTOBER 1983

Richard is still crying from his lone, beautiful eye when I silently repeat the words to myself:

Is he really dead?

He is. Finally, they all are.

"Excuse me for a moment," I say, although I'm not sure if the letters arrange themselves in the right order, if the words even emerge as words or if I've merely gargled and spat a string of nonsense syllables. I back away from the dining table and pass the wall of guns and find his bathroom and throw the light on. A chandelier's long, glass tinsel shivers and clinks above me, and I let myself exhale beneath its sound. I rest my forehead against the vanity, and I recognize the bleary, one-eyed monster staring back at me, the same monster I'd seen in the bathroom mirror at Exiles months ago, when I was lying to a boy I liked and Jude was lying to me. Jude is me and I am Jude and the one-eyed monster is us, melded so seamlessly I can't tell where she ends and I begin.

I am in the home of a man I tried to murder for reasons unknown to me.

I replay our conversation at his table, his patch off, his pointed questions: *Tell me about your accident. Do you know where you had been? Where you were going to? What you had done?*

Does he know?

He can't. He must. I can't think about it. I must think about it.

I lift my forehead from the mirror just enough to see two eyes and tell myself I'm Jude. I am Jude, and I am flushing the toilet and washing my hands and returning calmly to the dining room. Richard is wiping the last of his tears, and because I am Jude, I reach over and help him, dabbing with the lightest, most delicate touch. Because I am Jude, I am able to apologize for being so rude and abrupt, and confess that I'm not feeling so well—perhaps (and here I laugh Jude's bright, incongruous laugh) I have forgotten about a jambalaya allergy from my past.

"Are you sure you're okay?" he asks, so very sweetly. "I hope it wasn't something I said?"

"Don't be silly," I tell him. "Your conversation was enlightening, as always. Thank you for sharing so much with me."

"Likewise. Can I drive you home, at least? It's getting dark."

"No need. I think the air will help."

"I'll see you tomorrow, then?"

"Same time and place," I say, and ask a question straight from Jude's mouth: "By the way, would you happen to have a crowbar I can borrow? Verona is having a hard time with a rusty old lock on one of her trunks."

"I'm sure I have one in the basement. Be right back."

When he returns, crowbar in hand, I kiss him on the

cheek—a kiss filled with promise and meaning, and one that is entirely mine.

I begin to run. I run past the tattered rose bushes working themselves back into bloom, past the sculpted hedges and wrought iron gates, past the satisfied people stretching their arms and turning in for the night. I push faster, the cool fall breeze assailing my open mouth and unblinking eyes, the crowbar slicing the air. I push faster still, filled with the roar of my heart and the pump of my blood and the desire to know why I wanted to kill. I turn into Verona's driveway, where my car is parked next to hers, and scuttle around the side of the house. The kitchen lights are still on, and Wallis barks at my receding footsteps.

My mother had told me that the shed contains some of her rarer antiques; a burglar would never be able to find them. I had believed her, but no longer; I remember Jude's words of warning and now I understand that our past is stored in that small, windowless space. Five hundred paces back, five hundred more to the left, and the grove opens to a familiar clearing. I slip though the gash in the hedges and see the shed and approach its padlocked door. I plant my feet and wedge the crowbar into the first lock and summon all of my strength as I push down and away. The lock yields to me, easier than I expected. I do the same with the second and the third, bursting with my sister's lethal calm. From inside the house Wallis barks again—short and sharp, a warning.

I fling open the door and step inside.

I stop. I spin.

An army of what must be my father's inventions line the perimeter of the room, barbed wire spheres and rusty wheels and metal boxes with bulbs that once flashed. A clothing rack holds the costumes I'd seen in Richard's pictures: two balding monkey suits with moth-eaten tails; monkey masks with cracked plastic faces; a polyester scorpion onesie faded to pink and its crumbling, disembodied claw. I throw and kick and hack everything in my path, seeking and searching. Beneath an old sofa I find a loose floorboard that looks like a hidden drawer, with a piece of twine for the pull. Inside there's a large lavender box labeled *1971–1978*, a span of time that begins with our eleventh birthday and ends with the year we allegedly went to Europe. I lift the red lid and find photographs—dozens and dozens, tied up in ribbon, divided by year. I sit down and pry apart every last one.

I glance at the first photograph, the second, the third, the twenty-third, the fifty-third. I see myself, I see myself with Jude, I see myself with Jude and Violet, I see myself with dozens of children I once knew, I see myself naked on a bed with the lights casting shadows overhead, my body taking direction from some unseen conductor, arranging itself into poses my mind didn't understand. I see Richard with two strange men and find my mother's handwriting on the back: *Bash, Ronald, and Donald, The Think Is Games, 1976.*

I remember my mother's words: *Ronald and Donald. One by suicide, the other by accident.*

I remember Jude's words, spoken through Richard, whom she must know as Bash: *Finally, they all are.*

I now understand why Jude fled at the sight of Richard at the market; she believed he was dead.

I now understand that I have not merely tried to kill.

I have already killed.

I am a person who is capable of murder.

I am a person capable of murder because they killed me first— Before Kat, the Kat I no longer know, the Kat that my brain erased.

For some time—minutes, hours?—I stop existing. My senses abandon me. I can't see the things that were vivid just a moment ago, the crowbar smashing the lock or the ghostly moon or the stars like scattered dice, or hear the hoots of the owls or the shift of the branches, or taste the tart fall air on my tongue, or feel my tongue at all; it has abandoned the inside of my mouth, and then my mouth abandons my body, and my body sheds itself again and again, stripping layers of secret skins until there's nothing left. I can't move because there is nothing left to move. I can't exist because there are too many versions of myself for any one of them to be real.

"Katherine?" I hear my mother call. There's a panicky edge to her voice, and I worry that she can see me, that she is witnessing me see what I am seeing, that she knows that I know.

I push Verona from my mind and think of Jude. The accident relieved me of the burden of my past and left it all to her. She lied not to deceive me but to save me, to save herself, to save us. If she told me a story filled with lovely little lies, she could eventually make them be true.

I stuff the crowbar in my bag and run to the driveway and call up to my mother's open window: "I'll be back soon!" Before she can respond, I start my car and take myself home, watching for any deer along the way, certain my sister is waiting for me.

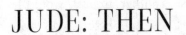

JUDE: THEN

Two Months before the Accident

JANUARY 1983

They had planned the second murder for the last Monday of the month.

On that afternoon, they stood on the corner of 10th and Spruce Streets carrying shopping bags filled with the necessary tools: Tragedy and Comedy, latex gloves, their handguns, and the same velvet scarf they had used with Ronald Lester.

News of Mr. Ronald's death shocked the Main Line and certain segments of the city proper. Imagine a man of his stature and wealth, his history of philanthropy and civic engagement, ending it all with a bathrobe belt, as undignified as it was tragic. He must have suffered financial setbacks in recent years, or grown despondent after his divorce, or become estranged from his children, or succumbed to a secret malaise. How disturbing for a delivery man to have found him three days later, smelling the body even before he reached the door. At his funeral, old friend Donald Lawson, the Donald half of the RonDon, shared a few words: "Wherever Ronald is, he's making that world work for him. What he thought, was. What his spirit feels, is."

In Jude's preliminary research, which entailed staking out the house for two weeks, she discovered that Mr. Donald had a girlfriend who occasionally spent the night—usually Wednesday, sometimes Thursday, but so far never a Monday. He also hosted a group of men on Tuesdays—for what, she didn't know. This evening he should be alone.

They needed to shake up their approach, differentiate this death from Mr. Ronald's. Another ambush would be unwise. Kat would not sweetly deliver a few lines before Jude made her move. They had to be patient and sly. They had to wear their masks: What if Mr. Donald rescheduled his group to Monday, forcing them to flee before completing the job? They had one hour to let every scenario, good and bad, tumble through their minds.

Kat huddled closer to her, shivering. All morning and afternoon it had snowed, the frothy piles not yet marred by dog piss or soot, and the wind's unrelenting shriek was the sound of a woman mourning alone. People passed, paying no attention. She and Kat could run screaming down the street waving Mr. Ronald's skull and no one would gaze in their direction. No one had time for anyone else's problems. There was no benefit in getting involved. Jude loved this about the city, the comforting anonymity, the aversion to superfluous connection.

"Let's start walking," Jude said. "Talk to me. Act like we're having a normal conversation."

Kat stepped over a puddle, gripping Jude's arm. "It's hard to have a normal conversation when you're being ordered to. What do you want to talk about?"

"Anything! The weather! What you ate for breakfast! The size of your shoes! Help me out here."

"You're doing great," Kat said. "Keep going, we're almost there."

"Weather, weather, weather, shoes, shoes, breakfast, breakfast, variables, variables, possible wrinkles," Jude said. They were almost inside. They were almost inside and they didn't know what or who might come in after them. Jude bent over and pretended to tie her shoe, fishing the key from her sock. The key had been a gift from Genesis, copied from the original years ago, when they all lived at the row homes and Gen was still alive, doing everything Jude asked.

"We're clear," Kat said. "No one is even threatening to look at us."

With a turn of the key and a push from Jude's shoulder, they were inside.

Mr. Donald's home was sparse and sleek, the bare minimum, save for his photographs along the walls, many of them self-portraits: the limp silver hair, the lantern jaw, the nose long and crooked as a beckoning finger. The shelves were absent of trinkets that might shatter during a struggle. Against the opposite wall stood a reclining couch made in the current decade. It was an obnoxious, hulking thing, done in gold vinyl and wide enough to accommodate two people, with a beverage holder built into one arm. It faced a teak stand holding a television set and small collection of books. Jude glanced at the spines: *Your Erroneous Zones*; *The Teachings of Don Juan*; *Illusions: The Adventures of a Reluctant Messiah*. She heard a buzzing noise behind her and turned to find Kat sprawled across the recliner, her body quaking.

"This thing actually vibrates," she said. "I'm a little disturbed."

"Did you touch a button without gloves on? Wipe it off and stop playing around—he will be home in forty-five minutes."

"Chill pill, please. It will take me two seconds to wipe it down." She swiped the button with the edge of her sleeve.

"Move over," Jude said. "Let me see behind it." She appraised the couch from the side, noting how the curved spine created a gap, cresting up and out like a wave. "We could fit behind this thing, don't you think?"

"Easily," Kat said.

Jude retrieved four latex gloves from the bag and gave a pair to Kat. They maneuvered themselves between the recliner and the wall; the space was just wide enough to conceal them both. "We'll have to wait here until he gets home, starts drinking, and passes out. This way we can leverage him from behind."

"There's no closet?" Kat asked. "I'm going to cramp back here."

"No, just a coat rack near the kitchen. The perils of an old house. We need to get the tub ready and hurry back down."

The second floor functioned as a sort of photography studio, with various cameras and tripods and black screens and the umbrella contraption that Jude could not look at for longer than a second. She turned on the bathtub and checked her watch: 5:35.

"What's more excruciating?" Kat asked. "Watching water rise or watching it boil?"

Jude ignored her. Her mind was entrenched in calamitous scenarios. If he walked in the door now, they'd jump from the bedroom window and land on concrete—a twenty-foot drop with no shrubbery to soften their fall. They'd likely break their legs or, at the very least, bust an ankle or knee, which would hinder a quick getaway. Not to mention that their equipment was stashed by the recliner. Nothing in the bags could be traced to her or Kat, but they would be clear evidence of an invasion. Mr. Donald would alert the police, an investigation would ensue, Mr. Ronald's suicide might be reconsidered as a murder.

Slowly, slowly, the water level rose; Jude estimated it had reached eight inches. It would have to be enough for now. She nudged Kat and they started back downstairs, the old pine staircase creaking with every step. With each passing second Jude expected to hear the lock turn and the door open.

"Turn around, Comedy," she said, and tied Kat's mask.

Jude was too afraid to speak as Kat returned the favor, transforming her into Tragedy. Her heart and stomach seemed to merge, both fluttering, both roiling.

"Relax," Kat said.

Jude stabbed Kat's side with an elbow. "Stop talking now," she said. Her watch read 5:53. Mr. Donald would be home any moment. She took a deep breath and willed her body to stay still inside its skin.

Seven minutes later, at exactly six o'clock, Jude heard the slide of a key, the click of a lock. A light flicked on.

"Do you want a drink?" Jude heard him ask.

He was not alone.

Kat gripped her arm, the nails sinking into Jude's skin. Silently she pleaded with her sister not to make another move.

"Definitely," a woman said.

Jude closed her eyes to sharpen her ears and everything quadrupled in volume. Mr. Donald let out a gusty sigh. A zipper made its shivery sound. Heavy steps thudded toward the kitchen. The sound of ice clinking and liquid pouring was absurdly amplified; Jude heard a hailstorm, a waterfall. On his way back, Mr. Donald turned on the television. "Kiss my grits," Flo quipped. Canned laughter sounded like a roar inside an amphitheater. The scratch of the woman's clothing against vinyl was a hundred records being stopped midplay.

Mr. Donald joined her, making the vinyl scratch again. Jude's body coiled tighter into itself. Kat was right; here came the cramping. A spasm galloped up her calf. She heard wet suction sounds, an army of plungers adhering and releasing, and realized they were kissing. Kat's hand clamped around her arm. Bile surged in her throat. She tried to coax it back down without making any hint of a noise.

There was a pause, a shifting, a freight train of panicky thoughts: *What if they are about to have sex? What if she gets on top and is high enough to peek over the crest of the recliner and see us? We can't hurt an innocent person. We can't have an outsider involved at all. If she sees us we will chop and kick and punch our way to the door as fast as possible, all the while trying to keep our masks on.*

She fought to keep her breath regular and silent. Her heart was a pinball inside her chest, shooting, spinning, jostling.

"Mmmmm," Mr. Donald murmured. "Can you stay?"

"You know I'd love to, babe," she said, "but the sitter's leaving soon."

Jude let out a tiny exhalation.

"Call her," he said. "I'll cover the extra hours."

Jude sucked in her breath.

"You know I wish I could, but she has plans tonight and can't stay longer."

She let herself exhale again, and felt Kat sink alongside her.

Mr. Donald and the woman pushed themselves up from the recliner.

"We didn't even get a chance to try the massager," he said.

"Next time. Soon."

The open door let in a whoosh of wind and cold, and then Mr. Donald believed he was alone again. Jude turned to Kat, and in that tiny sliver of space tried to mime her thoughts. *Back to the original plan: Wait until he passes out. Then you put him in a chokehold while I face him with the gun.* Kat nodded; she understood.

Jude knew that her sister did not want to wait, which is why she herself needed to hold the gun. They could not risk Kat pulling the trigger and making a mess Jude might not be able to clean.

Mr. Donald settled back into the recliner with his drink. "Who you calling crazy, honky?" asked George Jefferson. Sweat stung Jude's eyes. Ice cubes slid against the glass and she counted three gulps. Finally he was getting down to the business of knocking himself out. He got up again, and this time Jude heard slow footsteps up the stairs. Kat poked her and mimed popping pills. Jude folded her hands, miming prayer. Her ass felt like it had fallen asleep and her foot was close behind, tingling and halfway to numb. The stairs creaked again, signaling his descent. Jude heard a rattling in the kitchen, the scrape of glass against a counter; he was bringing the bottle with him.

She could not tell how long they sat there in the gap between the recliner and the wall, listening to Mr. Donald swallow and belch. Thirty, sixty, ninety minutes, who knows? She did not dare move. She cringed every time Kat readjusted herself. Mr. Donald farted. Kat's shoulders shook; of course her sister would laugh, even in this moment, when they were so ready. One more gulp, another belch, and he began to snore, a snarled knot sound coming from the bull's-eye of his chest.

They looked at each other: *Now.* Slowly they lifted themselves from the space, Jude gripping her gun, Kat making her arms into a noose. Jude crept to the front of the recliner, facing him, gun aimed.

It was time.

She watched as Kat wrapped her arms around Mr. Donald's neck. If he had been trained as Kat was, he would know to raise one shoulder and thrust the other down to weaken her grip. He might try to loop an arm over his head and spin, setting up to confront her head on, to pull her from her hiding spot and kick her in the groin. He would certainly push his chin down in order to breathe. But Mr. Donald did none of these things, and instead his glasses fell from his eyes, and his mouth burbled a splash of puke, and his head went slack inside her grip.

"You didn't kill him, did you?" Jude whispered.

Kat shook her head. "No, but just about."

"Good. We need to get him upstairs."

Jude pocketed her gun. She gripped Mr. Donald's torso as Kat hoisted his legs.

Together, gently, they lowered him to the floor and maneuvered him to the bottom of the stairs. They developed a system: Jude hoisted his shoulders while Kat lifted his legs, taking a step at a time, hoist and lift, hoist and lift, his ass the only part of him skimming the wood. He grew heavier with each hoist and her throat had gone dry. The Tragedy mask clung to her sweaty skin.

"Give me a few seconds," she told Kat. "I need to breathe."

She doubled over, hands on her knees, head hanging, and at that moment Mr. Donald's eyes flung open and he began to buck against the stairs. He grasped one of Jude's ankles and yanked, whisking her own body out from under her. He kicked at Kat's grasping hands. She saw Kat reach for her gun and aim it at Mr. Donald's head.

"Don't shoot!" Jude shouted, and the words reeled him back up to sitting. She lunged again, wrapping her arms around his neck, calibrating the pressure precisely, easing him toward the end but restraining herself just enough; he needed to die in the water. His breath thinned: a wheeze, a puff. She took off her glove long enough to press a finger against his neck, finding his slushy pulse.

"Still alive," she said, relieved.

They resumed their hoisting and lifting. At the top of the stairs they stripped him, piece by piece, and Jude dissected him in her mind: *His arm is just an arm, his foot a foot, his legs are legs, his torso is a torso, his thing—oh god, his thing—is really just a thing, and now he is almost just a body, a limp collection of bones and skin and rotting organs that will never function again.* Together they positioned him by the tub and Kat, still gloved, turned on the faucet; the jets released the water into bubbly spirals. "Poor Donald Lawson," they would say. "Got a bit too sauced and drowned in his own luxury tub." One more hoist and lift, and his body sank to the bottom of the tub.

With her own gloved hand, Jude threw off her mask. Let him see her now. Let him know that she is alive, not just alive but a beast—an indomitable monster that he helped to create.

"Now," Jude said, and sat down on the toilet to watch.

Kat cupped Mr. Donald's head and pushed him down. His eyes flipped open and widened, darting like minnows in their sockets; his legs spasmed into terse and feeble kicks. He gasped and gasped, and the bubbles popping around his open mouth would in any other context seem joyful and lively. *What shape is the water?* Jude thought. *The only prison is the one in your mind. What you think, is.*

Kat pressed until his limbs went still, and pressed another few moments just to make sure.

Two down, one to go.

KAT: NOW

Seven Months after the Accident

OCTOBER 1983

The door to apartment 4E is open, as if Jude has been expecting me, and she is pacing across the living room, back and forth. I think I see her lips move, and I realize she is having a conversation with me, playing both our parts. I know what she's saying, and what I'm saying back, and yet when my sister stops and turns, forcing me to look at my mirrored self, all of our words fail to come. "I don't know what to say," we both say. She steps right as I step left; I step right as she steps left; finally we do it correctly, moving in opposite directions. She locks the door behind me in a way that feels permanent, sealing us both inside.

She opens her mouth, closes it. She waves her hands. She shrugs, closes her eyes, and tries again, this time using the words only I will understand: "Ouy ownk." *You know.*

I nod, unable to speak.

The look on her face makes my heart clench; she is present but not here. She has stopped existing in the same way I'd stopped when I found the pictures: I can see the mechanics of my sister, her fulcrums and bolts and nuts and screws, the wheels and levers that activate and spin her brilliant brain, all come to an unnatural, jerky halt that drops her to her knees, without any instinct to break the fall. Her torso collapses next, sending her face directly to the floor with such blunt force that I hear the crack of her nose, and her blood spreads like a pillow beneath her. I kneel in her blood and rest her head on my knees.

"Jude," I whisper. "You don't have to say anything. You don't have to say anything you don't want to say ever again. And you don't have to lie."

For a long, long time, we sit this way. I grip a fistful of her hair like reins. I rock her back and forth. She looks at me without seeing, a different kind of blind from Richard, the blindness that comes from having seen too much.

"I do have to say something," she says. Her voice sounds clogged, rusty, as though she's forgotten how to use it. "You know about the murders."

I force myself to stay calm. I hold my broken, raggedy sister in my arms, her blood warm against my skin, and speak in an absurd, singsongy voice, the cadence of a nursery rhyme.

"I do know. And I know about a murder that didn't happen," I say, sweet, so sweet. "Deep breath, okay? I'm here now. I believe you. I'm sorry I ever doubted you."

My tone is working. She seems mollified, and responds in a shy, tentative whisper, like she's asking for permission.

"You saw there were two, Ronald Lester and Donald Lawson. We used to call them the RonDon. And then Sebastian Vance. We called him King Bash."

My hands squeeze her face. I try to picture the kind, self-deprecating Richard I know calling himself the king of anything.

"I know you know King Bash," she says. "You call him Richard and you are friends with him. I went to the market to try to talk to you and I saw him. He wasn't supposed to be there. He wasn't supposed to be alive."

"I know we did what we had to do," I tell her. "But it's okay now. It's in our past."

Jude shakes her head, breaking free of my grip. I can hear her think, *You don't understand* before she says the words. "No, it isn't. He has to die."

She can't mean this, I think. *This situation has no business in our future. If Richard suspects us, he has kept his thoughts to himself.* "What do you mean, Jude?" I say. A light tone, a curious tone. "Why would he have to die?"

"If he doesn't die, Violet will go to the police. She knows what we failed to do and she wants it done." She looks past my shoulder and addresses the wall, too embarrassed to face me straight on. "She has proof. My necklace ripped off in King Bash's house and she has it. And she had a tape recorder running during one of our meetings and I couldn't grab it in time and I am stupid and I've failed us. We have to do it."

I am not that person anymore, I want to tell her. *I am not her, and I no longer want to be her.* Instead I say: "Don't worry. You've worried long enough for both of us."

My sister becomes a person again, and the pain of her own presence hits her acutely. I let her cry, her nose blowing bubbles of her blood, and I promise, for the first time in our lives, to be the twin who concocts all of the explanations and tidies any mistakes. I will become Before Kat one last time, just for her.

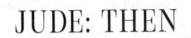

JUDE: THEN

The Night of the Accident
MARCH 1983

The forecast called for rain, but by the time it began to fall Jude expected they'd long be finished with King Bash, who lived in an old Tudor home just three blocks from their mother. Since dissolving The Plan in early 1982, Jude discovered, he had gradually down-graded his own life, receding from the public eye, selling his antiques full time, using his middle name, Richard, instead of Bash. But to Jude he would always be King Bash, who understood her from a very young age, who reassured her that her differences were an asset, who—despite her youth—treated her like a trusted confidant and important ally, whose betrayal imprinted on every cell in her body and surged through every nerve. She had loved him so much that her hate for him now pained her, a hate that did not respond to Reject and Release, a hate that pulsed inside her like a second deadly heart.

On that night, a Wednesday, she and Kat arrived in Norris Ford at five p.m., one hour before the antique market closed. Their bags held Tragedy and Comedy, their lucky velvet scarf, their pistols and flashlights, latex gloves, and a lock-picking kit. They parked their car down the road, belly-slithered like soldiers across the back of King Bash's lawn, and found their point of entry: double steel doors that opened to a dank basement. Jude remembered that basement well, and knew it had an internal door at the top of the stairs that led into his favorite room.

"They're heavy," Jude said. "You take one door and I'll get the other."

She let Kat descend first. When the doors were shut behind them, Jude waved her flashlight across the space. A cache of recollections opened in a vacant corner of her mind. She deployed her reject button, zapping at the images before they were fully formed, like stopping the development of a picture. A focused scan around the room would show mannequins wearing animal costumes, and a life-sized plastic rabbit, and a glorious portrait of Violet, age twelve, in a cracked frame. Rejected, they became a department store display, and a playground toy, and a sweet, hopeful smile on a face Jude could pretend not to know. Rejected, they existed only as objects and not as memories.

"I don't know about you," Kat said, "but I am rejecting and releasing all over the place."

Jude looked up to see Kat at the top of the stairs, her ear pressed against the door that led to the inside. "Do you hear anything?" she asked.

"Not yet," Kat said. "I looked beneath the crack and it seems like the room is still dark."

"Is the door unlocked?"

Kat jiggled the knob. "Nope."

"Damn," Jude said. She pulled on a pair of latex gloves. "Let me up there. We want to be ready to just spring inside when it's time."

She found the tension wrench and slid it into the keyhole, just as Marcus, her old rabbit, had taught her. Rotate the wrench back and forth, insert the pick and feel for the pins, press gently until you feel the farthest one click into place, repeat with each pin until you've touched them all. The lock will show no signs of damage, and the door opened with a quiet nudge.

"What are you doing?" Kat whispered. "If you're going in there, I'm coming with you."

Jude held up a hand, stopping her sister. "Let me just do a quick circle around the downstairs."

Behind her, she heard the sound of Kat cocking her gun.

The favorite room was just as Jude had remembered it. A long leather sofa spanned across the space, its back conveniently facing the basement door. In an adjacent alcove, a floor-to-ceiling cabinet show-casing antique guns faced a wall of rare coins. With a gloved hand she turned the tiny lock in the gun cabinet. She tried to put herself in King Bash's mind: Which would he choose if he'd decided to put a bullet through his brain? The pearl-handled Depression-era Smith & Wesson? The perfectly restored Smith Civil War carbine? The Springfield from the Second World War? She decided on a more modern pistol, maybe twenty years old—dark gray and sleek, with a long, thin barrel that resembled the snout of a whippet. Jude did not know its model or make, but it looked lethal enough. As expected, it was loaded. Kat's aim had to be perfect; they could not risk an errant bullet firing into the ceiling or wall.

Jude visualized how the evening should evolve: a surprise attack as King Bash sat on this couch, eating dinner or drinking one of his rare vintages. She would snag his neck in her arms while Kat crept around, aiming her own gun at his face. In the brief moment he was uncon-scious, Kat would place the vintage pistol in his hand and use his finger to pull the trigger. They had researched how to mimic suicide by gun: Shoot the temple at contact range, to ensure gunpowder residue and burn mark around the wound. The angle of the shot should veer slightly upward. Most important, there can be no signs of struggle—no marks, no scratches, no microscopic strips of skin left beneath fingernails.

She took the pistol from the case, closed the cabinet, and backed into the basement. Kat still had her gun cocked and ready to fire.

"Put that thing away," Jude said. "I have no idea how much longer we'll be alone, and we need to get ready."

As Kat tied the Tragedy mask around Jude's head, her heart began its nervous dance, moving out of beat with her breath. She urged her body back into synchronicity and reassured herself: they'd already gotten away with murder twice.

Together they sat at the top of the basement stairs, knees touching, ears flat against the door. They moved only to check their watches or find each other's eyes. Jude felt herself shaking—nerves or the basement's cold, dry air? She couldn't tell. Kat's shaking matched her own. They listened and listened. They swept their eyes down to the crack in the door, looking for a beam of light, a signal that he'd come home. An unknown number of moments later, the beam appeared: King Bash had arrived.

Slowly, so very slowly, Jude pushed the door open a fraction of an inch, just wide enough to see a sliver of the room. The long leather couch was still empty. She heard a banging in the kitchen, the sounds of dinner being prepared. And then music: Sinatra crooning about someone under his skin. *Damn.* Jude wanted to be able to hear him before she saw him. Hearing was such a vital component of knowing when to move. A half hour passed. Sinatra acknowledged it had been a very good year. At last, King Bash sat down on the leather sofa. He did not turn on the television. They could see his head and shoulders and the point of his elbow, raising and lowering his glass of wine.

Jude mimed the plan to Kat: *Let's wait until he's had a few glasses just so his reflexes are dulled. Then you point your gun, I knock him out, and you finish the job with his gun.* She pressed her hand against Kat's bag; the vintage pistol was there, ready to be fired.

Kat mimed back a message of her own: *I have to pee.*

Jude shook her head: *No. No you do not.*

Kat shrugged: *What can I do?*

This was a problem. Kat's miniscule bladder was a problem. Kat's expression of her desire to piss came only after hours of holding it in. When she said she had to piss, it meant *now*—not when they got home, not even at a stop along the way. It meant she was within five minutes of releasing herself wherever she happened to be. Jude could not allow this. What was Kat going to do? Rummage around in the basement to find a jar to piss in? And then what—leave it on the shelf for someone to find? She didn't think it could be traced to Kat, but still, there could be no hint that King Bash's death was anything but a suicide. Everyone who knew the RonDon and King Bash had to believe that their deaths came in a tragic cluster, one inspiring the next.

Kat mimed at her again, using her hands to scream: *We need to strike. Now.*

This was becoming too complicated for miming. Jude hissed at her sister: "Just fucking piss yourself! It will dry!"

Kat shook her head and hissed back: "It's time. We can take him. We have the element of surprise, like we had with Mr. Ronald. He'll have a gun at his head and his neck in a hold. We have him. We'll *have* him."

Before Jude could speak or mime a response, Kat cocked her gun and opened the basement door wide enough to fit her advancing foot. Whether or not Jude agreed, it was time.

They crept, their feet in unison, left right, left right. Sinatra crooned about strangers meeting in the night. King Bash sat two feet in front of them, his fork up and down, piercing the last bites of steak. Jude glimpsed a copy of the evening newspaper opened to the Arts section. At least he was preoccupied: music, food, words. He was not expecting Kat's movements, her sly shimmy to his right side, the gun raised and pointed. He was not expecting Jude's own movements, rising up like a cobra behind him, her arms taut and prepared.

He screamed and dropped his fork.

And there, right there and then, Kat began to piss herself.

Jude's arms lowered with the speed of a trap door. Her arms did what they had been trained to do. They stabilized and squeezed and stopped King Bash's body from working, the contracting of his diaphragm, the yanking of his rib cage. But then King Bash's body responded. It launched a series of moves—precise, learned moves— that were equal and opposite to Jude's, neutralizing her.

She saw it happening and was powerless to stop it: How could she, when his arms were making the same exact weapons but were twice as thick as hers? When his grip was tighter and his pull harder and his ability to unravel her so fast and clean? When his pointy elbow soared like a cannonball into her jaw? She felt her head hit the floor. She felt it bounce. She felt the tip of her incisor pierce her tongue and a rush of blood in her mouth. She swallowed it. She would not leave her own blood on this floor. She heard Sinatra warble about exchanging glances. She looked up and saw her sister pull the trigger.

Jude mimed at her: *No! Don't shoot!*

That one second encompassed the beginning and end of the world.

Kat pulled and nothing happened. Kat pulled again and nothing happened.

Jimmy the rabbit had warned them about Saturday night specials: the jamming, the unreliability. It didn't matter, they'd said, because shooting people with those guns was not part of their plan.

King Bash was standing, all six feet plus of him. He moved toward her sister with murderous intent. Their bodies collided and fell to the floor, twisting and roiling, giving and taking. She saw his hand encircle Kat's neck and launch her head into a table, the same motion one would use to christen a yacht with a bottle of champagne. She could feel the *pop* inside her sister's head, the unmooring of her brain inside her skull.

Jude felt her body crank itself, turning its knob all the way right. Her brain revved, her breath gusted, her blood boiled inside of her skin. Her limbs stretched and flailed, looking for something, anything, that would stop him from killing her sister. The object hit its target before Jude realized what it was: a fire iron lashing against the side of King Bash's head, once, twice, three times, marking the very spot where the bullet should have gone.

He stumbled as though drunk, landing on his knees. The blood bloomed so prettily across his white carpet. His hand gripped the table. He was trying to pull himself up. He was pulling himself up. He was almost up.

Kat, too, was almost up, resurrected by panic and adrenaline. Comedy looked at Tragedy and retrieved the fork from his dinner plate, a single leaf of lettuce hanging like tinsel from the tines. Tragedy looked at Comedy and raised the iron. Jude watched as Kat plunged the fork into the meat of King Bash's eye, digging it out like it was filling in a pie. He screamed and screamed, louder than one thousand Sinatras. Jude did not want to be the one who killed him but here she was, whacking the head of a man she once idolized and adored, again and again and again, and on the last blow his eyes closed shut. He was dead, he was dead, he had to be dead. Jude was sure of it.

They took five seconds to scan the room. It was a mess. King Bash was a mess. There was blood and piss everywhere. The cops would be called. There would be an investigation. But they had worn gloves that covered their fingerprints. Kat's blood could be anyone's blood. Kat's piss could be anyone's piss. There would be no reason to suspect it was them.

They gathered King Bash's vintage pistol and their bags and exited the way they came: through the basement, past the graveyard of rejected things, on their stomachs through the grass, to their car down the road. Kat had the keys and hurled herself into the car, her hands shaking against the wheel. She assured Jude she was fine; it was just a bump on the head. They had no time to argue; this was the sort of neighborhood where the cops came fast. Jude chose to ignore Kat's stumbling steps. She chose to believe her sister's slurred words. She chose to watch her sister turn the key and start the engine and hurtle off into the night, trusting that nothing from the past would ever catch them again.

The black street gleamed with rain.

JUDE AND KAT: NOW

Eight Months after the Accident
NOVEMBER 1983

Jude lied to Kat one last time, promising not to follow her to King Bash's house on a Friday evening, but here she is, standing idly on the street, pretending to read a map, waiting for her sister to round the corner. She knows she is making Kat do something she herself can't do—something that After Kat would also never do—and the knowledge of this spreads inside her, poisoning her from within.

As a small act of penance, she called Sab and confessed that she, not Kat, had been the one to end their relationship, for reasons she was not at liberty to disclose. If he were smart, he would win Kat back while he had the chance; he would never find another quite like her.

She knew, even after hearing Sab's relief at the news, that it was not enough. It would never be enough.

This new version of Kat, this After Kat, did all the advance research and preparation. She went shopping to buy some sort of large bird and various vegetables, which she told King Bash—Richard, to her—she would roast in his oven. Let her reciprocate his hospitality, she'd told him, calling from a pay phone. It has been a month since she's seen him, and she misses his company and conversation. And besides, she owes him a crowbar.

He agreed, as they both knew he would.

Jude watches as Kat pulls up the driveway and parks in its deepest curve, invisible from the street. Jude creeps closer, inching along the trees lining the side of the yard. Kat fidgets with her bag of food and bottle of wine. She is herself, but dressed like Jude: old jeans, a T-shirt, a face as bare as she can stand. Her old gun and King Bash's vintage pistol both hide in her purse, resurrected from their burial ground, loaded and cleaned of dirt. She will use his own gun against him but keep hers nearby, just in case.

King Bash—no patch this time—opens the door, takes the bag and wine, and ushers her in. Jude can picture the antique table, the long leather couch, the cases filled with old coins and older guns, the photos of her beloved, treacherous Violet on the wall, Kat setting the table, lingering over the forks, all too aware of what they'd done, the blood and the piss and the fevered excavation of his exquisite eye.

It's time for Jude to move.

She walks around the back of the house and belly-crawls across the yard, ending at the familiar basement door. She can hear the quiet refrains of music and bouts of loud laughter. She passes the dusty old relics of the Think Is Games: a scorpion costume, an inflatable rabbit, a monkey mask impaled on a rusty spike.

An hour passes, and for that hour Jude does not move. She prides herself on her lack of movement, for talking her body down, for ordering her cramps to dissipate, her ear to stop itching, her throat to stop tickling from the swirls of dust. She remembers Kat having to piss and then pissing herself at the moment the time came to aim her gun. Jude's own bladder is locked tight, her entire body on pause until she needs it to start again.

She presses her ear closer against the door and hears King Bash's voice, intermingled with her sister's. She presses her ear so hard that its flaps hurt against her head.

———————

"Kat, this looks delicious," Richard says. "Living on your own really seems to suit you."

I start arranging the food on our plates and continue this harmless conversation, this foreplay to murder. I try to imagine these same hands that are scooping vegetables holding a gun to this man's face, pulling a trigger, waiting for bullets that never shot.

Once Jude had stopped crying, once I'd made my promise to become Before Kat one more time, she told me everything about that night. She spared no detail, unburdening herself, and I absorbed it all.

Now, I hear myself say, "It does suit me. I miss my mother sometimes, but it was time to move on. And of course I can visit her, and you, any time you'll have me."

Our chat meanders in pleasant directions: new coins, new guns, new and strange customers, new ways to make them buy things they don't need. I think about Jude, no doubt pressing her ear against the door, the same position as the first time we had tried to kill him.

"Another glass of wine?" Richard asks. "I've been waiting for an occasion to open this Grand Cru from Burgundy, and this certainly qualifies."

"That sounds perfect," I tell him. "I'll sip while I do the dishes."

"Don't be silly," he says. I hear the cheery pop of a cork. "I'll do that when you leave."

"I insist," I tell him. "It's soothing to me, for some reason. One of those weird quirks that appeared after my accident."

"How funny," he says, handing me a glass. "I had similar experiences after mine. I became a bit obsessive about odd things—the way I folded my socks, for instance, or the arrangement of toiletries in my cabinet. I guess it's our subconscious way of seeking order after we've been through incredible chaos."

"That must be it," I say. I turn on the water, letting it get to scalding, watching it pink my skin. I pull a pair of latex gloves from my bag, resting on the floor by my feet. I think about the two guns inside of it, dormant, waiting. "Although I have a feeling my old self—I call her 'Before Kat'—specialized in chaos."

He must hear the thunderous bang of my heart over the sound of the running water; it is that loud. I remind myself of why I am here and who he actually is: *This is not my friend Richard but a stranger named King Bash, the man who collected children and transformed them into entertainment, the man who nearly destroyed my indestructible sister.*

"Did you say something?" Richard says. His voice is coming from somewhere behind me, maybe near the refrigerator. "If so, I missed it."

I'm so flustered I can't tell if I've spoken aloud, if I have whispered his old name and title from The Plan, a moniker I am not supposed to know. The water continues to run, heating my fingers through the latex gloves. "Nothing important," I say. "Just talking to myself."

"Look at me," he says.

I turn my head, a movement that feels as slow and ponderous as the rotation of the sun.

He is holding the vintage gun, *his* gun, which was supposed to still be in the bag by my feet. I have the same experience Richard described when we had our jambalaya dinner: the sensation of being separated from my body, being an observer of its form rather than inhabiting it, wondering when it stopped paying attention and allowed him to find his weapon.

"It was you, wasn't it?" he asks. "You and Jude."

I drop a dish at my feet, the pieces skittering across the floor.

"Take it from me if you want to," he says. "I won't stop you."

I can't move.

I think of Jude watching me and sense her disappointment; Before Kat would have already pulled the trigger. Before Kat would have been racing from the house already, speeding away into the rain.

"Kat," I hear him say, his voice so sweet, so kind. He raises his hands in supplication, the gun dangling from his thumb. "So now you know, and now you know *I* know. And I don't know if this means anything to you, but I am so sorry for everything. I am sorry to you and to Jude."

He brings his hands back down, puts his finger on the trigger, and extends his arm to me.

"This is your last chance to take it," he says, almost a whisper. "I told you I deserve it."

I conjure enough of my old self to extend my arm, too, meeting him halfway.

————————

Jude had heard enough to know that their past had been dragged into the present, belly up and exposed, waiting for someone to do something, for *Kat* to do something, to be the Before Kat she once was, the version of Kat who would have already pulled the trigger—but Kat isn't and she can't and she won't. Jude knows this, and in some strange way, it comforts her; Kat had always been true to herself. Jude should never have asked for a deviation from this loyalty, a regression into the past from which Kat would never return.

After Kat is a gift that Before Kat will not be permitted to kill.

Jude would rather take the blame for everything and go to prison. She would rather die herself.

She lowers her hand onto the knob of King Bash's basement door and turns.

She hears one flat, sharp shot, and then a terrifying echo of silence.

She rounds the corner and finds King Bash on the kitchen floor, a gun positioned inches from his hand, a smoking hole in the place of his stunning blue eye, now as blind as the other.

"He did it," Kat says. Jude sees that she is in shock, a veil of sweat blanketing her cold skin. "His took his own gun and turned it on himself and did it. Tis vore. Tis nafilly vore."

It's over. It's finally over.

Jude steps toward her sister. She wraps her hands around the back of Kat's neck and takes a deep dive into her sister's eyes. She clocks the oscillation of Kat's pupils, her quickened breath, the quake of her fingers. She is so close that the image of her sister warps and blurs. She sees Kat at age four, at age eight, at age ten, at age twelve, and all the moments in the ages after that, bad and good, dark and thrilling, defeated and triumphant, all of the many Kats she has ever known.

Even if Kat were lying, Jude would accept her words as truth.

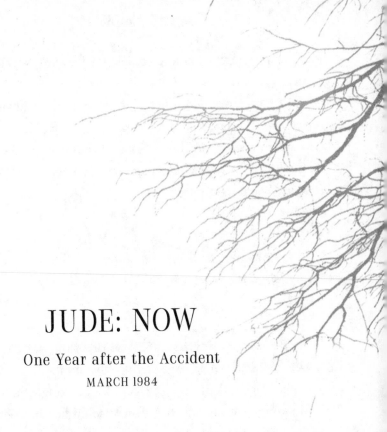

JUDE: NOW

One Year after the Accident

MARCH 1984

These are the things Jude Bird, formerly Jude Sheridan, knows to be true: One year ago, on a wet winter night, her mirror twin lost everything she ever knew about herself. She saved Kat, and Kat saved her in turn.

On March 13, the anniversary of the day Kat lost what she knew, Jude suggests they celebrate everything she's gained. She blindfolds her sister and walks her through the neighborhood, past a Catholic church, a playground, a rehab center, a check-cashing place, a McDonald's, a theater showing *Against All Odds*, Corropolese Tomato Pie. She opens the door of a tattoo shop and leads her sister inside and lays her down on a long leather table. Hours later they step outside, just in time to witness the last of the sun's brazen light, and examine each other's wrists: the old, identical scars have been transformed into identical arrows, pointed resolutely forward, beckoning what's to come.

The Plan is dead now, in both the external world and in her mind, rejected and released for good. She does not think of Violet until the day she comes home from work and finds an envelope bearing her name. Out falls Jude's nameplate necklace, perfectly polished, and a note in Violet's familiar script:

J,

I think you might have dropped this . . .
And the scorpion has lost its sting.

V.

She does not think about King Bash or the RonDon or the Island or kill-saving, the horrible weight of the monkey mask atop her head. She does not think of Verona except for one single Sunday evening in early spring. Kat says she has a surprise for her and leads her to their car, ordering Jude into the passenger seat. She drives with a concentration Jude hasn't seen since the murders—radio off, eyes unwavering, not a word of explanation, weaving in and out of traffic with an intense and deadly calm. After an hour they arrive at the old house, their childhood home, the place where they'd seen their father for the very last time, the place where they'd first met King Bash and the RonDon, the place where Jude had fled from Verona's dog, the place that still terrified her when she faced it straight on.

All this time Kat has not spoken one word. Now she turns to Jude and says, "You can do this."

Jude can't look at her, can't look at anything. She shuts her eyes and shakes her head and says *no no no no no*, feeling like a child on the verge of a tantrum, being dragged along when all she wants to do is sit down and stay put, safe in her stillness.

"Yes yes yes yes yes," Kat says. She exits her side of the car and opens Jude's door. She wrestles Jude's hand from her lap and traps it in her own. "You are doing it. *We* are doing it."

Kat pushes ahead as she has always done, oblivious to threats or consequences, pulling Jude along with her, down the curved brick driveway, all the way to the ancient front door. She raises and lowers the knocker, banging it again and again, until it swings open and reveals Verona, dressed in a gauzy robe, a cigarette glowing at her fingers. Her mouth drops open and her eyes flit left to right, taking them both in.

"Girls!" she says. "Katherine! Judith! What a—"

"Shut up," Kat says. "You just shut the fuck up." Her tone scares even Jude. She remembers her private description of Kat, one she'd never shared: a machine gun tucked inside of a tulip. Now the petals have fully opened, the barrel taking aim.

To Jude's surprise, Verona goes silent. The ashes drop from her cigarette.

Kat squeezes Jude's hand and says, "Go."

Jude knows she has no choice. "Ouy rea rou therom," she says. Her words sound disconnected from her own mouth, a voice being piped in from some distant locale.

"You are our mother," Kat translates. She squeezes Jude's hand again, so tight her fingers turn numb.

"Ouy rewe pupsosed ot cettpro su," Jude says. Her voice is louder this time, and closer.

"You were supposed to protect us," Kat says.

Verona is silent, her face unmoving. Another cluster of ashes drops.

Jude speaks one last line, her voice now fully her own: "Ouy rea thinong." She squeezes Kat's hand and they translate it together: "You are nothing."

They wait for a beat, hands intertwined, breath in sync. Again Verona's eyes dart back and forth, from Kat to Jude and back, until she lifts them to glance at something in the distance, a benign and empty place to land her gaze.

"Good gracious," she says to no one at all. "Good gracious indeed."

And with that, Very Sherry shuffles backward to step off the stage. Kat looks at Jude and Jude looks at Kat and together they thrust their hands against the door, slamming it shut, making her disappear.

Instead of thinking about all those things, now lodged deep into her past, Jude amplifies the minutia in her present, turning the small into big, the gray into color, the silence into sonic booms.

She thinks about the pleasure of the first bite of hoagie; of a table well dusted and a floor scrubbed clean; of Kat driving her own new car and getting lost on purpose; of their weekend trips with Wen to the topiary maze; of their poker nights with Sab in the dim, smoky snug room; of their growing collection of travel books about the places she said they'd been; of finding a new love, a *real* love, one that would corner and seize her heart; of spinning her very best lies into truth. Mostly she thinks about the long, wild challenge of learning who they are now, After Kat and After Jude—iterations that Jude believes will be their best ones yet.

And what she thinks, is.

ACKNOWLEDGMENTS

Making the leap from writing narrative nonfiction to writing fiction has been equal parts terrifying and thrilling, and I'm eternally grateful to so many people for cheering me on, offering invaluable feedback and encouragement, and generally ordering me to just sit in my chair and finish the damn thing.

Thank you to my brilliant and lovely editor, Sarah Crichton, for taking a chance on me and helping me to realize the best version of this story. She is a legend in this business for good reason. Her passion buoyed me throughout the process, and I'm so fortunate to have her in my corner. Thanks, also, to her intrepid assistant, Natalia Ruiz, who has a superhero talent for getting stuff done.

Thanks to the entire team at Henry Holt: Amy Einhorn, Marian Brown, Laura Flavin, Alyssa Weinberg, Gabriel Guma, Emily Mahar, Hannah Campbell, Vincent Stanley, and all the dedicated salespeople who advocated for and cheered on this book. You've made a harrowing and stressful process exponentially less harrowing and stressful.

Thank you to my agent, Simon Lipskar, for all the things over all the years. I can always count on you for honesty, unflagging support, a raucous evening of poker, and God's Ass Popcorn. I appreciate you more than I can say.

Thank you to my film agents, Sylvie Rabineau and Jill Gillett, for loving this book so much it makes me blush. I so appreciate all of your work on my behalf.

A very sincere thanks and exuberant "Yo" to two fellow Philadelphians, Liz Spikol and Patti Brett, who regaled me with tales of growing up in Center City in the 1970s. If you ever find yourself in Philly, check out Patti's bar, Doobies, which stands proud at 22nd and Lombard and is one of the city's most beloved dives. Thanks, also, to my trusted No-town scallywags: Mary Agnew Turley, Jason Buck, Laura DeSpain, and Melisa Monastero-Steinberg, with honorable mention to Billy "Yo Cuz" Abate, my two Sabs, Chinch, Booch, Guy, and other names I borrowed from real life.

Thank you to my luminous writerly accomplices who read various versions of this book and nudged me along: "The Lady" Joshilyn Jackson, Sara "Donkey Smoocher" Gruen, Emma Garman, Ada Calhoun, Susannah Cahalan, Gilbert King, Dan Conaway, Maud Newton, Denise Kiernan, Joseph D'Agnese, Anna Schachner, Lydia Netzer, Margaret Talbot, Liza Mundy, Kim Michele Richardson, Ginger Eager, David Bumke, and Alison Law. And thanks to a few more who listened to me vent and bought me cocktails: Erik Larson, Renée Rosen, Melanie Benjamin, Maureen Callahan, Lindsey Fitzharris, Adrian Teal, Diane Bierman, and Tom Hess.

Thank you to my voluble little dinosaur, Dexter, whose only contribution to this book was to literally crap on its pages. He is the best parrot in the world, regardless.

Thank you to Chuck, my unequal half, who will no doubt discern some reference to civil engineering in this story. He is my favorite person, regardless.

Most of all, thank you, person-holding-this-book, and all the smart and kind and generous booksellers and librarians who helped it find its way to you. Your interest in and commitment to old-school storytelling is a force of good in this world. I will keep writing as long as you keep reading.

ABOUT THE AUTHOR

Abbott Kahler, formerly writing as Karen Abbott, is the *New York Times* bestselling author of *Sin in the Second City; American Rose; Liar, Temptress, Soldier, Spy;* and *The Ghosts of Eden Park,* which was an Edgar Award finalist for best fact crime. She is the host of *Remus: The Mad Bootleg King,* an iHeartRadio podcast about bootlegger George Remus, and has written for *New York* magazine, newyorker.com, the *Wall Street Journal,* and the *Washington Post.* A native of Philadelphia, she lives in New York City and in Greenport, New York.